# TRAITOR

Chris Ryan was born in Newcastle. In 1984 he joined 22 SAS. After completing the year-long Alpine Guides Course, he was the troop guide for B Squadron Mountain Troop. He completed three tours with the anti-terrorist team, serving as an assaulter, sniper and finally Sniper Team Commander.

Chris was part of the SAS eight-man team chosen for the famous Bravo Two Zero mission during the 1991 Gulf War. He was the only member of the unit to escape from Iraq, where three of his colleagues were killed and four captured, for which he was awarded the Military Medal. Chris wrote about his experiences in his book *The One That Got Away*, which became an immediate bestseller. Since then he has written over fifty books and presented a number of very successful TV programmes.

To hear more about Chris Ryan's books, sign up to his Readers' Club at bit.ly/ChrisRyanClub

You can also follow him on social media:
Twitter: @exSASChrisRyan
Instagram: @exsaschrisryan
Facebook: ChrisRyanBooks

*Also by Chris Ryan*

Manhunter
Outcast
Cold Red

# CHRIS
# RYAN

# TRAITOR

ZAFFRE

First published in the UK in 2024 by
ZAFFRE
An imprint of Zaffre Publishing Group
A Bonnier Books UK company
4th Floor, Victoria House, Bloomsbury Square, London, WC1B 4DA
Owned by Bonnier Books
Sveavägen 56, Stockholm, Sweden

A CIP catalogue record for this book is
available from the British Library.

Hardback ISBN: 978-1-80418-591-9
Trade paperback ISBN: 978-1-80418-592-6

*Also available as an ebook and an audiobook*

1 3 5 7 9 10 8 6 4 2

Typeset by IDSUK (Data Connection) Ltd
Printed and bound in Great Britain by Clays Ltd, Elcograf S.p.A.

Zaffre is an imprint of Zaffre Publishing Group
A Bonnier Books UK company
www.bonnierbooks.co.uk

# One

General Gennady Nikolayevich Zorin, overall commander of Russian forces in Ukraine, was studying the latest reports from the frontline when he heard the knock on the door.

Zorin was grateful for the interruption. The reports made for grim reading. They spoke of demoralised soldiers, problems of resupply, faulty or missing equipment, poor intelligence. There were stories of exhausted troops pushed into battle without any military training whatsoever, forced to fight for months on end without being rotated out of combat. Men so hungry they had resorted to rummaging through bins for scraps of rotten food.

The general had been particularly disturbed by news of junkies in the trenches. Conscripts hooked on amphetamines and mephedrone to help relieve the boredom of life in a warzone. Zombie soldiers, the intelligence report called them.

All of which gave General Zorin a problem: what to tell his paymasters in the Kremlin.

The way he saw it, Zorin had two options. Neither of them good.

He could share the unedited reports with his superiors. Give them the full unexpurgated accounts of the situation unravelling seventy miles to the west, across the Ukrainian border.

There were advantages to this option. In recent days the forces under Zorin's command had suffered a series of embarrassing defeats. The Ukrainians had pushed his men out of several key villages. Only the line of defensive fortifications constructed by Zorin – the tank berms and minefields and network of trenches – had saved them from further humiliation.

The President would have heard the bad news by now. Inevitable. There would be the usual game of Kremlin scapegoating, people blaming one another in a bid to escape the firing squad.

So maybe it wasn't a bad idea to get his excuses in early. Launch a pre-emptive strike against accusations of incompetence. Anyone who read the reports would know that ultimate responsibility for the losses in Ukraine did not lie with Zorin, but with the people above him. The group of cronies, former butchers and opportunists who comprised the President's inner circle. They were the ones ultimately in charge of the special military operation.

But that approach carried significant risks. The President's confidants were powerful men. Greedy, yes. But also ruthless. They would not take kindly to being publicly held to account by a Russian general. They would surely seek revenge.

Zorin ruled out the first option.

Which therefore left option two.

He could sugarcoat the report. Sterilisation was how his colleagues referred to it. Accepted practice in the upper echelons of the Russian military nowadays. Strike out anything explosive. Anything that might contradict the President's distorted interpretation of events on the ground. Outright lies were unwise, of course. You couldn't make it too obvious. But you could always massage the figures downward. Minimise the casualties, gloss over retreats, reframe defeats as strategic withdrawals.

Most of Zorin's predecessors had done the same thing. Strategically the safer option. No one wanted to enrage the President. But professionally disastrous.

Zorin had been appointed to command Russian ground forces in the spring. It had not taken him long to identify the root cause of their many problems in Ukraine. Namely, incompetence and mismanagement at the top of the food chain.

His predecessors had been afraid to speak truth to power. They didn't have the balls to tell the President what was really going on. Already isolated, he had now become fully divorced from reality on the ground.

But no war had ever been won with a deluded Commander-in-Chief running the show.

Zorin considered himself a proud soldier. Forty years of service to the Fatherland. The failures in Ukraine burned deeply inside him, filled him with rage. He wanted to be remembered as the general who crushed the neo-Nazis in Kyiv. Instead, unless things changed drastically, Zorin would probably suffer the same fate as the previous commanders. Unable to achieve the unrealistic goals set by his masters, he'd be coerced into early retirement. See out his final years in his dacha in the Moscow suburbs, living on a modest state pension, his reputation in tatters.

*No good options.*

*So what to do?*

Zorin was still mulling over this question when he was interrupted by the sound of knuckles rapping on his office door.

'Come in,' Zorin said.

The door swung open. Zorin looked up. Major-General Maxim Solakov, his deputy, stood in the doorway. Solakov, the bull-necked thug, bald-domed and barrel-chested, with eyes like a couple of glass beads and a nose so wide you could plough snow with it. Zorin disliked his 2iC, had been looking for ways to get rid of him since his transfer to Rostov eight months ago. Solakov was one of the new breed of officers who'd cut their teeth in Syria. Extremists who believed the best way to defeat the enemy was to pulverise him into oblivion. More like gangsters than soldiers. Idiot had probably never studied Clausewitz or Zhukov.

'Yes, Major-General?'

'Message from the guardhouse, sir,' Solakov replied tonelessly. 'Advance party has arrived.'

'Party? What party?' Zorin snapped.

Solakov stared at him blankly. 'Security detail, sir. From Moscow. They have orders to clear the area before their principal shows up.'

'So we have visitors on their way. Why have I not heard of this until now?'

'The security detail says it's an unannounced visit, sir. Orders to keep it under wraps.'

'I see.' Zorin set down the report he'd been poring over. 'And did this advance party happen to mention which official shall be gracing us with their presence today?'

'No, sir. They just said he's on his way. That's all I know.'

Zorin frowned. Clearly someone in the top brass had decided to make an unannounced visit to Rostov-on-Don, the heart of ground operations in Ukraine. Which didn't wholly surprise the general. He'd half expected someone to travel down from Moscow after the recent losses on the battlefield. There had been the usual rumours of a Kremlin purge. The President's flunkies would be nervous. Therefore, they had to take action. They would send down one of the big guns. Defence Minister, maybe, or Chief of the General Staff. Demonstrate to their boss that things were under control. They'd meet with General Zorin, stare thoughtfully at maps, observe training drills. Make it look like they knew what the fuck they were doing.

'Where are they now?' Zorin demanded.

'Waiting in the lobby, sir.'

'Very well.' Zorin slid out from behind his desk, straightened his jacket, put on his peaked cap. 'We'd better go down and greet our surprise visitors.'

Zorin marched out of his corner office and made for the stairs, Solakov and his personal bodyguard, Colonel Dolgov, trotting alongside him. Zorin never took the lift. He liked to stay in shape. A ten-kilometre jog in the morning, followed by sets of sit-ups, push-ups and a four-minute plank. He was a man of iron discipline. Still weighed the same as he'd done as a young Spetsnaz officer forty years ago. His determination had seen him advance rapidly through the ranks. A veteran of Afghanistan, Chechnya and Georgia, Zorin had forged a reputation as one of Russia's most capable generals. Recipient of the Order of Military Merit and

Hero of the Russian Federation. Some had even talked about him as a potential successor to the President.

But then he had taken over operations in Ukraine. Zorin had been appointed by the President himself, with orders to restore morale among Russia's beleaguered troops. But from the start he had been hamstrung by those above him. Men more concerned with lining their own pockets than winning the ground war. They had their noses in the trough, skimming money from the defence budget while Zorin's troops were fed into the meat grinder.

Zorin's star had quickly dimmed. His bosses, he was sure, would try to make him the fall guy for the appalling losses they had suffered on the front. Cover their own arses. Conveniently ignoring the fact that without Zorin's methodical preparations, the Ukrainians would have already gone through their positions like a dose of salts.

*No way*, Zorin told himself. *I'm not taking the fall for those bastards in Moscow.*

*No fucking way.*

A group of bodyguards stood waiting for him in the lobby. Zorin counted four of them: mean-looking figures dressed in dark suits and crisp white shirts. Pancake-holstered pistols bulged beneath their jackets. Three of them wore wraparound shades, as if they were bodyguarding in Beverly Hills at the height of summer, not Rostov-on-Don on a dirty grey morning in late June.

One of the heavies caught sight of Zorin and beelined towards him. A tall, slender figure, fortyish, long-faced and thin-lipped. Eyes black as Siberian coal peered out from beneath heavily drooping lids.

Zorin felt his bowels shift. He recognised the bodyguard at once. Had seen the guy around various state functions and security council briefings, never more than arm's length from the President. Vadim Sergeyevich Lepsky, head of the SBP. The Presidential Security Service. Moscow's equivalent of the Secret Service.

There could be only one reason for Lepsky's unannounced arrival at the headquarters of the Southern Military District, Zorin knew. Because his boss was on his way.

A short, sinewy guy swaggered alongside Lepsky. He had hair the colour of piss, sculpted into a crewcut, like an army recruit about to get his first hazing. His eyes were like dots on a vast slab of pale flesh. Thin brows slanted downward, like a pair of pin-ball flippers. A subordinate, Zorin assumed. He swallowed the growing nausea in his throat, forced a smile and extended a hand to Lepsky.

'Vadim Sergeyevich. What a pleasant surprise.'

Lepsky pumped his hand. His lips spread into a peculiar grin. 'You're lucky you're a great soldier, General. Know why? No? Because you're fucking terrible at bullshit.'

Zorin smiled weakly. Lepsky flapped a hand at the guy at his side. The pale-faced heavy with the pinball flipper brows.

'This is Alexei Golikov,' he said. 'My second-in-command.'

Zorin smiled a greeting. Golikov stared back, face set like cement. After Zorin had introduced his 2iC to the heavies he turned back to Lepsky and said, nervously, 'What brings you here, Vadim?'

'The President is on his way here, General,' Lepsky said. 'He's coming to visit you.'

'When?'

Lepsky consulted his Patek Philippe watch and frowned. The guy probably had a drawer full of them back in Moscow, Zorin mused. There were rumours that Lepsky had amassed one of the biggest fortunes in the whole of Russia. A trillion roubles, some said.

'Motorcade should get here in fifty minutes. They're coming directly from the presidential jet.'

Zorin stood very still. He became aware of a faint tingling on the nape of his neck. He remembered to keep smiling.

'Excellent. May I ask the purpose of his visit?'

Lepsky must have picked up on the unease in Zorin's voice, because he placed a meaty hand on the general's shoulder and laughed gregariously.

'Relax, General. Nothing to worry about. You're not being sacked or anything like that. This is just a routine PR exercise. The boss wants to put in an appearance in front of the media. Thinks it's important to show people watching at home that he's not afraid. Especially after recent . . . events. You understand what I'm saying.'

Zorin nodded.

Two weeks earlier, the war had come to Russian soil. For four days and nights Ukrainian drones had struck targets across the border, in Rostov and elsewhere. Warehouses and factories had been damaged, army barracks destroyed. Dozens killed. Publicly the Kremlin had blamed the explosions on site accidents, but no one really believed that. Now the President was trying to get a grip on the situation. Change the narrative. Project an image of a strong leader taking personal charge.

*Routine visit.*

Lepsky said, 'You're a busy man, General. I appreciate that. I can assure you that we won't take up much of your time. An hour or so. No more. We'll have a quick meeting in view of the cameras, discuss the situation on the front, that sort of thing. Reporters will turn up fifteen minutes before the President himself.

'Obviously, my guys will need to clear the area thoroughly before then,' Lepsky continued. 'Beginning with this building. We've got another team outside, checking the surrounding streets.'

Precautionary measures, Zorin thought to himself. Standard operating procedure. The President was going to put in an appearance close to the Ukrainian border, in a city that had recently been hit by the enemy. They'd want to make sure the ground was safe before the Commander-in-Chief rocked up. Very fucking sure.

'Of course,' he said. 'My deputy will be happy to show your men around.'

Lepsky and his mute 2iC, Golikov, swapped a knowing look. Then Lepsky slanted his gaze back to the general and cleared his throat.

'Perhaps, General, you wouldn't mind accompanying us on the tour? There are some things I'd like to discuss with you before the President gets here. Issues of protocol. Unless you're too busy. . .'

'Not at all,' Zorin said. 'It would be my pleasure.' And this time he smiled like he meant it. Because he did.

*You're in the clear,* Zorin told himself. Relief flooded his bowels.

*The President doesn't suspect a thing.*

They went through the building floor by floor, with military precision. Zorin did most of the talking, Lepsky occasionally cutting in with questions. They covered the various entry and exit points, scoped out potential locations for the briefing with the President, ran through emergency drills, while Golikov relayed information into the push-to-talk mic fixed to his jacket lapel, communicating with his colleagues outside. The guys on the cordon team. They would be checking out the approach roads, searching neighbouring buildings for potential threats, assessing dead ground, establishing multiple routes in and out of the immediate area in case they needed to bug out at a moment's notice.

A full sweep. They were leaving nothing to chance.

'I must say, I'm surprised the President is joining us today,' Zorin said. 'I thought he was still in Krasnodar, greeting crowds of well-wishers.'

Lepsky shrugged. 'The President is a man of boundless energy. And besides, he cannot stay in Moscow. He must show his supporters that he remains fearless in the face of threats to his life. Even if,' Lepsky added, lowering his voice, 'it creates another headache for us.'

'Meaning?'

'The President's entourage is much bigger these days. Years ago, it used to just be the principal and two or three assistants, sometimes a guy with the nuclear codes. Now he insists on being accompanied everywhere by his personal doctors, his masseurs, his own chefs. Even his food-taster travels with him.'

'What difference does that make? Your men are not obliged to safeguard the lives of his underlings.'

'Pattern of life, General.'

Zorin shot him a puzzled look.

'Whenever the President decides to leave Moscow, it means a change to our routine as well. My guys stop using their personal phones or credit cards. They're not going out to dinner with their wives. Their pattern of life gets broken. That's what the enemy is looking for. Anything that might reveal our movements.

'That's how you get at someone these days. You don't target the principal. No. You look at what's around them instead. The outer circle. The weak point in any security team.'

'But you must have precautions, surely—'

'Of course. We're not fucking idiots. We travel data black nowadays. But now we have to worry about the President's entourage too. All it takes is one tiny mistake, General. Someone booking a flight online, or a hire car.'

'You assume that someone is smart enough to monitor the people around the President.'

'I assume the worst. It's my job.' Lepsky sneered. 'Trust me. One of these days, someone is going to try to kill the President. And it won't be because my guys were slack. It'll be because of some fucking idiot who got sloppy with his digital footprint.'

After they had finished scanning the top floor, Lepsky rubbed his jaw thoughtfully and said, 'This is all very good. Now, we will need to see the rooftop.'

'What for?' Zorin crinkled his brow. 'There's nothing up there.'

Lepsky smiled blandly. He said, 'The President wants to have a shot of him gazing towards the frontline. With you standing by his side, General. It'll go on the front of all the papers.'

Zorin shook his head slowly. 'We're too far away, Vadim. Seventy miles to the border. Further to the nearest battle. I'm sorry, but you can't see shit from the roof.'

Lepsky's grin stretched across his face. 'Actually, General, we've already taken care of that.'

Zorin stared quizzically at the SBP chief. Waited for him to go on.

'Our guys have parked a couple of oil tankers ten miles to the west,' Lepsky continued. 'They're rigged with explosives. We'll light them up when the President arrives. Put out a statement that the units were enemy saboteurs, sneaking across the border to carry out an attempt on the President. Ripped to shreds by heroic Russian soldiers before they could strike.

'You will stand on the rooftop with the President, pointing towards the rising smoke in the distance while he congratulates you on foiling the enemy scum. You'll be a hero, General. Medals will follow.'

Zorin felt a tremble of excitement as he listened. A staged attack, with Zorin standing alongside the President himself. Aside from the obvious propaganda value of such a photo, it indicated the General's elevated status. Marked him out as someone who'd caught the President's eye. A man on the up.

That would prove useful in the coming months, Zorin realised. Enhance his public profile. He'd have a certain level of celebrity. Name recognition. That would give him an edge over many of his colleagues.

Lepsky stared at him, waiting for an answer.

'Do you have a problem, General?'

Which was a pointless question. Both men knew that Zorin would have to agree to the proposal. You didn't say no to the President. Not unless you wanted to plunge to your death on a private jet. Or get thrown in front of an onrushing metro train.

'Not at all, Vadim. It's an excellent suggestion.'

They backtracked out of the conference room, walked down the ornately furnished hallway, passed Zorin's corner office and the smaller one belonging to Solakov, pushed open a fire door and climbed the maintenance stairs leading to the rooftop.

The wind bitch-slapped Zorin as he stepped outside. Lepsky, Golikov and Solakov followed close behind, fanning out among the rooftop ventilators and skylights, the radio masts and satellite dishes, the air filled with the hum of generators, the din of city life. Atop a metal flagpole, the Russian flag flickered in the strengthening breeze.

The headquarters building had been constructed in the style of an English country estate, with blocks on all four sides pierced by a central open-air courtyard. A tall wrought-iron fence topped with gold-painted spearheads ringed the neatly kept grounds. Beyond it stretched a slapdash muddle of modern office blocks, onion-domed churches and concrete high-rises hugging the northern bank of the Don River. Eventually, the city faded away towards a quilt of low, rolling plains and wheat fields dotted with tangled groves of mulberry trees. Cossack country. Old Russia.

To the west, somewhere across the horizon, lay the border with Ukraine.

A hundred thousand of General Zorin's countrymen had been slaughtered fighting against the enemy. Many more had been badly wounded. He did not share the pessimistic view of some of his fellow officers, that the war was unwinnable. A blood-and-soil patriot, he had been raised to believe in the innate superiority of the Russian military. The country of Peter the Great and Alexander Suvorov. Destroyers of Napoleon's Grand Army and victors at Stalingrad. Zorin believed there was no situation so dire that it could not be retrieved.

But Zorin was equally sure of something else. As long as the current regime continued to fuck things up, victory would elude them.

A few paces away, Lepsky and Golikov were talking in low voices. Discussing camera angles, presumably. Distances and timings.

Making sure it would all be set up for the Kremlin-approved hacks to capture the moment. Zorin waited patiently. Solakov stood close by, hands behind his back, saying nothing.

Lepsky and Golikov laughed about something. Lepsky broke off and jabbered into his mic. Conferring with the cordon team, Zorin guessed.

Lepsky swapped a quick look with his crewcutted deputy. Then he approached Zorin.

'The outer cordon has been cleared, General. We've given the green light to the President. Motorcade is approaching now. They should get here any minute.'

A panicked thought occurred to Zorin. 'I must return downstairs at once, Vadim.' He indicated his office uniform. 'I'll need to change into my ceremonial dress before the President arrives.'

Lepsky waved away his concerns. 'Don't worry, General. You're fine to meet the President dressed as you are. Make you look like a man of action. It'll be good for your image.'

Lepsky smiled. He glanced again at Golikov. Then he pressed a finger to his earpiece and resumed his chat on the comms frequency. Zorin watched and waited. There would be a continual flow of information coming over the channel, he knew. The guys on the advance party, the cordon team and the bodyguards travelling with the presidential motorcade. They would be updating each other on locations and timings, continually screening for threats. Working together, like a well-oiled machine.

After three minutes Lepsky said into his mic, 'OK. We're ready. Everyone is in place.'

He looked up at Zorin. Grinned.

'The President is pulling up now,' Lepsky said, moving towards the parapet wall fringing the rooftop. 'Come, General. You can see the motorcade from here. Best seats in the house.'

He waved Zorin over. Zorin approached the knee-high parapet and looked down at the central courtyard. Five storeys below, he descried a five-vehicle column slow-crawling down the access road leading from the front gates towards the flagstoned courtyard. An Aurus Senat limousine, with a pair of Mercedes-Benz G-Wagons in the front and two more in the rear. A pair of Ural model cT urban sidecar motorbikes rode in the van.

Both the G-Wagons and the Senat were armoured models. Ballistic windows capable of stopping a 7.62mm round, runflats, emergency on-board oxygen systems. Bodywork strong enough to absorb the blast impact of an IED or a landmine. Zorin figured four bodyguards per G-Wagon, plus two more in the Senat with the President in the back seat, along with his chief of staff and his press secretary.

The vehicles eased to a halt in front of the main entrance. The motorcyclists dismounted. Zorin waited for the President to emerge from his armoured limo. Solakov stood obediently at the general's shoulder, arms crossed over his barrel-shaped chest. Colonel Dolgov lingered a few steps away.

Immediately behind Zorin, at his six o'clock, he heard Golikov chatting into his mic. Coordinating with the heavies on the ground.

The passenger door on the Senat snicked open.

'Look, General,' Lepsky said. 'There he is.'

Zorin edged closer to the parapet, leaning over to get a closer look.

Then he felt a hand shove him in the back.

Zorin lurched helplessly forward, arms pinwheeling, clawing at thin air. He gave out a startled cry, then toppled over the parapet and plunged headlong to the ground five storeys below.

And the last thing Gennady Zorin ever remembered – the very last thing, a fraction of a second before his brains dashed against the flagstones, before the impact shattered his bones and turned his organs to pulp – was that he hadn't outwitted the President after all.

# Two

*Six months later. Campbell Barracks, Swanbourne, Perth*

Shortly after ten o'clock in the morning, on a sweltering hot day in early December, Sergeant Quade Dempsey strode purposefully into the senior NCOs' mess.

Sergeant Major Luke Carter spotted the Aussie as soon as he entered the room. Impossible to miss him. The guy was huge. Gargantuan. Bigger than he'd looked in the photographs in his file. He stood around six-three, sinewy and broad-shouldered. His chest circumference had to be at least fifty inches, Carter guessed. His arms had the approximate wingspan of a 787 Dreamliner. Short ginger hair and a flame-coloured beard encircled a freckled face.

*Like a matchstick injected with steroids*, the driver had told Carter on the ride down from the airport the previous afternoon, when he'd described Dempsey. Now Carter understood what the guy had meant.

Carter saw the Aussie scanning the room. Dempsey's gaze landed on the Brit. At a quarter past ten in the morning, most of the guys in the Australian SAS Regiment had finished their breakfast; a handful of NCOs sat around the mess, inhaling extra portions of carb-heavy grub. Carter sat alone at a table in the far corner, sipping black coffee. His fourth cup of the morning. He was practically mainlining the stuff now. Nineteen hours on a Qantas flight, direct from Heathrow to Perth.

*A long way to come to meet a candidate*, Carter thought.

But he was glad to get away from Hereford.

*Right now, I want to be as far from that fucking place as possible.*

Fifteen months had passed since Carter's older brother had died on a covert op in Ukraine. The head shed had moved quickly to hush up the circumstances surrounding Jamie's death. The usual post-op clean-up. The Regiment had form for burying the truth. Only Luke, the CO of 22 SAS and a few senior management types at Six knew the full story of how Jamie had helped to prevent a nuclear disaster. In doing so, he'd made the ultimate sacrifice. The lads had quietly mourned the loss of one of their own, then went back to work.

But Luke couldn't move on easily.

His brother had been shabbily treated by the Regiment. Jamie had rubbed people the wrong way from the moment he'd first walked through the gates at Credenhill. He'd refused to indulge in the politics and backstabbing, butted heads with the careerists and the gong-hunters, the guys who were more interested in advancing up the pyramid than the business of soldiering. In return, they made Jamie into an outcast.

Luke was different from his brother. Jamie had never been a conformist: he found it impossible to look the other way, whereas Luke had always been straight down the middle. A realist. He knew how to toe the party line, got along with the other lads. There was always a certain amount of corporate bullshit in any institution. A fact of life. He'd encountered it in the Paras, too, and learned to live with it. He didn't doubt that it existed in the Regiment. But he'd assumed that Jamie had made the situation worse, with his abrasive personality and short fuse.

Then Luke had followed in his brother's footsteps, passing Selection and earning the right to wear the winged dagger beret. At which point he'd learned an unpleasant truth.

When he'd joined the Regiment, Luke had his career all mapped out in his head. He saw himself getting posted to E Squadron, then a job in Training Wing. Maybe a commission to the officers' ranks, running one of the departments. Then retirement, followed by a lucrative gig on the private security circuit. But the more time he spent at Hereford – the further he went down that tunnel – the more he realised that life as a Blade wasn't as straightforward as it had looked from the outside.

Luke had always been a warrior, first and foremost. A dedicated professional. He wanted to soldier. Push himself to his limits. He'd never stolen, never been busted for drink-driving, never dabbled in drugs or any shit like that. In his naïveté, he'd assumed that would be enough to get ahead.

He'd been wrong.

All of a sudden, he'd found himself working with a group of ruthless, supremely motivated fuckers scrapping among themselves for an opportunity to climb the greasy pole. Some of the lads were prepared to shit on their mates in order to advance their own careers. Others were poor-quality soldiers, but they still won promotions – because they knew how to stitch somebody up.

Luke Carter had seen it happen to one of his best mates. A working-class Welsh bloke from the valleys. They had gone through Selection together, used to go out on the piss during their time in the Paras.

Then he'd got his commission. This same lad started wearing a tweed jacket and brogues, talking in a posh English schoolboy accent. He joined the Freemasons, even started attending the local church. Blanked his muckers in the other ranks. Did his best to try to fit in with the Ruperts; failed to realise that the Old Etonians would never accept the likes of him. Like trying to force a puzzle piece into the wrong jigsaw. You could dress in the same clothes as those rich bastards, share the same mess, go to the same officers' balls, but you were never going to be a part of their society. They would shit on you in the end.

Carter's own career had stalled once he'd transferred to E Squadron and took a two-year rotation with the Wing. He wasn't prepared to do the arse-kissing necessary to progress up the ladder. Gradually, he had become disillusioned with life in 22 SAS. He still loved the soldiering, but he no longer gave two shits about getting commissioned.

Soon after his brother's death, Carter reached a private decision. He would stay at the rank of Sergeant Major, focus on doing what he did best: fighting. Do something good with his life. Make a difference, then get out when he was good and ready. The NCOs were the backbone of the Regiment anyway. The guys in the thick of the action. Leave the management bollocks to the two-faced tossers.

*I won't end up like Jamie. No fucking way.*

But there was another reason why Carter had been eager to get out of Hereford for a few days.

In the weeks following Jamie's funeral, he'd heard disturbing rumours around the camp. Whispers about criminality in G Squadron. Senior Blades caught up in some seriously dark shit. Biker gangs. Theft. Drug dealing. Murder, even. His brother had briefly served in G Squadron. He'd cross-decked to A Squadron shortly before his deployment to Ukraine. And there had been those reports of a shooting outside a pub in Madley. A failed attempt on the life of an SAS man, according to the local gossip. Had Jamie been caught up in something sinister?

Luke had started to wonder.

He'd asked around. Spoke with Jamie's mates, the few he had left in the Regiment. They stonewalled him. No one wanted to talk. Code of silence.

And then, a month or so later, one of the old hands in G Squadron had reached out to Luke, asked to meet for a drink. Tom Farrell was a softly spoken Ulsterman. Family bloke. Decent guy. Or so Carter thought.

Over pints of London Pride, Farrell delivered a blunt warning.

*You want to back off, son. We both know what I'm talking about. Leave it well fucking alone, right?*

*The story will never come out. The top brass has seen to that. Dead and buried, lad. Dead and fucking buried.*

*I'm telling you this for your own good. Keep asking questions and it'll kill your career. Got it?*

Luke had been tempted to tell the older guy to go fuck himself. But deep down, he'd known that Farrell was right.

He'd heard of guys going over to the dark side. Blades who'd lined their pockets, or fabricated action-on reports so they could put themselves forward for a medal. The police never got involved; no one was court martialled or sacked from the Regiment. Instead, they were discreetly persuaded to resign, with the promise of a cosy gig with a private security company at the end of it.

*Regiment politics*, thought Carter.

It always came down to the same thing. *Self-preservation.* No CO wanted to be remembered as the guy who called in the police to investigate the SAS. The faintest whiff of scandal might scupper their chances of a knighthood.

*Fuck it.*

*Forget about those twats.*

*Cut out the noise. Focus on the task in hand.*

Which was why Luke Carter found himself sitting in a mess nine thousand miles from Hereford, waiting to interview an operator from the Australian SAS Regiment.

He'd arrived in-country the previous afternoon. One of the lads on the support staff had collected him from the airport, a scruffy-looking bloke called Brett Kozmina. The kind of guy who could wear an Armani suit and still look shabby. He'd ferried Carter to the SASR's main base, in the middle of a well-heeled Perth suburb, escorted him to his digs on the first floor of the combined mess, sorted him out with a late-night dinner of steak and chips. Then he'd told Carter to report to the canteen at ten o'clock the next morning.

*The guy you're interested in will RV with you there.*

He watched Dempsey march over to his table. Carter necked the dregs of his brew, rose to greet the heavyset sergeant. Dempsey nodded curtly.

'You must be the Pom they told me about,' he said in a bluff voice. 'Luke Carter, right?'

'That's right, mate,' Carter said.

The Aussie thrust out a hand that looked like it had been sculpted from granite. Carter pumped it.

'Quade Dempsey. Mates call me Ned.'

Carter looked at him questioningly.

'After Kelly. The outlaw.' Dempsey grinned. 'I'm related to him on my mum's side. Fourth generation. You're looking at the descendant of a genuine Aussie legend.'

Carter sized the guy up. With his wild eyes, tangerine beard and freckled skin he looked more Irish than a pint of Guinness. Like all the other SASR operators, he wore a specially adapted version of the Crye Precision gear favoured by the Regiment and Delta Force. The same basic uniform, but with a different camo pattern.

Carter laughed. 'Does that mean I'm supposed to bow?'

Dempsey frowned. 'That accent. Let me guess. Liverpool?'

'Blyth,' Carter said. He saw the blank expression register on Dempsey's face and added, 'Northumberland. I'm a Geordie.'

'Newcastle, eh? Never been that way myself. Did a year in Putney back in the day, though. Pulling pints. Pulled a lot more than that, too, if you know what I mean.'

Dempsey's grin stretched across his face.

'Pom women. Telling you, they can't get enough of this,' he added, pointing to his crotch. 'Guess you Brits must be doing something wrong in the sack.'

'Either that,' Carter responded drily, 'or the women down south haven't got any taste.'

Dempsey threw back his head and laughed. 'Pom humour. Can't beat it. Well, I suppose you lot have got to be good at something. Not like you can boast about the cricket these days, is it?'

Carter didn't reply. Dempsey folded his huge arms; his expression became serious.

'So, here's the deal,' he continued. 'I've booked out the squadron briefing room for the next hour. We'll walk over, and then you can tell me why your bosses have sent one of their own halfway round the world for a handshake. That work for you?'

'Sounds fine, mate,' Carter said. 'Lead the way.'

Dempsey started towards the exit. Carter followed the burly Aussie out of the mess building.

Morning sunshine blinded the two soldiers as they stepped outside. Summertime in western Australia. Pastel-blue sky, temperature in the high twenties. A warm breeze drifted in from the Indian Ocean, mussing Carter's salt-and-pepper hair.

*Maybe I'll move here once I'm done with the Regiment,* he thought. *Spend my evenings sipping beers, watching the sunset. There are worse places to live.*

*Either way, I won't be sticking around Hereford.*

Dempsey made for a cluster of three-storey glass-and-brick buildings north of the mess. The Ops Precinct. The brains trust of the SASR. Regimental headquarters, plus separate HQs for the individual squadrons. The camp itself had been built on a parcel of land due west of Perth, facing out across the coastline. As they approached one of the squadron HQs Dempsey pointed out the different areas: stores, recovery centre and support services to the east; admin blocks at their twelve o'clock. Strip of beach to the west.

'You from around here?' Carter asked.

Dempsey shook his head. 'Darwin. Northern Territory. Hot, humid and boring as fuck.'

'I'll remember to leave it off my bucket list.' Carter laughed.

'So would most people. It's not a bad place. Just, you know – flat. Nothing much going on. Kind of why I ended up joining the army.' He glanced sidelong at Carter. 'How long are you staying here?'

'Six days. I'm on a flight back home Friday morning. Seven-day turnaround.'

Dempsey clicked his tongue. 'Too bad. You'll miss the game next weekend. We're playing your lot at the Gabba. Gonna be a big one, that. You into your cricket, Pom?'

'Not really my bag, mate.'

'Aussie rules. Now there's a proper sport. Not that you lot would be any good at that, either. Ain't much you Brits are good at these days. Except drinking and shooting yourselves in the foot.'

He laughed at his own lame joke.

'I'll show you round the training area in a few days,' Dempsey continued. 'Check out the sights. If we've got time, we could grab a few pints. There's a good microbrewery up the road in Claremont that serves some top pale ales. You a beer man, Luke?'

Carter grinned broadly. 'I'm a Geordie. We can drink your lot under the table any day of the week.'

Dempsey smiled. 'Is that a challenge?'

'Not really. Just a statement of fact.'

Dempsey laughed heartily. They entered the reception area, passed the guardroom, climbed the stairs to the first floor, marched down a long corridor flanked by briefing rooms. No one paid the two men any attention; everyone else minded their own business. Which was how it should be. They were in the nerve centre of ops for 4 Squadron, the SASR's covert military intelligence team. Their equivalent of the Wing, the clandestine unit within 22 SAS tasked with working alongside the intelligence services. A lot of secret stuff went on inside these walls.

'Must be something big,' Dempsey was saying. 'Why they've sent you over here. Long way to travel just for a meeting. Haven't you Poms heard of Skype?'

Carter shrugged. 'Wasn't my call, mate. Orders from the people above. Said they wanted this thing done face to face.'

'Hey, it is what it is. Who knows what the bosses are thinking half the time. Right, this is us.'

Dempsey had stopped in front of an unmarked door at the far end of the corridor. He jerked the handle, stepped aside, gestured for Carter to enter.

Carter stepped into a blandly furnished briefing room. Practically identical to the one used by E Squadron. As if someone had ripped it out and shipped it Down Under. The same dull grey carpet and walls, the same recessed ceiling panels emitting weak squares of light. But also highly secure. The SASR lads would regularly sweep this place for bugs; there would be counter-jamming equipment on the roof, everything necessary to create a sterile environment. A place where they could talk freely.

'Sit down, mate,' Dempsey said.

They took their seats at the near end of the walnut table, Carter on one side, Dempsey crowbarring his hefty frame into one of the executive chairs opposite.

A few moments later there was a sharp knock on the door. A smooth-faced guy with badly receding hair stood in the doorway and introduced himself to Carter.

'Major Paul Rogers,' he said as they shook hands. 'OC of 4 Squadron, as I'm sure you know.'

'Yes, sir,' Carter replied tonelessly.

Rogers nodded stiffly. He had the hair of a middle-aged bloke and the skin of someone twenty years younger. Carter wondered how you got skin like that in your mid-forties. Probably a combination of exercise, genetics and a low-stress existence. Rogers didn't seem like someone who'd ever carried the weight of the world on his shoulders.

'Don't mind me,' Rogers said. His accent was subtly different from Dempsey's, Carter noted. Less rough, somehow. The same basic notes but planed down at the edges.

'Just thought I'd say hello and see how our guest is settling in,' he went on.

Which was bullshit, Carter knew. Rogers wouldn't give two shits about Carter on a personal level. No doubt he had orders from the SASR top brass to check up on the Brit. He wouldn't want any problems to feed back to 22 SAS. Rogers and his chums would want to make a good impression on their opposite numbers in Hereford.

'How is everything? Your digs all right?'

'Everything's fine, sir,' Carter replied diplomatically.

'Good, good,' Rogers said. 'Well, if there's anything you need – anything at all – don't hesitate to ask.'

'Thank you, sir.'

'Matt Banbridge is in the Regiment these days, isn't he?'

'Yes, sir. He's the OC of B Squadron.'

Rogers nodded sagely. 'Our paths crossed while I was at Sandhurst. Top bloke. Tell him I said hello, won't you?'

'Yes, sir. Will do.'

Rogers straightened up, frowned at his G-Shock.

'Right. I'll let you two get on. Perhaps we can catch up later, Luke? Have a beer on camp?'

'That'd be great, sir.'

Rogers nodded again. Then he left. The door closed. Dempsey skimmed his gaze towards Carter.

'Is that true?' he asked, jerking a thumb at the door. 'About that Banbridge fella being a good bloke?'

'Is it fuck,' Carter said. 'I served under him in E Squadron for a while. He's an arrogant twat. Thought he was Robin Hood leading his band of Merry Men. We all hated him.'

Dempsey threw back his head and laughed.

'So, what's the craic? Why are you here?'

'What has Rogers told you?'

'Fuck all, mate. He just took me aside a couple of days ago, told me some Pom was flying over. Wanted to speak with me in private about a joint op. That's it.'

'I can't tell you what the job is,' said Carter, 'because I don't know the details myself. '

'Reckon it must be a training op,' Dempsey speculated. 'Or close protection work.'

'Maybe. But I think it's bigger than that.'

'Based on what?'

'Experience. The top brass won't tell us a thing until the full mission briefing. Which is in Germany. Ramstein Air Base. Eleven days from now.'

'Who's running the show? Our lot, or yours?'

'Six,' Carter said, 'Six is leading the op.'

Dempsey pulled a face. 'This isn't gonna involve anything illegal, is it? No offence, but we've had enough trouble recently. You might have heard.'

Carter nodded. 'That business with 2 Squadron being disbanded.'

'Too fucking right.'

Everyone in the SF community knew the story. There had been a lengthy inquiry into rumours of war crimes committed by SASR personnel in Afghanistan. The subsequent report had carried details of the alleged murders of civilians and prisoners and the planting of foreign weapons to cover up their crimes. In the wake of the inquiry the government had removed 2 Squadron from the Order of Battle.

Carter said, 'The job's been signed off by the Foreign Secretary. We've got a green light right up to the Prime Minister himself. It's nothing dodgy.'

Dempsey laughed cynically. 'Do you actually trust those arseholes?'

'Not really. But look at it this way. Would your head shed have signed off on this thing if they thought there was the slightest chance it might come back to bite them on the arse?'

Dempsey stroked his orange beard as he considered. 'Fair point. But why me, specifically? Why not any of the other blokes in 4 Squadron?'

Carter said, 'I understand you're the best drone pilot in the unit.'

'That's what people say. I specialise in training other SF teams in how to use them. Did a four-month rotation in Ukraine last year. Showed them fellas how to use different bits of kit. Nano-drones, cameras, robots. All kinds of cool shit.'

'How did you get on?'

'Well enough. They're not the best soldiers in the world, but they're honest and motivated. Plus, they like a drink. My kind of people. It took a lot of work, but we brought them up to a professional standard.'

'Have you been in any trouble before? Any disciplinary issues I should know about? Arrests for drunk and disorderly behaviour?'

'Isn't that in my file?'

Carter stared at him. Dempsey shrugged.

'You want to hear it from the horse's mouth. Fair dos. Well, I've kept my nose clean. Spotless record. Ask Rogers if you don't believe me.'

'When did you join SASR?'

'Six years ago. I started out in the Signals Corp, trained at Kapooka, did my courses in drone piloting, electronic warfare and battlespace comms, information systems. Anything technical, that's my bag. That and beer.' He grinned. 'I served as a chook in 152 Signals here at Swanbourne. Three years later I applied for SAS Selection. Passed first time.'

Carter nodded. Absorbing the int Dempsey was feeding him.

'Can you at least tell me how many guys you're recruiting for this team?' the latter asked.

'Four,' said Carter. 'It's a four-man team. Two of our lads, plus two of yours.'

'Who's the other bloke from our unit?'

'That slot is still up for grabs. I haven't sounded anyone out yet. Wanted to sit down with you first. See if there's someone you think might be a good fit.'

'Why don't you ask Rogers?'

'He's a Rupert. If I want to know about the art of arse-kissing, I'll consult him. I need the opinion of a professional.'

'Anything else you can tell me about the job?' Dempsey asked, scratching his ginger beard. 'If you want my help, you've got to throw me a bone. Tell me what skillsets you're looking for, that sort of thing.'

Carter said, 'We need a sniper for the team. Ideally someone who knows their way around Eastern European weapon systems.'

Dempsey furrowed his brow. 'There is one person who might be worth checking out.'

'Who?'

The Aussie hesitated to go on. 'This bloke, he's good. Fucking good, you know? Top marksman. But he's not perfect.'

'What do you mean?'

'Let's just say he can be a bit too honest.'

Carter said, 'Who is he?'

'Steve Lazarides. Greek-Croat heritage and bloody proud of it. Never misses a chance to remind anyone, either.' He chuckled.

'What squadron is he in?'

'None of them.'

Carter shot him a questioning look.

Dempsey said, 'He's out of circulation. Left 2 Squadron after the report about Afghan hit the headlines. This was three years ago.'

'Was he implicated?'

Dempsey shook his head firmly. 'He's clean. That I know for a fact. Before he cut away the head shed offered him a posting to another squadron. Which he rejected. They wouldn't have made the offer if they suspected he might be involved in any way.'

'So why did he leave the squadron?'

'You'd have to ask him, mate.'

'Can you vouch for him?'

Dempsey nodded eagerly. 'I did Selection with him. He's a top professional. Brilliant sniper, too. The best shot I've ever seen, hands down. Expert in camouflage and concealment. Spent his time in Afghan giving overwatch to SF operators.'

'Knows his weapon systems?'

'Better than his own mother. If it's been engineered somewhere in the world, this guy will know about it.'

'Where is he now?'

'Steve went back home after the Afghan business. Runs a farm over in the back of Bourke.'

'Where?'

Dempsey saw the puzzled look on Carter's face and said, 'It's a saying. Means a long way from here. He lives in a place called Denmark. The town, not the country.'

'Is it far from here?'

'Not really. Three hundred miles or so.'

'What makes you think your man would be interested in the job? If he's turned his back on the unit, he might not want to return into the fold.'

'Steve couldn't stand the politics. Never had any time for it. But he loved to soldier. Lived and breathed it, mate. Besides, three years on a farm is enough to drive anyone stir-crazy. Bloke's probably itching for a chance to get stuck in again.'

'But there's a chance he'll say no.'

'There's always a chance. Like you Brits beating us at the cricket.' Dempsey grinned.

Carter said, 'Can you get him in? For a chat, like.'

The Aussie clicked his tongue. 'Better if we drive down to see him. He left under something of a cloud. If we ask him to return to what he considers a hostile environment – he'd probably tell us to go fuck ourselves.'

'Is he around right now?'

'Reckon so. Steve doesn't travel much these days. Bit of a loner, if I'm honest. Always has been. Makes the occasional trip into Albany for supplies, but otherwise he stays put on the farm. Cut himself off from the SF community after he checked out of the army.'

'He must really love those pigs.'

Dempsey laughed.

He said, 'We'll take a run down there tomorrow. I'll have to drop him a message. Let him know we'll be in the area. He ain't keen on visitors turning up unannounced.'

'Roger that. In the meantime, I'll notify Hereford. Tell them we've got a possible fourth candidate for the job.'

'Does this mean that I've passed?'

Carter glanced inquiringly at the Aussie. 'Passed?'

'The interview.' Dempsey swept an arm in front of him, indicating their surroundings. 'I know what this is all about. You were sizing me up. Checking to see if I'm the right material for your team. So, am I in?'

Carter paused. His first impressions of Dempsey reinforced what he'd heard on the grapevine. A first-class soldier. Sports-mad. The best drone operator in the business. The kind of bloke who never stopped talking. Fine in small doses, but after a while he got on your nerves. The prospect of a long rotation in his company didn't appeal to Carter.

But he wasn't in Australia to make friends. He had orders to assess Dempsey's suitability for a highly secretive mission. A role that required a tech-savvy soldier, with battlefield experience using drones. Someone who could be trusted to get the job done.

*We can't afford any blowback on this one*, the CO of 22 SAS had told him shortly before he'd left the country.

'Yes, mate.' Carter smiled. 'You're in.'

# Three

Carter found Dempsey waiting for him in the mess at nine o'clock the following morning. The two soldiers helped themselves to mugs of steaming hot coffee and servings of crispy bacon, sunflower-yellow eggs, grilled mushrooms and tomatoes, hash browns. Better than the greasy fare served up in the cookhouse in Hereford, Carter decided. It was worth getting a posting to SASR just for the food.

A short time later they emerged from the mess and made their way to the regimental car park due north of the ops precinct. Carter followed Dempsey towards a white Toyota Land Cruiser at the far end of the rain-slicked tarmac. The Aussie seated himself behind the wheel; Carter climbed into the shotgun seat. Dempsey gunned the wagon, K-turned out of the car park, stopped at the guardhouse and traded a few words with a chubby-faced sentry. Then they hit the main road.

The drive to Denmark took them nearly five hours. They cut through the Perth suburbs, then hit the Albany highway east of Armadale. The route funnelled them on a rough southerly trajectory, past dense sprawls of woodland and low hills, on butter-smooth roads almost devoid of traffic. Carter thought of the long hours spent sitting in traffic in Britain and wondered why he hadn't already emigrated.

An hour later the forests abruptly gave way to a patchwork of crop fields, irrigation systems and gently rolling hills. Wheatbelt country. Grain silos the size of tower blocks, vineyard-carpeted slopes. Wind farms dominated the horizon, turbine blades turning lazily in the cool air. Almost like an English country scene, Carter thought. Without the mud and rain.

The radio was tuned to a local sports station. There was a lot of shouting, a lot of baiting and angry invective. At one o'clock the news came on. The headlines sounded depressingly familiar. Inflation was still high. House prices were still rising. The war in Ukraine risked turning into a hopeless stalemate, according to a slew of experts. In Russia, a high-profile politician had been killed in a hit-and-run. The latest in a string of suspicious deaths, the report said. Beginning with the suicide of a top general several months earlier. The Kremlin had issued a statement denying involvement and blaming Western insurgents.

Ninety minutes later Dempsey veered off the highway onto Route 102. They were nearing the coast now. Half an hour until they reached Denmark, according to the on-board GPS. They carried on west and then south through the town. Which seemed pleasant enough, thought Carter. Brick-built Federation houses and gable-roofed Californian-style bungalows fringed wide sun-dappled streets; decorated verandas gazed out over trimmed front lawns. There were worse places to live.

Since the death of his older brother, the idea of quitting Britain had grown on Carter. Always a Regiment man, he had grown weary of life in 22 SAS. The political in-fighting had become much worse since the winding down of ops in Afghan and Iraq. All of a sudden there were fewer opportunities for guys to get promoted. Highly experienced lads found their careers hitting dead ends. That was when things turned poisonous. People stabbed their mates in the back, scrapped with one another for the handful of job openings. So far Carter had managed to steer clear of trouble, but he wondered how much longer he could stick it out.

Jamie had been a fighter. Tough as they come. He wasn't the kind of bloke who broke easily. But in the end, the Regiment had ground him down.

*Maybe the same thing will happen to me*, thought Carter. *Maybe it's finally time to start thinking about a life beyond Hereford. A fresh start.*

*Get away from the greasy-pole monkeys. The rumours about Jamie. Get as far away from the place as fucking possible.*

30

Dempsey interrupted his thoughts.

'Something I don't understand. You reckon this mission is a big one. A game changer.'

'That's my personal assessment,' Carter said. 'But I could be wrong.'

'But if it *is* something big, why are your bosses keen to share the glory with us? If we were running the show, we wouldn't be recruiting blokes from outside our own unit.'

'The top brass didn't give me a reason.' Carter hesitated.

'But?'

'It could be a question of resources. We're badly overstretched. The usual deal. Guys tied down all over the shop, running training packages, close protection work. We've lost a few veterans from G Squadron lately, too,' he added.

'It's four blokes. We're not talking about a whole fucking squadron. Are you seriously telling me your head shed can't pull a couple of lads from another job?'

'This is the way Six works, mate. Pointless to second-guess their motives. Might as well search for water with a stick.'

They drove on through a windblown landscape of dilapidated farmsteads, lumber yards, rusted pickup trucks and empty caravan parks.

*Fuck me*, Carter thought. *This place really is the back of beyond.*

He said, 'What did you mean yesterday? When you said this Lazarides fella was too honest for his own good.'

'I'm a loyal soldier. Loyal to the system. That's my MO. The unit might piss me off sometimes, but it always comes first. Brotherhood of the warriors. A lot of the other lads feel the same way.'

Carter stayed quiet. He waited for Dempsey to go on.

'Steve was different. For him, doing the right thing always comes first. That was more important than loyalty to the unit. To his mates. Saw everything in black and white. There were hills he was willing to die on, no matter who he pissed off. You see what I'm saying?'

Carter nodded.

'There were rumours that Steve was the whistleblower in 2 Squadron. Or one of them.' Dempsey paused. 'You can imagine how that went down with some of the lads in the camp.'

'Like a cup of cold sick, I'd imagine.'

'Pretty much. He denied it, of course. But it didn't stop the other guys from turning on him all the same. Some accused him of being a traitor to the Regiment.'

'Do you think he did it?'

Dempsey hesitated while he considered. 'Look, all I know is that if Steve saw something he didn't like – if he was a witness to anything disturbing – he wouldn't be able to keep his mouth shut. That's not who he is. So read into that what you will.'

They continued south past Denmark. Four minutes later, Dempsey slowed the Land Cruiser to a crawl and hooked a hard right off the main road, pointing down a rough track flanked by strips of grazing pasture and neat rows of gum trees. Five hundred metres away, the track bowed off to the left, terminating at a patch of dirt fronting a cluster of farm buildings. Cattle grazed in the nearest paddock.

The Land Cruiser shuddered along the trackway, tyres churning up clods of loose earth. Dempsey pulled up in front of the farmstead and cut the engine. The two men debussed; Carter walked round the property, brushed flies away from his face, grateful for a chance to stretch his legs after the road trip.

The place looked old, and tired. Litter tumbleweeded across the ground. Chickens pecked at the dirt in a nearby coop. The smell of manure hung thick in the air, mixing with the odour of burnt wood.

The farmhouse itself was in a state of disrepair. Breeze-block walls surmounted by a rusting iron roof. Dirty net curtains, thin as onion skins, covered the windows. To the right of the main house was an open-fronted storage shed with a mud-spattered red Toyota Hilux parked beside it. Fifty metres further downstream stood a slurry pit, a fenced-off sheep yard and a couple of galvanised steel sheds. Workshops, Carter figured. Or machinery sheds. There were piles of timber planks lying around the place, bits of farming equipment. Tendrils of smoke drifted up from the crumbling chimney.

Carter looked round again.

No sign of Lazarides. No sign of anyone at all.

'Mate? You home?' Dempsey called out.

The farmhouse was silent. Carter heard nothing except the grate of the windpump blades slowly turning, the low rumble of a diesel generator, the bleating of sheep from the other side of the estate.

'You sure he's here?' Carter asked.

'Must be.' Dempsey waved a hand at the chimney. 'He's got the log fire going. He'll be around somewhere. Come on.'

They stepped through the rusted gate, crossed the weed-choked lawn, climbed the veranda. A gust of wind blasted across the land, slapping the front door against the timber frame.

'Steve? Mate?'

No answer.

Dempsey pushed open the front door and moved down the hallway, Carter close behind. They searched the farmhouse, starting with the living area. A quick and dirty room clearance. Minus the flashbangs and the weaponry. They checked the kitchen, the storeroom, the main and guest bedrooms, the bathroom.

The place was filthy. Empty mugs on the kitchen table, dirty plates in the sink. Empty bottles of Teachers and Ballantine's on the counter, the bin bag overflowing with beer cans. Dust everywhere.

'Does anyone else live here?' Carter asked. 'Wife, girlfriend?'

'Fuck, no. Steve's not the domesticated type. A great soldier, but he ain't house-trained.'

Carter nodded. He'd known guys like this in the Regiment. Capable warriors, but outside the narrow world of military expertise they were hopelessly lost. Lads who could conduct a flawless stronghold assault but were out of their depth when it came to

33

table manners and polite conversation. For some of the guys, being a Blade was fundamental to their existence, but Carter had never felt that way. It had primarily been a way out of poverty – a chance to do something useful with his life, a gateway to a decent career, allowing him to buy nice things. An escape route from Blyth.

They left the farmhouse and checked the storage shed on the opposite side of the dirt patch. Carter saw boxes filled with tools, paint-scabbed filing cabinets and work benches.

'Where the fuck is he?' Carter wondered aloud.

'Let's try the sheds.'

Dempsey strode towards the metal gate at the far end of the housing block, stepping around the tangle of hosepipes. Carter followed him through the gate. They made for the steel sheds fifty metres away, across a stretch of beaten earth and mud. Further east, sickle-shaped leaves rustled in the strengthening breeze.

They approached the nearest shed, walked through the open entryway. Inside was a sprawl of agricultural equipment: spreader, backhoe, flatbed trailer, utility tractor, sack truck, cement mixer. Plus bits of irrigation kit, batteries, tilling blades, manure forks, stacks of wooden pallets, shovels and pickaxes.

Dempsey stepped back from the shed and tried the second building. The roller shutter curtain had been lowered over the main entrance, Carter noticed. There was a small tractor parked outside, next to a hundred-gallon steel tank filled almost to the brim with boiling water. A fire crackled and popped beneath the tank; ash flakes drifted across the dirt.

They approached the steel security door on the side of the building. Dempsey levered the handle, pushed the door open.

'Steve? You in here?' he shouted.

A sickening stench of shit and blood hit Carter as he stepped through the opening behind Dempsey.

He stopped a couple of paces inside and looked round. Carter saw several animal carcasses hanging from meat hooks. Sets of cleavers, axes and bone saws on a metal bench to one side of the room. An old hunting rifle propped against the wall.

Not a machinery shed.

A slaughterhouse.

In the middle of the room a scruffy-looking guy in a butcher's apron was skinning a pig hanging head-down from a gambrel and chains. Blood leaked from the animal's guts into a drainage canal cut into the concrete floor. Heavy metal blasted out of a radio.

The guy in the apron had his back to Carter and Dempsey. He seemed oblivious to the presence of the two figures as he worked the knife down the side of the carcass, slicing through the flesh as if he was cutting fabric.

'Mate,' Dempsey said, raising his voice to make himself heard above the music. 'Steve.'

The guy in the apron stopped eviscerating the pig. He whipped round, still gripping the butchering knife in his right hand. He glanced at Carter before his gaze landed on Dempsey. The knife arm lowered. His face cracked into a grin.

'Ned Dempsey. As I live and breathe. Fucking hell.'

Lazarides set down the knife on the cutting bench, scrubbed his blood-lacquered hands in a bowl of water, dried them on his apron. Switched off the radio. Approached his two guests.

'Must have lost track of time,' he said, shaking Dempsey's hand enthusiastically. He jerked a thumb at the carcass. 'Caught this bastard digging up my patch this morning. Thought I'd get him skinned and carved up before you got here.'

'Hogs still causing you trouble, mate?'

Lazarides snorted. 'War of attrition. Buggers breed faster than we can wipe them out. Reckon we had an easier time fighting against the Taliban back in the day.'

The two Aussies shared a laugh. Lazarides turned his attention to Carter.

'Who's your friend?' He was addressing Dempsey, but kept his gaze fixed on Carter. 'Didn't tell me you were bringing company, Ned.'

Dempsey said, 'This is Luke Carter. He's over from England for a few days. One of our brother warriors from Hereford.'

'Fucking Pom, eh?' Lazarides hawked and spat out a wad of chewing tobacco. 'Like there's not enough of you in the country already.'

Carter ignored the dig as he looked the guy up and down. Lazarides stood four or five inches shorter than Dempsey. Five-ten, or thereabouts. The guy had an outdoorsy face: windblown and leathery, with a salt-and-pepper beard, crooked teeth and wild bug eyes. The sleeves of his checked shirt were rolled up to the elbows, revealing thick forearms inked with tattoos. His faded jeans were smeared with dirt; his desert boots were caked in an inch of mud. He looked like he'd spent the night sleeping in the bush.

'Heck of a drive down from Swanbourne. Get you fellas a cold one?'

'No, mate,' said Dempsey. 'We can't stay for long. Hitting the road after this. Straight back up to camp.'

'What type of pig is that?' Carter asked, nodding at the slain animal dangling from the gambrel. It looked huge, he thought. Bigger than any pig he'd seen before. A hundred kilograms at least. The tusks were still attached.

'A whopping big one, mate,' Lazarides said.

Dempsey said, 'It's a razorback. They're feral pigs. Solid as fuck. They barrel through the farms, digging up roots, wrecking fencing. Some of 'em have been known to kill sheep.'

'Bloody nightmare to deal with,' Lazarides chipped in. He studied Carter with a contemptuous look. Like he was something he'd scraped off the sole of his boot.

'You pure Pom, mate?'

'Far as I know.'

'Shit. That's rough. Better luck in the next life.'

There was a hard, flinty edge to his voice.

'What about you?' Carter asked. 'Your family from round here?'

'Nah. We're a bit of everything. My grandmother's Croat. Came over here after the war and married a Greek bloke. He owned this land, passed it down to his kids. The other side of my family comes from Albania. Even got a bit of Scottish in the mix somewhere too. But do you know something?'

'What's that?'

'There's not a drop of fucking English in our blood.'

Lazarides spread his lips into a wicked smile. Dempsey burst into laughter. Carter could feel the hatred coming off the farmer in waves. He had the sense that Lazarides genuinely despised the Brits. With Dempsey it seemed more like friendly piss-taking, but this guy evidently had a serious grudge.

Carter gritted his teeth. Reminded himself that he was on a recruiting mission.

*Don't jeopardise the op. If this idiot wants to rip the piss, that's his problem, not mine.*

*I don't have to get on with him. I just need to know if he's capable or not.*

Although Carter had agreed to the meeting, he had some doubts about Lazarides. Three years was a long time to be out of the system. Three years without any training or range work, the guy was bound to be rusty. Fact of life. No doubt working on the farm kept him in decent shape, but there was a massive difference between general fitness and the elite standards demanded by the Regiment. And they were on a tight schedule. Ten days from now, unless the situation changed, they would be in Germany, getting ready for the briefing from Six. Not enough time to dust off any cobwebs. Not nearly enough.

*Whoever joins this team, they need to be ready to roll as soon as we're green-lit.*

Carter changed the subject. He pointed towards the remains of a skinned animal dangling from one of the meat hooks. The head and legs had been chopped off, leaving an unrecognisable lump of bone, skin and meat.

'What's that thing?'

'That?' Lazarides glanced over his shoulder at the carcass Carter had indicated. 'That's a roo, mate. Hind and forequarters. And that one over there,' he added, nodding at a horse-sized trunk, 'is a camel.'

'Camel?' Carter stared at him in surprise. For a split second he wondered if Lazarides was joking.

The ex-soldier ran a hand through his greasy hair. 'Maybe you look at 'em differently where you're from, but round this way we consider them rodents. Fucking pests. They ain't the only threat, neither. We get foxes, rabbits, rats, mice. Wallabies. All sorts. Digging up the crops, getting into the paddocks. Crafty sons of bitches.'

'Keeps me in target practice, though,' Lazarides continued. 'Shot me couple of hogs last week. How I learned to shoot, as a matter of fact.'

'Killing hogs?'

'Among other things, yeah.'

Lazarides thrust a hand into his jeans pocket and fished out a pack of Winfield cigarettes. He plucked one out, sparked up.

Carter thought, *Heavy drinker. Smoker. No way this guy is in good shape.*

*If we bring him onto the team, it could backfire.*

He pointed at the hunting rifle propped against the wall. Recognised it immediately. A Springfield 1903. Bolt-action, chambered for the 30.07 calibre round. Five-shot capacity, walnut stock, Tasco power scope mounted on the top side of the receiver. An old American army weapon. Later adapted for the civilian market by Klein's Sporting Goods. One of the true classics of the rifle world.

'That's a tasty piece,' he said. 'Where'd you get it?'

'A present. From my uncle Greg. On my thirteenth birthday. My first gun. Still works like a beaut, too. On a clear day I can hit a pig's arsehole from six hundred metres away. My uncle was the one who taught me how to shoot. Right here, on this farm.'

Lazarides took a long drag on his ciggie, tapped ash into an empty beer can. He stared at a point past Carter's shoulder, seemingly lost in his memories.

'Had some good times, the two of us. Hunting roos in the bush. Uncle Greg was the one who pushed me into joining the army, actually. Guess he saw a skillset that might prove useful. Best decision I ever made. Worst, too,' he said bitterly.

He exhaled heavily, returned his gaze to Dempsey.

'What's going on, Ned? Reckon you didn't drive all the way down from Swanbourne just to shoot the breeze. My company ain't that special.'

Dempsey grinned. He said, 'Luke's assembling a team. For a joint operation with the Brits. Covert mission.'

'Good for him. Good for you, Pom.'

'We want to bring you on board.'

A deep groove formed above Lazarides' brow. 'This your idea of a fucking joke, Ned?'

'No, mate.'

Lazarides said nothing for a long beat. He took a final pull on his cigarette, crushed the butt beneath his heel, looked up at Carter.

'What the fuck are you interested in me for? You need a good marksman, there's plenty of blokes left in the unit. Recruit one of them fellas. I'm out of the system.'

'I don't need a good sniper,' said Carter. 'I need the best.'

'That's why we're here,' Dempsey cut in.

The look on Lazarides' face darkened.

'Piss off. Think you and your friend can just rock up here, blow smoke up my arse and sweet talk me into going back into it? After what happened with 2 Squadron being abolished?'

'That was a long time ago. Ancient history. Things are different now.'

'Says you.'

'It's the truth, mate.'

'Doesn't matter. I'm out of it. End of.'

'Don't you miss it?'

Lazarides let out an ugly laugh. 'Course I do. But half the job is politics. Frankly, I miss that side of it about as much as I miss gonorrhoea.'

Carter stayed silent. A deliberate strategy. They'd discussed it on the drive down from Swanbourne. Better to let Dempsey do the talking. He knew Lazarides; they had history, had suffered the ordeal of SASR Selection together. Dempsey knew what made his mucker tick, how to appeal to him.

'You're the best shot I've ever seen,' he said. 'Are you going to let your skills go to waste out here?'

'I told you, I'm not interested.'

Dempsey shook his head slowly. 'This is an opportunity to reset everything, mate. We're offering you a way back in. You can finally put all that business with 2 Squadron behind you. Get back to doing what you do best.'

Lazarides took a step towards Dempsey, trembling with barely suppressed rage.

'You don't get it, do you, mate?' Lazarides pinched the air between his thumb and forefinger. 'I was *this* close to getting dragged into the shit because of that investigation into Afghan. Christ, I could have been sacked for something that had nothing to do with me.'

'Is that why you left?' asked Carter. 'Because of the report?'

'Among other things, yeah. It was a toxic environment,' Lazarides said. 'Figured I was better off out of it.'

'That's not what I heard,' said Dempsey.

'What's that supposed to mean?'

'There are rumours around the camp. Some of the lads are saying you spilled your guts to the investigators.'

'I don't give a crap what they think.'

'Come back, then.'

Lazarides shook his head furiously.

'I sweated blood for the army. Put my neck on the line. Always did the right thing. Never broke the rules. I was a bloody good soldier. Fucking loved it, you know? I believed we were the good guys.'

'We are, mate.'

Lazarides said nothing.

'Don't you want to hear us out, at least?'

'I said I ain't interested.'

Lazarides gave his back to the two men. Walked over to the bench, started arranging his tools. Dempsey tried again.

'Look, Steve, I know you're racked off after everything. Honestly, I don't blame you. But this is a chance to rewrite the narrative.'

Lazarides said nothing. Carter could see that Dempsey was losing the argument. His best shots had failed to land. He stepped forward and said, 'I don't know what went on in Afghan. Frankly I don't give a shit. The past is a dead end. But here's what I do know. This mission is a big deal. We've got the chance to make a real difference in the world, by doing something important.'

Lazarides shook his head and said, bitterly, 'They said the same thing before the Afghan deployment.'

'This is different. I've done a lot of jobs with Five and Six. The way this one is panning out, it's going to be something big. And we're going to be right in the thick of it.'

Lazarides hesitated. His gaze drifted back to the bench, brow heavily creased. A guy wrestling with a decision. Then he let out a deep sigh.

'It doesn't matter. The Regiment would never allow it. The guys I worked with think I'm a snitch. They'd hit the fucking roof if I came back.'

'You don't need to worry about that. Everything's been cleared at our end.'

'There's a job waiting for you with 4 Squadron,' Dempsey added. 'You'll be working with my lot.'

'I can't, mate,' Lazarides said. 'I can't . . .'

His voice faded into nothing. Dempsey stepped towards him.

'This isn't you, Steve. Spending the rest of your life out here, skinning hogs. You're better than this.'

Lazarides rounded abruptly on his former colleague, expression stitched with anger.

'You fucking deaf? I ain't coming back. So take your offer and shove it up your bollocks. Now, if you'll excuse me, I've got work to do. Nice seeing you, Ned.'

He returned to the hog carcass, pulling open the chest cavity. Intestines oozed out, slopped into the bucket beneath the pig's head.

Dempsey glanced at Carter and shrugged. As if to say, *Well, we gave it our best shot.*

They left the shed and walked back across the open ground towards the housing block. Crossed the farmstead, hopped into the Land Cruiser. Dempsey gunned the engine and pointed the vehicle down the rough track.

After a few minutes Dempsey thumped a fist against the wheel in frustration. 'Shit. I really thought we could bring him round.'

'What now?'

'Head back to camp and ask around, I guess. There are one or two other blokes who might fit the bill. I'll introduce you to them tomorrow.'

'Any of them as handy with a rifle as the pig-killer?'

'Does it matter?'

'You're asking the wrong person. I'm in the dark, remember? They just told me to recruit the best drone operator in the unit, and the best sniper. No one told me why.'

'But what difference does it make? A shit-hot marksman like Steve won't be much use on a training mission.'

Carter pursed his lips. 'Maybe it's not a training mission. Maybe it's something else.'

Dempsey glanced at him. 'Like what?'

'I don't know.'

They drove on in stony silence. Dempsey arrowed the Land Cruiser back down the main track, past the rows of thirty-metre-high blue gums, before he hung a right on the main road and tooled north in the direction of Denmark. Dempsey upped the volume on the radio. There was a preview of an upcoming Rugby World Cup fixture. Australia versus Wales. In Lyon, France. A big match, apparently.

Dempsey leaned forward, frowned heavily at the rear-view mirror. 'What the fuck . . .?'

Carter glanced over his shoulder at the rear windscreen. Then he saw it too. A red Toyota Hilux roaring into view at their six o'clock, throwing up palls of dust in its wake. The same pickup Carter had seen parked outside the shed on Lazarides' farmstead.

The truck was closing fast.

'What does he want now?' Carter muttered.

Dempsey didn't answer. He downshifted to second, steered the Land Cruiser towards the lay-by. A few moments later the Hilux pulled up right behind them. Lazarides dismounted from the wagon while Carter and Dempsey got out and met him halfway.

'This mission,' Lazarides said, addressing himself to Carter. 'Can you give me your word it won't land us in the shit?'

Carter said, 'That's what I've been told. But I can't offer more guarantees than that.'

'And I'll be joining 4 Squadron, right?'

'That's the deal,' said Dempsey. 'It's been signed off by the CO. Everything's agreed.'

Lazarides looked away, eyes fixed on a point in the middle distance, brow heavily wrinkled.

'All right,' he said finally. 'I'm in. What's the plan?'

Dempsey said, 'You'll report to Swanbourne. Admin staff will need to get your paperwork processed before the job goes live.'

'When?'

'Soon as. Have you got someone who can look after your place while you're away?'

Lazarides thought quickly. 'My neighbour. He runs a dairy farm up the ways from me. I'll speak with him tomorrow. Ask him to man the fort for a spell.'

'Good. Then I'll meet you at the camp gates. Two days from now.'

'Do I need to bring anything?'

'Just yourself. I'll notify the guardhouse in advance. Tell them we're expecting you.'

Lazarides hesitated. 'What's this all about, anyway?'

'I don't know,' Carter responded. 'There's gonna be a full briefing once we land in Germany. Until then, they won't tell us a thing.'

'You won't regret this, Steve,' Dempsey said.

'Yeah, well. Guess we'll see, won't we?'

He strolled back over to his pickup truck. Fired up the engine, U-turned in the road, bulleted south down the main road. Carter and Dempsey folded themselves back into the Land Cruiser. A huge grin spread across Dempsey's mug.

'I knew I could convince him. The old Irish charm, Pom. Never fails to work its magic.'

He pointed the Land Cruiser back onto the main road. A light rain was seething over the land, drops beading the windscreen. After a few minutes of silence Carter said, 'Are you sure your man will be up to the job?'

'Course. Why wouldn't he be?'

'He's hardly in the best shape.'

Dempsey batted away his concerns with a wave of his hand. 'Don't sweat it. Steve might not look like he's up to scratch right now, but the guy's as tough as boiled leather. Trust me, he'll be ready.'

'I hope you're right.'

*Otherwise,* he thought, *we'll be going into this thing half-cocked. And that's when mistakes happen.*

# Four

Carter spent the next couple of days killing time at Swanbourne. The worst part of any op. Waiting for the green light. He reported back to Hereford using the secure line in the SASR ops room, briefed the Regiment ops officer on the two recruits. That information would be relayed to Vauxhall, he knew. Support staff would take care of the necessary admin for the new members of the team: plane tickets, documentation, bank cards, onward transportation from Heathrow to RAF Brize Norton. Military flights to Germany.

On the third morning, Steve Lazarides rocked up at the barracks in his Hilux. The admin staff confiscated his phone – personal electronic devices were forbidden around the camp – and put him up in the accommodation wing on the first floor of the mess.

'You're provisionally booked on commercial flights,' Carter explained as they convened in the squadron briefing room the same afternoon. 'Qantas. Leaving Perth on Monday. Seven o'clock in the evening. Landing at Heathrow six thirty Tuesday morning. Direct flight. This is assuming we're green-lit, of course.'

'What happens when we get to London?' asked Dempsey.

'We'll have someone collect you from the airport. One of the drivers from Vauxhall. They'll ferry you straight to Brize Norton. Then an onward flight to Ramstein Air Base. Military transport.'

'Where are you in all of this?'

'I'll be flying out to Germany on Wednesday. Day after you arrive. I'll meet you on the base.'

'And the fourth bloke?'

'Same deal. He'll be travelling with me.'

'Who is he?'

'The ops officer hasn't told me. Reckon I'll only find out at the pre-op shake-out.'

'What about equipment?'

'Any requests, put them through on an indent. I'll make sure it's passed on to the relevant people at Ramstein. Everything will be waiting for you when you land.'

'Going to be tricky to draw up a list of kit,' Dempsey said, 'considering we don't have a fucking clue what the job involves. We're flying blind here.'

'Can't be helped. Just let me know what you might need. Any specialist kit that might be useful.'

'And if we need something else? What then?'

'We'll source it once we're on the ground at Ramstein. The Regiment has a coordinator based there. Rank of Sergeant Major. He runs the Q stores on the base. He can get hold of almost anything.'

'Are we going in uniform?'

'Civilian wear,' Carter said. 'You know the drill. One fresh set, plus a change of clothing. Mobiles will be issued on arrival as per usual. Burners with local SIM cards. Anything that might leave a footprint has to stay behind at Ramstein.'

'Guess they want us fully sterilised for this job,' Lazarides commented.

'They could do with sterilising your clothes first,' Dempsey joked, wrinkling his nose. 'What the fuck have you been doing on that farm of yours, mate? You smell like you've been skinny dipping in a pit latrine.'

'Piss off, Ned.' He looked back towards Carter. 'What about my paperwork? I ain't lifting a finger before I'm rebadged and back on the payroll.'

'Your admin team's taking care of that. They'll process all your documentation while you're in the air. By the time you land in Germany, everything will be official.'

'Will we be travelling on our own passports?' Dempsey asked. 'Once we're on the job?'

Carter said, 'I don't know. They won't tell me.'

Lazarides gave him a long, searching look. 'What's this really all about, Pom? You can't be completely clueless. Your people must have told you something, for fuck's sake.'

'They didn't.'

'Bullshit. They wouldn't send you here without briefing you first.'

'I know as much as you. The situation is still fluid. They're looking at multiple options. Different plans, depending on the situation on the ground. The people running the show won't share anything with us until they're ready.'

Lazarides' face tightened. 'So you say. But how do we know you're being straight with us? For all we know, we could be walking into a fucking trap.'

'I'm not known for stitching people up.'

'You're a Pom. That's practically your national fucking pastime.'

Carter ignored the remark. 'Just make sure you're both packed and ready to fly out on Monday night. Once we're on-site in Germany, we'll get a full mission briefing. We'll run through everything then. Plans, SOPs. Operational guidance. Actions-on. The works.'

*And then*, he thought, *we'll finally find out what Six has got planned for us.*

*   *   *

On the Wednesday morning Dempsey showed Carter round the barracks. Like a guided tour, minus the hordes of selfie-takers and overpriced gift shops. Carter looked round the training areas, armoury, vehicle workshops, the comms centre. The camp had been heavily redeveloped several years ago, Dempsey explained. When he'd passed Selection, the place had been falling apart at the seams. The old structures had been torn down, replaced with state-of-the-art facilities. As good as anything at Hereford. Back then the SASR had been the pride of the Australian military. Politicians had been falling over themselves to throw money at the project. Then the Afghan scandal had dominated the news. Now no one wanted to touch the unit with a barge pole. There was a lot of anger among the soldiers. A lot of bad blood and mutual suspicion.

That afternoon Carter hit the gym. Dempsey was already there, busting out deadlifts on the Smith machine. Across the floor, Lazarides trained on one of the treadmills. The guy looked in shit shape, struggled to keep up with the modest pace of the conveyor belt. A few minutes later he slapped the stop button, cutting the workout short. Lazarides staggered away from the machine, gasping for breath, his gym T-shirt drenched with sweat.

'Jesus Christ,' Carter muttered to Dempsey in an undertone. 'I'm starting to think this guy isn't up to soldiering.'

'He'll be fine,' Dempsey said dismissively.

Carter stared at him with raised eyebrows. 'He doesn't look fine. Fuck me, he can barely manage a short jog without hacking his guts up.'

'He's a bit rusty. That's all. Wait till you see him shoot.'

'It's not his shooting I'm worried about.'

'He'll pull round.' Dempsey dropped his voice. 'Listen, I know Steve as well as anyone. He might not look like it, but he was one of the fittest guys on Selection. Once he's got all the shit out of his system, he'll turn it around.'

Carter gritted his teeth and sighed wearily. He'd known guys at Hereford with similar attitudes. Soldiers who let their hair down when they weren't in training, smoking and drinking heavily, but when it came to the exercises, they were the ones left standing at the end. Fitness was about the strength of the individual. Human willpower. Determination. Some guys had it. Maybe Lazarides would surprise him on the day.

*Then again*, he thought, *maybe he won't.*

The following evening, the day before Carter flew back home, the three soldiers took a stroll down to the Starboard Tavern on

Claremont Crescent. Which advertised itself as a microbrewery but looked more like a saloon from a 1950s western. A mahogany bar the size of a train carriage dominated the middle of the room. Rustic cross-beam lights hung from the timber ceiling. A fire roared in a stone-dressed fireplace. On the far side of the room a group of burly rugby fans were watching the big game on a bank of TV screens.

Carter had suggested meeting up for a few beers before he left Swanbourne. He didn't give a shit about the social scene in suburban Perth, and he wasn't a big drinker – not by the standards of some lads in the Regiment. But he figured the three of them would be spending a lot of time in each other's pockets over the next few months. Maybe longer, depending on the job.

*Might as well share a few jars with these lads. Find out as much as I can about them.*

*One day, I might have to rely on them to save my neck.*

'Take a load off, fellas,' Dempsey said. 'I'll get the beers in.'

'Make sure the Pom gets the next round,' Lazarides cut in. 'You know what those sneaky bastards are like when it comes to money, Ned. Tighter than a nun's arse.'

Dempsey's chest rippled as he burst into laughter. He strolled over to the counter and returned a few minutes later carrying three beer glasses, and planted himself on an empty stool. Carter sipped his pint of Carlton Draught. Across the bar, the loose knot of rugby fans jeered as the Welsh scored a try against the Australians.

'Shame you're heading back tomorrow,' Dempsey said.

Lazarides grinned. 'One less Brit in the country? I'd say that's a cause for celebration, mate.'

Dempsey gave a lopsided smile. 'There's that.' He slid his gaze back to Carter. 'But if you were over here for longer, we could have taken a trip east to Glenrowan. Ned Kelly country. Could have shown you the house where Ned made his last stand. Still got relatives there, you know.'

'Didn't that bloke kill a couple of police officers?'

'Self-defence, mate.'

'If you say so.'

Lazarides snorted contemptuously. 'You want to show a bit more respect. Ned's a fucking hero to most people round these parts.'

'Strange idea of a hero,' Carter said. 'A thief and a murderer.'

'He hated you British. That makes him a legend in my book. Anyone who shits all over the Poms deserves a medal.'

Carter glowered at him. Dempsey set down his drink, placed a matey hand on each of his colleagues' shoulders.

'Easy, fellas. We're all on the same team here. No need for any aggro.'

Lazarides didn't reply. He just sat there staring meanly at Carter.

Dempsey tipped his head at Carter. 'Did you always want to be in the SAS, Luke?'

*Smart move*, thought Carter. *Steering the chat onto safer territory.* He marked Dempsey down as a pragmatic character. The peacekeeper. The kind of bloke who could get along with anyone and didn't take things personally. That was good to know. Four guys on a job, things could get claustrophobic after a while. The last thing you wanted was the operators at each other's throats like a pack of wolves.

He said, 'It was always on my radar. Growing up in Blyth, there weren't many opportunities. You either got a job at the port, worked in a factory, or signed on the dole. Or joined the army. My brother, he served in the Paras, then passed Selection.

'I knew how much Jamie loved to soldier. He used to talk about how he liked being part of a team. Being part of something bigger than himself. The army made his world bigger. That made me want to follow in his footsteps. So I did.'

'Is he still in the SAS? Your brother?'

'No,' Carter said flatly. He coughed and said, 'What about you? Why did you join up?'

Dempsey contemplated his pint. 'It was different for me. Signing up, that was never part of the plan. I was big into tech as a kid. Spent my spare time taking stuff apart. TVs, DVD players, computers. Anything that I could pick apart with a screwdriver, I was all over it. Drove my old man nuts.' He chuckled at the memory. 'I used to hack those old cable TV receiver boxes. Take out the smartcard, order one online from China, stick it in the box, get access to all the films and sports for free. Flogged them to my mates at school. Made a killing.' He shrugged. 'I was just a bored kid in the suburbs having a bit of fun. Leastways, that's what I thought at the time. But it turned out to be a slippery slope.

'When I turned eighteen I started stealing cars. This was in the early noughties. Fucking easy, back then, if you understood the technology. Me and a couple of mates, we'd jack a ride, take it for a spin round Darwin, dump it somewhere. We weren't doing it to make money by selling the parts, or anything like that. We were just having a laugh.

'Then one night I got caught. Happened over in Karama. Me and a buddy were lifting a Holden Commodore when the cops pounced. Figure one of the neighbours called the police on us. I usually drove but that night I let Scott take the wheel. Stupid fucking mistake. He took a turn too fast and lost control. Ploughed straight into the road barrier. Miracle neither of us was badly hurt. He managed to leg it on foot. Next thing I knew, the cops were dragging me out of the wreck and slapping me in handcuffs.

'When it came to trial, I was bricking it. Everyone told me to prepare for the worst. I was definitely gonna get banged up. Then my solicitor cut a deal with the judge. Told him that I'd agreed to join the army in exchange for a reduced sentence. Which was fucking news to me, I can tell you.

'But it worked. I got off with a warning. Slap on the wrist. Stern talking-to from the judge about mending my ways, all that shit. Then it hit me: I had to join up. Like, this was really happening. No way out of it. My old man marched me down to the recruiting office the next

51

day. I had no intention of sticking it out, of course. But turns out it was the best thing that ever happened to me. Never looked back.

'If I hadn't signed up, I'd probably be in jail right now. A lot of mates ended up that way. Clever lads who got into trouble. Truth be told, I've loved every minute of it. This is the life for me. Even with all the shit that went down with 2 Squadron, I wouldn't give this up, not for anything. And best of all I still get to muck around with the tech. More so than any job I could have landed on Civvy Street. I've done drone flying courses, electronic warfare, cyber, you name it.' Dempsey paused, took a long pull of beer. 'Yeah, I fucking love being a soldier. And you know what? If I ever bumped into that solicitor again, I'd owe him a pint.'

Dempsey fell silent. The three soldiers sipped their lagers and small-talked. Across the bar, the rugby fans shouted abuse at the screen as the Welsh scored another try, drowning out the Keith Urban song and the faint hubbub of conversation.

A while later Carter noticed Lazarides staring at him. The guy was already half-cut; cold blue eyes glazed beneath heavily drooping lids.

'What are you holding back from us, Pom?' he asked.

'Nothing. I already told you, mate. The suits are keeping their cards close to their chests on this one.'

'But they must have dropped a few hints. Weather forecasts in the area we'll be operating. Equipment indents. Local geography. You must have your suspicions.'

'I don't,' Carter replied stiffly. He clenched his jaw. 'Now drop it.'

'But—'

'I said drop it.'

Dempsey said, 'He's right, Steve. This ain't the time or place. Let's not talk shop when we're having a few beers, eh?'

'Fine,' Lazarides growled. He necked the rest of his pint, slammed the empty glass down, wiped beery foam from his mouth. 'I'll take another one, Pom. Your round.'

Carter stared right back at him.

'You sure that's a good idea?'

Lazarides creased his brow. 'The fuck is that supposed to mean?'

'I've seen your kitchen. More whiskey bottles than a Scottish distillery.'

'I like a few looseners. So what?'

Carter said, 'Maybe it's time to lay off the juice for a spell. Let's get the op done first. Then we can get fucking wasted.'

Lazarides said, 'Starting tomorrow, I'll be as dry as a witch's tit. But tonight, I'm getting pissed. That's final.' He looked a challenge at Carter. 'You got a problem with that?'

'Depends.'

'On what?'

'Will you be all right once you're off the drink?'

'Jesus, mate. I'm not an alkie. I'll be fine.'

'Didn't look that way yesterday. You were hanging out of your arse in the gym. I've seen slop jockeys with better stamina.'

'Sweating it out. Best form of detox.' Lazarides relaxed his features into a crooked grin.

'I'm not joking.'

'Me neither. Just you watch me. I'll turn it on when the time comes. Besides, I could do with a dry spell. My fitness is the last thing you need to worry about.'

Carter said, 'Fine. But this is the last one for me. Then I'm back to the camp.'

Lazarides grinned. 'What'd I tell you, Ned? The Pom can't hold his beer. He's got hollow legs, this one.'

The Aussies shared a laugh. Carter gave them a frosty look and said, 'I've got a long-haul flight tomorrow. I'm not getting on that plane with a thumping hangover.'

Dempsey said, 'Your choice. But you're missing out. An hour from now this place will be heaving with Regiment groupies.'

'More fun for us then, mate.' Lazarides smiled, rubbing his hands excitedly.

Carter slid off his leather stool and threaded his way towards the bar. Women glanced in his direction, hungry eyes mentally undressing him. Which came as no surprise to Carter. He was in the shape of his life. Ninety kilos of honed muscle. The sleeves of his polo shirt strained around bulging biceps; plain trousers bear-hugged his colossal thighs. Like Hercules jacked up on steroids, an ex-girlfriend had told him.

He was looking forward to getting his head down. Had a rapid turnaround once he landed in Britain. Four days on the ground. During which time he had to take care of his personal admin, attend a final briefing with the ops officers at Hereford, find out who else was on the team. Then he was on a flight to Germany.

*Better to go back to your digs*, Carter told himself. *Get some shuteye.* Oldest rule in the SAS book. Rest when you can before an op.

He ordered three pints of Carlton Draught, shouting over the din of rugby match noise and bar chatter. Had to repeat the order three times before the barman understood his thick Geordie accent. In the corner of his eye he noticed one of the supporters on the fringes of the crowd staring at him with heavily glazed eyes.

'Hey, Pom!'

Carter ignored the man. Waited for his drinks.

The Aussie moved towards him. Raised his voice.

'You deaf? I'm talking to you, Pommie bastard!'

Carter still ignored him. The barman finished pulling the pints, set them down on the drip tray.

'Here, lads! Look at this tosser,' the rugby fan called out to his mates. He pointed at Carter's sculpted biceps. 'Got a Pom over here who thinks he's fucking Superman.'

Carter paid for his beers. At his nine o'clock three of the drunk guy's mates had turned towards him. Sizing Carter up.

'Think you're hard, do you, Pom? Think you're the big man?' the drunk guy rasped. 'Oi! Where are your manners? Say something, you Pom prick.'

Carter calmly wheeled round to face the Aussie.

The man in front of him was tall and heavily built, with a silvery beard and flared nostrils. He had an Australian rugby union jersey stretched over his beer belly. His bulky frame suggested a guy who enjoyed the good life. Beer and cookouts and meals in fancy restaurants. Muscle buried beneath a costume of fat.

'What d'you bench press, mate? Bet it ain't as much as me.'

Carter didn't reply. By now three of Silver Beard's muckers had turned away from the match to see what was going on. One of them was heavily suntanned, with skin the colour of mahogany and a shock of blond hair. He had the same sort of running-to-fat build as Silver Beard.

The guy next to Suntan had a glistening bald dome, small eyes set too close together; a walrus moustache drooped down either side of his thin lips. With his flannel shirt and beanie hat he looked like a lumberjack who'd clocked off work for the day.

The fourth man was a Samoan. He was undoubtedly the biggest bloke Carter had ever seen. Had to weigh north of twenty stone, he guessed. At the very minimum. His chest was the approximate width of a forty-five-gallon drum. His legs were as thick as concrete bridge piles. His hands were the size of kettlebells.

Silver Beard started shadow-boxing in front of Carter. Dancing around him, aiming fake jabs and hooks at the SAS man. 'Come on, Pom. Show us a few moves,' he said as he feigned another strike at Carter's solar plexus.

Suntan, Walrus and the Samoan laughed.

Carter thought, *I really don't need this.*

*Not tonight.*

'Fuck off,' he said.

Silver Beard stopped boxing. Dropped his arms by his sides and glared at Carter, the skin pulled tight across his face. Anger pulsed behind his narrowed eyes.

'What did you say?' he rasped.

'Fuck off back to the rugby,' Carter said, coolly. 'You might see your lads actually score a point if you're lucky.'

'You gonna take that, Tate?' Suntan called out.

'Hit the cunt!' Walrus shouted. 'Knock his fucking teeth out!'

In his peripheral vision Carter spotted the nearest drinkers edging backwards. Smelling trouble, no doubt, and wanting to get as far away from it as possible.

He refocused his attention on the four rugby fans. Sensed the situation turning ugly. He'd been in plenty of similar situations in the past. He knew how it would go down. The Aussies were looking for a scrap. A volatile combination of titanic quantities of alcohol, testosterone and seeing their team getting destroyed in the rugby.

Silver Beard took another step towards Carter. Invading his personal space. Staking out his territory. He was close enough for Carter to smell the beer on his breath.

Suntan, Walrus and the Samoan drew closer. Crowding round Carter.

'Pom bastard!' Silver Beard roared madly.

Then he shaped to throw a punch.

Carter read the move a whole second before it happened. Which didn't sound like much. But in a close-combat fight, a second was the difference between countering an attack and getting smashed in the face. Silver Beard had a lot of bulk, a lot of slow-twitch muscle fibre. He could probably lift more weight than Carter. On a one-rep max deadlift, he'd beat Carter hands down. But he didn't have speed of movement. The sprint gene had evidently skipped a generation.

Carter saw Silver Beard lifting his right shoulder, his hand bunched into a tight fist as he twisted at the core. Throwing all of his kinetic energy into the blow. Winding up for a strike to the jaw. Which was theoretically a good tactic. A clean hook, executed correctly, could end the fight in a single punch. But Silver Beard's immense mass let him down. The guy looked like he was moving through treacle. Carter could have finished reading the complete works of Tolstoy before the blow landed.

Carter slapped the Aussie's fist away with his left hand, diverted it down and away from his body. In the same movement he rocked back on his right foot and punched up at an angle, driving his clenched fist at Silver Beard's throat. The Aussie gasped as Carter's knuckles slammed into his windpipe. He dropped to the floor like a sack of hot bricks, hands pawing at his neck.

Then all hell broke loose.

Walrus was the first to lunge at Carter. He roared madly, throwing wild punches. Not the most sophisticated attack in the world. He was betting on pure male aggression succeeding where his friend had failed.

Carter tacked to the right, narrowly evading a ragged blow aimed at his chin, swiped an empty pint glass from the bar and smashed it against Walrus's head. Glass shards waterfalled over his bald dome. The Aussie grunted as he fell backwards, slack weight crashing to the beer-slicked floor.

Carter had no time to admire his handiwork. He spun round, saw Suntan and the Samoan simultaneously rushing towards him. A coordinated assault. Carter threw up his arms, desperately shielding his face. Pain flared in his ribs as one of the Aussies caught him with a low blow. Another punch found its way through his raised hands and struck him on the side of the head. The next thing Carter knew he was landing on his back. Suntan and the Samoan swarmed over him, delivering savage kicks to his torso, while the other customers scrambled away from the fight, knocking over bar stools and beer bottles.

Then, through a gap between his attackers, Carter caught sight of a pair of blurred figures charging towards him.

Lazarides and Dempsey.

They sprinted across the bar, shouting challenges at Suntan and the Samoan. Suntan turned to face the new threat and walked right into a flurry of punches from Dempsey. He took a meaty fist to the temple and grunted in pain. At the same time Lazarides sprang forward, catching the Samoan with a devastating left hook. The Samoan stumbled back out of range, blood streaming out of his mashed-up nose. Before he could recover Lazarides was on him again, feinting another left hook. The Samoan moved to block the attack; Lazarides shovelled a punch into the guy's bread-basket, winding him, followed through with a brutal uppercut. The Samoan groaned as his jawbone slammed into the roof of his skull. He crumpled to a heap at Lazarides' feet, clawing at his mashed-up nose.

The fight was almost over. Carter picked himself off the floor. Pain scraped fingernail-like down the sides of his skull. Through the brain fog he spied Dempsey finishing off Suntan with a mean right hook that sent him flying backwards against the bar, arms windmilling as he knocked over racks of empty bottles and wine glasses. He slumped down amid a sea of broken glass and spilled booze.

Walrus climbed groggily to his feet. So did the Samoan. The two Aussies stood facing Lazarides and Carter, staying well out of punching range, eyeing the soldiers warily. Blood streamed down Walrus's face. A few paces away, Silver Beard writhed in agony, clutching his throat. Suntan was still out of the fight, lying face down on the floor as if someone had glued his lips to the boards.

'Come on, then? Which one of you fucking wants it?' Lazarides thundered. The veins on his neck bulged, thick as winch cables.

The two Aussies hesitated. Which was understandable. Their world had been turned upside down. They had anticipated a four-on-one scrap with Carter. Now they found themselves outnumbered and badly beaten. They saw the maddened look on Lazarides' face and edged backwards. A small gesture, but loaded with significance. They were signalling their retreat from the battlefield.

Lazarides waved a hand in the general direction of the entrance.

'Fuck off, then,' he snarled.

Walrus and the Samoan didn't argue. The Samoan helped Silver Beard stand up, threw an arm round him; Walrus hauled Suntan upright. The four battered rugby fans staggered towards the entrance, picking their way past the throng of stunned onlookers. A moment later they were out of sight.

The barman hurried over from behind the counter and started sweeping up the debris. Behind him an older man approached the soldiers, hair shot through with grey, glass crackling underfoot. The manager, Carter guessed. Lazarides stood glowering at him.

'The fuck do you want?'

The manager said, 'I'm not looking for trouble. But this is a family establishment. I'm going to have to ask you fellas to leave.'

'Wasn't our fault. Fuck's sake, those twats started it. We just did you a favour, getting rid of those wankers.'

Dempsey held up his hands in a peaceful gesture. 'We're from up the road, mate. We're just looking to enjoy a few drinks. That's all. You won't hear another peep out of us.'

The manager paused, sized up the four well-built men and reached a decision. 'All right,' he said grudgingly. 'But any more shit and you're out. Understood?'

'Roger that, mate.'

The manager walked back over to the bar with his dignity intact. The other drinkers returned to their beers, stared at their phone screens or gossiped with their companions. On the TV screens, the rugby match had finished. The Australian players trudged off the field, looking dejected, while the Welsh team celebrated wildly.

Carter nodded his thanks at Dempsey and Lazarides.

'That was one hell of a left hook you put on that lad,' he grinned.

Lazarides chuckled. 'Still think my drinking is a problem, Pom?'

'Just as long as you're on the orange juice once we're on the job.'

'Don't worry about that. By the time we've finished getting smashed tonight, me and Quade won't be thirsting for a beer for a while.'

'That's all I wanted to know.'

Carter smiled with relief. He knew then that his doubts about Lazarides had been misplaced. The guy didn't have the honed fitness of an elite athlete, maybe, but he had something even better, in Carter's eyes: raw fighting ability. The desire to go down into the trenches, into the dark places no one else wanted to go. The willingness to do anything to win. Not something you could hone on a machine in the gym, or boost with a pill. A combination of the genetic lottery and a lifetime of hardship.

'Stay for another round, Luke?' Dempsey asked.

Carter shook his head. 'I'm out. Heading back to camp. Don't want to fly back with a black eye.'

'Suit yourself.'

Carter left them at the table knocking back pints of cheap lager. He stepped around the staff cleaning up the mess and headed outside. Emerged to the mild Perth night. Smell of damp earth in the air. A possum scuttled across the road and disappeared down a gloomy alleyway. Carter started back up the main street towards the barracks and felt a familiar prickle of anticipation. The same feeling he always had before a job.

*Six days*, he reminded himself.

*Six days before the op begins.*

*And then there's no going back.*

# Five

Carter took the redeye Qantas flight from Perth. At five o'clock in the morning he stopped in Dubai for a two-hour layover. He navigated a shopping zone the size of a cruise ship, took a table outside a French chain store bakery, knocked back several cups of strong black coffee, then caught his connection to Heathrow. Landed at noon on a grey-as-ash Saturday. A pot-bellied Regiment driver with talcum-white hair and a black beard greeted him in the arrivals hall, ferried him up the M4 in foul West Country rain. By the time the car pulled up outside Carter's three-bedroom cottage in the village of Credenhill he'd been travelling for a solid twenty-four hours. Swanbourne, with its blazing sunshine and Instagrammable beaches, felt like a long time ago.

A short while later, his Regiment-issue phone hummed.

'Luke, it's Christopher,' a silvery voice said.

Carter knew the voice. Christopher Smallwood was the Regiment ops officer. A career Rupert. One of the many that infested the SAS. Forever looking down on the NCOs, treating them like an inferior species. The English class system in action. Smallwood had recruited Carter for the op, ordered him to Australia to interview suitable candidates. Carter had been expecting his call on his return.

'Good trip, Luke?' Smallwood asked in a tone that suggested he really didn't give a good fuck either way.

'Fine,' said Carter. 'Everything went fine.'

'And productive, I hope?'

'I met some interesting lads.'

Smallwood coughed to clear his throat. 'Listen, we need you to come in. Discuss a few things before you set off. Latest updates, final shake-out, that sort of thing. You know the drill.'

'When?' Carter asked.

'Tomorrow morning. Ten o'clock. Report to my office.'

'Roger that.'

\* \* \*

Shortly before ten o'clock on a bleak Sunday morning, Carter ditched his BMW X3 in the Credenhill car park and beat a path towards a three-storey concrete-clad building on the far side of the camp.

Everyone knew it as the Kremlin: the beating heart of operations for 22 SAS. The name had survived the cull of all things Russian that had followed the invasion of Ukraine. Probably they would still be calling it the Kremlin fifty years from now, Carter thought as he breezed through the entrance. He climbed the stairs to the second floor, stopped outside the door to the ops officer's private office, heard a roar of laughter from inside. Carter rapped his knuckles twice on the frame.

The laughter cut out. A muffled voice from the other side called out, 'Yes? Come in!'

Carter ducked into a large room decorated like something out of an early 2000s office furniture catalogue. White desk, computer monitor, strip lighting, cabinets and shelving, Cisco phone system. Rectangular meeting table ringed with cantilever chairs.

Christopher Smallwood sat at the head of the table, his head crowned with a few tragic strands of thinning brown hair. As if a crow was in the early stages of building a nest on top of his head. Two figures were seated either side of the ops officer. To his right was Peter Hardcastle, the CO of 22 SAS. To his left, the adjutant, Nick Waddell. Carter was staring at the three most powerful men in the Regiment. The Holy Trinity of Credenhill.

Across the table sat a fourth man. A whippet-thin guy with acne-scarred skin and a slab-like forehead. His Adam's apple protruded from his neck so far you could hang a coat from it.

Carter recognised him instantly.

Karl Beach, aka the Food Monster, was a fellow Blade. One of the guys who ran the courses on the Dems wing. Which made him an explosives nerd. A South London lad with a dirty sense of humour, Beach was famous around the camp for his legendary appetite. He always seemed to be eating, and yet he didn't look like he weighed a gram over seventy kilos. How he put away so much junk without piling on the pounds was one of the enduring mysteries of Hereford.

Beach had been part of the same intake as Carter. They'd passed Selection together, lifted each other's spirits during the gruelling Hills Phase. Since then, their paths had crossed a few times on various training packages.

'Hello, Geordie,' Beach said. 'How are you, pal?'

He looked up at Carter, grinning from ear to ear. On the other side of the table, Waddell and Smallwood were both stifling laughs, as if they had been listening to the punchline of a filthy joke.

Carter stood in the doorway, momentarily taken aback.

'What the fuck are you doing here?' he demanded.

The grin fell from Beach's face. Waddell and Smallwood stifled their laughs.

'Karl's joining your team,' Smallwood explained. 'We've just been bringing him up to date on things.'

'Take a seat, Luke,' Hardcastle said tersely. 'Close the door behind you, there's a good chap.'

Carter frowned. The sight of Beach looking chummy and cracking jokes with the Regimental bigwigs had put him on the back foot. He had the uneasy feeling that he'd been hoodwinked.

*How long has Beach been sitting here chatting with this mob?* Carter wondered. *What have they been talking about without me?*

He dropped into the empty chair next to Beach. Hardcastle leaned forward, bony hands laced in front of him.

'I understand,' he began, 'that you've found a couple of suitable lads for the operation among our friends Down Under.'

Carter nodded. 'That's right.'

Hardcastle nodded briskly. Waddell, the adjutant, sat with crossed arms. The junior member of the Trinity. Smallwood would do most of the talking, Carter assumed. As ops officer he was running the show, moving pieces on the board. Hardcastle had probably insisted on sitting in on the briefing to make sure he was up to speed on the plan.

*And to shield himself from any blowback if this thing goes south,* Carter thought.

'Well, out with it, man. What's your assessment?' Hardcastle asked. 'Are they on the level?'

'They're sound,' Carter replied. 'Experienced lads. Capable, as far as I can tell. Obviously, I haven't seen them train or anything like that.' He shook his head. 'I still don't see why you needed me to go down there on some fucking jolly. Surely you could have got all of this stuff from their files?'

'Files can only tell us so much. They don't give us the full picture. I wanted you to look them in the eye. Man to man. Only way to know if they're up to the job.'

'Any other issues we should know about?' Waddell chipped in. 'Anything that isn't in their files?'

Carter met his gaze. 'You mean that business with 2 Squadron being disbanded?'

Waddell shrugged. 'Among other things, yes.'

'Well, Luke?' Hardcastle asked.

Carter said, 'They're clean as a couple of hound's teeth. You've got no worries on that front.'

A look of relief played out on the CO's face as he eased back in his chair. He gave a slight nod in Smallwood's direction, giving the floor to his subordinate. The latter sat upright and said, 'Karl is coming over to E Squadron from the Dems wing. We've brought him on board for his particular knowledge. That should have you covered for all the skillsets you're going to need.'

'So we've got the green light?'

Smallwood nodded. 'Everything's still set for Wednesday. Which means you'll need to get your prep done in the next forty-eight hours.'

'What's the itinerary?'

'You'll both be leaving on a C-17 from Brize Norton. Wheels in the air at 0700 hours Wednesday morning. Landing in Germany at around 0900 local time. Sergeant Major Mike Beattie will be there to meet you on the other side.'

'Mike's been notified,' Hardcastle said. 'He's expecting you.'

Smallwood said, 'He'll arrange a doss-up area for you on-site. Briefing rooms. Personal kit. All of that will be supplied on arrival. You'll be going in data black, of course. The Scaleys will sort you out with phones and tablets. Everything you'll need for the mission.'

Carter nodded his understanding.

In recent years data black had become standard operating procedure for the lads on covert jobs. Carter and his colleagues wouldn't be taking any personal electronic devices with them – anything that might leave a digital footprint. But equally, a bunch of guys strolling through an airport without a phone between them would automatically arouse suspicion. So 18 Sigs had started issuing the guys with burners fitted with local SIM cards. To a casual observer they looked like bog-standard Android handsets. But entering a certain code on the unlock screen triggered a secret distress signal, transmitted back to the Hereford ops room.

'What about the Aussies?' asked Beach.

'They're flying out of Perth on Monday. Landing at Heathrow around nine o'clock Tuesday morning, then onward to Ramstein. They'll be waiting for you both at the base.'

Carter said, 'Who's going to brief us in Ramstein?'

'Our friends at Vauxhall,' Smallwood said. 'They're sending some of their chaps down. Three officers. We understand they'll be landing early Tuesday morning.'

'Have they said anything more about the op?'

'Only that the situation remains extremely fluid.'

'Blame the suits down in London, Geordie,' said Hardcastle airily. 'Nature of the beast. The usual concerns about the plan being compromised. Won't tell us a damned thing.'

He wrinkled his nose. Carter kept his mouth shut. But he didn't believe for a second that Six would have cleared the op without briefing their Hereford counterparts on the bare bones. No doubt they had made it clear to Hardcastle that they didn't want any int shared with the team until they had landed in Germany. By which point, Carter knew, it would be too late to abort.

He said, 'Can you at least tell us what the weather's going to be like where we're operating? Conditions on the ground?'

Irritation flickered across Smallwood's face. 'Are you getting twitchy, Geordie? Cold feet about the mission?'

Carter shook his head. 'I just want to get my prep done properly.'

'It's a fair question,' Beach said. 'No point packing our thermals if we're deploying to the Maldives, is it?'

Smallwood said nothing. He darted a glance at Hardcastle. As if seeking permission. Waddell scribbled notes on a pad. Hardcastle pressed a finger to his lips and considered for a long beat. Then he tipped his head at the ops officer. *Permission granted.*

'It's a cold weather environment,' Smallwood said.

'What's the temperature? Forecast?'

'It won't get above one or two degrees. Low of minus five or six, but with the wind it'll feel colder. Above average rainfall for this time of year. That's really all I'm at liberty to share with you.'

Hardcastle glanced at his watch. Looked round the table. 'I think that should just about cover it, gents? Unless you have any further questions? Geordie? Karl?'

Carter and Beach glanced at one another. Beach shrugged. Smallwood levered himself up from his chair, signalling an end to the briefing.

'Right, lads. I suggest you finish your preparations. Sort out any life admin. Report to the camp at 0500 hours Wednesday morning with your bags packed. One of the drivers will shuttle you down to Brize for your flight. No need to bring along your passports or any other documentation, Six will take care of all that at the briefing.'

'Good luck, gentlemen,' Hardcastle said, soberly. He leaned across the table, looked the two soldiers hard in the eye. 'I shouldn't have to say this, but I'm going to anyway. Don't fuck this one up. Don't you bloody dare. We've had enough problems in this unit lately. Give me any more trouble – either of you – and I'll skin you both alive.'

Carter and Beach filed out of the ops office, left the Holy Trinity sitting around the table talking shop. They emerged from the Kremlin to the grey gloom of midday. Carter started across the tarmac towards his BMW. Beach walked at his side, wearing a troubled expression.

'What was all that about, Geordie? All that stuff the CO said at the end, about problems in the unit.'

'He was talking about G Squadron.'

'Why?' Beach's frown deepened. 'What's the craic with G Squadron?'

Carter glanced at him in surprise. 'Haven't you heard the rumours?'

'Been out of the loop, pal. Spent the last two years teaching dems.'

Carter brought him up to speed on the gossip surrounding G Squadron. The stories he'd heard about some of the lads in the squadron. Guys getting involved with shady biker gangs. Stealing loot during stronghold assaults. Selling weaponry and ammunition on the black market. The recent exodus from the squadron.

Beach lifted an eyebrow. 'Fucking hell. Sounds like some of them lads were up to no good.' A thought played out on his face. He stared at Carter curiously. 'Half a mo. Wasn't your brother in G a while back?'

'He was. Not for long, though.'

'Fucking tragic what happened to him.'

Carter nodded but didn't reply. In the days after Jamie's death the head shed had put out a story that he had been killed by a stray round fired from a Russian position while bodyguarding a top Ukrainian general. Karl Beach and the rest of the guys knew nothing about the general's betrayal, or that the enemy had been minutes away from causing a disaster at the country's largest nuclear power plant.

'Either way,' Beach continued, 'it's good to get back to some proper work. Tell you the truth, I was getting bored out of my nut teaching the course.'

Carter said, 'I thought you were mad about dems.'

'I love the theory. The maths, the formulas. But you try teaching the same shit for two years. Enough to do my head in.'

Carter chuckled and said, 'You might change your tune a few weeks from now. We're heading into the unknown here,' he added quietly.

Beach looked at him carefully. 'Any idea what this is all about?'

'I was hoping you might tell me.'

'Meaning what?'

'Meaning,' Carter responded, 'you were friendly back there with Hardcastle and his arse-kissers.'

'Fuck off, Geordie. I was just telling them a few jokes, like. Breaking the ice. Nothing more than that.'

'As long as that's all it is.'

'I don't know a thing,' Beach insisted. 'I'm in the dark, same as you. Playing catch-up. Figured you might know more than me.'

Carter said, 'I don't. They've fobbed us off every time I've asked for clarity. Been the same story since they pulled me onto the op.'

'But if you had to guess?'

'I'd say it probably involves Ukraine.'

Beach nodded. 'My thinking exactly. Why else would they fly us out to Ramstein? Every fucker knows that's the nerve centre for SF ops in Ukraine. Guess that counts as a cold weather environment, too.'

Carter laughed. 'Definitely ain't tropical at this time of year.'

'Probably a training op,' Beach speculated.

'That's what the Aussies reckon.'

'And you?'

'I don't know,' Carter said. 'But whatever those fuckers at Six have got planned for us, they're desperate to keep it a secret.'

Beach shrugged. 'Either way, it'll be better than teaching another course on Dems wing. Had enough of that to last me ten lifetimes.'

They had stopped midway across the car park. Beach jerked a thumb in the direction of the sergeants' mess.

'Grab a bite to eat, Geordie? Don't know about you but I'm hungry as fuck. Could eat a horse right now.'

He patted his washboard stomach.

'You could always eat a horse, you greedy bastard.'

'What can I say?' Beach grinned. 'I'm a man of big appetites. Need all that energy to satisfy the ladies in bed.'

'Yeah,' Carter said. 'Those two-minute performances must really take it out of you.'

'Prick.'

They parted ways. Carter headed towards his BMW.

He thought, *Four-man team.*

*Sniper specialist.*

*Drone operator.*

*Dems expert.*

*And a team leader.*

*Tasked with a job in Ukraine.*

Maybe Beach and the Aussies were right. Maybe they were being sent out to instruct Ukrainian SF personnel. But he wasn't convinced. The Regiment had been running training packages in

Ukraine for several years, teaching local forces how to fight. Some of Carter's colleagues on the Wing had been part of those rotations. Not routine jobs, perhaps. More exciting than a stint on Dems wing. But not out of the ordinary, either. Certainly it wouldn't justify the veil of secrecy Vauxhall had insisted on.

*Something else is going on here,* thought Carter.

*Something much bigger.*

*Whatever it is, we'll find out soon enough.*

# Six

Carter spent the next thirty-six hours sorting out his pre-op prep. Tying up loose ends. He packed his leather holdall with personal kit which consisted of two pairs of civvy clothes, suitable for sub-zero temperatures, bivvy bags, portable stove, webbing, toiletries, canteen, sterilising tablets, carb-rich snacks, pen-torch, binoculars. Everything he might conceivably need for the mission. He downloaded the latest David Fincher film to his Reg phone, along with several episodes of *Ozark*. Enough to keep him entertained at Ramstein. Carter figured there could be a lot of sitting around, waiting for updates from Six.

On the Monday afternoon he dropped off his spare keys with his neighbour. Ken Greening was one of the many ex-SAS guys who lived in and around Credenhill. Carter often dropped round for a chat over a brew. He liked to listen to the old Blade's war stories. The stunning raid on Pebble Island in the Falklands. Operating behind enemy lines in Iraq in the First Gulf War, cutting around in Land Rover 110s and knocking out targets. Those tales were a powerful reminder that Carter was following in the footsteps of giants. Men who had gone out and done the business, faced down impossible odds. Men who had changed history.

*Now we're about to do the same,* Carter told himself.

*I just hope we're ready.*

The next morning he left for Germany.

* * *

The Regiment driver was waiting for them at the camp car park. The same guy who'd collected Carter from Heathrow four days earlier with his powder-white hair and dark beard. As if he'd dyed his facial hair but had run out of colour before he could get to work on his head. Carter and Beach dumped their luggage in the rear of the Volkswagen Caravelle and sat in the middle row of seats. The driver buzzed the sliding door shut, climbed behind the wheel, rolled out of the camp.

The first bluish light of dawn tinged the horizon as they shuttled east towards Oxfordshire. The driver stayed silent during the journey. He coasted along a few miles below the speed limit, Classic FM spilling out of the car speakers at a low volume. Part of the training for the job. Don't ask questions. Stay invisible.

Carter spent most of the ride staring out of the window, lost in his thoughts. Beach periodically worked an app on his smartphone, fingers swiping and scrolling through screens filled with numbers.

'What's that?' Carter asked.

'Gambling app,' Beach explained. 'Just laying a few last-minute bets before we leave the country.' He looked up from the screen. 'Enjoy a flutter, Geordie?'

'Mug's game,' Carter said. 'I've got better things to do than piss away my hard-earned dough.'

'It's not pissed away if you win.'

'Is this what you've been doing on Dems wing all this time? Betting on the horses?'

'I don't bet fixed odds. That really is a fool's game. Me, I'm more interested in spread betting. Keeps my mind exercised. I like to study the maths behind it.'

Carter laughed. 'You sure that isn't your inner addict speaking?'

Beach gave him a look. 'There's more to spread betting than slapping a few quid on the 12.20 at Lingfield. A lot more. The rewards are huge, too. You can make big profits.'

'Wasting your time. If it was that easy, every fucker in the country would be a millionaire by now.'

'I never said it was easy. You need to have a head for numbers. Statistical patterns and trends. It's a whole system, Geordie. I could show you sometime, if you want?'

Carter managed to disguise his horror at the prospect of a prolonged maths lesson with Karl Beach. 'Let's get the op out of the way first.'

They settled in for the rest of the journey. At 0650 they reached RAF Brize Norton. The Reg driver cleared security at the main gate, drove past a cluster of maintenance buildings and rolled straight onto the tarmac stand. He pulled up downstream from a C-17 Globemaster. The Caravelle side door whirred open. Carter and Beach retrieved their holdalls from the back seat and trotted across the tarmac towards the waiting cargo transporter. Dawn had broken in the distance; a ribbon of rose-gold light flamed the horizon, silhouetted the clumps of woodland beyond the perimeter.

A loadie stood beside the lowered ramp aft of the C-17, watching the two SAS men as they approached. Behind him a number of sturdy pallets had been tethered to the centreline with cargo straps. Resupplies for Ramstein, Carter supposed. Ration packs and other essentials. A huge amount of stuff would be flown into Germany each week, keeping the SF teams on the ground fed and clothed and supplied with all the hardware they needed for ops in the east. A complex logistical operation. Perhaps not the most glamorous aspect of warfare. But just as vital if they were going to defeat the Russians.

Carter and Beach stepped round the tangle of metal chains and straps, flipped down two of the sidewall seats at the far end of the fuselage, next to the loadie's station. Dumped their bags at their feet and buckled up. The loadie came over clutching two pairs of Ear Defenders. Distributed one set to Carter, the other to Beach. They were sitting a few metres away from four Pratt & Whitney turbofan engines. Powerful beasts, but also fucking loud. Carter fished his wireless earbuds out of his holdall, popped them in, placed the defenders over the top. Unlocked his iPad, tapped open Netflix.

The loadie carried out his pre-flight routine, checking straps, conversing over his mic with the pilot and co-pilot. He kept throwing suspicious glances at Carter and Beach. Jealously guarding his territory. The fuselage was his domain. No doubt he wanted to know more about the two soldiers dressed in civilian gear, wondered what the fuck they were doing on a cargo flight to Germany.

The loadie finished his checks, plodded back over to his station. Strapped himself in. There was more chatter between the loadie and the pilots. The engines cranked up several notches, reached an incessant whining pitch. The aft ramp closed, sealing the guys inside the belly of the C-17. Carter upped the iPad volume to the max setting to muffle the background noise, while the C-17 crept forward, taxiing towards the runway.

Four minutes later they were in the air.

*   *   *

They touched down at Ramstein exactly fifty-nine minutes later. Nine o'clock on Wednesday morning. The engine drone dialled down to a faint whine as the C-17 ground to a halt on the apron. There was a burst of chatter between the loadie and the pilots. The aft ramp dropped, Carter and Beach snatched up their holdalls and hurried down the ramp, passing half a dozen members of the ground crew wearing high-vis jackets over their standard-issue uniforms. The crewmen dropped down beside the cargo pallets, loosening the straps with rehearsed speed.

Almost a year had passed since Carter had first visited Ramstein Air Base. Back then he'd arrived as part of a team tasked with body-guarding the Ukrainian President. Not much had changed since then. The place still swarmed with frantic activity. Across the apron several ground staff were busy unloading cargo from a grounded Atlas transport craft. The continual grind of the war effort, thought Carter. A vast operation. Billions of taxpayer dollars in action. Tens of thousands of service personnel working round the clock. All of it dedicated to one end: defeating the ambitions of the madman in the Kremlin. He wondered how long the overlords of the West could keep up the momentum. Already the news channels were carrying reports of war-weariness among the NATO members. Beleaguered politicians were threatening to turn off the spigot. A year from now, unless the mood changed, Ukraine might find itself standing alone against the Russian aggressors.

Two figures marched over to greet the SAS men. One of the guys was in his early fifties with porcupine hair and sandpaper-rough features. Carter had met him on his previous visit to Ramstein. Sergeant Major Mike Beattie. Hereford's man on the ground in Germany. Air Base Quartermaster. One of the NCO lifers in the Regiment.

Alongside him walked Christopher Smallwood.

'What the fuck is he doing here?' Beach muttered under his breath.

'No idea, mate,' said Carter.

Smallwood nodded stiffly at the soldiers as he approached. 'Guys. How was your flight?'

Carter stared at him in confusion. 'You didn't tell us you were flying over.'

'Last-minute decision,' Smallwood replied matter-of-factly. 'Hardcastle wanted me to take personal charge of this one. Hands-on approach. Liaise with our friends in Six on the planning and prep.'

'When did you get in?'

'Yesterday morning. Came over on the same flight as the suits from Vauxhall.'

Carter said nothing more. He just stared at Smallwood, his mind racing ahead of him.

*I don't know what they're planning for us*, he thought. *But I know this much. This is definitely a big job. They wouldn't have sent Small-wood over here. Not unless it was something massive.*

'Back already, Geordie?' Beattie broke in with his strong Ulster brogue. He grinned broadly as he shook Carter's hand. 'Fucking hell, didn't we only just get rid of you?'

Carter shrugged. 'Guess I'm a glutton for punishment.'

'Either that, or you can't get enough of my famous brews.'

'Yeah, that's definitely it, Mike. Your shite tea is why I'm back here so soon.'

Beattie threw back his head and laughed. 'I'm guessing you must be the other lad they told me to expect,' he said to Beach.

'That's right,' Beach said.

Beattie scrutinised him. 'Fuck me, son. Look at you. Skin and bloody bone. What did your mother feed you as a wee kid? Scraps from the local curry house?'

'Piss off.'

'Where are the Aussies?' asked Carter.

Beattie said, 'Doss block.' He indicated the steel hangar on the far side of the apron. 'Everything's all set up for you. This way. Let's get you lads settled in.'

He turned and led them across the tarmac at a brisk pace, Small-wood at his side, Carter and Beach following a couple of paces behind, carrying their holdalls. Beyond the airbase the last shreds of mist clung to the distant wooded hills. Dirty clouds bulged like sandbags overhead, heavy with the threat of rain. Ramstein Air Base, thought Carter. The only place in the world that could rival Manchester for crap weather.

As they neared the hangar Beattie fell in next to Carter.

'You heard about that shitstorm with G Squadron?' he asked quietly.

'None of my business,' Carter replied.

'Course not, Geordie. Course not. Fucking shocking, though. What they were supposed to have done. Word is, the DSF hit the roof when he found out. Threatened to sack half the squadron.'

Carter kept walking. He couldn't be sure where Beattie's loyalties lay. He knew the guy had been part of G Squadron back in the day; had good friends in that group. Including some of the soldiers who'd quietly left the Regiment in the summer. The men suspected of involvement with the biker gangs.

Beattie kept up his questions. 'Is it still going on? The investigation?'

'I wouldn't know. I haven't been in camp much lately.'

'Your brother was in G for a spell, wasn't he? Did he say anything to you?'

'Not a peep. We didn't really speak much. Moved in different circles.' He rounded on Beattie. 'Why are you interested, anyway?'

'No reason, mate,' Beattie said defensively. 'Just curious about the latest gossip from H, that's all.'

Carter carried on towards the hangar. Not for the first time, he wondered what his brother had been up to during his brief stint in G Squadron. Had Jamie known – or suspected – his colleagues of wrongdoing? Or perhaps he'd been involved himself . . .

Carter instantly dismissed the thought from his mind. Jamie would never have allowed himself to get involved in anything shifty. It would have gone against everything he stood for.

They followed Beattie and Smallwood past the duty guards and swept into the hangar. The layout was instantly familiar to Carter. He could have walked around the place blindfolded. He listened as Beattie pointed out the various areas to Beach. Planning section at the opposite end. Designated zone for the Scaleys in 18 Sigs. To the left, separate spaces for the cookhouse, gym, kitchen, breakout area. Storage facilities, so the guys could securely cache their kit prior to deployment. Accommodation for the air crews.

A dozen SF lads were milling about the place, decked out in their Crye Precision gear. Some were doing weights; others sat around watching shows on their iPads. Waiting for the call to deploy forward to Ukraine on covert ops.

*We might be making the same journey a few days from now.*

Beattie and Smallwood ushered them towards the doss house on the right side of the hangar which consisted of a series of prefabricated steel units, each one roughly the size of a shipping container, stacked up like Jenga blocks, with gantries leading to the uppermost structures.

'You're on the ground floor,' Beattie said. 'Crocodile Dundee and his mate are bunking on the first floor.'

He stopped just short of their bunks. Thrust out a hand. 'I'll have to ask you to surrender your devices. You know the rules. We're in a sterile environment now.'

Carter and Beach took out their phones, handed them over to Beattie. Then Smallwood checked his watch and said, 'Right, guys. Initial briefing is in an hour. Briefing room three. I'll see you then.'

He turned on his heels and headed over to the planning section. Beattie straightened his back, nodded tersely at Carter and Beach in turn. 'I'll let you lads get settled in. Questions?'

'Where's our kit?' asked Beach.

'Storage area. It's all there. Equipment, stores. Drones, sniper rifles, explosives. Everything you and your mates requested.'

'What if we need anything else?'

'I can usually source it from somewhere in Germany or the US. Get it delivered to base in a few days. Within reason, of course. But if you're after a sex doll you're shit out of luck.'

'No worries on that front,' Carter quipped. 'Karl's gone so long without any he's probably got weeds growing down there now.'

'Fuck off, Geordie. I do all right with the ladies.'

'Really?' Beattie lifted an eyebrow in surprise. 'Things must have changed in H since I was last there, then.'

'Yeah? How's that?'

'If you're doing well for yourself, there must be a thriving market for stick-thin blokes who've smacked into every branch on the ugly tree on the way down.'

Carter and Beattie laughed easily. Beach glared at the Ulsterman, his lips pressed into a hard line. He started to reply, but Beattie was already walking away, making for the signallers' units.

Carter and Beach dumped their holdalls on their bunks and crossed the hangar to the breakout area. They found Lazarides and Dempsey sitting at one of the tables. Dempsey was reading a paperback biography of the Kelly gang; Lazarides watched Sky News on a TV screen so big you could map the stars on it. They rose from their chairs at the sight of the approaching Blades, introduced themselves to Beach. Small-talked about their flights and what they had been doing since they got in.

Dempsey said, 'Any news on when we're getting briefed?'

'An hour. With Smallwood.'

'Thank fuck for that,' Lazarides groused. 'Been bored out of my arsehole since we got here. Nothing to do except watch crap TV and drink brews. We're not even allowed off-base to get a beer.'

Carter said, 'You're supposed to be off the sauce now.'

'We're not on the job yet. I was hoping for a final tinny or two before the big briefing.'

'Should have brought a few books with you, Steve,' Dempsey said. 'Educate yourself.'

'Why bother, when I've got your sad arse for company? President of the Ned Kelly fan club. Heard so many stories since we got on the plane, I could write a book on him myself.'

Beach patted his flat stomach. 'How about we get some scran? Bloody starving, me. Haven't had a bite since we left Brize.'

Carter stared at him in disbelief. 'We were only in the air for an hour, you greedy bastard.'

'Long enough.'

Lazarides said, 'What's the deal with your ops officer? You didn't say anything about him joining us.'

'Because I didn't know,' Carter said. 'No one told me he was coming.'

'He told us it was a last-minute decision,' Dempsey said.

'It's possible,' Carter replied.

'You think he's lying?'

Carter said carefully, 'I've done plenty of jobs for Six since I joined the Wing. Never had the ops officer flying over for the general briefing. Sometimes an int officer will join us, but the ops chiefs are usually tucked up in bed back home.'

'So why is he here?'

Carter shrugged. 'Maybe our CO wanted him to sit in on the briefing.'

'What for?'

'To keep a close eye on us, maybe. Make sure we behave ourselves. The CO wouldn't want to rely on feedback from Six. He'd want someone he can trust. Someone who can report back to him on the QT.'

Dempsey furrowed his brow. 'You reckon your boss is *spying* on us?'

'Do you have a better explanation?' Carter said.

Dempsey didn't reply. He contemplated the dregs of his coffee cup, as if he could read his fortune in it. Beach stared longingly at the grub being served up in the kitchen.

'Guess we'll find out what's going on sooner or later,' Lazarides said, breaking the silence. 'But one thing's for sure, Pom. I don't trust your bosses a fucking inch.'

# Seven

Forty minutes later, Beattie summoned the team to the briefing room. He led them across the hangar floor, towards a row of sound-proofed units at the far end. Ramstein's planning section. Beattie stopped in front of the nearest cell, plucked a plastic key card from his jacket pocket. Tapped it against the card reader fitted above the chrome escutcheon. The reader beeped twice; the light glowed bright green. The locking mechanism clicked. Beattie wrenched the door open, gestured for Carter and the others to enter.

They stepped into a long and narrow briefing room illuminated by a quartet of standing lamps. Carter, Beach, Dempsey and Lazarides seated themselves on the chairs on one side of a scuffed beechwood meeting table. Smallwood sat opposite them, scowling at his phone like he had a personal beef with it. A pair of sixty-inch TV screens had been rigged up to trolley stands at the far end of the table. There was a landline in the middle of the table, a tablet, a Dell laptop, a discus-shaped conference speakerphone, bottles of mineral water, coffee cups, thermal jugs. Like someone had preserved a turn-of-the-century conference room in aspic.

Smallwood waited for the men to take their seats. Beattie closed the door, sealing them inside. The ops officer set his phone screen-down on the table, laced his hands together.

'Where are the suits?' Carter asked.

'They're tied up,' Smallwood said. 'Busy getting clearance for everything, as I understand. They'll join us later. For now, we'll cover the basics. Operational and planning briefings to follow.'

Dempsey folded thick arms across his front and said, 'Just tell us the craic.'

Smallwood said, 'Guys, I'll get straight to it. You're going to be running a training team. Your mission is to instruct a group of pre-screened Ukrainian soldiers, teach them your specialist skill-sets and bring them up to the necessary standards, preliminary to conducting a series of clandestine operations on foreign soil.'

Carter said, 'Who are we instructing?'

'Your students will be drawn from Alpha Group. The most elite unit within Ukrainian Special Forces. I'm sure those of you who have operated in Ukraine before will have heard of them.'

Carter nodded. 'I've met one or two of their lads. They work under the Ukrainian Security Service. Sort of like the Wing.'

'Are they capable?' asked Beach.

'They're not Regiment standard. But they're not a million miles away, either. Honest soldiers. Dependable. I've worked with a lot worse.'

Carter had encountered a few of the Alpha Group guys during his previous rotation on the President's bodyguard. They had carved out a reputation as Ukraine's most efficient SF team, snuffing out Russian sleepers and double agents, launching snap ambushes on enemy columns.

*At least these lads will be well motivated. And they'll know how to fight,* Carter reassured himself. *We won't have to spend our time going over the basics.*

Smallwood continued the briefing in his nasal voice.

'You'll carry out the training package at a GROM camp in Poland. Eastern outskirts of Warsaw. Six has already cleared it with Polish security chiefs. They're expecting you. Geordie, you've trained with GROM before, I understand?'

Carter nodded. 'Aye.'

GROM was the leading Polish SF unit. He'd seen a few of them at Hereford over the years, flying over for joint training exercises with the SAS. The Poles had a long history with the Regiment; some of the Reg lads had helped to train the first GROM recruits, instructing them in the fundamentals of covert ops. There was a mutual professional respect between those guys and their Hereford counterparts.

'Is the site secure?' asked Dempsey.

'Ultra,' came the reply from Smallwood. 'The Poles are well drilled on opsec. Way of life when you share a border with Russia. You won't have to worry about anyone bothering you while you're in-country.'

'I hope you're right,' said Carter. 'The last thing we need is a Russian drone detonating on top of us because someone got slack about their camp security.'

'It won't happen. The Poles have given us cast-iron guarantees on that front. Next question?'

Lazarides said, 'What's the distance on the camp ranges?'

'There's an outdoor range for sniper practice. Two thousand metres at its maximum. Should be sufficient for your needs. Separate indoor facility for close-range pistol shooting.'

'Have they got somewhere to practise camouflage and concealment? Approaching targets, stuff like that?' asked Carter. 'Somewhere we can work on fieldcraft.'

'There's an area of woodland adjacent to the camp. Should be perfect for your needs, Geordie.'

Dempsey said, 'I'm gonna need a built-up space for flying the drones, mate.'

'The Poles have a series of mock-up buildings they use for practising counter-terrorism ops. You can use them for drone training. Same goes for you, Karl,' Smallwood added, nodding at Beach. 'Anything they blow up, you're welcome to use for teaching your dems instruction.'

'How many lads are we gonna be working with?' Carter asked.

'Eight. Two four-man teams, operating in rotation.'

'What's the plan? Once they're whipped into shape?'

'I can't discuss that yet. We're still waiting for clearance from above. Once we've got it, we'll talk through the operational side of things.'

Dempsey said, 'We'll need enough time to get it right. Can't turn them into elite SF overnight, mate.'

'I'm well aware of that,' Smallwood replied stiffly. 'I've asked the question, but Vauxhall hasn't shared that information yet. The situation is extremely—'

'Fluid. Yeah, we fucking get it,' Lazarides said.

Smallwood stared daggers at the Australian.

'You will have more information as and when I receive it. In the meantime, I suggest you start working on the training package. You need to be ready to deploy as soon as we get the go-ahead.'

'Do the Poles know why we're there?' Carter asked.

Smallwood shook his head. 'If anyone asks, you're in-country to train up a new bodyguard detail for the Ukrainian President. But I doubt they'll take an interest.'

'What's the deal with comms?'

'Scaleys will cover that stuff later. After the operational briefing.'

'What if we need any more kit?' asked Dempsey.

'Draw up an indent for Beattie. He'll make sure any extra items are forwarded to the GROM camp.'

'We're gonna need guidance on protocols,' said Carter. 'How to respond if there's a diplomatic incident, all of that.'

'Our friends from Six will brief you on that side of things. They'll go through restrictions, actions-on, SOPs.' Smallwood glanced at his watch. 'They should be ready for you in an hour or so. Now, if that's everything, guys? Good. Then get on with it. I'll let you know as soon as the suits are ready.'

They trooped out of the briefing room. Smallwood remained at the table, hastily tapping out messages on his phone. Carter, Beach and the Australians made their way back over to the breakout area.

'Just my bloody luck,' Beach muttered. 'Two years of my life teaching dems. I joined the Wing so I could do something more exciting. And my first job is showing a bunch of Ukrainians how to blow shit up.'

Carter chuckled. 'Welcome to the Wing, mate. It's not all about door-kicking.'

'I'm starting to realise that,' he replied moodily.

Beach hesitated. 'What do you think them Alpha lads are gonna be doing? Once we've schooled them?'

Carter thought briefly. 'Sabotage ops in the east. That's the most likely scenario. Blowing up bridges, disrupting supply lines, hunting down Russian collaborators in regained territory. Anything that's beyond the capability of the green army ranks.'

'As long as we're not incriminated in anything dodgy,' Lazarides cut in. 'I didn't fly all the way over here to get dragged into any dark shit.'

Dempsey was staring past Carter's shoulder at the planning area, frowning heavily. Like a guy trying to remember where he'd left his car keys. 'It doesn't make any sense.'

'What's that?' asked Carter.

'This is just a bog-standard training job, right?'

'Far as we know, aye.'

'So why were your bosses so keen to bring us on board? Any number of your blokes could have handled the drone and sniper training. No need to fly us halfway round the world.'

'Ned's got a point,' said Lazarides. 'We're good, but we ain't *that* good.'

Carter shrugged a reply and gritted his teeth. He felt a tightening in his stomach.

*I don't know what's going on here*, he thought. *But there's something they're not telling us.*

Beach fixed a round of brews while the others gathered round one of the tables. Then they started writing up their training doctrine. Planning. The cornerstone of any Regiment mission. They drew up a detailed schedule: skills to be taught to the students, training scenarios. Weapon systems the candidates would need to master. Principles of movement. How to operate in specialist environments. Following which the team checked their kit. Making sure they had everything they needed for the training job. They didn't want to waste valuable time on the ground waiting for equipment to arrive.

Lazarides inspected the sniper rifles, optics and rangefinders. Dempsey took the drones on a test flight. Beach ran his eyes over the dems. A short while later, Carter noticed three figures dressed in civvy suits ducking inside the briefing room. Two men and a woman. The officers from Vauxhall, he assumed.

An hour passed. Then two.

After three hours, Carter began to wonder what was going on.

'What the fuck's taking them so long?' Beach grumbled. 'Why haven't they called us back in yet?'

'Operational snags,' Carter suggested. 'They're probably waiting for someone in Whitehall to sign off on the job.'

He figured the chiefs would want to make sure they had covered their arses before they gave the green light. That was priority number one. Or there might have been a hold-up at the Polish end. Could be any number of things. Could be something as simple as trying to sort out accommodation for the team at the GROM camp.

Beach grunted. 'Whatever it is, they'd better get a move on. I didn't transfer to the Wing to sit around on my arse all day.'

At five o'clock Carter grew tired of waiting and went looking for Beattie. He checked the clerks' quarters. Questioned the guards. Nobody had seen him since the morning. Meanwhile Smallwood remained cooped up in the briefing room with the three suits.

*Everyone's here*, Carter thought.

*Smallwood. The folks from Six. The training team. Even if there's been some sort of delay, they should have called us in to give us an update. Instead they've left us in the dark.*

*What's going on?*

He wondered if something had gone wrong with the mission. New information filtering through, perhaps. Or a change of mind in Whitehall. Someone getting cold feet.

*The situation remains extremely fluid,* Smallwood had said back in Hereford. Like putting an asterisk next to the plan. Everything could change in the time it takes to make a brew.

*Nothing we can do except wait.*

They finished drafting the training doctrine. Checked their kit a second time, made a list of extra items they'd need to get sent over to Warsaw. Packed everything back into their civilian rucksacks. Dempsey returned to his Ned Kelly biography. Beach raided the kitchen in search of more snacks. Carter drained his four hundredth cup of coffee. Lazarides napped, demonstrating the universal ability of snipers to remain static for long stretches of time.

At seven o'clock in the evening Beattie strode back into the hangar through a side door. He crossed the floor and made straight for the breakout area. Stopped in front of the soldiers.

'They're ready for you now, fellas,' he said.

'Thank Christ for that,' Lazarides muttered as he rose to his feet. 'What took you so long? Thought you Poms prided yourselves on your time-keeping.'

'You'll have to ask Smallwood. Come on. This way.'

Beattie escorted them towards the planning area. Approached the same briefing room, stopped in front of the door, repeated the entry procedure. Tapped the key card against the reader. The unit beeped and glowed.

Carter and the rest of his team shuffled inside. Smallwood stood up to greet them, wearing a pale expression. He smiled weakly. The ops officer looked knackered, Carter thought. Several empty cups of coffee cluttered the table in front of him.

'Guys. My apologies for keeping you waiting. Sit down. We'll explain everything. Thanks, Mike. We'll take it from here.'

Beattie turned and left, closing the briefing room door behind him, while the soldiers took their places round the table. Carter dropped into the chair facing Smallwood. Next to the ops officer sat the three smartly dressed figures he'd seen entering the room several hours ago.

The guy immediately to the right of Smallwood looked to be in his early sixties, Carter judged. He had slicked-back grey hair and a long face terminating in a dimpled chin. Small eyes peered out from behind a pair of black thick-rimmed spectacles. His cheeks were flushed from a lifetime of booze. With his tweed jacket, loafers and badly creased shirt he looked like an academic in the humanities department at a second-rate university.

The man next to him looked young enough to be his son. Late thirties or early forties. He wore a quilted Barbour coat over a plain Oxford shirt, dark corduroy trousers, a pair of polished walnut brogues. One of the Vauxhall fast-trackers, Carter guessed. Hyper-motivated. Switched on, whip-smart. But also naïve. And therefore dangerous. The young thrusters were proactive, in Carter's experience. Keen to make a name for themselves. They had a habit of sanctioning risky missions, disregarding the potential for things to go wrong. That was how mistakes were made. Mistakes that ultimately cost lives.

The woman was around the same age as the guy in the Barbour jacket. Another fast-tracker. She was dressed in a dark trouser suit and a crisp white shirt, black leather court shoes. Her brown hair had been cut short; kind green eyes softened the downturned mouth and high cheekbones.

'What the fuck's going on?' Dempsey demanded. 'Why the big delay?'

Smallwood said, 'We'll come to that in a minute. Let's get the introductions done first, shall we? Then we'll give you a full update.'

'About fucking time,' Lazarides muttered.

Smallwood glared briefly at him before he composed his features and pointed towards the man sitting to his left. The one dressed like a shabby academic.

'This is Tony Vallance. Director of Operations at Vauxhall.'

'Gents,' Vallance said. 'A pleasure.'

Smallwood indicated the guy in the Barbour jacket. 'Julian Heald runs the Russia Desk. And this,' he added, nodding at the woman in the trouser suit, 'is Ellen Kendall. Julian's number two.'

Kendall smiled at Carter.

'Hello, Luke,' she said. 'Good to see you again. You're looking well.'

Beach jerked his head back in surprise. 'You two know each other?'

'We met once,' Kendall said, her voice betraying her Lincolnshire roots. 'A year ago, wasn't it?'

'That's right, ma'am,' Carter said. 'At H.'

He recalled the scene. Kendall had been at the post-op debrief after his return from Ukraine. They had been gathered in the CO's office, Hardcastle listening in silence while Kendall recounted the details surrounding Jamie's death. Carter disliked most Six officers, but he found himself warming to Kendall. Mainly because she was a straight-talker, much like himself. She seemed to have a zero-tolerance policy towards bullshit. Nothing like the Old Etonian dynasts who still dominated the upper echelons of the service.

Smallwood cleared his throat and carried on. He introduced Beach, Lazarides and Dempsey to the three Six officers. Took a sip from a bottle of mineral water.

'I'm sorry to keep you waiting, guys,' he said. 'But the situation was quite out of our hands.'

Lazarides said, 'Just tell us the fucking score.'

Smallwood glowered again at the Australian. He continued.

'As I was saying. We couldn't call you back in until we had clarity from the Foreign Office. Things have been moving fast – very fast. The picture on the ground has changed. There have been some rather worrying developments.'

Carter waited for Smallwood to go on. Instead, the ops officer glanced anxiously at Vallance. The most senior man in the room.

The director of operations shifted his considerable weight and crossed his legs.

'A few hours ago,' Vallance began in his gravelly accent, 'we received an urgent intelligence report from the SBU. The Ukrainian State Security Service,' he added. 'It appears there has been a breach at their end.'

'Breach?' Carter frowned.

'Earlier today, a number of key individuals within Alpha Group were arrested. It's too early to draw any definite conclusions, but it appears the men in question have been supplying confidential information to the Russians.'

Heald, the guy in the Barbour jacket, said, 'They're working for Moscow. Traitors to the state. Been going on for a while, the Ukrainians think.'

'The Russians have form for this sort of thing, of course,' Vallance said. There was a hint of admiration in his voice as he continued. 'Blackmailing vulnerable elements in the enemy ranks. Par for the course when you're dealing with men who cut their teeth in the KGB. Those of us who've been with the service for a long time have seen this happen many times before. Frankly I'm surprised the Russians got away with it for as long as they did.'

Although he addressed himself to the soldiers, Carter had the distinct impression the ops director's words were meant for his subordinates. Vallance was asserting his credentials. Establishing dominance. The seven-hundred-pound silverback in the room, reminding the others of his seniority.

'How many blokes are we talking about?' asked Dempsey.

'Half a dozen. A relatively small number. So far.'

'You think there might be more?'

'We're not ruling anything out. Not until we get to the bottom of this thing. For all we know half the unit might be dirty.'

Heald said, 'SBU agents are questioning the suspects as we speak. We'll know more soon. How much information has been handed over to them, what they know. Who else might be involved.'

'Naturally,' said Kendall, 'we're working on the assumption that the training mission has been compromised.'

Lazarides scoffed. 'I'd say it's more than an assumption, love. Reckon that's a nailed-on fucking certainty.'

'We don't know that. Not for sure. Right now, we're dealing purely in hypotheticals.'

Vallance cut in, 'Worst-case scenario, the Russians will know the full details of the clandestine operations Alpha Group have been planning. Which includes the mission they were going to carry out once you had brought them up to scratch.'

'What was the job?' asked Carter.

Vallance and Heald traded a look. The operations director nodded at his subordinate. Giving him silent permission.

Heald said, 'What we're about to tell you is in the strictest confidence. It doesn't leave this room. Is that clear?'

'Crystal. Go on.'

'Alpha Group had been tasked with eliminating a high-value target. A senior figure in the Russian government.'

Several gears clicked into place inside Carter's head.

*So that's why they insisted on the very best for the job. Because this isn't an ordinary team.*

*They wanted us to train up a group of stone-cold killers.*

'The target in question is one of the key figures in Vladimir Putin's inner circle,' Vallance explained. 'One of his most trusted advisers. Our source has provided us with detailed information regarding their whereabouts and movements. Security routines and so on.'

Heald coughed and said, 'This a continuation of established Kyiv policy. Since the war began the Ukrainians have sanctioned several high-profile hits on alleged traitors. Opposition politicians, SBU officers, mayors, journalists. Anyone suspected of collaborating with the Russians is considered fair game.'

'That's different,' Carter insisted. 'Far as I recall, those other targets were living on Ukrainian soil when they got slotted. Most of them were Ukrainian nationals. You're talking about going proactive, for fuck's sake. Taking the war to Russia.'

Dempsey squished his eyebrows. 'Why are you telling us this stuff now? The job's dead. Null and void, mate. You just said so yourself.'

'Not quite,' Vallance said.

Dempsey stared at him, waiting for an explanation. Smallwood sat with folded arms, watching the soldiers closely. Vallance went on.

'The security breach has disrupted our plans. That much is clear. We have to assume that the intended target will soon go to ground. Which means the window of opportunity to liquidate them is closing fast. What's equally clear is that we don't have the time to train up a dedicated kill team. So that means you're going to have to do the job yourselves, gents.

'New orders. We want you to eliminate the target. And you need to do it as soon as possible. Before they drop off the grid.'

# Eight

No one said anything for what seemed like a long time. Carter felt his stomach muscles automatically tensing. Silence hung heavily in the briefing room. Like coconuts from a palm tree. A thought occurred to Carter as he listened to the Six officers outlining the op. One he hoped wasn't true. He parked the thought as Lazarides spoke up.

'Does Whitehall know about this?' he asked.

'That's none of your damn business,' Heald snapped.

'Actually, it fucking is, mate,' Dempsey cut in. 'We're the ones having to put our necks on the line here. We've got a right to know if this thing has been approved by someone at the top of the food chain.'

Heald looked towards Vallance. The ops director said, 'The Foreign Secretary has been fully briefed. Hence the delay in getting you back here. We wanted the thumbs-up before briefing you.'

'That's not an answer. Have they rubber-stamped it or not?'

'They procrastinated, as one might reasonably expect. I doubt they make a decision on what tie to wear each morning without consulting a focus group first.' Heald chuckled at his own lame joke. 'But they understand the situation. We have been presented with a golden opportunity to take out one of Putin's leading figures. This could change the mood of the war. Put Russia on the back foot for a change.'

Vallance leaned back and recrossed his legs, revealing a pair of bright-pink socks.

'So, yes,' he continued. 'To answer your question. We have sign-off from the secretary. In fact, we've even got the document to prove it.'

He produced a sheet of letterheaded paper from a folder in front of him, passed it to Carter.

'What the fuck is this?'

'Private letter, drafted by the Foreign Office and personally signed by the Foreign Secretary, addressed to the Chief of Six, confirming her approval of the mission as discussed. This is proof that the operation has been sanctioned at the very highest levels of government. So you can put to bed any idiotic notions that this is some sort of amateur-hour stitch-up. Because it's not.'

'Is the int solid?' Beach asked.

'Like a rock,' Vallance said, snatching the letter back.

'We're gonna need a lot more reassurance than that,' Lazarides said. 'Who's your source?'

Vallance smiled paternally at Kendall.

'Ellen, perhaps you'd care to answer? You've been running the asset, after all. You're best placed to give them the background, I think.'

Not a request. But an order. Delivered with a thin smile and a posh accent. Vallance was putting on a show for his audience. Demonstrating who was in charge.

Kendall said, 'For the past several months, we've been cultivating a high-level source inside the FSB.'

Carter's ears pricked up.

*Federal Security Service*, he thought. *Successor agency to the KGB. Glorified thugs.*

Most senior Russian officials, he knew, had served in the FSB at one time or another. Including Putin himself.

Kendall continued, 'The asset's identity is a closely guarded secret, and we plan on keeping it that way. Outside of this room, only half a dozen people are aware of their existence. Even the Prime Minister doesn't know their real name. Just so we're clear.'

'Can we trust him?' asked Carter.

'Not him,' Kendall corrected. '*Her.*'

Kendall reached across the table and picked up an iPad. She flipped open the cover, swiped and tapped. Delicate fingers performing a complicated dance on the glass. A few moments later a photograph appeared on one of the sixty-inch TV screens at the end of the room.

Carter found himself looking at a picture of a woman in her mid-thirties. Slender-faced and high-cheekboned, with short side-swept red hair and an upturned nose. Absinthe-green eyes stared boldly at the camera. Her lips teased into a playful smirk at the corners. As if she was in on some private joke between herself and the photographer.

Kendall said, 'Yulia Volkova. Aged thirty-seven. Born into a military family in Nizhny Novgorod, five years prior to the collapse of the Soviet Union. Father was a Russian general. Mother worked for the local branch of the Communist Party. Yulia studied engineering at Samara State University, before going straight into the service. Four years ago, she moved to FSB headquarters in Moscow, taking a job in the economic security department.'

'Politics may have well had something to do with her rapid rise,' Heald interjected. 'Yulia's father was regarded as a national hero. Earned his stripes in Afghanistan in the eighties.'

'She sounds like a classic nepo baby.' Dempsey laughed.

'In part. But she's also extremely well connected. Yulia has several friends and relatives in the upper ranks of the FSB and SVR. An uncle in the Duma. People she meets with regularly. People who trust her.'

'She has contacts with loose lips,' said Vallance. 'As we say in the trade.'

Kendall said, 'Volkova has been providing intelligence to us through an interlink. A contact in the Ukrainian security services. Eduard Ruznak. Operations officer in the counter-intelligence section.'

She tapped the tablet screen again. Another photo filled the second TV screen. A square-faced man with a haunted expression. Deadened eyes studded a face so pale it practically blended into his creased white shirt. A patchy beard smothered his jaw. The guy looked like he hadn't cracked a smile since the invention of the printing press.

'Ruznak was Volkova's original point of contact. She reached out to him, asked him to arrange a meeting with our people. Said she had information that would be of interest to us. Gave us the details of four Russian sleeper agents operating in Britain. Albanian nationals. She's been working for us ever since.'

Heald cleared his throat and said, 'The point is, guys, Yulia is the most important agent we've had in a very long time. She has unfettered access to Putin's inner circle. The power-brokers inside the Kremlin. She knows who they are, where they live, where they go on holiday. When they're vulnerable.'

'What's she getting out of the arrangement?' asked Lazarides. 'Wonga? A new life in Pom-land?'

'Neither,' said Kendall. 'She wants revenge.'

'Yulia's father died several months ago,' Heald explained. 'General Gennady Zorin. Commander of Operations in Ukraine. Probably the second most popular man in Russia. Right up until he plunged to his death.'

Carter nodded slowly. He recalled the report he'd heard on the radio several days ago. The drive down to Lazarides' farm. The string of high-profile suicides in Russia in recent months. Politicians and bankers and intelligence chiefs. Among them, the top general who'd fallen from the rooftop of his office in Rostov-on-Don in the summer.

Beach frowned. 'Wasn't that guy bent? Caught with his hand in the till?'

'Smear campaign. Typical Moscow tactics. Selective justice,' Vallance pronounced. 'If the Kremlin went after every senior official who'd lined their pockets there wouldn't be anyone left to turn out the lights.'

Heald said, 'Yulia is determined to take her revenge for her father's death, by inflicting as much damage on Putin's regime as possible.

She's supplying us with premium-grade intelligence. Including the whereabouts of the target.'

Carter noticed that Heald kept referring to the FSB officer by her first name. He wondered about the relationship between the pair of them. How involved they were. Whether there was something else going on.

'It could be a trap,' Dempsey speculated. 'For all we know, your asset might be leading us to our deaths.'

'I sincerely doubt it,' Heald replied. 'Yulia has been excellent for us. Never let us down in the past. She's fully committed to the cause.'

Kendall saw the doubtful look on Dempsey's face and said, 'We have verified her information independently where possible. It checks out. As I said, it's gold-plated intelligence.'

'You'd personally vouch for her?' asked Carter.

Vallance smiled. 'We're sitting here, aren't we? Discussing the operation with you. I'd say that's ample proof of how we see things. If we had the slightest doubt, this wouldn't be happening.'

'Who's the target?' asked Beach.

Vallance removed his spectacles, wiped the lens on his shirt. 'Ellen, will you do the honours?'

Vallance was treating the junior officer more like his personal assistant, Carter thought. *He'll be asking her to make the tea soon enough.*

Kendall worked the iPad again.

A close-up shot of a round-faced man replaced the photo of Eduard Ruznak. He had the look of a retired heavyweight boxer. That was Carter's first impression. Someone who'd been in plenty of scraps. Small eyes peered out from subterranean sockets either side of a bulbous nose. Scar tissue criss-crossed his chin. He had pockmarked cheeks, hair the colour of burnt wood.

'This is the target,' Kendall began. 'Konstantin Ternovsky. Some of you might recognise him from the news. Russia's Defence Minister. Served as Putin's bodyguard for over a decade. Entered politics twelve years ago. Had a spell as director of the Russian secret service before he moved into his current post as one of Putin's placemen.'

'As you're no doubt aware,' said Vallance, 'the President has become extremely paranoid since the beginning of the war. People he trusted let him down, pulled the wool over his eyes. Sold him lies about Ukrainians waiting to welcome the troops with open arms and bouquets of flowers. The subsequent purges of top officials have left the President more isolated than ever. He relies heavily on his old bodyguard.'

'No surprises there,' Lazarides said. 'Those fellas are paid to stop a bullet for the big boss. Can't get much more fucking loyal than that, can you?'

Heald said, 'Loyalty is an understatement when it comes to Ternovsky. Putin was best man at his wedding. He's godparent to Ternovsky's daughter Darina. They go on hunting trips together. Spend their summers hanging out at Putin's dacha, shooting bears, drinking home-brewed vodka and riding around on horseback.'

Dempsey puffed his cheeks. 'Bloke must be fucking minted, if he's that close to the President.'

Smallwood chuckled. 'Let's just say that Ternovsky won't be struggling to pay his credit card bill anytime soon.'

'Why kill him?' Carter asked. 'Just because he's chummy with the President?'

Kendall said, 'Ternovsky is much more than that. He's being lined up as Putin's successor.'

Heald grinned. 'Worst-kept secret in Moscow. Everyone knows Ternovsky is the prince in waiting. That makes him politically untouchable. And a very attractive target.'

'Knocking him out will also send a message,' added Vallance. 'A number of Putin's supporters are concerned about the way the war is going. They're not entirely oblivious to the public unrest, the crippling effect of the sanctions on Russian society. They're worried about the direction of the economy and asking themselves whether supporting Putin is a lost cause.

'There's a chance Ternovsky's death might persuade some of them to abandon ship. At the very least, it'll make Putin look weak. And in Moscow, weak men,' the senior Six man added with a savage glint in his eye, 'tend not to survive for very long.'

'You're sending us on a suicide mission,' Lazarides remarked. 'This guy will have round-the-clock security. How the fuck are we supposed to get to him in Russia?'

'You won't have to, gents. Ternovsky is going to come to us. In a manner of speaking.'

Kendall said, 'According to the information Volkova has given us, Ternovsky has a secret wife. In Minsk, Belarus. Arina Gluschenko. An actress. Twenty-eight years old.'

On the left screen, another photograph appeared in place of Volkova's face. A blonde-haired woman reclining on a yacht deck, dressed in a tiny swimsuit. Toasting the camera with a flute of champagne.

Beach whistled his admiration.

'Lucky bastard. Wouldn't mind a bit of that action myself.'

Carter laughed. 'This is as close as you'll ever get to shagging a model, mate. More chance of you skipping a meal than bedding a good-looking woman.'

'Piss off, Geordie.'

Kendall stared at the two SAS men in silent disapproval.

She said, 'Most senior Russian politicians have an unofficial family. Common practice. Ternovsky met Arina at a nightclub in Moscow eight years ago. He's been with her ever since.

'Shortly before the war broke out Ternovsky bought her a villa in a suburb of Minsk. He flies out once or twice a month on his private jet for a dirty weekend. That should give you a window of opportunity in which to strike.'

'When's he next due to visit?'

'Two days from now. He'll be staying at the villa for three nights, before returning to Moscow. That's according to Volkova's source.'

Heald said, 'Yulia has a contact in Ternovsky's office. This individual has access to the minister's itinerary. When he's flying to Minsk, how long he'll be staying, his plans while he's in-country.'

'Could be misinformation,' Dempsey put in. 'False RV. Throw any surveillance teams off the scent.'

'We considered that. Which is why we've got eyes on the villa as we speak. The place is usually graveyard-quiet, but there's been a whirlwind of activity in the past twelve hours. Cleaners, gardeners. Food deliveries. Flowers. Bodyguards reporting for duty. Electricians testing the gates and alarms. Trust me. Ternovsky is definitely flying there for his usual frolics.'

'What's security like?' asked Carter.

Kendall said, 'Heavy. Eight-man BG team patrolling the grounds. Guard dogs. Night-vision cameras covering the entry points. Bespoke safe room with reinforced concrete walls. Two-metre-high perimeter wall. State-of-the-art alarm system. Direct link to the nearest police station.'

'Fuck me. Sounds more like a military compound than a residential home.'

Heald said, 'Ternovsky is nervous about his security arrangements. Hardly surprising, I'd say, given the gruesome ends some of his colleagues have met lately. Yulia's father among them.'

Dempsey clicked his tongue. 'Going to be tough to take him out at his gaff, mate. Sounds like his place is locked down tighter than a Wuhan virus lab.'

'I'm sure you can find a way. That's what you chaps are paid to do, isn't it? Kick in doors and shoot people?'

Carter shook his head determinedly. 'We're soldiers, not fucking supermen. Assaulting the villa isn't a four-man job. We'd need a full Regiment Troop for that kind of operation. Choppers to ferry us to and from the compound, the works.'

'Out of the question. Downing Street would never agree to expanding the operation beyond its current parameters.'

Dempsey said, 'Then we'll have to do it outside the villa. Wait until your man Ternovsky sticks his head above the parapet. Hit him while he's vulnerable.'

'Has he got any engagements while he's on the ground?' asked Carter. 'Any meetings in Minsk? Bookings at fancy restaurants, things like that?'

Kendall shook her head. 'Ternovsky tends to keep his head down.'

'Although,' Vallance said, 'there is one event in his diary.'

Carter looked towards the senior Six man. Waited for him to go on.

'There's a performance at the Bolshoi Theatre in central Minsk. Day after Ternovsky is due to land. Seven o'clock in the evening. He's set to attend a performance of *The Barber of Seville*. Honorary guest of the Belarussian Minister of Defence. The Director of the Belarussian KGB will be there too.'

'Those guys still call themselves KGB?'

Vallance smiled. 'It's Belarus. Hardly the world's most progressive society, old bean. The guys in charge are all ex-spooks. Many of whom have fond memories of the Soviet Union.'

'Where's the theatre?'

Kendall said, 'Trinity Hill neighbourhood. The old part of Minsk.'

Carter stroked his stubbly jaw and pondered. The professional part of his mind hard at work, processing theoretical scenarios and probabilities. In the corner of his eye, he noticed Dempsey watching him closely.

'You thinking what I'm thinking, Pom?'

Carter nodded in agreement. 'Best chance of taking him out.'

*Better than a suicide attack on the villa.*

He turned to Smallwood and continued, 'We'll need mapping of the area around the opera house. Up-to-date satellite images. Everything you can get your hands on.'

'Consider it done,' Heald said. 'You can discuss the operational nitty-gritty post this briefing. In the meantime, we'll keep you updated on developments from our side of things. We're expecting to have confirmation from Yulia on Ternovsky's plans imminently.'

'Have you got a secondary int source? In case she's bullshitting you?'

Kendall nodded and said, 'We're keeping track on flight manifests from Moscow. As soon as we've independently verified that Ternovsky has departed for Belarus, you'll fly to Warsaw. From there, you're on a private charter flight to Minsk.'

'Why not a civvy flight?' asked Dempsey.

'There aren't any. Not from within the EU, leastways. EU carriers have been forbidden from flying over Belarussian airspace since the authorities in Minsk diverted a commercial flight and forced it to land in the capital a few years ago. They arrested a journalist and his girlfriend. Since then, the country's been off limits.'

'Won't we stand out like sore thumbs?'

'Far from it. There are still plenty of flights coming in from elsewhere. Dubai, Turkey, some other places. Besides, your cover story should place you above suspicion.'

'Which is what, exactly?'

Heald said, 'You're an advance party from a TV company. You're in the country to carry out a pre-filming recce for a reality TV series. Celebrities surviving in the ancient forests of Belarus. You're scoping out suitable accommodation, filming areas and so on.'

Beach puckered his brow. 'Surely we need a licence for that.'

'Not in this case,' Kendall responded. 'You're only there to check the place out. Initial site visit. No specialist equipment or permits necessary.'

'You'll be flying with false travel documents, naturally,' Vallance said. 'We've prepared everything for you. Passports, driving licences, bank and credit cards.'

'What about our accreditation?'

'We've already sorted that out,' Heald replied smoothly. 'In addition, our tech team has created a fake website for a UK-based film and TV production company. Fake address in Soho. Ditto for email and social media accounts. LinkedIn and IMDb profiles for the four of you. Under your false names, of course. Anyone tries to contact the company, their inquiries will be rerouted to a room at Vauxhall.'

'Do we need visas?' asked Carter.

'Not unless you're planning on an extended stay. British nationals are free to enter Belarus without a visa when arriving by air. Thirty-day limit. Same goes for Australian citizens.'

Dempsey said, 'What about facial recognition? What if one of us gets flagged up?'

'Ned's right,' Lazarides said. 'Last thing we need is some border guard giving us the silver bracelet treatment.'

Vallance threw back his head and laughed. 'This isn't Beijing, chaps. You're going into Belarus. Agricultural country. Dictionary definition of an Eastern European backwater. The government's not using cutting-edge tech.'

Smallwood said, 'The Scaleys will come in and talk you through the comms side of things after we're done here. You'll be travelling with standard handsets with local SIM cards; the phones will be populated by the signallers to reflect your cover story. Which means search histories related to Belarussian parks and forests, car hire. Phone calls to a hotel in Minsk. Pre-paid booking at the same place. You get the picture.

'We'll also supply you with receipts from a Polish hotel and restaurant, spanning several days, to make it look like you've spent a week on the ground in Warsaw. Corresponding entry stamps in your passports. Some local currency. Belarussian rubles and Polish zloty. Along with a log of recent calls to a Polish TV company based in Warsaw. Any British crew would need a local fixer to help them navigate the language barrier.'

Vallance said, 'It's a good cover story, gents. And you can use it to your advantage. Appeal to their sense of national pride. If anyone gets suspicious, tell them how beautiful their country is, how much you're looking forward to capturing the mystical splendour of their forests on camera. Or something. Use your imagination.

'The point is, people in those parts are always keen to impress foreigners with their national heritage.'

'What language do they speak in Belarus?' asked Beach.

Heald said, 'Officially, Belarussian and Russian. In reality, almost everyone speaks Russian. So Volkova will do the talking while you're on the ground. She also speaks fluent English.'

'And Ruznak?'

'Him too.'

Carter said, 'What's the plan once when we get into Minsk?'

Kendall said, 'You'll RV with Eduard Ruznak. The SBU officer. He'll meet you at the airport. Volkova will be waiting for you there too. She's in charge of local arrangements. Transportation and what-have-you.'

'How are we supposed to get our kit across?' Carter asked.

Smallwood said, 'There's a criminal group. Inside Russia. Smugglers. They control the largest smuggling route from Europe to Moscow, which runs via Belarus. The Ukrainians are paying them to deliver your equipment to a pre-designated location not far from Minsk.'

That made Carter sit up straight. 'We're gonna be working with a bunch of Russian thieves?'

'Only at arm's length. This is the only way we can guarantee delivery of your kit.'

Heald said, 'We can trust the smugglers, if that's what you're worried about. They have every reason to hate the system as much as Yulia. One of the gang leader's brothers was arrested last year and sent to a Siberian gulag.'

'I don't give a fuck about their sympathies. Just as long as we can count on them to get our equipment across the border.'

'They won't let us down,' Heald said confidently. 'These guys have worked for the Ukrainians before. They've got a whole system. Tunnels across the Russian border. Border officials on their payroll. They know all the key crossing points.'

Smallwood raised his palms in mock surrender. 'Look, I know this is far from ideal. But given the time pressures on this mission, it's a risk we're going to have to take. There's no time to supply you locally.'

'It's a big fucking risk,' Carter said. 'There's no guarantee the smugglers will get the goods across to us. They might get caught en route. Or they might stab us in the back and make off with the money. There's a lot that could go wrong.'

'In that case, you'll have to forage. Make do and mend.'

Beach said, 'What's the deal with getting out of the country once we've done the hit?'

Heald said, 'That depends on the situation. If it's deemed safe to fly, you'll leave the same way you came in. If that's not possible, for whatever reason, you'll have to drive out. Land crossing. But again, Yulia and Ruznak will take care of that side of things.'

'We're putting a lot of faith in them two,' Lazarides growled.

'We don't have a choice. But as I say, they've never let us down before.'

'First time for everything,' Beach said.

'Too right,' said Carter. 'There's even a whisper of a chance you might get laid one of these days.'

'Geordie bastard.'

Dempsey said, 'Let's assume that this job goes to plan. What then?'

'Then,' Smallwood said, 'you'll return here for the usual post-op debrief.'

Vallance glanced impatiently at his watch. 'Let's wrap this up, shall we? As soon as we've confirmed that the target is en route to Minsk, we'll let you know. Until then, I suggest you get on with your detailed planning.'

Smallwood looked round the table. 'I think that just about covers everything for now, guys?'

He stood up. So did Kendall and Heald.

Carter remained seated.

'What happens if we get caught?' he asked.

He directed the question at Kendall. The junior officer. Subordinate to Vallance and Heald. But the most honest person in the room. And therefore the least likely to sell him a pack of lies.

'Don't,' she said. 'That's my honest advice. Because if that happens, there's no coming back. We'll deny any knowledge of the operation. There won't be any deals. No one will be coming to rescue you. At that point, you're on your own.'

* * *

The Six officers left the room. Smallwood stayed behind with the guys on the team, making small talk with the Australians while they waited for the signallers to arrive for the next briefing.

Carter thought about the false passports. The credit cards and driving licences. He thought, too, about the pre-populated phones. The search histories and booking emails. The bundles of local currency and restaurant receipts from Warsaw.

*This is a sophisticated operation.*

*Planned right down to the tiniest detail.*

*Not something that was cobbled together in a few hours.*

*Not even close.*

After the Scaleys had finished walking them through their equipment, Carter took Smallwood to one side. The ops officer said, irritably, 'Yes? What is it, Geordie?'

Carter waited for the others to leave the briefing room. He dropped his voice so low it could have crawled on its belly across the floor.

'I smell a rat here,' he said.

'Pardon?'

'Be honest with me,' Carter said coolly. 'There was never a training mission, was there? It never existed. This was the plan all along.'

Smallwood gave Carter a blank hard stare.

'I don't know what you're talking about, and frankly I resent the implication. I'm not privy to the discussions that take place inside Vauxhall, as you bloody well know.'

'So you're telling me you're not in on it?'

'For God's sake, man,' Smallwood hissed, 'there is no "it". Now stop jumping at shadows and get on with your fucking job.'

# Nine

Carter and the rest of the team took a short break while Smallwood pulled together the int they needed to start their planning. They made their way over to the cookhouse, feasted on plates of steak and chips, followed by generous portions of cherry pie and ice cream. Their last meal for a long time, potentially. As important as checking their equipment and getting their heads down. No good army ever marched on an empty stomach.

'Think we can pull this off, Geordie?' Beach asked as he tucked into his second helping of dessert.

'It'll be tough,' Carter said. 'We're not dealing with some small-time mayor or journalist. This bloke is the Defence Minister. One of the big beasts. And he's careful.'

*Ternovsky is nervous about his security arrangements*, Heald had said at the earlier briefing.

*Keeps his head down.*

Carter continued, 'A lot depends on the int we're getting from Six's FSB asset. If she's as good as they claim, we've got a chance.'

'*If*,' Dempsey emphasised.

Beach shoved another spoonful of pie into his mouth and said, 'Let's say we do the op and nail this guy. Bang. Mission accomplished. So what? Putin will just parachute in another crony. Business as usual. Nothing changes.'

'It's not as simple as that,' Carter said. 'It's not about slotting one bloke. Putin doesn't have many mates left. You heard what the suits said. The guy's isolated and paranoid. That's a dangerous combination. Taking out Ternovsky will put him on the defensive. He'll start wondering who else he can trust. And his mates will wonder if they're next.'

'So we're doing this to Putin to piss him off?'

Carter shook his head. 'Take a step back and Google Earth it. The Ukrainians aren't going to win this war on the battlefield. They haven't got the numbers. So they need some other way of disrupting Putin's regime. Such as taking out his number two.'

'Hate to say it, but the Pom's got a point,' Dempsey put in. 'Simple question of numbers. Russia can absorb mass casualties and still feed more guys into the meat grinder. The dregs of their society. The Ukrainians haven't got that luxury.'

Beach shook his head. 'We're talking about a war. Not a fucking maths problem.'

'Same outcome. Any way you cut it, the Ukrainians aren't strong enough to claw back their territory.'

'For now. Things might change in the spring.'

'Or they might not. The big counteroffensive this year didn't work. Who's to say how things might look a year from now? New bloke in the White House, new Prime Minister. Maybe they decide Ukraine isn't worth the cost. You've already got politicians wondering why we're pissing away billions on military aid to Kyiv.'

'They're just grandstanding. Dickheads in suits trying to make a name for themselves.'

'Doesn't matter. If you're in Putin's boots, that's music to your ears. Because he doesn't have to seize Kyiv to win the war. Not anymore. All he's got to do is hold the line and wait until the West loses interest.'

Lazarides nodded his agreement. 'Same thing happened in Afghan. War fatigue. Once the media spotlight goes elsewhere, Ukraine's well and truly fucked.'

Beach said, 'What are you saying? Six are running this op because they can't win the ground war?'

Carter said, 'They're trying to find a way to change the narrative. Disrupt the Kremlin from the inside. Chisel away at the power structure. Like testing for weaknesses in an old building. See if it's a house of cards waiting to collapse.'

'It'll send a message to Putin's supporters, too,' Dempsey said. 'What your man Vallance said. It'll let them know Putin is a marked man. Even the Kremlin's propaganda machine won't be able to gloss over the death of the crown prince.'

'It's still fucking dicey,' Lazarides remarked. 'This could go badly wrong. We're putting a lot of faith in this Russian woman.'

'You don't trust her?'

'I don't trust anyone. Force of habit.'

'Kendall vouched for her,' Carter pointed out.

'So what? She's looking at this thing through a different lens. You know what these spooks are like. Always have one eye on their career progression. Maybe she's ignoring the warning signs. Or maybe she's prepared to gamble with our lives for the sake of a promotion.'

Carter shook his head. 'Kendall's not like that. She's not the same as the rest of them pricks. She's sound.'

'Heald says the int's solid, too,' Beach added.

'That bloke? He's fanny-struck,' Lazarides replied witheringly. 'And fucking naïve. He'd believe anything that bird told him.'

'You don't think the plan will work?'

'They're being reckless. That's what I think. Rushing into a job without looking at the consequences. Because there's a lot that could go wrong. Once you pull the trigger on this op, there's no telling where it'll end up. Look what happened with Saddam, when we knocked him on the head. Fucking chaos.'

Carter looked steadily at the sniper. 'Are you getting cold feet?'

'Fuck off, Pom.'

'That's not an answer.'

Lazarides snorted in disgust. 'Look, I didn't travel all this way just to throw in the towel. I'm committed. You've got no worries on that front. I just hope your mates know what the fuck they're doing.'

Carter studied him carefully. Remembered what Dempsey had told him back in Perth. His reservation about Lazarides.

*Let's just say he can be a bit too honest.*

Which concerned Carter on several levels. Lazarides had walked out on his muckers once before. Turned his back on them out of principle. What if he quit on them again? Walked away from the mission? Or worse, what if he decided to blow the whistle on the job? Tip off someone outside of the loop. Carter decided he'd have to watch him closely from now on. Look for any signs that he might be getting twitchy.

Lazarides and Dempsey left the table and went off in search of Beattie to notify him of the change of plan. Expedite their kit requests. Get everything packed and ready to be shipped on to Warsaw before being handed over to the Russian smugglers. From there it would be loaded onto the back of a lorry filled with farming equipment, destined for Belarus.

Carter watched the Australians move out of earshot before he said, quietly, 'There's something strange going on here.'

'What d'you mean?' Beach asked.

'This morning we were preparing for a training op in Warsaw. All of a sudden, they're calling us back in and saying the situation's flipped. That's a fast turnaround. Too fast,' he added darkly.

Beach shrugged. 'They're working against the clock.'

Carter shook his head. 'It's not just that. There's the letter from the Foreign Secretary, too. That wouldn't have been drawn up in a few hours. Something like that, it's got to be drafted and approved by the PM, the Attorney General, the Vauxhall chiefs. All of that takes time.'

Beach looked steadily at him. 'Are you saying they stitched us up?'

'I think they needed a way of getting us all into the room without creating any suspicion. They'll want to keep this thing tightly controlled. No loose lips. Explains why they'd want the Aussies on board, too,' he added softly.

'Why's that?'

Carter tapped the side of his head. 'Think about it. What happens if this job goes tits-up? Vallance and his mates need plausible deniability. Which means layers between themselves and the top. Four Reg lads on a mission looks official. But with Crocodile Dundee and his mate on board they can spread the blame. If there's an inquiry down the line, they can hold up their hands and say the Aussies were the ones pushing the mission.'

'You're saying they need a scapegoat?'

'Not a scapegoat. A buffer. They can publicly point to the allegations about the SASR and argue that this is more of the same. Rogue soldiers taking the law into their own hands. Or they could go to the SASR chiefs, have a quiet word, persuade them to hush it up. Those guys wouldn't need much encouragement. They'd be desperate to avoid another public scandal. That would spell the end of the unit.'

Beach looked pale. 'Would Six really do that?'

Carter laughed. 'I've worked with these people before. They're slippery. You don't go into that line of work unless you're prepared to lie to people and get them to do stuff that's not in their best interests. Who knows what they've told their mates in Oz?'

'Christ.'

Beach looked away. Across the hangar Beattie was running through the kit indents with the Australians, checking the drones.

'But if they're prepared to trick them lads,' he added, 'what's to stop them from shafting us down the line?'

\* \* \*

At ten o'clock in the evening the team reconvened in the briefing room. They spread out around the table and began studying satellite imagery, terrain and road maps of Minsk. Orientation. The most important part of an operation after the job itself. Familiarising themselves with the target environment. Getting a feel for the place. You didn't want to be going into a hostile situation without knowing the area as well as the back of your hand.

They began with Minsk itself. A sprawling mass of Soviet-era housing, grand palaces and public parks set in an area of rolling hills and pine forest, encircled by a traffic-clogged ring road. Like a moat enclosing a medieval castle. The soldiers zeroed in on the Bolshoi Theatre, an imposing structure at one end of Troitskaya Gora Park, on the eastern bank of the Svislach River. Slap bang in the heart of Minsk. They assessed the surrounding streets, looked at the lines of sight to the opera house from adjacent buildings. Entry and exit points. Routes to and from the theatre. Likely traffic levels during the concert. The layout of the Trinity Hill district. Roads to avoid in rush-hour. Distances to the nearest police stations. Emergency escape routes if the police threw up checkpoints. Planned roadworks and diversions.

Then they widened the lens. Taking a broad view of life in general in Belarus. They looked at the distances from Minsk to the land borders. Crossing to Ukraine was out of the question. The Belarussians had fortified their southern frontier since the start of the war, mined the crossing points. Nor could they head east to Russia. Which left Poland, Latvia and Lithuania as potential escape routes. Four hundred and fifty miles of border. The smuggling gang would know the weak points in the chain. Or so Carter hoped.

They studied weather forecasts. The outlook for the next week. Temperatures of around minus one in the day, plunging to a low of minus eight at night. But no rain. No fog or snow. No conditions that might materially impact on their plan.

Every so often Smallwood popped his head round the door to check in with the team. Updating them on the situation.

By two o'clock in the morning there was still no news from their FSB asset. Carter started to wonder if Volkova had gone to ground. Would Vauxhall have told her about the Russian collaborators in Alpha Group? He wasn't sure. On balance, probably not. They wouldn't want to spook her. But she might have heard the news from a third-party source. One of her FSB or SVR contacts, perhaps.

Or maybe one of the collaborators might have warned off Ternovsky before they'd been arrested. *They're coming for you, Minister. Stay low. Don't leave the country for now.* Maybe Ternovsky had aborted his plan to fly to Belarus at the last minute? Any number of things might have happened.

Carter shook his head. Pointless to speculate. All they could do was plan the job in meticulous detail, and wait.

Shortly after four o'clock Smallwood strutted back into the briefing room, accompanied by the three Six officers. They sat around the table. Vallance removed his glasses, rubbed heavily bagged eyes; Heald gulped down coffee from a paper cup. Kendall addressed the soldiers.

'We've heard back from Volkova,' she said.

'About fucking time,' Lazarides muttered.

'What's the news?' Carter asked.

Kendall said, 'Ternovsky is flying out of Moscow eight o'clock tomorrow morning, on his private Learjet. Accompanied by four BGs. Skeleton crew. Due to land in Minsk at around nine thirty.'

'So it's on,' said Beach.

'Looks that way,' Smallwood said. 'You'll be wheels up as soon as we've received confirmation that our man is in the air.'

Carter said, 'Any word on those Alpha Group suspects?'

'Not yet. The SBU are still questioning them.'

'They're taking a long fucking time to wring the truth out of them.'

'Like I said. No news. You'll have it when we have it.'

'Aren't you worried about a leak?'

Smallwood said, 'Ternovsky is sticking to his schedule. We can safely assume that the collaborators weren't able to alert their Kremlin friends in time to the target package. So we proceed as planned.'

'What about our kit?' asked Lazarides.

'We're preparing to forward it to Warsaw as we speak. Journey time by HGV from Warsaw to Minsk is around seven hours, depending on traffic and the particular route taken by the smugglers. Either way, it should be waiting for you by the time you get to the safehouse.'

'Which is where?'

'A cottage. Forty miles outside Minsk. Ruznak will have the details.'

Tiredness fogged Carter's brain. His eyelids felt as heavy as ten-kilo weight plates. He stifled a yawn, checked the time on his G-Shock: 0419. Almost twenty-four hours since he'd set off from Hereford.

'Let's get some rest,' he said. 'Doss up and reassemble here at 0930. We'll continue the planning then.'

The team spent the next day and night fine-tuning their preparations for the operation. They had identified a window of opportunity between the target stepping out of his armoured vehicle and making his way up the steps leading to the opera house. A distance of roughly fifty metres. Therefore they would have around thirty seconds in which to take down the Defence Minister.

They quickly ruled out a sniper attack. Too much risk of accidentally hitting someone else in the crowd. They were working on the assumption that Ternovsky's BGs would accompany him to the concert. He'd have guys in front and behind. Other people would be in close proximity too. Executive assistants, media advisers. No guarantee of an unimpeded line of sight to the target. So they looked at other options.

In the afternoon they settled on a plan. One that would provide them with the maximum chance of success, while reducing the risks of getting caught and collateral damage. The attack required patience, coordination and two kilograms of C4 explosive.

'We're going to need rooftop access,' Dempsey said. 'Somewhere close to the target. Maximum range of five hundred metres.'

Beach said, 'And we'll need a van. Something inconspicuous.'

Carter nodded. He thought, *Two-man reaction force. Another guy on overwatch duties. Plus a fourth operator on the rooftop.*

*We're going to be spread thin.*

'I'll speak to Smallwood,' he said. 'Put the request through to Ruznak. Get him to sort it while we're en route.'

They kept at it throughout the night. Walked through the operation step by step, went through it again. Then a third time. They rehearsed everyone's role until they had committed everything to memory. They had one chance to get this right. Getting arrested wasn't an option.

*There won't be any deals. No one will be coming to rescue you.*

*You're on your own.*

Later on, Carter caught an item on the ten o'clock news. A report on the Russian President. Putin was up for re-election the following year, the reporter said. Which Carter assumed was a foregone conclusion. Like the rising of the sun, or longer NHS waiting lists. But the guy still went through the motions. Performing the rituals of an election campaign. Stadium rallies, kissing babies' heads and shaking the hands of adoring supporters. Which prompted a question. *Why show your face in public, if you're worried about someone taking you out?*

The team waited and prepared.

Biding their time.

Then, at precisely six minutes past eight the following morning, a message came through from the asset.

*Target is in the air. Wheels down in eighty-five minutes.*

Twenty minutes later – two days after they had landed in Germany – Carter and the rest of the team departed for Warsaw.

# Ten

They left Ramstein Air Base on a C-21A transport aircraft. The US military variant of the Learjet Model 35 executive jet. The same basic airframe, with swept-back wings and twin turbofan engines, but stripped down to the bare bones. There was seating in the cramped interior for six passengers, plus a stretcher and boxes of medical equipment, allowing the C-21 to double up as an air ambulance in an emergency. Cargo hold at the rear. Maximum range of well over two thousand miles. The Americans kept a C-21A on standby at the base at all times, ready to ferry high-ranking officials across the border to Ukraine. Not heads of state, but those a step or two down the ladder. Senior diplomats. The ones whose job descriptions didn't include a complimentary private jet.

Carter and his colleagues travelled light: holdalls packed with spare sets of civvy clothing, laptops and tablets, chargers, binos. Fake passports and driving licences, along with the phones issued to them by the Scaleys in 18 Sigs. Indistinguishable from regular handsets, but highly encrypted, allowing the team to communicate with each other while they were on the ground.

Each guy also carried ten thousand Polish zloty – two grand in British currency – and four thousand Belarussian rubles, equivalent to around a thousand pounds sterling. Double the average monthly salary in Belarus. Enough to bribe their way out of trouble.

In addition, the team travelled with two hard-shell travel cases, each one containing an advanced drone capable of carrying a payload of up to four kilograms. Flight time of twenty-eight minutes. Front-mounted night-vision camera. Fourteen grand's worth of high-grade machinery. The kind of thing used by professional film crews. And integral to the team's plan to liquidate the Russian Defence Minister.

The flight to Warsaw took eighty minutes. The C-21A touched down at Chopin Airport a few minutes before ten o'clock in the morning. Carter, Beach and the Australians snatched up their luggage and descended the airstairs. A doughy-faced Polish intelligence official stood waiting for them a few metres away. He flashed his ID, shook Carter's hand and introduced himself as Jakub Urbanski.

Smallwood had briefed the team on the arrangements at Warsaw prior to their departure.

*Someone from the Internal Security Agency will meet you airside,* the ops officer had said. *You're expected. No need to pass through immigration. Our Polish friends will take care of that. Charter flight will be waiting for you on the apron.*

*The Poles don't know about the job. They think you're on bodyguard duty. Providing muscle for a Six officer attending a meeting in Minsk.*

An icy wind lashed across the airfield, knifing Carter in the face as he followed Urbanski across the apron. The Polish officer led them towards an Embraer Legacy 450 parked on the tarmac a hundred metres away, engines low-burring, pilots sitting in the cockpit. Presumably running through the standard pre-flight checks.

As they neared the jet Carter's burner vibrated. He unlocked the handset with a hard stare, tapped open the new text message. Sent from an unknown UK number.

*Congratulations! Your package has been delivered.*

Carter deleted the message. Stuffed his phone back into his jacket pocket.

He said, 'Update from Six. Kit's arrived at the safehouse. No problems.'

Beach made a quick mental calculation and said, 'They must have made it across the border a while back. Four hours ago, minimum. Guess they didn't run into any trouble on the crossing.'

'Looks like our luck's in, fellas,' Dempsey said.

'Early days,' Lazarides cautioned. 'Plenty of time for this job to go tits-up yet.'

A smooth-faced steward dressed in purple and white, the colours of the charter flight company, greeted them beside the Legacy. Six had arranged the booking with a charter flight company based in Farnborough, with the invoice paid from a bank account linked to the fake film production company. All part of their effort to distance themselves from the operation. Arse Covering 101. Practically the MI6 motto these days. The people behind the desks wanted to make sure they were covered before giving the go-ahead.

*If this job goes south, they'll be safe and sound.*

*Unlike us.*

They stowed their holdalls and the drone cases at the rear of the galley and settled into their seats. The smell of polished wood and new leather hung in the air. Classical music tinkled softly in the background. The steward came over to Carter, asked if he could get them anything.

'We're fine,' Carter said. 'But there is one thing I need you to do.'

The steward smiled blandly. 'Yes, sir. How can I help?'

'Do you have any premium-quality booze on this flight?'

'Of course, sir. We've got bottles of Louis Roederer Cristal, Moët, Grey Goose, Patrón tequila, Johnnie Walker Blue Label, Cîroc . . .'

Carter thought for a beat. Put himself in the shoes of a Belarussian border guard. Imagined living in a cramped apartment in Minsk. Making ends meet on a piss-poor state salary. Dealing with tourists who earned vast riches compared to him. Asked himself what such a guy might want to drink if he had the choice of anything behind the bar. Something Scottish, probably. Something he'd have heard of and perhaps seen advertised on TV. Something that represented a certain lifestyle choice. Something aspirational.

Carter reached a decision.

He said, 'When we land, the Belarussian immigration officer will stick his head through the door and ask to see our passports. What he's really after is some good quality booze. Give him a couple of bottles of Johnnie Walker and bill them to our company account.'

'May I ask why, sir?'

'We're on a tight schedule. I can't afford to have our team stuck on the jet because he's got the hump. Just make him happy, OK?'

'Of course, sir.'

'Good man.'

The steward stretched to his full height, still wearing the same bland smile. Headed down the aisle. Dempsey took out his paper-back biography of Ned Kelly. Beach flipped through the compli-mentary copy of the *Telegraph*. Lazarides reclined his seat and closed his eyes, like a Zen Buddhist practising the art of stillness.

Ten o'clock in the morning.

Midday in Belarus.

*Thirty-one hours to go*, Carter thought.

*Thirty-one hours before the performance begins at the opera.*

*And if this job goes to plan, the target will never make it to his seat.*

The steward came back over, took his seat at the front the cabin. The jet trundled across the apron, the engines blasted, roaring to a crescendo as the Legacy rocketed down the runway. Then they were climbing into the sky, leaving Warsaw behind.

Heading for Minsk.

*     *     *

They landed in Belarus forty-five minutes later. One o'clock local time. Carter remembered that Minsk was two hours ahead of Warsaw and adjusted his watch as the Legacy steered round to the tarmac apron.

The engines died down, the jet shuddered to a halt, the steward dropped the airstairs. A glum-faced immigration official barrelled into the cabin. He glanced round at the passengers, spotted the drinks trolley stowed in the aft galley. He took a cursory look at their passports and driving licences, quizzed them about their business in Minsk. Carter did most of the talking, a smoke-blowing exercise. He told the official about their plans to recce the national forests. The major TV production coming to Belarus in the very near future. Z-list celebrities surviving on grubs and wild mushrooms in the wild. *We're here to visit your beautiful country and report back to our bosses.* The officer feigned interest in their business.

'Very good, very good,' he said, handing Carter's passport back to him. His gaze snapped back to the steward. 'Any nice whisky on this flight?'

As if on cue, the steward produced two bottles of Johnnie Walker Blue Label from the bottom of the trolley, handed them over to the officer. The guy admired the labels, licked his lips in anticipation. Tipped his head at Carter, wished them all the best with their TV programme, and left the jet with a bounce in his step. Which the team took as their cue to deplane. They retrieved their holdalls and the drone cases from the rear of the cabin and headed for the exit, Carter nodding his thanks at the steward.

They descended the airstairs, into the teeth of a vicious winter wind. Two vehicles had pulled up a short distance from the jet on the apron. A white Toyota Highlander and a palladium-grey Škoda Octavia estate.

A man and a woman waited beside the two motors. The guy had a medium build, with a scraggly beard, peppercorn hair and skin so pale it looked like someone had drained the blood from his head. Carter recognised his face from the op briefing back in Germany.

Eduard Ruznak, the Ukrainian SBU officer.

Yulia Volkova stood beside him, puffing on a cigarette.

She was around five-six or seven, with the kind of slim-hipped build Primrose Hill yoga mums would die for. She seemed somehow different in real life, Carter thought. More naturally beautiful. Like an Instagram filter, but in reverse. At first, he couldn't put his finger on it. Then he realised it was the eyes. They were brighter than they had seemed in the photograph; they pulsed with magnetic intensity. The kind of eyes that could make a vicar burn a stack of Bibles.

She thrust out a hand at Carter.

'Luke, yes? Luke Carter?' she asked in thickly accented English.

'That's right.'

'Yulia,' came the reply. 'And this is Eduard.'

She flicked ash, gestured towards Ruznak. The Ukrainian security officer. He greeted the four soldiers with an upward jerk of his chin.

'First time in Belarus?' he asked.

'Yes, mate.'

Ruznak sucked the air between his teeth. 'I cannot say welcome. This is shit place. Land of our enemies. Too bad we must breathe the same air as these scum. But it will be worth it in the end, yes? Two days from now we shall be celebrating a great victory.'

Carter nodded back as he sized the Ukrainian up. Hatred for Russia emanated from every pore of the guy's body. More so than some of the SBU officers Carter had met during his stint on the President's BG team. He looked serious, Carter thought. Humourless. Not a guy who indulged in small talk. That was fine with Carter.

*We're not here to make lifelong buddies.*

*We're here to do a fucking job.*

He introduced the other members of the team. Then Ruznak said, 'Your package arrived a short time ago. Our friends delivered it to the safehouse. Everything is waiting for you.'

'Any problems? Anything we need to know about?'

'No problems. All good, my friend.'

'What's the news on the target?'

Volkova said, 'Ternovsky landed a few hours ago. My contact sent me a message. They're currently at his girlfriend's villa on the western outskirts of the city. All OK.'

Carter glanced at the FSB officer. She seemed anxious. Jittery. Eyes darting left and right, as if she expected to get arrested at any moment. He could smell the nerves coming off her like a bad scent.

'We should get going,' she said. 'We've got a lot to discuss before tomorrow.'

Ruznak said, 'Something I must ask. Why the sudden change of plan? Two days ago, I was told we would be directing Alpha Group to the target. Now everything has changed. Why?'

'Surprise to us too,' Carter replied tonelessly.

'They must have told you something?'

Carter pursed his lips. At the final shake-out before leaving Ramstein Smallwood had told the soldiers to deny any knowledge of the Russian collaborators inside Alpha Group.

*Only five people know about the infiltration. Ruznak isn't one of them. Volkova doesn't know anything either. Six doesn't want anything getting out. Not until they've established how many people are involved. What int has been compromised. How deep the rot runs.*

'Sorry, mate. No fucking clue,' Carter replied after a pause. 'They just told us there was a change of plan and wanted us to do the mission instead. That's it.'

Ruznak's eyes narrowed to slits. 'You are sure they didn't tell you anything else?'

'Not a fucking thing. We're just the hired muscle. Door-kickers. Our spooks don't tell us stuff like that.'

Ruznak examined his face for a long moment, as if searching for a tell. Then he stuffed a hand into his jacket pocket, chucked a key fob at Carter.

'This is you,' he said, indicating the Highlander. 'We're in the Škoda. We'll drive ahead to the safehouse. You follow us. Stay close behind, OK? Don't lose sight. GPS is not good in some places.'

'How far is the safehouse from here?'

Volkova stubbed out her cigarette, grinding it under her heel. She said, 'Forty miles to the north. Outside a village. A place called

Brosino. Very small. Nothing there except farms and fields. Not many people. Forty-five minutes by car. But an easy drive. We will discuss the mission later, OK?'

Carter frowned at his watch. A little after one o'clock local time. They would arrive at the safehouse at around two o'clock in the afternoon. A full twenty-nine hours before the big curtain raiser at the theatre.

'Fine,' he replied. 'Lead the way.'

Volkova and Ruznak hopped into the Škoda. The soldiers dumped their luggage in the back of the Highlander and piled inside the vehicle. Carter took the wheel, stamped the accelerator, tailed the estate out of the airport car park. Eight minutes later they were cantering north along the motorway, staying well below the regulation speed limit of a hundred kilometres per hour. Traffic was surprisingly light. The EU ban in action, Carter thought. No incoming flights from the major European carriers. Probably not a big loss to the national economy. Minsk wasn't a big tourist destination. Not unless you had a passion for farming techniques and brutalist Soviet architecture.

'What do you reckon, Geordie?' Beach asked after a pause of silence. 'Can we trust the Russian?'

'Can we fuck,' Lazarides interrupted before Carter could reply. 'You ask me, she looks nervous. Got an edge to her.'

Dempsey said, 'She's taking a major risk working with us. I'd be shitting bricks if I was in her shoes.'

'That's one way of looking at it.'

Beach twisted round in his seat, looked quizzically at Lazarides. 'What's the other, mate?'

The Australian shrugged. 'Maybe she's nervy because she's leading us into a trap.'

'No. That can't be it. Six checked her out. They told us her previous int has been solid.'

'Doesn't mean anything. For all we know she might have been feeding good information to Six deliberately. Reel them fuckers in by earning their trust. Classic Moscow technique.'

'It's a possibility,' Carter reflected. He could see the logic. The Kremlin would leap at the chance to use someone to earn the trust of Six officers. See what they might throw up. Find out what they know, who else they were handling inside Russia.

Lazarides grunted and said, 'It's a lot fucking more than that. I'd say there's a decent chance she's working for the other lot. Maybe she's shagging Heald, too. Get him on her side.' Lazarides screwed up his nose, as if he'd just trodden in shit. 'You've seen the way that posh twat talks about her. He'd give Volkova his pin number if she asked for it.'

Beach glanced at him in the rear-view mirror, wearing a pensive expression. 'You're saying she's a sleeper?'

'What I'm saying, Pom, is that we've got no idea who she really is. Do we? All we've got is the word of your friends in the service. And I don't fucking like it one bit.'

'Nature of the beast,' said Carter.

'Meaning what?'

'I've done loads of deniable jobs with the Wing. Always the same. We're operating in a vipers' nest. A lot of people working to their own agendas. We're only seeing a small part of a much bigger picture.'

'What the fuck difference does that make?'

Carter gripped the wheel hard, fixed his gaze on the flat land-scape ahead.

He said, 'There's no point worrying about Volkova right now. It's out of our control. All we can do is concentrate on the job. And watch our fucking backs.'

# Eleven

They carried on for forty minutes, staying close to Volkova and Ruznak in the pickup as they motored past harvested fields and drab farms. Carter saw a lot of grazing cattle and complicated irrigation. Crows swarmed over acres of rotted wheat stalks. Crude single-storey dwellings lined the unmetalled roads, punctuated by the occasional gated villa. Drainage ditches overflowed with rubbish. Stout old ladies in headscarves tramped along the roadsides, lugging sacks of potatoes. Old men ambled past on rickety bicycles. The descendants of nineteenth-century serfs, theoretically enjoying a better quality of life than their forebears but still tethered to the land. Still scraping a living from the unforgiving earth.

After thirty-five miles the Škoda took a hard right off the main road and shuddered along a dirt track that ran like a spear through the village of Brosino. They passed run-down farms, weed-choked yards and worn timber outbuildings, neatly trimmed graveyards lined with rows of gleaming marble headstones.

The track grew increasingly rough. Carter shadowed the guys in the Škoda, took a hard left and juddered down a stony path for three hundred metres before they eased to a halt outside a clapboard dacha.

The house fitted in with the decaying landscape. Peeling exterior paintwork, as if the building was shedding its old skin. Corrugated metal roof scabbed with rust. Gaps in the picket fence, like missing teeth. There was a vegetable patch to one side of the track, a timber-framed storage shed with a stack of worn tractor tyres beside it, an overgrown meadow dotted with alder trees. An empty pigsty enclosed within a chain-link fence. Dense woodland to the rear, and beyond the fields to the east and west. No other buildings in sight. Just a series of barren fields studded with utility poles.

*No prying eyes*, Carter noted. *Only one way in or out of the property. Long approach road, giving the team plenty of warning if any strangers unexpectedly showed up.*

*As good a place as any for a safehouse.*

Beach, Lazarides and Dempsey climbed out of the Highlander, Gore-Tex boots squelching on the muddied ground. They stretched journey-stiff legs, fell into step behind Ruznak and Volkova as they approached the dacha.

'Who owns this place?' Carter asked the Ukrainian.

'Smuggling gang,' Ruznak said. 'We're on the main trafficking route from Moscow. It runs through Smolensk, then on to Bialystok on the Polish side of the border. There are many places like this along the route. Old dachas owned by families loyal to the smugglers.'

'Let's hope the cops haven't got eyes on this place,' Lazarides grumbled. 'Last fucking thing we need. A drugs bust, right when we're sitting on a cache of weaponry.'

Ruznak gave a dry laugh. 'No chance. The police would never raid the safehouses. They have strict orders to leave the gang alone.'

'Says who?'

'The Russian government.'

Carter's mouth hung open. 'They know about the smugglers?'

Ruznak grinned. He said, 'The Kremlin relies on the smugglers to bring in all the things they cannot get on the open market these days. Medicine, computer chips, even spare aviation parts. In response, they turn a blind eye to the drugs and cigarettes going the other way. The sanctions have been very good business for the gangs.'

'Just as long as we don't have to worry about them guys stitching us up.'

'Relax, English. We can trust them. The smugglers are no friends of Moscow. Some of them hate Russians almost as much as we do.'

He smiled thinly at Volkova. Carter sensed a friction between them. He guessed the Ukrainian would have mixed feelings about

127

working with an FSB officer. Mistrust, mingled with pure hatred for the enemy.

'What's the deal with security at this place?' he asked.

'There's usually a guard or a house sitter. Someone the gang trusts to watch for thieves and squatters.' Ruznak gestured towards the bleak sky. 'At this time of year, the dachas are empty. Too cold. Everyone has returned to the city. That is when the vagrants move in.'

'Anyone here now?'

'No. The usual guard has orders to remain in Minsk until the job is done. For now, it's just us. No one to disturb us.'

Ruznak stopped beside the entrance, shoved a key in the lock, swung the door inward. Carter followed him inside a pinewood-cladded front room. Dust motes swirled in the sunlight thrusting through the gaps in the moth-eaten curtains. In the middle of the space stood a cast-iron stove with a brick-built chimney. There was a chintzy sofa pushed up against the far wall, a table and chairs opposite. Bottle of local voddie on the table, along with three smeared glasses, a cheap ashtray and a bank of monitors showing live feeds from cameras positioned around the dacha. There was a tiny kitchenette to the rear, a bathroom, a sparsely furnished bedroom.

Volkova knelt beside the stove, threw in some scrunched-up balls of newspaper and kindling, sparked up a match, chucked it inside. Carter and his colleagues dumped their holdalls beside the sofa. Ruznak paced over to the kitchenette, dropped to his haunches and pulled back a frayed Persian rug covering the floorboards. He prised up a pair of gnarled planks, revealing a rectangular opening cut into the flooring, leading to a hollow space beneath the suspended floor. The sort of thing a peasant family might have used to hide potatoes and other goods from local Communist officials. But also a good place to keep drugs and other contraband, Carter reckoned.

Ruznak reached down into the hollow and retrieved half a dozen weapon cases, plus a waterproof rucksack.

'Your equipment.' He passed up the last packet to Beach, wiped his hands on his trousers. 'Delivered by the smugglers.'

'This is everything?' asked Carter.

Ruznak nodded. 'This is it.'

Beach laid the cases out on the kitchen floor and unzipped them. Carter ran his eyes over the hardware. He counted two longs and four pistols. The longs were L119A2s. Rifle of choice for UKSF. The shorter variant, designed for CQB ops, with a ten-inch barrel, vertical foregrip, collapsible buttstock and rear sling. Both weapons were pre-fitted with Surefire suppressors and top-mounted Trijicon ACOG 4 x 32 sights. Chambered by the 5.56 x 45mm NATO round, effective to around four hundred metres.

The pistols were standard-issue Glock 17s, capable of holding seventeen rounds of nine-milli Parabellum. Internal safety mechanisms, so the operator didn't have to manually flick off a safety before discharging a round. They had under-mounted tactical red-light lasers. Pancake holsters for concealed carry.

Beach took out several boxes of ammunition from the rucksack and stacked them next to the guns. Enough rounds for three full mags for each long, plus two mags apiece for the Glocks. A total of three-hundred-plus bullets. They'd only need to use their weapons if they ran into trouble, but Carter prayed to fuck it wouldn't come to that.

Also inside the rucksack: four trauma kits, a bunch of US Army MRE ration packs, sterilisation tablets, baseball caps.

The team broke down the weapons, inspected the individual parts, reassembled them. Leaving nothing to chance. Carter took a wild guess and assumed that the Russian smugglers weren't paragons of integrity. They might have skimmed a little cream off the top. Helped themselves to some of the kit to sell on to the black market.

'Is it all there?' Ruznak asked.

'Aye,' said Carter. 'Everything's here, mate.'

The Ukrainian replaced the two planks and the threadbare rug. Volkova stood over his shoulder, watching him as she sparked up another tab. She scraped a hand through her hair. Said, 'We should go over the plan. We don't have much time.'

'Agreed,' said Carter.

She said something to Ruznak in what sounded to Carter's ear like Ukrainian. He'd served alongside Ukrainian SF during his rotation on the Presidential BG team and knew enough of the local lingo to distinguish between their language and Russian. Ruznak stood up, headed into the kitchen, filled the kettle and got a set of brews on the go. Meanwhile Volkova cleared the clutter from the table and spread out a detailed map of central Minsk.

'How much have they told you about the target's plans tomorrow night?' she asked between quick draws on her cigarette.

'The basics,' said Carter. 'We know he's due to arrive at the theatre tomorrow night for the opera. Approaching from the main entrance facing the park.'

Volkova nodded. 'That's correct. My source in the minister's office has confirmed the plans. Everything is set for tomorrow night. Ternovsky will be accompanied by his usual bodyguard team. Arriving at the theatre in his chauffeur-driven car.'

'What's the model?'

'Mercedes-Maybach GLS. One of the armoured versions, imported from Germany.'

'Bodyguards?'

'Eight men, my contact says. Four came in on the jet with Ternovsky.'

'And the others?'

'They landed in Minsk ahead of the target. Went straight to the villa to set things up for Ternovsky's arrival.'

'Are they all going with him to the theatre?'

'My source thinks so. Ternovsky might leave one or two men to guard the compound, but we won't know for sure until tomorrow evening.'

'What about security at the theatre?'

'Minimal. Maybe a few police officers out on the streets, but you shouldn't expect anything heavy.'

Dempsey said, 'What are the BGs driving?'

'G-Wagons. Two of them.'

'Anything out of the ordinary? Any breaks with his routine? Any unusual activity?'

'Not as far as I know. My contact says the minister doesn't suspect a thing. Business as usual. He spent most of yesterday in bed with Gluschenko, popping Viagra and drinking champagne.'

'Who's your source?' asked Lazarides.

'Ternovsky's private secretary. He has access to the minister's business diaries, his phone calendar, his email. He knows everything that goes on in the minister's life.'

'Is he travelling to Minsk?'

'Of course. He travels everywhere with Ternovsky. They're practically joined at the hip.'

'Why would he betray his boss?' asked Carter.

'The SBU have got him over a barrel. They know he's been stealing funds from his boss. Millions of roubles. If Ternovsky finds out, he's a dead man.'

'Do you trust him?'

Volkova looked levelly at the Australian. 'He's a man. He enjoys my company. We've known each other for a few months. Does that answer your question?'

Lazarides sat back, nodded in satisfaction. 'Good enough for me.'

Ruznak brought coffee over to the table. Carter took a sip and decided it was the vilest brew he'd ever tasted. Like drinking watered-down soil. Worse than the freeze-dried shit some of the lads at Hereford knocked back. The Ukrainian dropped into the chair next to Volkova, bummed a cigarette from her pack.

'So,' he began, blowing smoke towards the ceiling, 'we have waited long enough. What's the plan? How are we going to kill the Russian pig-dog Ternovsky?'

131

Carter pushed his coffee cup to one side and walked them through the plan. A step-by-step account. Like a dress rehearsal for a play, the day before opening night. Centre-stage on the map was the opera house, bordered on its western side by Maksima Bahdanoviča Street. A series of steps led down from the opera house to Troitskaya Gora park on the southern side of the square. A parcel of prime real estate in the heart of Minsk, situated on a bend in the Svislach River. Chain hotels lined the waterfront south of the park. Hostels and apartments due west. North of the theatre stood a row of businesses, with the Ukrainian Embassy four hundred metres to the north-west, next to Sciapanauski Garden.

'Access to the rooftop is from here,' Ruznak said, tapping a finger at a point on the map approximately four hundred metres west of the opera house. 'A two-bedroom penthouse apartment just off Storozhovsky Street. Private entrance, rooftop terrace. Month's rent paid in advance using a Ukrainian SBU slush fund.'

'Who owns the place?' asked Dempsey.

'A young couple. They inherited the flat from the woman's grandmother, renovated it and turned it into a rental property. She lives in Brest nowadays, rarely visits the city. A real estate company handles the lettings. Yulia has organised the contract.'

'Anyone else use the rooftop?'

Volkova said, 'The estate agent says no. It's only accessible from the apartment. You won't be disturbed.'

'Anyone likely to see us come and go?'

'I doubt it. Most of the apartments in this neighbourhood are short-term lets. And we're outside of the holiday season. Low occupancy. Not many tourists here, even in the summer.'

'Parking?' Lazarides said.

'Underground garage. We reconnoitred the area yesterday when we visited the apartment. Security cameras in the garage, but there are dead spots. I'll point them out to you before we leave.'

Carter said, 'What about the van we requested?'

'The smugglers will supply us with one of their vehicles. A breakdown recovery van. The smugglers use them to transport goods across the country. We'll collect it tomorrow, from an address in the city.'

Beach looked round at the SBU man. 'Where are you gonna be in all of this?'

'I will leave here same time as you,' Ruznak replied curtly. 'Flight to Poland. Then back to Kyiv.'

'You're not taking part in the job?'

Ruznak grimaced and made a helpless gesture. 'Out of my hands. Orders from the top. I am allowed to help with information and planning. But I cannot get involved in the execution. My bosses were very clear on that point.'

'Six didn't say anything to us about you sitting this one out.'

'Operational deniability. Kyiv is worried about escalation. You have a problem, take it up with your people.'

'Bollocks,' Lazarides spat. 'You're already involved, for fuck's sake. The only reason you're stepping back is because you're worried the job might go south.'

Ruznak shook his head firmly. 'We cannot give Putin a reason to escalate the conflict. If I am arrested in Minsk, what do you think will happen? Putin would force the Belarussian President to declare war on us. We will find ourselves fighting two enemies, instead of one. No. I must stay back.'

Carter stared at him for a long moment. Figured the Ukrainian was telling the truth. He had no reason to bullshit them. He shifted his gaze back to the map.

'I'll set up an overwatch here,' he said, indicating a side road a hundred and fifty metres west of the theatre steps. He squinted at the map, grappling with the strange name. 'Zaborskogo Street. Should give me a good line of sight to the target area.'

He drew his finger across the map, tapped on the row of shopfronts two hundred metres north of the opera house. Parking spaces lined the street outside.

'What's here?' he asked Volkova.

'Customer parking. For the shops. Bakery. Café. Bank. Pharmacy.'

'Parking restrictions?'

'None.'

'Fine. That's where we'll set up the reaction force.' He nodded in turn at Lazarides and Beach. 'Steve, Karl, you'll wait in the van here.'

Volkova said, 'What about me?'

'You'll be positioned half a mile away, at the transfer RV. Here.' Carter pointed out a backstreet to the north of the emergency rendezvous. A patch of blacktop at the rear of a printing shop, a computer repair business, an accountancy firm.

Carter went on, 'Quade, once you've done the job you'll head out of the apartment, make your way over to the Škoda at my overwatch point. We'll drive over together to the transfer RV. Steve and Karl, you'll head separately to the RV and meet us there. We'll ditch the van and Škoda, get in the Highlander, bug out of the city and make for the Polish border.'

Dempsey said, 'What if it goes tits-up?'

'Then we'll make for the emergency RV at Sciapanauski Garden, hide out and wait to be picked up.'

'You won't have long,' Beach pointed out. 'Twenty minutes at most. Any longer and there's too much chance of getting boxed in by the local plod.'

'Better hope it doesn't come to that, then,' Lazarides said with a grunt. ''Cos if that happens, things will have gone fucking badly wrong.'

* * *

They discussed the plan throughout the evening, fine-tuning it. Carter went over the details with Volkova until he was certain she had committed everything to memory. They identified escape routes, public transport, the best roads to take to the Polish border.

Volkova occasionally interrupted to clarify points or add details, filling in the blanks in the intelligence picture. Carter grilled her about parking spaces around the opera house, whether any of the nearby roads had been closed off. Any changes on the ground, anything that differed materially from the mapping the team had obtained at Ramstein.

Ruznak contributed little. Maybe because he didn't know Minsk as well as the FSB officer. This was Volkova's backyard, after all. Belarus was practically home turf for the FSB.

At nine o'clock they took a break. Ruznak served up tinned soup, followed by beef stew and potatoes. Carter and the rest of the team grazed on their MRE ration packs. Like chewing on wet cardboard, but Carter didn't care. He just needed the carbs.

They would have no further comms with Six, not until they were back on friendly soil. Their burner phones contained an emergency number, stored in their Contacts book, only to be used if the op had to be aborted. But strictly a last resort. As soon as you made the call, there was a good chance the enemy might detect the signal.

At around eleven o'clock they called it a night. The soldiers unfurled their foam mats on the floor and settled down for some shuteye in their doss bags. Ruznak took the sofa. Volkova kipped on the lumpy single bed.

The next morning, shortly after seven o'clock, Ruznak and Beach left in the Škoda to collect the van from his smuggling contact in Minsk. They returned ninety minutes later, Ruznak pulling up in the Škoda. Behind him Beach parked a white Volkswagen Crafter with blacked-out windows and a vinyl decal down the side carrying the logo for a highway recovery business.

At nine o'clock Beach left again with Ruznak in the Highlander. Bound for Minsk airport. From there the SBU officer would catch a flight to Poland before his onward journey to Kyiv. The guy seemed supernaturally calm, thought Carter. He showed none of the anxiety that normally gripped spooks on the eve of a big op. Maybe he had supreme faith in the Regiment. Or maybe he just had a really fucking good poker face.

Beach returned to the safehouse at ten. Then the team members began their final preparations. Lazarides hauled a ten-litre petrol can out of the Škoda boot, lugged it over to the Crafter, dumped it in the footwell in the front cab. Beach loaded the hardware and holdalls into the back of the Škoda. Dempsey checked the drone battery units. Making sure they were all fully charged. No one wanted to be going into action with half-dead kit.

Carter fixed himself a weak brew in the kitchen. He found Volkova sitting at the table, nervously pulling on a cigarette.

'You are sure this will work?' she asked Carter quietly.

'It's risky. But if everyone sticks to the plan, we've got a good chance of pulling it off.'

'But it could go wrong?'

'No job ever goes according to plan. First rule of warfare. Anyone tells you otherwise, they're a fucking liar. All we can do is focus on our prep and stay flexible.'

Volkova shook her head, extinguished her tab.

She said, 'I don't like it. There's a lot that could go wrong.'

Carter eyed her suspiciously. 'Are you getting nervous?'

'I'm betraying my country. I would have to be an idiot or a drug addict not to be worried. There are no rules in this game. If I am exposed, it is over for me.'

'You must have worked out a deal with Six. New life, all that shit.'

She laughed bitterly. 'Your people can't protect me. They don't understand how our organisation works. The lengths my bosses are prepared to go to get their revenge. Do you know what the punishment is for FSB officers who are caught spying for the enemy?'

'I can guess,' said Carter.

'No. Trust me, you cannot. It's not a bullet in the back of the head. It's far worse than that.'

Carter waited for her to go on. Volkova plucked another cigarette from her packet, reached for one of the bottles of cheap voddie, poured herself a thumb measure of firewater into a dirty glass.

'There is a special punishment for traitors in my country,' she carried on. 'There is a crematorium in Moscow in the basement of a building owned by the FSB. They take you from your prison cell, drive you to this place. Strap you to a metal stretcher. Then they shove you into the furnace. Alive. Feet first, so it takes longer for you to die. Sometimes they film the execution on their phones and send it to your family members, to warn them against speaking out. That is the fate that awaits me, if I am caught.'

Volkova necked the vodka. She puffed on her cigarette and poured another shot, spilling some of the clear liquid on the tablecloth.

'Jesus Christ.'

'That is one way it might end for me,' Volkova said. 'There are others. Maybe it happens a week from now. Or maybe nothing happens for twenty years. Then one day I come back to my nice cottage in the English countryside and there is a man waiting for me inside.

'Or maybe I put my hand on the door handle, and the next day I'm infected with a deadly nerve agent.' She laughed mirthlessly. 'The FSB are very creative when it comes to making their enemies suffer. And they are patient. They are prepared to wait a very long time. After this is over, I will never be able to rest.'

Carter contemplated telling her that she wouldn't be getting a cottage in some idyllic village in the Cotswolds. No Whitehall pen-pusher would ever sign off on that sort of deal. More likely, they'd set her up in a shabby mid-terrace in some drab new town in Hampshire. A modest monthly retainer. Enough to pay the bills and do her food shopping, but no more than that. Wheeled out for the occasional interview at Six. Condemned to spend the rest of her life in suburban irrelevance. A fate worse than death, when you had been used to moving in the corridors of power.

'So why are you doing it?' he asked. 'If you're worried about your old mates getting their revenge, why take the risk?'

'They killed my father. A decorated Russian general. A man who served his country all his life. Loved by his soldiers. And they threw him to his death.'

'I thought it was suicide,' Beach said.

'They always say that. But he was killed. Orders of the President himself. I know this for a fact.'

'But if your dad was a hero, why would they want him dead?'

'Because he was planning a move against Putin.'

Carter stared at her. 'Your old man was plotting a coup?'

'Papa, and several others. My father had been a strong supporter of the President at first, you see? Everyone at the time craved a strong man. You people in the West, you don't know how it was for us back then. We were humiliated. The whole world looked at poor Russia and laughed at our stupid oligarchs and drunken President. What we needed was someone who could restore order after the chaos of the Yeltsin years. And for a while, it was possible to ignore the corruption, the murder of oligarchs and journalists and politicians, because these things have always been part of life in Russia. But everything changed last autumn when my brother was killed on the eastern front. Another Russian sent to his death.

'My father started drinking heavily. He became disillusioned with the war. Realised that it had turned into a millstone around the Russian neck. That it would ruin our country. Eventually Papa and some other officers decided to do something about it.

'He never told me any of this, of course. I only found out the truth later, from one of the other organisers.'

'What happened?'

'Someone tipped off the President. Who this person was, I don't know. But once Putin heard about their plans, he moved quickly to get rid of the ringleaders. Including my father.'

Volkova downed another slug of vodka. She looked out of the grimy net curtains at the stubbled fields beyond, her gaze fixed on some vague point in the middle distance.

'Papa practically raised me by himself, you know. My mother died when I was four. For as long as I can remember, it was just me and Papa, and my grandparents when they weren't sick.

'We'd play soldiers in the garden. Go on fishing trips together. At bedtime he'd tell me stories about the great heroes of Russian history. Zhukov, Bagration, Peter the Great. He was the whole reason I joined the FSB. I wanted to follow in Papa's footsteps. Serve the Fatherland, just like Papa had done. He loved his country, and this is how they rewarded him. So when I heard what happened, I swore I would take my revenge.'

'You must really hate your bosses.'

'More than you can imagine.'

'What will you do?' he asked as she got up from the table. 'After this is done? Will you be coming back with us to Ramstein?'

Carter had assumed that she would be met by the Six team on the ground in Germany. Following which she would be processed and escorted to London to begin her new life.

'No. There's a safehouse in Warsaw. One of several owned by the service. I'll lie low there for a while.'

'Won't your bosses get suspicious?'

She laughed. 'I'm an FSB officer. We are not like your MI6 bureaucrats, with their expense forms and performance reviews. We have a lot of freedom in the field. It's not unusual for one of us to go dark for a while. No one will be asking questions.'

Carter said, 'You're taking a big fucking risk. If it was me, I'd want out as soon as the job was complete.'

Volkova blinked. A tiny frown grooved her brow. 'But our mission does not end with Ternovsky.'

Carter jerked his head back in confusion. 'What are you talking about?'

'You mean . . . you don't know?'

'Know what?'

Volkova said nothing. Hot rage spread through Carter's chest, boiled in his veins.

'What aren't they telling us, Yulia?' he demanded.

Volkova shook her head. 'I – I can't say. Your bosses aren't being straight with you. You need to ask them. That's all I can tell you.'

'Tell me. What the fuck is going on?'

Volkova, seeing his rage, backed away from Carter. 'I've said too much already.'

'Bullshit.' Carter drew closer to her. 'You know what's happening. What's this all about? What haven't they told us?'

Volkova stood her ground. 'I'm sorry, I can't tell you. You need to speak with your bosses. If they haven't explained things that's their problem, not mine.'

The sound of approaching footsteps drew Carter's attention towards the door. Lazarides stood in the entrance to the kitchen, eyes narrowed at the Russian. 'What's going on here?'

'Nothing,' she said.

Carter pulled back. Volkova hurried out of the room, barging past Lazarides on her way out. The latter watched her in puzzlement, shifted his gaze back to Carter.

'What the fuck was that about, Pom?'

Carter hesitated. He made a split-second decision not to tell the others about his conversation with Volkova.

*We've got a job to do.*

*We can't afford any distractions.*

He said, 'Just a petty disagreement. Nothing to worry about. Get everything ready. We leave in an hour.'

# Twelve

At exactly midday – seven hours before the start of the perform-ance – the kill team bugged out of the safehouse in a three-vehicle convoy. Volkova led the way in the Highlander. Carter followed in the Volkswagen Crafter. Dempsey, Beach and Lazarides brought up the rear in the Škoda.

They took the motorway towards central Minsk, past rolling fields and belts of woodland. After a while the farmland gave way to blocks of Soviet-era high-rises, looming over a sprawl of factories, supermarkets and gated villas. The route shuttled them along Maksima Bahdanoviča Street, a jumbled stretch of old and new Minsk: sushi bars and nineteenth-century gardens, lavish museums and trashy shopping malls.

At the first ring road Volkova hung a right. The team took the same turn, carried on for a quarter of a mile, sticking close to Volkova as she made a series of quick lefts and rights before she drew to a halt in a litter-strewn back road abutting a row of busi-nesses. Commercial dumpsters overflowed with rubbish. The kind of place where you only ever saw knee-tremblers, junkies or people stopping to take a piss.

Volkova parked the Highlander, hopped out and scurried over to the Crafter. Hopped into the front cab alongside Carter.

'OK,' she said. 'Let's go.'

They rejoined the traffic flowing south on Maksima Bahdanoviča. Continued for half a mile, passed the opera house, then hooked a right and crawled down a wide street running parallel to the river. After seventy metres Volkova indicated a parking space outside a bookshop.

'Pull over here,' she ordered.

Carter steered into the spot, engaged the handbrake, kept the engine humming over while the guys in the Škoda pulled up in the space directly aft.

Volkova pointed towards a five-storey apartment block at the far end of the street. A grand old structure, with a rose-pink façade, wrought-iron balconies, tall sash windows and projecting cornices beneath the rooftop.

'Wait for me here,' she said. 'I'll go up and meet the estate agent, get the keys and clear the rooms. Don't move until I give the signal.'

Volkova sprang open the front passenger-side door and stepped outside. Through the mud-splashed windscreen Carter watched her hasten down the street. She reached the entrance to the building, climbed the front steps, stabbed a button on the intercom panel. Several moments passed. Then Volkova moved inside.

Carter scoped out his surroundings. There was a tanning salon, a restaurant, a discount clothing shop. He saw an old man walking his dog. A jogger. A middle-aged woman in too-tight acid-wash jeans wheeling along a kid in a pram. Routine life in Minsk. Nothing out of the ordinary. Nothing that struck him as suspicious.

Eight minutes later, the front door to the apartment block swung open and a primly dressed woman emerged from the lobby, moving at a quick trot down the street. She crossed the road, unlocked a Peugeot 308 parked twenty metres away. Ducked inside, reversed out of the space and puttered south. A few moments later she turned the corner and disappeared from sight.

The team waited while Volkova swept the apartment for bugs. Twelve minutes, Carter's phone buzzed. Volkova was using an ultra-encrypted device, issued to her by Ruznak before he'd left. A departing gift from the Ukrainian intelligence service. Practically identical to the phones the team had been given by the Scaleys back at Ramstein.

Volkova said, 'Everything's clear. Head to the underground garage. I'll meet you upstairs.'

Carter said, 'Roger. On our way.'

He tapped out a message to Beach, relaying the message to the three guys in the Škoda. He pointed the Crafter back onto the main road, hooked a left past the apartment block, the Škoda at his six o'clock. Midway down the side street Carter turned into the underground garage. He stopped in front of the security barrier, worked the buttons on the mounted control panel. Dialled up to Volkova in the penthouse apartment. There was a brief pause before the barrier lifted, and Carter arrowed the van down the ramp.

He steered towards the spaces at the far end of the garage. One of the dead spots Volkova had identified during her recce of the garage the previous day. The Škoda pulled up immediately to the left; Carter clambered out of the wagon, walked round to the rear of the Škoda and grabbed the weapon cases from the storage compartment. Beach, Dempsey and Lazarides retrieved their holdalls.

The four soldiers cut across the garage, slipped through a fire door, climbed the access stairs to the top floor. Padded down a short corridor and stopped outside the penthouse apartment. Carter knocked twice. Volkova unlocked the door, ushered them inside. They dumped their kit in a wide living space decorated like a Swedish homewares store showroom.

She said, 'I've had an update from my source.'

Carter said, 'Everything OK?'

'Everything's still on. Ternovsky is scheduled to take part in a conference call with his junior staffers this afternoon, followed by a visit from his regular masseuse at four. Dinner at five o'clock. He'll leave for the theatre immediately after.'

'Curtain-up's at seven o'clock sharp,' Volkova added. 'Ternovsky is scheduled to arrive at the theatre at six to meet the KGB Director and the Belarussian Defence Minister.'

'Why so early?'

'There's a champagne bar at the Bolshoi. They'll talk shop over a bottle of Laurent Perrier before the performance, then take their seats.'

Carter nodded and looked down at his phone screen.

*1321.*

*We've got less than five hours to get into position.*

They started unpacking the hardware. Carter handed out the Glock 17s. One per operator, plus two full mags of 9 x 19mm Parabellum rounds. One clip in the feed, spares stuffed in their front pockets. The guys strapped the pistols into their pancake holsters, concealed the pistol grips beneath their untucked civvy shirts.

At the same time Dempsey broke out the two drones from their cases. He attached the propellers, checked the spare battery packs nestling in the boxes. Half a dozen per drone. Two of the packs had been tagged with strips of red tape. They looked exactly like the other batteries, except each one contained a kilo of C4 explosive encased in plastic film over a set of metal ball bearings, with an electric detonator fuse triggered by a button on the drone controller. Like a miniature Claymore. Only airborne.

Lazarides watched the pair of them with barely disguised contempt and moaned about the dying art of the sniper. Volkova paced anxiously up and down the front room, smoking furiously and checking her phone screen every few seconds.

'Shit,' Dempsey cursed.

Carter had been busy thumbing rounds into the long clips. He stopped what he was doing and looked up. 'What is it?'

The Australian held up one of the drone batteries and scratched his head. 'This one's a dud. Lost half its juice since yesterday. Fucking thing ain't holding its charge.'

'So plug it in.'

'I would, mate, but I can't find the adapter. Must have left it back at the safehouse.' Dempsey shook his head in frustration. 'Schoolboy error.'

Lazarides walked over to the kitchen. Unplugged a chrome kettle and returned to the living space. He nodded at the portable drone tool kit Dempsey had brought with him from Germany.

'Give us a crosshead screwdriver. I'll need a set of cable strippers, too. I can wire the charger up to the kettle plug.'

While Lazarides unscrewed the plastic case, Dempsey took the stairs leading to the rooftop terrace to get his bearings. Calculating distances and angles and battery longevity.

Volkova periodically checked in with her source. The Defence Minister's love-struck private secretary. Getting updates on the target's movements. Lazarides finished wiring up the drone charger to the kettle plug. He shoved the adapter into the socket, flicked the switch. Four green lights blinked on, indicating that the battery was charging.

A while later Volkova's source confirmed that Gluschenko wouldn't be accompanying the minister to the theatre. No explanation. Maybe she wasn't thrilled about the prospect of sitting through three hours of nineteenth-century comic opera.

Carter said, 'Is the secretary travelling with him?'

'No. He'll stay behind at the compound. Only the bodyguards are going to accompany him to the theatre.'

'Anyone greeting him on arrival?'

'A junior flunky, my source says. One of the Belarussian Defence Minister's underlings. His counterpart will be arriving ahead of Ternovsky. Same deal with the KGB chief.'

'No press, no big greeting from the theatre director? Nothing like that?'

Volkova shook her head. 'Ternovsky insists on a media blackout whenever he travels.'

'What about the other guests? Are they using the same entrance?'

'There's a staff car park on the western side of the opera house. Separate entrance. The other guests will be directed over to that side. Only the VIPs are permitted to use the southern entrance.'

A troubling thought had been brewing at the back of Carter's mind. 'What are we missing here?'

'Missing?' Volkova repeated.

Carter said, 'Ternovsky is a high-level minister. And he's an ex-bodyguard. No one knows the tricks of the trade better than him.'

'What's your point?'

'This guy is running a major risk, attending a performance in the middle of Minsk. But according to your contact he won't be taking any extra precautions. No body doubles, no extra security, nothing to reduce the chances of someone knocking him on the head.'

'Maybe he's getting lax,' Beach suggested. 'Maybe the fucker thinks he's untouchable.'

Carter considered this briefly, then shook his head. 'That's not it. We know this guy is normally very careful. Fuck me, he barely leaves the villa when he's in-country. Plus he's got all them extra security measures. Attack dogs, infra-red cameras. Panic room.'

Lazarides set down the kettle plug he'd been unscrewing. 'What are you saying, Pom?'

'Ternovsky doesn't seem like the kind of bloke who cuts corners on his personal safety. He wouldn't go out tonight, not unless he was confident no one could have a pop at him.'

Dempsey shrugged and said, 'Won't make a blind bit of difference. He's still planning to rock up at the opera house, ain't he? As long as our man does that, he's fucking toast.'

\*   \*   \*

At two o'clock Carter and Volkova left the apartment to conduct a walk-around recce of the target area. Standard procedure. Get a mark-one eyeball on the environment. Check for any unexpected threats or obstacles. Volkova played the role of the local guide, showing the big-shot British TV producer the major sights in Minsk. Both of them wore baseball caps to shield their features from any CCTV cameras. They did a wide clockwise loop of the neighbourhood. Started north until they hit the Ukrainian Embassy and the fringes of Sciapanauski Garden, then cut east past the football stadium, carried on for half a mile. Took a right onto Kuybyshava Street and continued south towards the theatre.

Then they spotted the police officers.

Carter estimated two dozen of them, guarding the various entrances to the public park and patrolling the grounds. Four more guys paced up and down the road parallel to the theatre. Two men in police uniform and a couple of heavyset thugs decked out in black civvies. KGB muscle, Carter assumed. Orders to assist the local plod in clearing the area ahead of Ternovsky's appearance. They worked in pairs, stopping to peer into the windows of the cars parked at the roadside.

Carter glared accusingly at Volkova. 'I thought you said security was lax round here?'

The Russian looked pale. 'Normally this is true. I – I don't know what's going on.'

'I do,' Carter replied through gritted teeth. He indicated the policemen. 'This is why our man's not worried about tonight. He's got the whole fucking area on lockdown.'

'What are we going to do?'

'We'd better tell the other lads. Come on.'

They walked south at a quick pace, past the theatre and the gardens. Hurried west on Janki Kupaly Street, turned right at the riverfront and hastened back to the apartment. Inside, Volkova smoked another coffin nail while Carter briefed the rest of the team on the heightened security presence around the opera house.

'Which means the original plan is dead. I can't sit in a vehicle and get eyes on the target,' Carter said. 'No chance. If I park up anywhere near that building the cops will notice me. They'll order me to move on or stick me in the back of a police van. We're going to need a new plan.'

'What have you got in mind, Geordie?' asked Beach.

'First things first, I need a power drill.' He turned to Volkova. 'Is there a hardware shop somewhere close by?'

Volkova unlocked her burner phone, opened Google Maps, pinched and swiped across the screen. She said, 'There's a place on the other side of the river. Open until eight o'clock.'

'How far is it?'

'Three miles away.'

Carter nodded. 'Listen carefully. Get down there right now and buy a power drill. A cordless one, with a pre-charged battery. I'll also need a box of different drill bits. Got all that?'

Volkova made frantic notes on her phone, grabbed her purse and the keys to the Škoda. Hastened out of the apartment. Carter checked the time again: 1508 hours.

*We're going to be cutting it close.*

Minutes passed. Dempsey finished fitting the explosive packages to the brackets on the undersides of the two drones and carried the units up to the rooftop terrace. At four o'clock Volkova returned to the apartment clutching a plastic shopping bag.

'Bad traffic,' she said. 'Police everywhere.' She handed the bag to Carter. 'Everything I could find. OK?'

Carter fished out a Makita cordless power drill with a couple of battery units, plus a separate case with an assortment of masonry, wood and HSS drill bits, countersinks and nut drivers and hole-saws. Carter depressed the check button on one of the lithium battery packs. An indicator lamp briefly illumed. Two bars. Fifty per cent capacity left in the unit. Good enough.

He slid the battery into the grooved underside of the drill, plugged the spare unit into the charging base, flipped the drill switch to high speed, gave the trigger a quick pull to check that it was working. Then he snatched up the kit, grabbed the car key fob from Volkova and took the access stairwell down to the car park. He walked casually over to the Škoda, scanning the garage.

The place looked empty. No one else in sight.

Carter halted next to the boot. He dropped to a knee, took a 3mm drill bit from the set and secured it in the jaws of the chuck.

Aimed the bit at a point just above the licence plate and below the car badge. Depressed the trigger and drilled a pilot hole through the bodywork.

Carter twisted the sleeve counter-clockwise, released the bit and replaced it with a larger one, gradually enlarging the hole in increments. He repeated the process until he had an opening roughly the circumference of a pound coin. Big enough to get an eyeball on the target.

Satisfied with his work, Carter locked the wagon, trotted back up the steps to the top floor. Woke his phone again.

Four thirty in the afternoon.

Ninety minutes to go.

He retrieved a set of miniature binoculars from his holdall, set down the drill and bit set, joined Volkova at the kitchen table. Reached for the iPad next to an empty Coke can doubling up as an ashtray, opened the map and zoomed in on the streets around the theatre. Assessed potential OP sites. He needed somewhere with an unobstructed view of the opera house, in an area where a parked – and seemingly unoccupied – vehicle wouldn't attract unwanted attention.

He pointed to a side road a hundred metres upwind of the theatre. Said, 'Here's what we're going to do. I'll crawl into the boot of the estate. You'll drive me over to this point and park at the side of the road. Make sure you're not double-yellowed, so we won't get any hassle from parking wardens or shit like that. Have the boot facing south-east, towards the theatre. That way I'll have eyes on the target when he arrives.'

'Like a Trojan horse?'

Carter nodded. 'Lock the car, but make sure you turn off the interior monitoring before you get out. Should be an option on the infotainment settings menu. Once you've done that, walk away and make your way back to the garage. Steve and Karl will meet you there.'

'What if the cops search it?'

'They won't. From the outside the car will look unoccupied. They won't have any reason to take an interest in it.'

'How will you get out? Once it's done?'

'Give Quade the keys. As soon as the target's liquidated, he'll head over to the car, get behind the wheel and head to the transfer RV point. As we discussed earlier.

'Just remember to switch off the monitoring before you debus. Otherwise the sensors will go off with me inside. Last thing I need is those KGB thugs coming over to take a good long look at the car.'

'When do we leave?'

Carter dropped his eyes to his G-Shock. 'Ten minutes. I'll need to be in position for five o'clock. An hour before the target arrives. I'll have my phone with me, so keep me updated on the minister's movements. Anything changes, let me know.'

'OK,' Volkova replied uncertainly.

They went through final checks. At four fifty Carter stood up, slipped on his jacket and red baseball cap, grabbed his phone and binoculars. Tipped his head at the others.

'Right,' he said. 'Let's go.'

# Thirteen

They packed away their kit and bugged out of the apartment. Dempsey stayed behind and ascended to the rooftop with the two explosive-loaded drones. The rest of the team made their way down to the underground garage. All five members had plugged in their military-grade earbuds. Designed to look like standard civilian models, with built-in mics and Bluetooth connectivity, but capable of withstanding extreme weather conditions. They would allow the team to communicate throughout the op via a five-way chat group on their burners.

Beach loaded the longs and holdalls into the back of the road recovery van and climbed inside the front cab. Lazarides took the wheel. Reversed out of the spot, steered up the exit ramp, disappeared down the street towards its designated position. Volkova watched them go before she unlocked the Škoda. Carter smuggled himself into the empty boot space, setting the binoculars down beside him. Burner phone in his jeans pocket. Volkova slammed the lid shut, entombing him in the back of the estate.

The journey to the OP site took eleven bone-jarring minutes as the Škoda rattled over potholes and skewed round corners. Carter was dimly aware of muted street noise: motorcycles backfiring, car horns, gypsy music thumping out of sound systems, people shouting, the faint hubbub of conversation. The Škoda lurched to a halt and backed up, and Carter guessed that Volkova must be parallel parking. The engine silenced. He heard the muffled thump of a door as Volkova hopped out, the sharp click of the car locking behind her. Carter hoped to fuck she'd remembered to deactivate the motion sensors.

He adjusted his position in near darkness, drawing his eye towards the circle of daylight leaking in through the gap above the rear licence plate. From his position on the street corner facing east, Carter had a clear line of sight across the main road towards the opera house. A distance of no more than a hundred and fifty metres.

A red carpet had been laid out in front of the entrance, trailing down the front steps like a tongue. At the base of the steps a block-paved access road cut through the park on an east-west trajectory. An ornate fountain faced the southern park entrance on Janki Kupaly Street. To the north stood a row of businesses: a hotel, a health spa, a Chinese restaurant. Further east was a secondary school; beyond that, Carter descried the offices of the Belarussian Ministry of Defence.

A good OP.

But with one problem.

Volkov had said the target would approach from the north, heading along the main thoroughfare before turning into the park and making its final approach on the access road. But from his position Carter was too far away to confirm the target with the naked eye. In order to verify the minister's identity Carter had to use his binos. Which meant kicking out the cargo shelf, sitting up in the back of the Škoda and peering through the rear windscreen. And which risked exposure. A passer-by might catch sight of the stranger popping into view from the car boot and raise the alarm. But no way round it. They had to eyeball the target. No one wanted to slot the wrong guy by accident.

The cops were out in force, Carter noted. Working in pairs with their KGB minders as they prowled the park and the surrounding streets. Full court press. Two of them grabbed a couple of youthful protestors waving placards, marched them roughly out of the park. A bald-headed guy in a black leather jacket with a silver chain around his neck, and a short, stocky cop with dark bushy eyebrows. They shoved the protestors into the back of a police van. Returned to their posts guarding the western entrance to the access road.

Carter glanced down at his illuminated G-Shock.

17.06.

Fifty-four minutes to go.

*　*　*

Five hundred metres away to the north-east, Lazarides and Beach sat in the front cab of the Crafter, L119A2 longs pointing barrel-down next to the side doors. They had parked the van in a free space outside a grimy-looking café on Chychernya Street. Two hundred metres from the opera house. Early evening in Minsk, and the coffee shop staff were winding up for the day. A bored-looking kid mopped the floor; a portly woman carried out bags of rubbish, tossed them into a nearby dumpster.

Lazarides steepled his fingers on the wheel. Counting down the minutes.

*　*　*

Half a mile to the north-east, Volkova moved swiftly across the filthy backstreet where she had stowed the Highlander a few hours earlier. She sidestepped a pile of stinking rubbish, shooed away a stray dog. Unlocked the car, scooched behind the steering wheel, tugged the door shut. Caught her breath.

'In position at the transfer RV,' she reported over the comms channel.

Dempsey's voice sounded in her earbud.

'What about Geordie?'

'He's ready,' she said.

'Same here,' Dempsey replied. 'Reaction force in place.'

Volkova reached for her cigarette packet. Lit a tab with a shaking hand. Took a quick nervous pull and glanced at the clock on the dash display.

17.24.

Thirty-six minutes to go.

* * *

Six hundred metres to the south, Dempsey set down the two drones on the rooftop. He took one of the fake battery packs loaded with explosives and secured it between the mounting bracket arms on the underside of the first drone. Did the same with the second unit.

Carter had the role of overwatch on the mission, providing a stream of live intelligence on the goings-on in front of the opera house. As soon as Carter had confirmed the target was making his final approach, Dempsey would fire up the drones. Then it was simply a case of waiting for a visual confirmation from Carter before guiding the drone towards its destination.

Dempsey had a second aircraft for backup, in case the first one failed. Not an outlandish scenario. Any number of things could go wrong. The explosives might fail to detonate. Dud blasting fuse, maybe. Someone might shoot the drone out of the sky before it reached its target. Or Dempsey might miss. Unlikely, but stranger things had happened.

The team had one chance to take out Ternovsky. Fail, and the guy would go deep underground. Disappear off the radar. His security cordon would be strengthened. Once that happened, it would be damn near impossible to get at the fucker.

*If we're going to kill him, it's got to be today.*

17.38.

Twenty-two minutes.

* * *

A minute later, Volkova's phone vibrated urgently with a message. She grabbed the handset from the dashboard. Skim-read the text.

Got back on the five-way chat with Carter, Lazarides, Beach and Dempsey.

She said, 'I've heard from my contact.'

'What's the news?' asked Carter.

'Target has left the compound,' Volkova replied. 'Two minutes ago. He's en route with his bodyguard team. Heading our way now. Twenty-seven minutes out.'

'Roger.'

\* \* \*

Carter waited.

Dusk began to settle across the city. Streetlamps burned around the park, bathing the opera house in warm light. At 17.42 four vehicles bowled down Maksima Bahdanoviča Street before making the turn onto the access road leading to the steps at the bottom of the opera house. A Mercedes-Benz S-Class rode in the middle of the crocodile, with a pair of Chevrolet Suburbans to the rear and an Aurus Arsenal armoured minibus in the lead. No sign of a Mercedes-Maybach GLS among the fleet, or a pair of G-Wagons. Therefore not the target. Carter assumed the convoy belonged to one of the other VIPs attending the evening's performance.

He watched as the fleet pulled up in front of the steps. Half a dozen figures promptly disgorged from the vehicles. Carter counted them off. Eight thickset bodyguards in cheap suits and earpieces. Plus two smartly dressed older men with moustaches. The Belarussian Defence Minister and the KGB big boss, Carter guessed. Hard to tell at this range, but according to Volkova's inside source this entrance was reserved for Ternovsky and his Belarussian counterparts. No one else had permission to approach the theatre from this side.

A reedy younger man in an ill-fitting suit vaulted up the steps after the VIPs. The Belarussian minister's junior flunky. He paused beside the entrance, took up a spot next to the doorman. Presumably he had orders to await the arrival of Ternovsky. The guest of honour. RV with him and escort him to the champagne bar.

As Carter looked on, the crowd of BGs and VIPs disappeared inside the opera house. The column of vehicles eased further east along the access road, exited the park with a right turn onto Kuybyshava Street, continued south until they reached the corner of the park and hung another right on Janki Kupaly Street. They pulled up outside the southern entrance to the park, a hundred and fifty metres from the theatre. A secure area, guarded on either side by police patrols. The cars would wait there and collect their guests at the end of the performance.

Minutes ticked past.

More cars arrived at the theatre. Traffic cops directed them to the large western parking lot. The area reserved for non-VIPs. Men and women in evening wear flocked towards the side entrance.

At 17.51 a tramp stopped on the street corner four metres from the Škoda, unzipped his trousers and relieved himself against the wall with a satisfied groan. Piss splashed down the brickwork, puddled around the guy's tattered shoes.

A few seconds later Carter noticed a pair of figures hustling across the road from the western side of the park. Silver Chain and Eyebrows. The two guys he'd seen manhandling the protestors into the back of a police van a short time ago. They were heading in his direction, shouting angrily at the tramp. Eyebrows stopped short of the vagrant and pointed to the west. A clear order. *Get the fuck out of here.*

The homeless guy finished pissing. Slurred a response as he hitched up his baggy, piss-stained trousers. He grabbed his plastic bags of worldly possessions, shuffled along.

In the back of the Škoda Carter stayed perfectly still. The Belarussians were less than two metres away from him now. The slightest noise might alert them to his position.

*No choice but to wait for them to move on. Return to their posts in front of the access road.*

But the Belarussians didn't budge. Instead Silver Chain paused to light a cigarette, offered one to Eyebrows. The cop gratefully accepted. Muttered a few words to the KGB thug. Complaining about the problems of homelessness in Minsk, maybe. They were in no hurry to return to their positions. Two disgruntled employees having a smoke, chatting shit, putting the world to rights before going back to work.

Silver Chain gave his back to the Škoda. Carter felt the vehicle sag as the KGB thug leaned his hulking frame against the bodywork.

Blocking his view out of the spyhole.

Carter felt his blood freeze.

He couldn't move. Couldn't alert the other guys on the team to his predicament. Not with only a thin sheet of metal separating him from the Belarussian cops. He could hear Silver Chain hack-coughing between drags on his ciggie, drowning out the chatter on his earbuds.

Five minutes to go.

Carter stayed very still. Sweat glossed his palms. He was running out of time. Unless Silver Chain and his mucker moved away in a few minutes he wouldn't be able to get a visual on the target. They'd have to postpone the job, at the very last moment.

Seconds crept past.

At 17.56, Carter feared the mission was dead. He decided to give it another two minutes. Then he'd have to tap out a text message to the others, telling them to abort. They couldn't risk detonating the drone blind. Too much chance of collateral damage. Better to call off the job and wait for another opportunity to present itself.

*Assuming there is one.*

Another minute passed. Silver Chain laughed hoarsely at something Eyebrows had said. A dirty joke, maybe. Eyebrows hawked and spat on the ground.

Still neither of them moved.

*Two minutes to go.*

*Shit.*

*We're almost out of time.*

Then Carter heard the distinctive squawk of a police radio.

Eyebrows and Silver Chain stopped talking. A scratchy voice came over the net. The police officer barked a reply, exhaled noisily.

The weight pressing down on the vehicle abruptly shifted. Light flooded into the spyhole as Silver Chain pushed away from the Škoda. Carter heard the fading patter of footsteps. He peeked through the opening, felt his stomach unclench as he watched the KGB heavy and Eyebrows dash their fags in the road and walk smartly back across the street, heading towards their posts at the western entrance to the access road.

In the same beat a movement drew Carter's eye to the north. He looked towards the main road running parallel to the nearside of the park and spotted a motorcade gliding along the thoroughfare. A slick armoured Mercedes-Maybach GLS, buttressed front and rear by a pair of black G-Wagons. The vehicles carrying Ternovsky and his BG team.

Carter felt his pulse quicken.

*We're in business.*

The motors slowed down as they steered onto the access road. Carter whispered into his earbud mic.

'Target approaching,' he said.

\*　\*　\*

On the penthouse rooftop, Dempsey got to work.

He slid back the gripper on the side of the explosive battery fixed to the belly of the first drone, arming the bomb. Flipped up the antennas on one of the controllers, thumbed the power button above the seven-inch high-resolution monitor. The engine started; the propellers on the first attack drone began spinning rapidly. The aircraft lifted slowly off the ground and hovered three feet above the rooftop while the system went through its own pre-flight diagnostics. Dempsey watched the drones for any signs of instability, checking to see that all the props were turning smoothly.

He looked round the rooftop, making sure no one was watching him. A legitimate danger. The drone was noisy. Someone at a neighbouring property might hear the sound and poke their head out of the window. But the area remained clear.

Dempsey went through the same process for the backup drone. At that point both units were live and ready to detonate.

The drones had a maximum speed of sixty miles an hour. Equivalent to twenty-five metres a second. In windless conditions, Dempsey estimated around fifteen seconds to reach the target.

Fifteen seconds to strike before he was safely inside the opera house.

A narrow window.

No margin for error.

But all they needed.

'Drones ready,' he said.

*   *   *

Two hundred metres away, Carter observed the motorcade slowing to a halt in front of the opera house, at the point where the carpeted steps met the access road. The doors on the two G-Wagons swung open. A couple of guys dismounted from the lead vehicle, a third from the car at the rear. Rent-a-toughs in matching blue suits and crewcuts, each guy rigged up with an earpiece for covert comms.

Ternovsky's bodyguards.

One of the BGs from the front G-Wagon strutted round to the rear passenger-side door on the Maybach, popped it open. He stepped back. Giving the boss room to exit the vehicle.

A thickset figure stepped out of the Maybach. Carter couldn't see him clearly. At a range of a hundred and fifty metres, with his view partially obscured by the rear G-Wagon, it was impossible to be sure. Carter kicked upward, knocking the cargo shelf from its plastic clips, so he could sit upright. He scooped up the binoculars, centred them on the five figures converging beside the Maybach.

He spied three heavies, plus the heavily built principal. Plus three more bodyguards behind the wheels of the G-Wagons and the Mercedes-Maybach. Therefore six BGs in total. Volkova's source had stated that the Russian Defence Minister had eight guys on his BG team. Carter presumed the other two guys were back at the villa with the girlfriend and the secretary. House-sitting duties. *Ternovsky might leave one or two men to guard the compound, but we won't know for sure until tomorrow evening.*

The Belarussian ministerial flunky trotted down the steps to greet Ternovsky. He said something to one of the principal's BGs, gestured towards the fountain to the south. Telling them where to park. The drivers would steer the vehicles round to the southern side of the square, pull up in the secure area behind the Suburbans and the minivan, then wait until the performance had finished before collecting their principal. Standard procedure when ferrying a high-value target around. But indisputably the most boring part of any BG job. Hours of sitting around doing nothing.

Ternovsky followed the flunky's pointing finger. And for a fleeting moment Carter got a good look at the guy. He noted the thick nose, the pinprick eyes buried in the fleshy face, the cross-hatched scar tissue on his chin.

'Target confirmed,' he said. 'That's him, lads. Mission is go. Repeat, mission is go.'

*　*　*

As soon as he heard Carter's voice Dempsey thumbed the joystick on the right side of the controller, pushing it up. The first drone pitched forward, surging clear of the rooftop, gradually increasing its speed.

160

The backup aircraft remained in its hover mode, propellers turning and burning. If he needed to deploy the second drone he didn't want to lose valuable seconds starting it up.

Dempsey switched his attention to the controller screen for the first drone. The monitor relayed a crystal-clear feed from the on-board camera. Dempsey worked the two joysticks, pitching and rolling the aircraft through the sky as he guided it towards the opera house.

As soon as Dempsey had the principal within killing range, he'd press the Home button on the controller, sending a signal to the electric detonator, triggering the on-board bomb.

Four hundred metres to the target.

Three hundred.

Two.

# Fourteen

From his OP in the back of the Škoda, Carter looked on as one of the BGs spoke into his sleeve mic. He figured the heavy was relaying the flunky's information to the drivers over the secure comms channel. A logical assumption. At once the two G-Wagons and the Maybach chuntered further along the access road, taking the same route as the earlier motorcade, while Ternovsky started towards the theatre entrance. Two BGs walked in front, with a third guy at his six o'clock as the tail-end Charlie and the flunky at his right shoulder. Forty metres away the doorman stood holding the door open, ready to admit the evening's star guest. A few plain-clothed KGB toughs and police officers hung around the front of the building, facing outward, keeping a close eye on the park grounds.

The bodyguards scanned the area as they moved, like professionals. Looking for anything that didn't fit the picture. But they had made a fatal mistake. They were working on the assumption that any threat to the principal's life would come at him from ground level. They weren't expecting an airborne attack.

Ternovsky had almost made it halfway up the steps when the tail-end Charlie abruptly halted.

Carter heard the faint insect buzz of the drone bearing down on its target. He figured the rear bodyguard must have detected the noise too. Because he wheeled away from his principal and lifted his head skyward.

On the step immediately above the tail-end Charlie, Ternovsky had stopped too. The flunky at his side pointed at the sky. At the drone swooping down towards them.

Then he shouted in terror.

Several steps further up, the two BGs in the vanguard had also halted and spun round. Eyes drawn towards the flunky and the principal five or six metres below their position.

The tail-end Charlie was closest to the principal. A distance of no more than a metre between the two men. Therefore, the best placed to react to the threat. His training automatically kicked in; he lunged desperately at Ternovsky, shoved the flunky aside and threw the minister to the ground, landing on top of him. Like a gridiron player sacking a quarterback before he could make a game-winning pass.

A few paces away, the doorman dashed forward to help the dazed flunky to his feet.

In the next breath the first drone detonated its payload.

The explosion engulfed the steps in a savage fireball, fragging the tail-end Charlie. Ball bearings flew outward, peppered the nearby flunky and the doorman. Like a shotgun blast pattern. The resulting overpressure blew out the windows at the front of the theatre. Glass fragments rained down on the red carpet. Someone screamed in agony. Others yelled in shock and terror.

When the smoke cleared, Carter glimpsed the rag order bodies of the junior flunky and the doorman sprawled amid the broken glass, debris and blood spatter. The dead weight of the shredded tail-end Charlie lay slumped over Ternovsky, pinning the latter to the ground.

The two BGs further up the steps had survived the explosion. At a range of six metres from the blast they would have caught some of the fragmentation, but otherwise they seemed to be OK. A lot fucking better than their colleague. They sprinted over to the principal, grabbed hold of the dead BG and threw him aside. One of the surviving bodyguards seized the minister by his left bicep and hustled him down the steps while his companion shouted into his sleeve mic. Alerting the other guys to the situation.

On the eastern side of the park, the motorcade screeched to a halt.

*Shit*, thought Carter.

'Drone missed,' he said into his earbud mic, fighting to keep his voice controlled. 'Target's on the move. Get the other fucking bird in the air, Quade. *Now.*'

'On it,' came the reply from Dempsey in his ear. 'Where the fuck are they? I need a location.'

Carter searched for the principal through the binos. Cops were running around like headless chickens, drawing weapons and yelling pointlessly into radios. They would be wondering what the fuck had just happened. Had there been a suicide bomber? Had someone planted a bomb? Were terrorists launching a siege on the theatre? Minds would be racing with all sorts of nightmare scenarios.

Amid the confusion one of the BGs manhandled Ternovsky towards the waiting motorcade. The other guy ran along just behind, still bellowing into his mic. The G-Wagons and the Mercedes-Maybach had stopped on the corner of Kuybyshava Street. A distance of no more than a hundred metres from the close protection team. Carter grasped their plan at once. The bodyguards would want to get their principal as far away from the theatre as possible. Bundle the minister into the armoured Maybach and speed back to the compound on the outskirts of Minsk. Hunker down there until it was safe to emerge. A sound strategy.

*That's what I would do.*

The BGs were seventy-five metres from the vehicles now.

'I've got them,' Carter said in a low voice. 'Targets heading east on the access road. Making for the exit on Kuybyshava Street. Get that fucking drone on them, mate.'

'Roger,' Dempsey replied. 'I see them. Drone two in the air now.'

Carter tracked the targets. They were moving fast. But not fast enough. The lead BG tried to hurry the minister along, but the guy was dazed from the first blast and clearly struggling. Twice he stumbled and almost fell over, slowing the team down.

Fifty metres between the bodyguard and the wagons.

Forty metres.

They were thirty metres from the wagons when Carter heard the propeller-whir of the second drone zipping through the air. He looked up, glimpsed the aircraft plunging out of the sky, like a bird of prey, descending towards its human meal. Dempsey was handling the drone masterfully, planing and pitching, adjusting its flight path at speed.

*No escape now.*

The bodyguard to the rear of the principal glanced over his shoulder, spotted the drone closing on him, stopped in his tracks and whirled fully round, snapping his pistol from his shoulder holster in a blur of motion. Making a split-second calculation. He realised they couldn't hope to outrun the aircraft. They were too far away from the motorcade. A simple matter of time and distance. No way round it. So he went for the next best strategy. Shoot the threat out of the sky. Like a warship in the Pacific, trying to down a Japanese kamikaze pilot before it crashed into the hull.

Last-chance saloon. A desperate move.

But necessary.

The bodyguard took aim at the drone.

His pistol barked twice.

Missed.

The drone kept plummeting towards the team.

Beyond the shooter, the third BG and Ternovsky were fifteen metres from the nearest G-Wagon. Agonisingly close to safety. The drone was right on top of them now.

The target was nearly home and dry when the bomb detonated.

A cloud of hot smoke and flame instantly swallowed the three figures. One kilo of high-grade C4, mixed in with the ball bearings, had about the same kinetic impact as a Claymore mine. Serious killing power. Powerful enough to destroy a car or take out multiple enemy combatants on the battlefield. The windows on the side of the G-Wagon shattered. Car alarms squealed. Bystanders shrieked in panic.

The smoke drifted upward. The two remaining bodyguards and the minister had disappeared from sight. Like a vanishing act at a magic show. They were there one second, then they were gone. Severed and burned limbs scattered the block paving. Shoes and smouldering scraps of fabric. Charred bits of flesh. Nothing identifiable as a human body. The clean-up job for the emergency responders was going to be a nightmare.

'Target down,' Carter reported to the others. 'Repeat, target is neutralised. Got the fucker.'

The scene in front of him was chaotic. People were running in every direction, diving for cover behind the fountain or the sculptures dotted around the park. The fleet of armoured vehicles parked beside the southern entrance K-turned on the main road and raced round to the parking lot on the western side of the theatre. Ready to collect the Belarussian Defence Minister and the KGB chief and speed them out of the danger zone.

'Quade, mate. Get down here,' Carter said. 'Steve, Karl, arses into gear. Before they close off the neighbourhood. We'll meet you at the transfer RV.'

'Roger that,' said Beach.

Police officers were swarming over the park now, weapons drawn. Some ran over to the dead guys. Carter didn't know why. Hoping to apply CPR to a bunch of body parts, maybe. Others were shouting into their radios, presumably demanding backup.

Everyone had turned their backs to the surrounding streets. They had their attention fully locked on the carnage in front of the opera house. No one was looking in Carter's direction. The plan was going smoothly. Better than he could have hoped.

*All I've got to do now is wait for Dempsey to scurry over from the apartment, and get the fuck out of the city.*

Then he heard the voice, and the plan went to shit.

* * *

At that moment Dempsey was ramming the controllers into their pre-moulded slots in the shell boxes. He lugged them over to the A/C unit on the far side of the rooftop, jammed them out of sight behind the metal casing. Someone would inevitably discover them a few weeks from now, but that didn't matter. He just needed to ensure no one stumbled upon the drone kits in the next day or two. Buy the team some time to bug out of the country. Twenty-four hours from now, they would be out of Belarus and back at Ramstein Air Base, celebrating a job well done.

Dempsey stood up. Legged it downstairs.

*Time to get the fuck out of here.*

* * *

The voice shouted hysterically at Carter again in Russian. It sounded close. Had definition. Therefore, not someone at the park, but much closer to his position on the side street. Coming from his nine o'clock.

He looked out of the rear window. Spotted the tramp ten or twelve paces away from the Škoda. The same guy he'd seen earlier, with his piss-stained trousers.

The tramp's eyes had popped wide with alarm; his plastic bags had dropped at his feet, spilling junk over the pavement as he pointed an accusing finger at Carter.

The tramp shouted once more. Louder this time. His panicked cries must have caught the attention of the cops further to the east. Because in the next beat Carter heard a chorus of figures bellowing at him from the direction of the theatre.

'*Stoyat! Politsiya!*'

Carter felt his stomach drop.

The tramp had rumbled him. He'd seen the Brit sticking his head above the cargo shelf just before the attack. The cops would have heard the guy's manic yells. They would have looked up, seen the guy pointing at the parked-up Škoda, the suspicious figure sitting upright in the boot compartment. And understood that Carter was somehow connected to the opera house bombing.

In a matter of moments, he knew, they would be swarming over his position.

He couldn't risk staying in the Škoda a moment longer.

*Only one thing for it.*

*Time to bug out.*

Carter removed the panel covering on the emergency boot release, tugged on the lever. The tailgate sighed open. He bomb-burst out of the luggage compartment, scooped up the portable binos. To the east the four nearest cops broke into a run and sprinted towards the Škoda, drawing weapons while simultaneously hollering to their comrades, drawing their attention to the suspect to the west.

Carter turned away from the theatre.

And started to run.

# Fifteen

In the front of the Crafter, Lazarides twisted the key in the ignition. Ready to execute the next phase of the plan. Which involved motoring round to the designated transfer RV, where Volkova was waiting with the Highlander. They'd link up with Carter and Dempsey, torch the van and the Škoda; then everyone would bundle into the back of the wagon. Once they were clear of the city limits it was a straight run to the border with Poland.

Then Geordie Carter's voice came over their earbuds.

'I'm compromised,' he said breathlessly. 'Exfilling on foot. Police all over the fucking shop.'

'Shit,' Beach muttered. He sat bolt upright.

Lazarides said, 'Where are you now?'

'I'm running west on Zaborskogo Street,' Carter replied. He was barely audible above the background noise. People were shouting. Police sirens wailed. Car alarms screamed.

He continued, 'No way I can make it to the transfer RV on foot. Heading to the emergency RV. Meet us there.'

'Got it. Leaving now, mate.'

'What about Quade?' asked Beach.

There was a beat of silence before Dempsey's voice came over the line. 'On my way to the emergency RV too. Four minutes out.'

'Hurry,' Carter said. 'Fuckers are closing on us.'

Lazarides shifted into Reverse, mashed the pedal and backed out of the parking space. The Crafter swerved onto blacktop and lurched to a halt, front bumper aiming northwards. Lazarides upshifted and stomped the accelerator again. The diesel engine growled. They swung hard to the left at the next T-junction. Motored west down the main road towards Sciapanauski Garden.

Then they spotted the roadblock.

* * *

Five hundred metres away, Carter rounded the corner and pelted north on Starovilensky Street. As he sprinted past the American Embassy, he took a quick glance over his shoulder. Three cops were tearing after him, a hundred metres further back. One of them hefted up his service pistol, aimed it in Carter's general direction and loosed off a wild round.

There was a sound like cracking ice as the gunshot split the air. The bullet missed Carter by a good half metre and starred the windscreen of a nearby parked Volkswagen Passat. The cop fired twice more. Rounds ricocheted off the stem of a streetlamp to Carter's right. A woman out for her evening jog screamed and dived for cover behind a parked Tucson.

Carter kept on running.

Two hundred metres to the emergency RV.

He had no interest in shooting it out with his pursuers. His absolute priority was to put as much distance between himself and the police officers as possible. Trading rounds would only slow him down, give the Belarussians time to close the net around him. Better to keep running. Outpace the enemy. Get to the emergency RV. Wait for the lads in the Crafter to scream over and jump inside.

He checked his watch: 1806. Six minutes since the first drone had detonated its lethal payload. At that moment the cops would be throwing up roadblocks, sealing off the district from the outside world. Forensics teams would scour every square inch of the crime scene. Very quickly, investigators would establish certain facts. They'd logically conclude that one of the attackers must have been within radio range in order to direct the aircraft onto its target. Buildings and cars in the neighbourhood would be searched. There would be intense pressure from the Kremlin to arrest and punish the killers. No stone would be left unturned. Half an hour from now, escape would be impossible.

*We've got to get clear of Minsk before then.*

He detoured to the west, darted down a side street, ran on past the Ukrainian Embassy. Tacked a right at a steel-and-glass shopping mall, bolted north down a one-way street and vaulted over the metal fence bordering Sciapanauski Garden.

Carter slowed to a walk as he scanned the grounds. Breath misting in front of his mouth, heart pounding in his chest. He couldn't see anyone sitting at the benches or walking along the various footpaths. It was freezing cold, and dark. A winter's night in Minsk. Hardly ideal conditions for a stroll in the public garden.

He spied a movement in the corner of his eye. Coming from his nine o'clock. The west side of the garden. Carter looked round. In the glow of the streetlamps he spied Dempsey running over from an entrance between two blocks of flats. He stopped beside Carter, chest heaving up and down from his exertions.

'Fuck happened?' Dempsey gasped.

'Later,' Carter said. 'Anyone see you?'

'Don't think so, no.'

'Good. Come on.'

They tacked north of the monument, made for the northern fringes of the garden. Focused on their immediate priority.

*Get behind cover. Wait until the van can rescue us.*

They approached a thick knot of shrubs and bushes running alongside the perimeter fence. The area the team had previously identified back at the safehouse. The perfect hide-out spot. No street lighting. No nearby benches or walkways. No reason for anyone to pay attention to it. Less risky than waiting out in the open.

Carter dropped to his knees and crawled in among the bushes. Twigs and discarded bits of rubbish were strewn across the damp earth. Dempsey crept in after him. They rested close to the fence, staying concealed among the shadows. As soon as the van pulled up they would shoot to their feet, leap over the fence and dive into the back of the Crafter.

*Now all we've got to do is wait*, Carter reassured himself.

*Stay calm.*

*Help is on the way.*

\* \* \*

Four hundred metres to the east, Steve Lazarides eased his foot off the gas pedal. Beach automatically lowered his gun hand to the long resting against the passenger door. Twenty-five metres ahead, four police officers stood in the middle of the road. Two of them had their pistols drawn while their muckers made their way down the line of stationary motors, leaning into driver-side windows and checking ID. Another team armed with sniffer dogs searched the boots and back seats, frisked down the passengers.

Roadblock.

'Shit,' Lazarides said. 'They set that fucker up quick.'

Beach stared at him. 'Keep driving.'

Lazarides nodded. They both knew the score. They couldn't allow themselves to get stopped by the police. He white-knuckled the steering wheel. Swerved out of the traffic piling up at the roadblock, lined up the van with the middle of the road. Stamped on the pedal. The Crafter shot past the static motors and ploughed straight towards the cops. Two of them swivelled towards the van, waving their hands frantically. Shouting at them to stop. Lazarides surged forward.

The cops dropped their arms.

Turned to flee.

The front end of the van clipped one of the guys before he could dive out of the way. He bounced off the windscreen, limbs flailing like a rag doll, tumbled off to one side. The Crafter jolted violently as the second cop went under the wheels with a cry of despair.

The other two police officers had scrambled for cover at the side of the road. Lazarides saw them in the rear-view as the van roared past the roadblock. The cops climbed to their feet, reaching for their guns. Muzzles flashed. Half a dozen rounds hammered against the back panels.

'Bastards are giving chase,' Lazarides reported. 'Two cars behind us.'

'Take a right here, mate,' Beach said as they bombed towards the crossroads.

Lazarides spun the wheel clockwise. Beach gripped the passenger grab handle as the Crafter skidded into the turn. The wagon fishtailed, then straightened out and bulleted north on the thoroughfare. Behind them the cop cars took the same corner at speed. The lead vehicle was fifty metres behind Lazarides and Beach now. No doubt they were radioing across to their mates, alerting them to the van. In a few minutes they'd have half the force in Minsk on their case.

After two hundred metres Beach pointed at a junction directly ahead and said, 'Hang a right at those lights. We'll block those fuckers off on a side street.'

'Roger.'

Lazarides kept his foot hard to the floor. The Crafter screeched as it slewed to the right. They took the next left and shuttled the wrong way down a one-way street. A cyclist ambling down the road caught sight of the van accelerating towards him, leaped off his bike and dived towards the pavement a few moments before the Crafter struck, crushing the frame beneath three tonnes of machinery.

As they reached the midway point Lazarides lifted his foot off the gas and spun the wheel all the way round. The Crafter dropped its speed; then Lazarides depressed the clutch and lifted the hand-brake. The wheels shrieked as the back end of the van swung round. The Crafter rocked to a standstill side-on, blocking the road.

'Get out,' Beach ordered. 'Torch the fucking van. I'll start put-ting rounds down.'

The two operators hefted up their longs, sprang the side door handles. Boots thudded down on the asphalt. Lazarides hooked round to the back of the van while Beach took up a firing position behind the front cab, trained his L119A2 sights on the eastern end of the side street.

The first cop car slid round the corner, lights flaring and pulsing. Beach lined up the front windscreen in his sights. Double-squeezed the trigger. Two rounds spat out of the suppressed barrel in quick succession. The windscreen splintered. The passenger's head exploded. Blood sprayed the cracked glass. Two women stand-ing outside a karaoke bar cried in terror and threw themselves to the ground.

The driver dived out of the police car and scuttled behind a row of parked motors, leaving behind his dead mate with his brains splattered across the windscreen. Meanwhile the second cop car skidded to a halt; two officers jumped out and took cover behind the rear fender. A wise move. One of their mates had just been slot-ted. They would think twice before engaging. They weren't being paid enough to be heroes.

Lazarides hefted up the plastic petrol can from the footwell. He unscrewed the cap, poured the contents over the front seats, soak-ing the upholstery in flammable liquid.

At the front wheelbase Beach discharged two more rounds at the cops. Suppressive fire. A time-honoured tactic. Keep the enemy pinned down while you tried to gain an advantage, or make a tactical withdrawal.

Lazarides fished out a Zippo lighter from his trouser pocket. He rolled his thumb over the sparkwheel, drawing a flame.

'Get back!' he yelled at Beach.

The latter let off another round before he pushed away from the Crafter. Lazarides tossed the Zippo into the front cab. There was a low roar as the back seating burst into flames.

'Time to go! Move!' he thundered.

Lazarides and Beach broke into a sprint down the one-way road. Away from the blazing Crafter. The few civilians left in the street were running for their lives. A mother grabbed a kid in an Argentina football jersey and dragged him screaming into the stairwell of a block of flats.

Behind them the fire was spreading quickly. Jets of apricot flame licked out of the shattered windows, smothered the upholstery. The noxious smell of burning plastic and fuel choked the air.

'We've run into the cops,' Lazarides said over the comms channel. 'Two officers down. Had to ditch the van. On our way to the emergency RV now. We're on foot.'

The two operators ran on. Aimed for an alley directly ahead of them, opposite a nail salon. Lazarides figured the makeshift roadblock would give them a two-minute head start over the cops. At the most. Two minutes in which to lose their pursuers and join the other guys at the emergency RV on the north side of Sciapanauski Garden.

Enough time.

He hoped.

From there they would have to somehow make their way to the transfer RV half a mile to the north. But there was no point thinking that far ahead. They forced themselves to focus on the immediate task. Pushed everything else from their minds, like all good SF veterans.

*Prioritise.*

*Concentrate on surviving the next sixty seconds. Worry about everything else later.*

\* \* \*

Half a mile to the north, Yulia Volkova sat in the front of the Toyota Highlander, listening to the reports filtering through from the kill team.

'On our way to the emergency RV on foot,' Lazarides was saying.

'Where are you now?' Volkova asked.

'Kisialiova Street. Seven hundred metres from the RV.'

Volkova closed her eyes. She visualised the layout of the streets around the Bolshoi Theatre. Pictured Lazarides and Beach fleeing down the road on foot, a trail of destruction behind them. Mapped out the route from their position to the emergency RV on Sciapanauski Garden. Guesstimated the time it would take for the Belarussian police to put a ring of steel around the Trinity Hill neighbourhood, versus the distance between the scattered team members and the transfer RV. Reached the inescapable conclusion.

There was no way the team would be able to make it.

They were too far away. Too much ground to cover. The cops would be flooding the area in a matter of moments. Might already be doing so, in fact. Two of their own had been taken out. Shit had just got personal. They would be extra motivated.

Volkova reached a decision.

She said into her mic, 'Wait at the emergency RV. I'm coming to get you.'

Volkova fired up the engine. Backed out of the alleyway.

Took off down the main road.

\* \* \*

To the south, Carter heard Volkova's voice in his earbud, telling him that she was en route to their position.

In the distance, police sirens chorused.

At that moment every officer within a mile radius would be rushing towards the Bolshoi Theatre. Like filaments drawn to a magnet.

They would have been alerted to the shootout with the van. The two figures legging it on foot. The third guy who had been seen running away from the back of the Škoda estate. The cops would be organising themselves. Cordons would be thrown up. Search teams would be going through the area. Very soon the whole city would be sealed off.

With Carter and the others trapped inside.

'Karl, Steve, fucking hurry,' he whispered urgently over the ear-bud mic. 'Get over here fast as you can. Yulia, what's your ETA?'

'Sixty seconds out.'

'Don't come straight to us. There's a nursery directly opposite our position. Pull into the parking lot next to it. Entrance on Starovilensky Street. Wait there but keep the engine ticking over. We'll give you the signal to swing past as soon as we've got sight of Karl and Steve.'

There was a pause. 'Police are setting up roadblocks everywhere. I can't wait for very long.'

'You won't have to.'

\*   \*   \*

Lazarides and Beach raced towards the RV. Running as fast as their legs could carry them. They had to take a circuitous route to Carter's position. No choice. The area was crawling with police. They heard the mechanical wail of sirens at their six o'clock, dropped to their bellies and wriggled underneath a parked pickup truck seconds before a pair of cop cars hurtled past. They waited until they were sure it was safe, crawled out from under the wagon and ran on. Took the next backstreet, stopped when they caught sight of a cluster of blue lights popping at the far end. Retraced their steps to the main road and sprinted north for a hundred metres until they hit the next block and took that turn. Boxing around the trap.

A laborious tactic, lengthening the distance they had to travel and delaying their arrival at the RV. But the only sure way of avoiding capture.

They barrelled down the pavement. Still five hundred metres from the RV.

Five hundred metres from safety.

* * *

At that moment, Volkova was pulling into the parking lot on Starovilensky Street. A hundred metres upwind from Sciapanauski Garden. She stopped the Highlander a short distance from the nursery building. Left the engine running, as per Carter's instructions.

'In position,' she said.

* * *

At the emergency RV, Carter shifted his position and reconnoitred the ground immediately east of the garden. Watching and waiting. Looking for any sign of Lazarides and Beach.

Counting down the seconds.

'Where the fuck are you, lads?' he asked in a hushed tone.

'Three hundred metres out.'

Two ambulances bombed past the line of cars waiting at the cross-road traffic lights, closely tailed by a cop car. Shadowed figures peered out of balcony windows. Local residents, no doubt wondering what was going on below. Further away, the faint whump-whump of a helicopter carried across the evening air.

'That's it. We're out of time,' said Volkova, her voice strained with anxiety. 'We've got to go now. I'm coming round to collect you.'

Carter said, 'Wait one. We're not ready yet.'

'Are you crazy? They're about to seal off the district. We won't be able to get out.'

'Just give us another fucking minute. That's all I'm asking.'

Volkova said nothing.

Carter went back to scanning the crossroad.

Ten seconds.

Then twenty.

'Where are you, Steve? Pom?' Dempsey hissed impatiently.

No reply. Nothing but dead air.

Carter kept his eyes nailed to Kisialiova Street due east of the garden. Fighting to stay calm, even as his heart thumped savagely in his chest.

*If those two don't show up in the next thirty seconds,* he thought, *we're going to have to bug out without them.*

Twenty seconds left.

Carter's mind scrolled through potential scenarios. He wondered if Beach and Lazarides had been captured. Cornered by the cops, maybe. Or cut down in a gun battle with the local KGB. Maybe the poor fuckers were bleeding out at that very instant.

Fifteen seconds to go.

Still nothing.

Then he heard Beach on the comms saying, 'We're a hundred metres away. Get that wagon ready, for fuck's sake.'

'Roger that,' Carter replied. 'Yulia, get moving. Stop at the traffic lights on the junction directly east of my position. Make sure them side doors are unlocked.'

'On my way,' Volkova said.

Carter skated his gaze towards the road running north to south at the intersection. Agonising seconds passed. The police sirens were deafening now.

Then the Highlander rocketed into view. It lurched to a halt at the lights forty metres from the garden. Carter signalled silently to Dempsey. They broke free of the bushes, cleared the fence, dashed across the street towards the wagon. Flung open the rear doors and dived inside.

Volkova twisted round in her seat, eyes popped wide with panic. 'Where are the others?' she asked.

'There! Look!' Dempsey said, pointing beyond the crossroad.

Volkova looked. So did Carter. Lazarides and Beach bolting towards them from the opposite end of Kisialiova Street, lugging their rifles. Charging past terrified bystanders.

The howl of unseen police cars grew even louder as Beach threw himself into the back seat next to Dempsey, gasping for breath. Lazarides jumped into the front passenger seat, screaming at the top of his voice, 'Go! Go! Fucking go!'

Volkova stomped on the pedal, ran a red light and made a sharp right at the junction. As they motored west Carter glanced out of the rear windscreen. A trio of cop cars screeched wildly to a halt outside the entrance to Sciapanauski Garden. A dozen officers dismounted and began spreading out across the grounds.

'Shit,' Beach said, breathing heavily. 'That was fucking close. Another ten seconds and we would have been shafted.'

'We're not out of the woods yet,' Carter cautioned. 'This city is gonna be on full lockdown soon enough. Keep your eyes fucking peeled.'

They drove out of the city in tense silence. Volkova stuck to the backstreets, careful to avoid any main roads or busy intersections. Carter kept his eyes nailed to the road ahead, alert to the first sign of a police checkpoint. In which case they would have to box around it. Or ram their way through. But they hit the first ring road without running into further trouble and carried on through the western suburbs at a steady speed, obeying all the laws of the road. Doing nothing that might draw attention to themselves. After eight miles they cleared the outer ring road and mounted the motorway leading west out of the city.

'Thank fuck,' Beach said, breathing out. 'I don't know about you lads, but I'm gonna need a few beers after that.'

'Speak for yourself, Pom.' Lazarides made a face. 'Me, I'm gonna need a whole fucking crate.'

'What now?' Volkova asked.

Carter said, 'We stick to the plan as discussed. Head to the border near Grodno. We'll cross there and make for the Polish Air Force Base at Lask. They'll be expecting us. From there we'll catch a military flight back to Ramstein. We'll drop you off en route.'

Volkova said, 'We might get stopped. At the border. The guards will have been alerted to the attack.'

'So what? They won't know who to look for, not yet. It'll take a while for the cops to piece things together. Right now, all they know is that there have been two explosions at the Bolshoi, a bunch of people are dead and three male suspects in baseball caps were seen leaving the area on foot. They won't know about the drones or the apartment. Most likely they'll wave us past.'

'And if they kick up a fuss?'

'Show them your warrant card. The guards will shit bricks once they know they're dealing with the Russian FSB.'

'What about the guns?'

'We'll take care of that. Just keep driving.'

*　　*　　*

They raced west for two hours. Putting some serious distance between themselves and the crime scene. Volkova flicked on the radio, tuned into the state-owned news station. Details on the attack were thin on the ground, Volkova said as she translated the report. The station described a terrorist attack in the heart of Minsk. Several persons had been killed, among them the Russian Defence Minister, Konstantin Ternovsky. An anti-Russian guerrilla group based in Belarus had claimed responsibility for the bombing.

Carter smiled to himself. He knew that statement would have been put out by Six. A distraction, intended to help the team's escape from the country. The Belarussian authorities would be directing their efforts into hunting down the guerrillas. Therefore, they would be looking for local suspects. Embittered ex-service personnel, with the expertise necessary to carry out a drone attack in the middle of the capital. No one would pay much attention to a few foreign nationals.

They drove through a moonlight-bathed landscape of bare fields, lumber yards, industrial processing plants. At around nine o'clock they reached a village called Korolovtsy, and Carter ordered Volkova to turn off the main road. She guided the Highlander down an unlit gravel track for a hundred metres. Then Carter said, 'Stop here. That's far enough. This will do.'

He started to get out.

'Where are you going?' Volkova asked.

'To get rid of the evidence.'

Carter climbed out of the wagon. Lazarides debuckled from the front passenger seat and joined him at the roadside. The cold scraped Carter's hands as he took one of the longs and knelt down in front of the headlamps. He ejected the rounds from the rifle chamber, removed the clip. Detached the sights and suppressor, took the guts out of the weapon breach, disassembling all the working parts of the rifle. Repeated the process for the second weapon, while Lazarides took apart the four Glock 17s. Then Carter placed both rifles in front of the Highlander, with the barrels propped against the kerb.

He waved at Volkova. She inched the wagon forward, driving over the longs. There was a splintering crack as the rifles broke apart under the weight of the vehicle.

Volkova backed up. Lazarides cleared away the smashed-up rifles. Carter laid the Glocks flat on the ground next to the front tyres, two per side. Volkova nudged the Highlander slowly forward once more, crushing the four pistols beneath the tyres.

Carter and Lazarides gathered up the damaged Glocks and carried them over to the edge of a patch of woodland. They dropped the hardware into a hollow in the ground, chucked in the longs, covered everything with a mound of rotting vegetation. Not as effective as burying the guns, but the ground was rock-hard with night frost, and they had no entrenching tools. Too cold to dig with their bare hands. They tossed the spare clips, holsters and cases into a nearby ditch, scattered leaves and bracken on top. Hastened back over to the Highlander.

Carter was reasonably sure that the weapons wouldn't be discovered for a while. On the off-chance a civilian did stumble upon them, they wouldn't be serviceable. A small thing, maybe. But Carter didn't want some teenager discovering a fully loaded piece in a field and causing an accident.

'OK,' he said. 'We're done. Let's get the fuck out of here.'

# Sixteen

The team hit the western border ninety minutes later. Eleven o'clock in the evening local time. They joined a slow procession of long-haul lorries and tankers waiting to cross into Poland. When they reached the front of the line, Volkova smiled at the potato-faced guard as she handed over their documents. The guy glanced cursorily at their passports and fired a few questions at Volkova in Russian. From the look on his face, he found her answers unsatisfactory.

He beckoned to one of his colleagues. A second guard stepped out of the sentry box and strolled over to join Potato Face beside the Highlander. He asserted control of the situation, peppered Volkova with more questions in a stern tone. Carter sensed things growing tense. Then Volkova flashed them her security service ID. Her get-out-of-jail-free pass. Literally. The guard leaned forward, squinted at the card with his razor-blade eyes. The colour dropped so quickly from his face Carter almost heard it thud against the ground. He stepped sharply back from the Highlander. Nodded at Potato Face. An unspoken signal. But clear enough.

*Let them through.*

The barrier arm lifted.

A short time later they cleared the Polish side of the border. They refuelled at a petrol station in the next small town, paid in cash from the team's walk-around fund, stocked up on bottled water and snacks. From there it was a five-hour dash across the country to the air force base at Lask, with a quick stop at an FSB safehouse in Warsaw.

At three in the morning, they dropped Volkova outside a slick new apartment block on Ludna Street, on the western bank of the

Vistula. As he watched her disappear inside the building Carter's weary mind drifted back to his conversation with Volkova the previous morning.

*Our mission does not end with Ternovsky.*

What had she meant by that? Clearly the head shed had lied to the team; that had come as no great surprise to Carter. But what had they been hiding? *What else do they want with us?*

Carter had pushed these questions to the back of his mind during the mission. Compartmentalisation. One of the mental skillsets you learned to master in the Regiment. Cut out the external noise. Concentrate solely on the task at hand. Forget everything else. Distractions meant you weren't fully focused. Which could be fatal to your life expectancy. But now the job was done, and he found himself thinking ahead to Germany. The debrief.

*I don't know what's going on here,* he told himself. *But once we're in a room with the head shed, I'm going to get some fucking answers.*

They continued towards Lask. Beach took the wheel; Carter punched out a message to Kendall on the emergency number stored on his burner.

*Everything is done,* he wrote. *Target liquidated. We're out of the country. En route to Lask AB now.*

There was a long pause. A sequence of typing bubbles popped up at the bottom of Carter's screen as Kendall composed a response. Ten seconds later a new message appeared.

*Any casualties?*

Carter wrote, *Negative. We're all fine. But law enforcement had to be engaged. Two police officers dead.*

*And the asset?*

*At the safehouse.*

*OK,* the next message read. *Good job.*

They spent another two hours on the road. By which point the adrenaline rush of the job had faded. All the tension and stress Carter had felt before the mission ebbed away. Now he was just exhausted. The other guys looked equally knackered. No one had slept in more than twenty-four hours.

Shortly before five o'clock in the morning they reached Lask Air Force Base. The duty officer at the guardhouse had been notified in advance of their arrival; he directed them past the hangars, towards the apron. Whereupon they ditched the Highlander and climbed aboard a military jet waiting for them on the tarmac.

Ten minutes later they were on their way back to Germany.

\* \* \*

They landed at six thirty in the morning. Sergeant Major Mike Beattie was there to greet them on arrival. They deposited their luggage at the rear of the hangar and mainlined coffee while they waited to be called in for the debrief. After a while Smallwood emerged from the unit housing the 18 Signals team. Three suits followed the Reg ops man out of the room. The Six officers. Vallance, Heald and Kendall. They crossed the floor before disappearing inside one of the secure briefing rooms. Carter watched them, unease bayoneting his guts.

'That doesn't look right to me,' he muttered.

Beach blinked and said, 'Something wrong, Geordie?'

'Aye. *That*.' He pointed with his head at the Vauxhall suits. 'The job's done.'

'So what?'

'So why are the Six bods still here? They should be back in London right now, breaking open the bubbly. No reason for them to be hanging around this dump.'

'Maybe they're tying up loose ends.'

Carter thought back to his conversation with Volkova at the safehouse and shook his head. 'I don't think that's it, mate,' he said quietly.

Half an hour later, Beattie strolled over to the breakout area and announced that Smallwood and the others were ready to begin the debrief. Carter led the others towards the same secure room they had gathered in three days ago. They found Smallwood seated on one side of the conference table with Kendall, Vallance and Heald occupying the chairs next to him. The latter still wrapped in his quilted Barbour jacket. Maybe the guy had a collection of them, Carter mused. One for every day of the week.

Carter took another step in the room – and stopped dead.

Sitting next to Heald was a fifth guy. A pale-skinned man with a mottled beard and unkempt hair, dressed in a crumpled suit. As if he'd spent the night sleeping rough on a bench.

Eduard Ruznak greeted the soldiers with a tight smile.

Carter stared dumbfounded at the Ukrainian.

'What the fuck are you doing here?' he demanded.

Ruznak smiled but said nothing.

Vallance said, haughtily, 'Take a seat, gentlemen. We shall explain everything in due course. There's plenty of ground to cover before your next operation.'

'Next op?' Lazarides screwed up his face. He looked round at Carter. 'What's this cunt talking about, Pom?'

'You have questions, no doubt,' Vallance cut in smoothly before Carter could reply. 'By the end of this meeting everything will be perfectly clear, I assure you. Now, for God's sake, sit down. We're wasting valuable time.'

The soldiers looked at one another. Carter reluctantly dropped into one of the chairs facing the suits. So did the others.

Vallance said, 'First of all, allow me to congratulate you on the Ternovsky hit. Excellent handiwork. Shame about the police officers, and we'd have preferred it if there hadn't been any civilian casualties, but those are minor quibbles. Well done.'

Carter snorted. 'Just tell us what the fuck is going on.'

Vallance smiled diplomatically. He said, 'You're angry. That's perfectly understandable. But you must see that we had to keep certain things from you. For your own good.'

'Keep what?'

Vallance dipped his head at Smallwood. The latter said, 'You're being re-tasked, guys. Immediate turnaround.'

'You mean—'

Smallwood nodded gravely. 'There's a second target. You're going to take out another one of Putin's confidants.'

# Seventeen

The words punched Carter in the face. For a long beat he simply stared at the ops officer, too stunned to reply. Then the shock hardened into cold anger. Invisible fingers clamped around his throat. His hands balled into tight fists.

'Why didn't you tell us about this before?' he demanded.

'Opsec, Geordie.'

Vallance spread his hands and said, 'If you were captured in Belarus, the KGB would have tortured you. Doubtless you would have resisted for a while, but eventually you would have spilled your guts. The Belarussians are very good at that sort of thing. Of course, that would have compromised the mission. The second target would have gone underground before we had a chance to nail him.'

'You fucking lied to us.'

'"Lied" is a rather strong word,' Heald said. 'We merely withheld certain key details of the mission from you, in order to protect our wider strategic interests.'

'I don't give a shit what you call it.'

Heald shot him a withering look. 'We've already explained why we couldn't put you in the loop. Quite frankly I find your protests rather tiring. Get over it, man.'

Carter cocked his chin at Ruznak. The Ukrainian SBU man. 'Did you know about this?'

Vallance cleared his throat and said, 'Eduard has been helping us to coordinate the second operation. We've invited him here to assist with the planning.'

'So that's a yes.'

The Six director stared at Carter with his lips pressed into a hard line. Smallwood rubbed his hands together and said, 'Let's get down to it, shall we? This op is extremely time-sensitive.'

'Who's the target?' asked Dempsey.

Kendall said, 'Pavel Grabakin. First Deputy Director of the FSB. Previously he served as Director of the GRU. Russia's military intelligence agency. You've probably heard of them.'

'Rings a bell,' said Beach, rubbing his chin. 'They're the ones behind the Salisbury poisonings a few years back.'

'Among other operations, yes. They've got form for carrying out jobs on foreign soil. Assassinations, spying, bribery. Illegals networks. Grabakin is responsible for dozens of killings over the past twenty years. Now he's the second most important spook in Russia.'

Dempsey said, 'Never heard of the bloke.'

Vallance smiled. 'You wouldn't. Grabakin is a classic grey cardinal. He works in the shadows. Avoids the limelight at all costs. Never gives interviews. We don't even have an up-to-date photograph of him. There's a black-and-white profile from his days in the KGB with Putin, but that's almost forty years old.'

'They're old friends,' Heald chipped in. 'Grabakin and the President. Probably the only chum Putin has left from his St Petersburg days, after the latest cull. He's being lined up for Director of the FSB. Russia's spy chief.'

'They already have one of those, don't they?'

'For now. But the FSB are taking the rap for the intelligence failures in Ukraine. The current director is in a rather uncomfortable position. Word on the street in Moscow is that he'll be fortunate to last the winter. Grabakin is a man on the up.'

'And now,' Vallance smiled, 'you're going to kill him.'

He reclined in his chair, indicated Ruznak with a broad sweep of his arm.

'Eduard will run through the nitty-gritty.'

Ruznak leaned forward and said, 'Yulia has cultivated a source in Grabakin's household. One of the housemaids. She's got a son fighting in Ukraine and hates the fact that he has to risk his life every day while the rich kids stay at home. She's provided us – Yulia – with information on Grabakin's movements.'

190

'Where is he now?' asked Beach.

'Staying at his house on Lake Geneva. Big meeting with his money men, we understand. His wife and kids live there in exile too. We also know that he's planning to travel to Courchevel for a skiing holiday.'

Beach scrunched his face. 'How the fuck can he move around Europe that freely? He must be on a blacklist.'

Heald smiled faintly. 'Officially the Swiss support the EU-wide sanctions, of course. But there are loopholes for those willing to exploit them. Many Russians still live there.'

Vallance said, 'Money is a great facilitator. It's remarkably easy for someone as rich as Grabakin to take a private flight from Geneva to Courchevel, land on the altiport and hit the slopes. But that also works in our favour. Because it gives you an ideal opportunity to get at him.'

Heald said, 'Naturally, you're going to need someone who knows the lay of the land. Which is where Eduard comes in.'

All eyes in the room turned to the Ukrainian who said, 'Since the war began, the SBU has been running surveillance operations on suspected Russian war criminals. People responsible for the atrocities in Bucha and elsewhere. Many of those pieces of shit own properties in Geneva. Some live there. And some,' he added, 'spend their holidays in Courchevel.'

'Eduard has spent time on the ground, coordinating efforts with his colleagues,' Vallance said. 'So he knows the local area as well as anyone. He'll walk you through the place before you set off. How to get around, entry and exit points and so on.'

Carter said, 'Are we certain your man Grabakin is going to travel to Courchevel? What if Volkova's source is wrong? What if he decides to stay put in Geneva?'

'Then you'll have to plan accordingly. Stay fluid, and so forth. Isn't that what you gents are paid to do?'

Carter stared hard at the Six director. Visualised the impact of his fist colliding with Vallance's nose.

'When does the target get in to France?' asked Dempsey.

191

'Two days from now. He'll spend a week on the slopes with his family.'

'Could be disinformation,' Carter speculated.

Kendall said, 'We think that's unlikely. We've been able to break into the daughter's phone. Zarina Grabakina. Seventeen years old. Very much a daddy's girl. Yesterday afternoon she sent a message to her father. Told him she's had his skis waxed and serviced, and she's looking forward to burning him on the slopes.

'Zarina is into her winter sports. Just like her father. Her private social media profiles are full of pictures of the family on previous skiing trips. She's also posted a cryptic message about a special guest joining them in Courchevel in a couple of days. Trust us, Geordie. Grabakin is definitely going up there.'

'What about his family?' asked Carter.

Heald said, 'They arrived at Courchevel last night via private aircraft. Zarina, her younger brother Kirill and their mother, Irina. They dumped their bags at the chalet, had dinner in town. Accompanied by four of Grabakin's bodyguards. Rest of the BG party is currently with Grabakin, but we believe they'll travel with him to France.'

A look of irritation flickered across Vallance's face. 'I think the picture is perfectly clear, gentlemen. Grabakin is planning on spending some quality time with his family in Courchevel. And if fortune favours us, he'll be coming back in a casket.'

Dempsey said, 'Is anyone else accompanying the principal?'

Heald shook his head. 'Not as far as we know. This is a private family affair. For planning purposes, you should assume it'll be just the target, his wife and children and his bodyguards.'

'How long's the holiday?'

'They're staying in Courchevel for seven nights. Grabakin's private aircraft is scheduled to collect them from the altiport ten days from now. Should give you ample time to execute your mission.'

Carter said, 'Assuming the trip doesn't get called off.'

'Geordie's got a point,' Beach said. 'This bloke will have heard about the Defence Minister getting plugged in Minsk by now. What if that changes the picture?'

'We've not seen or heard anything to suggest that,' Vallance replied glibly. 'Kremlin cronies dying in suspicious circumstances is hardly big news. Men like Grabakin are supremely arrogant. Comes with the territory, when you're a high-level spook.'

'There's arrogant,' replied Carter, 'and then there's completely fucking reckless.'

'Naturally, Grabakin's BG team will be on high alert,' said Kendall. 'They'll be extra vigilant. They won't leave anything to chance. You'll have to factor that into your planning.'

Heald said, 'Our friends at Cheltenham will continue to monitor the daughter's phone. If the situation changes, we'll let you know. But for now, the mission is go.'

'Ruznak will assist you with the planning,' Vallance said. 'We'll leave the details to you; that's your area of expertise. But make sure you limit the collateral damage on this one. A few casualties in Minsk we can live with. Courchevel is much closer to home. This has to be a clean operation. No civilian casualties.'

'We'll try our best.'

'You'll do a damn sight better than that. A Russian crony getting killed won't cause much fuss in Whitehall, but I won't have innocent people getting caught up in the attack this time. Is that clear enough for you?'

He stared at Carter, a hard glint in his eyes.

Dempsey said, 'How are we getting in?'

Heald said, 'By car. You'll cross the border south of Saarbrücken. It's a straightforward trek down past Nancy and Lyon. Shouldn't take you more than about eight hours to reach your destination. Rather pleasant journey, actually. Done it myself once or twice. Spectacular scenery down there.

'Your cover story is that you're a group of tourists going on a skiing holiday. Hardly original, but it's the best we can come up with at short notice, and at this time of year you won't stand out.'

'Why don't we fly direct to the resort?'

'You can't. Only light aircraft and choppers are able to land at the altiport. It's used exclusively by high net-worth individuals. Everyone else drives in from Geneva or Chambéry, the nearest major town. A few coarse Englishmen and Australians landing at Courchevel would stand out like sore thumbs.'

Carter said, 'It'll be busy at the resort. Ski season started a couple of weeks ago. Kids are on their school holidays. Lots of families. Going to be tricky to isolate the target.'

'No doubt,' Heald responded coolly. His lips parted into a thin smile. 'But that's your problem, not ours.'

'Twat,' Beach muttered under his breath.

'We'll need hardware,' Lazarides said. 'Weapons. Skiing equipment to support our cover story. All of that.'

Smallwood said, 'Beattie will sort you out from the on-base supplies. That should cover the basics. Anything else, you'll have to buy in town or scrounge from the Americans prior to your departure. There's no time for any other arrangement.'

Carter said, 'How are we supposed to identify the target, if we don't know what the fucker looks like?'

Heald and Kendall looked at one another. As if deciding who should answer the question.

'Yulia will be joining you on the mission,' Heald said. 'She's met Grabakin a few times at official functions. She'll confirm the target prior to the execution of the job. She also speaks French, so that should come in handy in terms of finding your way around.'

'She knows about the plan to kill Grabakin. No details, obviously, just broad brushstrokes. We'll brief her fully after this meeting,' Kendall said. 'She'll be waiting for you at Grenoble airport. Her flight lands at two o'clock tomorrow afternoon. Collect her on your way to Courchevel.'

'Should help with your cover,' Heald said. 'Less suspicious than four burly blokes travelling by themselves.'

Carter nodded, half listening. He clenched his jaw tight with suppressed rage. Felt the blood pounding between his temples. He thought back to his chat with Volkova at the safehouse.

*So that's why she didn't return to Moscow after the Minsk job,* he realised. *Because she knew there was another job in the pipeline.*

*Volkova knew the truth all along.*

Another question scraped at the base of his skull.

*Is that all Six have held back from us?*

*What else aren't they telling us?*

'And Ruznak?' he asked, indicating the Ukrainian. 'Is he coming too?'

Vallance gave a brisk shake of his head.

'Eduard will stay behind here. Orders from Whitehall. They're worried about a known Ukrainian officer getting mixed up in an assassination on French – or possibly Swiss – soil. That would make life rather complicated for all concerned. Particularly at a time when Ukraine is in dire need of additional resources from her allies.'

'But you're prepared to let Volkova risk her neck?'

Vallance merely shrugged.

Smallwood made a big show of frowning at his watch. 'Right, guys. I think that just about covers the basics. Unless you've got any more questions?'

They ran through a few more points. Specifically, actions-on, emergency procedures, comms protocols. Each member of the team would be issued with a brand-new burner, plus a clean fake passport, bank card and matching driving licence for the mission, since the identities they had used for Minsk would be too hot to employ again.

There was a brief discussion about the risks of facial recognition. The assassination of Russia's Defence Minister had made global headlines. Putin had remained silent so far, but some media commentators were claiming that the strike was beyond the limited capabilities of Belarussian insurgents. There was speculation about possible involvement of Ukrainian intelligence. All agreed that the murder of Konstantin Ternovsky had shaken the Kremlin and left the President looking vulnerable.

No one suspected British involvement in the killing. The team was unlikely to run into trouble at the border. Checks at the crossing point at Saarbrücken were practically non-existent, Smallwood assured them. Frictionless travel. More chance of Karl Beach going on a hunger strike.

Vallance wrapped up the briefing. The suits checked out of the room. The team broke for scran. Their first hot meal in two days. Beach went back for seconds, then thirds. Going for some kind of personal calorie-consumption record. Half an hour later they reassembled in the briefing room and knuckled down to the business of planning how to kill a top-level spook at a French ski resort, at the height of the Christmas holidays.

'What d'you reckon, Geordie?' Beach asked as he ran his eyes over a satellite map of Courchevel. 'Can we do it?'

Carter rubbed his jaw and said, 'It's a tough gig. Place will be rammed with tourists. Party-goers and families. There's a lot of potential for things to go sideways.'

He visualised packed slopes. Restaurants heaving with holidaymakers. Long queues at the gondola lifts. The logistics would be a nightmare.

'We could hit him at the chalet,' Dempsey suggested.

Ruznak shook his head vigorously. 'Sorry, but that won't work. Yulia says Grabakin has twelve men on his BG team. Security is very tight. Even the famous SAS won't be able to get him there.'

Beach clicked his tongue. 'Drones are out, too. Can't use 'em in Courchevel, lads. Not with the head shed insisting on a clean kill.'

'Then we'll have to find another way,' Carter said.

Ruznak slipped outside the room for a smoke. Lazarides watched the door slam shut behind the Ukrainian. He said, quietly, 'Maybe we shouldn't be doing this one.'

'What are you talking about?' Beach growled.

'We pushed our luck in Minsk. We were a cunt hair away from getting nabbed. This could go very wrong.'

Carter looked evenly at the Australian. 'Is it the job that worries you? Or is something else on your mind?'

Lazarides shrugged and said, 'Fine. Cards on the table. I don't like the Russian spook. Not one fucking bit. I've got a bad feeling about her, Pom.'

'You think she's dodgy?'

'She bullshitted us in Minsk. She knew about this other hit but kept it to herself.'

'So did the Vauxhall bods.'

'There's more. She didn't want to come back here. Why?'

'Maybe she's worried about blowing her cover. The Russians know about this place. They'll know Ramstein is the hub of SF ops in Ukraine. They've probably got eyes on it, making a note of who's coming and going.'

'That's one explanation.'

'What's the other?'

'Maybe she wants us to think that. Maybe she's meeting with her Russian bosses right now, working out how to knock us on the head.'

Carter considered briefly. He said, 'I don't think that's it. Yulia had the chance to leave us in the shit on the last job. But she didn't. She saved our arses. If it wasn't for her, we'd be in a police station in Minsk right now, getting the crocodile clips treatment from the local branch of the KGB.'

'She might have done that to earn our trust.'

Carter shook his head. 'No. She helped us nail the Defence Minister. Putin's anointed successor, remember? If she was really working for the other side, why would they let us get away with killing him?'

'Maybe that wasn't the plan. Maybe they tried to get a message to the principal to warn him off, but it didn't get through. Could be any number of reasons.'

'You're reaching, mate. Clutching at straws. Look at the evidence.'

'You're saying you trust her?'

'I'm saying,' Carter said, 'she's not done anything to suggest she's working against us.'

Lazarides folded his arms, curled his lips in contempt. 'You're starting to sound like that fanny-struck wanker Heald.'

Beach grunted and said, 'Yeah, well. Maybe Volkova's not the one we should be worried about.'

Lazarides rounded on him, face twitching with rage. 'What'd you mean by that?'

'From what I heard you betrayed your mates in the SASR. Maybe you're thinking of snitching on us, too. Blow the whistle on us because you've had a sudden crisis of conscience.'

Lazarides exploded. 'Go fuck yourself, Pom. I've got no problem icing a few Russian scumbags. I just want to be sure no one's going to stick a knife in my back while I'm doing it.'

Carter could sense the atmosphere turning frosty. He held up his hands and said, 'We're wasting our time. There's fuck all we can do about Volkova. She's on the op with us, whether we like it or not. Nothing we can do to change that. Let's focus on what we can control. Besides,' he added, 'we may not be the only ones who are having doubts about Volkova.'

Dempsey looked at him. 'You think the suits are suspicious?'

'Not them. The Ukrainians.'

'What makes you think that?'

'Simple logic. Why is Ruznak on the team? He doesn't need to be involved in the planning stages. He could just as easily have taken a back seat after introducing Six to Volkova. Instead, he's out here, rolling up his sleeves and getting stuck in. There's only one reason for that.'

'Go on.'

'His bosses in Kyiv don't trust Volkova. They want someone on the mission, keeping eyes on her. Someone who can report back to the SBU.'

Beach let out a heavy sigh. 'Christ. This thing is getting dark. Too many moving pieces. I'll be glad when the job's done.'

'Assuming it's just two hits,' Dempsey said quietly, running a hand through his ginger beard.

Beach shot him a screw-face. 'You think there might be more?'

'They kept this op from us, didn't they? They were happy to keep us in the dark until the last bloody minute. Why would they 'fess up to future targets?'

'Ned's right,' Lazarides said. 'Your bosses are a pack of liars. Clear as fucking day, that. For all we know, there might be another target lined up after this one.'

Carter said, 'That doesn't change anything for us. We've still got a job to do. So let's find a way to get it done. Because if this goes wrong, it's gonna be almost impossible to bug out. We'll be in a world of shit.'

*And if that happens*, thought Carter, *Volkova's loyalties will be the least of our problems.*

# Eighteen

The next morning, as the sun burned up the last scraps of dawn mist, two Land Rover Defender 110s quietly slipped out of Ramstein Air Base and took the westbound autobahn towards Saarbrücken.

Carter and Lazarides rode in the front wagon; Beach and Dempsey had the second Defender. All four team members wore Gore-Tex trousers and North Face jackets over jumpers and thermal base layers. The roof boxes mounted on top of the Defenders were crammed full of equipment: Blackcrows skis and Fischer boots, artificial ski skins, mountaineering boots, ski poles, daysacks, ski socks and helmets. Their rucksacks were crammed full of high-protein snacks, carb gel packs, ski jackets and trousers, spare clothing, camping gear, gloves, hats and goggles.

Both Defenders had been fitted out with winter tyres; in the boots they carried snow chains and essential recovery gear. French officials were notoriously fussy about vehicles getting stuck on the Alpine roads. Snow-trapped cars meant blocked roads, which meant delays keeping the resorts well-stocked with caviar and Dom Perignon.

Also stashed in the front Defender: a Sig Sauer Cross bolt-action hunting rifle, sealed in plastic, with the stock folded down, hidden under the passenger seat. A fine piece of weaponry, in Carter's opinion. Sixteen-inch barrel, with a fitted suppressor and bipod, and a Vortex Razor LHT 4.5-22 x 50 scope attached to the rail. Chambered for the .308 Winchester. Built in the Granite State. Rural New Hampshire. Hunting country. A place where even the governor went out to hunt turkey. What they didn't know about rifles probably wasn't worth knowing.

Prior to leaving Ramstein the team had also stripped down four Glock pistols, wrapped the individual components in plastic and shoved them into their ski boots, concealing them beneath pairs of woollen ski socks stuffed down the ankles. Boxes of nine-milli Parabellum and a Glock suppressor had been distributed among their camping equipment. A lump of C4 explosive with a remote-activated electric detonator had been secreted in a box of hexi stove tablets.

Lazarides had also brought along an Osprey trekking backpack filled with extra kit. Inside he'd packed a white snow-camouflage net, the kind of thing you could buy from army surplus stores or prepper websites; a handheld Magnum 1200 laser rangefinder; a Gerber folding shovel; a foam roll-up camping mat; a Kestrel anemometer to gauge wind speed and direction; two pairs of binoculars; shooting gloves, and a snow-cam pattern ski jacket and matching trousers. Which might have looked suspicious twenty years ago. But Carter had been surprised to learn that all the cool kids wore snow-cam gear on the slopes these days.

A huge amount of kit. Everything the team might theoretically need. But necessary. Killing a high-level spook wasn't going to be easy. They had to keep their options open. Stay flexible. They would be operating in a busy environment crawling with civilians.

But that also worked in their favour. Because Carter strongly felt that Grabakin wouldn't be expecting an attack. In Belarus they had been operating in Putin's backyard. The Near Abroad. France was different. Grabakin wouldn't act recklessly; no professional BG team would allow that. But the guy might unconsciously relax a little once he touched down on French soil. Not by much. One or two per cent, perhaps.

*But that's all we need. He just has to drop his guard once.*

*And that's when we'll strike.*

They crossed the border west of Saarbrücken at nine o'clock. A stony-faced border guard glanced briefly at the soldiers' passports, while a dog handler walked a Belgian Malinois round both vehicles. Which didn't surprise Carter. In this area drug smuggling was the main threat. Most likely the Malinois would have been trained to detect coke and heroin. It wouldn't recognise the smell of ammunition or high explosive.

He assumed.

The dog sniffed disinterestedly at the air. Looked away in boredom. The owner said something to him in French and stroked his head. He moved on to the next vehicle in the line.

Another guard ordered Beach out of the second Defender in broken English. Beach swung up onto the sidestep, reached up to the roof box. Unlocked it. The black shell yawned open. The guard glanced briefly at the mound of junk threatening to spill out of the storage box and stepped back down. Evidently deciding it was too much hassle to search through it all. The famous French work ethic in action. The guard said something else to Beach. The latter forced the box shut with some effort, hopped back behind the wheel.

They drove on.

*First hurdle cleared.*

Carter had long ago learned to break missions down into smaller parts. Like deconstructing a weapon. A lesson he'd been taught by his older brother, back when Jamie had helped him to prepare for the ordeal of SAS Selection. Jamie had shared the same advice he'd been given by a Reg veteran before he tackled the Hills phase.

*Don't think about the total distance.*

*Shut down that part of your mind.*

*Look no further ahead than the next step.*

Luke had taken that lesson to heart. He'd worked on training his brain as much as his body. He possessed a superhuman ability to focus on the immediate task. Reduce everything else to mere background noise. So he wasn't thinking ahead to slotting Grabakin, or exfiltrating from the Alps. He thought only about crossing the border.

Then get to Grenoble. RV with Volkova. Get to the chalet.

*Step by step.*

*Absolute focus.*

The journey to Grenoble airport took six hours. Carter drove for the first two hundred miles. They paid in cash at the automated toll points, took a piss break at a rest stop outside Dijon and topped up the fuel tanks. Lazarides regularly checked his burner for updates from Six. If Grabakin called off his skiing trip at the last minute, the team would change direction, head over to Geneva, locate the target's vehicle and stick the block of C4 under it. The nuclear option. Nobody wanted to set off a bomb in the middle of a city. But the powers-that-be didn't think it would come to that. They were confident that Grabakin would stick to his original plan.

Carter hoped to fuck they were right.

Lazarides took the wheel for the second leg of the journey. At two thirty Carter dug out his Samsung and fired off a message to Volkova's SBU-issued burner.

*Five minutes out. We'll be in the short-stay parking zone. Look for two Land Rover Defenders. German plates. Head for the metallic grey one.*

They reached the airport four minutes later. The wagons manoeuvred round to the drop-off zone and parked side by side, front passenger windows facing the arrivals hall. Thirty seconds later Volkova walked out of the building, dressed in a Patagonia down jacket, softshell trousers and Ugg boots, wheeling along a small black suitcase. She crossed the road, stopped briefly, scanned the rows of parked motors. Spotted Carter and Lazarides in the grey Defender and hustled over.

Volkova shoehorned her luggage into the boot. She climbed into the back seat, nodded at the two soldiers sitting up front. 'OK,' she said. 'I'm ready. Get moving.'

Lazarides kept the wagon in Park. He shot a glance at her in the rear-view, eyes as thin as lines of coke. A mixture of suspicion, and hate, clouded his expression. Volkova tilted her head to one side and stared a challenge at him.

'Yes? You have a problem?'

'No problem,' Lazarides replied tetchily.

Volkova jerked her chin at the exit. 'Then what are you waiting for? Let's go, please.'

Lazarides navigated out of the drop-off zone. Ninety seconds later they were back on the main road and heading east.

* * *

They passed through Chambéry and began the long climb to Courchevel. The last leg of their journey. The Defenders skated around the southern fringes of the Bauges Massif and followed the A-road running parallel with the course of the Isère river, up through Albertville and then south towards Moûtiers.

The route quickly steepened; the snow-cleared road corkscrewed sharply up the slopes, a tarmac snake twisting this way and that through a snow-blanketed landscape picketed with pine trees. At five o'clock the team finally reached their destination. Dusk was already creeping across the Three Valleys as they steered round to Rue des Chenus in Le Plantrey. A five-minute drive north of the Michelin-starred restaurants, luxury spas and designer shops in the centre of Courchevel 1850.

They parked on a patch of loose gravel in front of a small stone-and-timber chalet, booked in advance by Six via the business account of a shell company registered in Delaware. A last-minute cancellation, Smallwood had claimed. Hence why they had been able to land a luxury chalet in the heart of Courchevel with two days' notice. Carter wasn't so sure.

*If they knew about the op all along, maybe they had this place booked out weeks ago. Maybe longer.*

*Maybe this is another of Vauxhall's lies.*

Volkova unlocked the electronic key safe box using an app on her phone. She kept one set of keys, handed the other set to Carter.

They unpacked the two Defenders and the roof boxes, dumped everything in the front living room. Carter checked out the upper floors. The first-floor balcony faced out towards the peak of Sommet de la Saulire. There was a separate ski room, a sauna, a kitchen with a Smeg fridge and a Gaggia bean-to-cup coffee machine, an expensive-looking bottle of complimentary champagne. Six small bedrooms, three bathrooms. The place was modest by Courchevel standards. Self-catering. No indoor pool or gym. No private driver or daily visit from the cleaners. That was good. Nobody else would enter the property while they were in town. They wouldn't have to worry about anyone rooting through their private possessions and accidentally stumbling upon their weaponry.

'How much was this place again?' Beach asked as he tramped round in amazement.

'Six didn't say,' Carter replied. 'But for half a dozen people for a week, I reckon they must have paid about ten or fifteen grand. Minimum.'

'Fucking hell.' Beach whistled.

Volkova said, 'This is nothing. You should see the chalets near the altiport. Some of them are as big as palaces. That's where the real money is in Courchevel.'

'Speaking of which,' Carter said. 'We'll have to take a run past the target's chalet before he's due to get in. Recce the area. See what the deal is with security around the town. Steve, you'll come with me. Quade, Karl, secure the gear.'

'What about me?' Volkova asked.

'Stay here. Check in with your contact. The housemaid in Geneva. See if she knows when the spook is due to land tomorrow. Once we've got a rough ETA, we'll set up an OP near the altiport. That's our best chance of getting eyes on the target.'

Dempsey said, 'Won't that look suspicious? Couple of people sitting on their arses eyeballing the runway? I know fuck all about this place, but I'm guessing you don't get many plane spotters up here.'

205

Volkova said, 'There's a restaurant opposite the runway. Le Pilatus. People often gather there to watch the planes coming in. We can park there and wait for Grabakin to arrive, and no one will give us a second look.'

Dempsey looked bemused. 'People spend their time watching fucking airport traffic?'

'Courchevel is the highest airport in Europe. Which makes it one of the most dangerous in the world. It's a big attraction.'

Dempsey shook his head. 'Europeans.'

In the fading light Carter and Lazarides cruised through the town centre in one of the Defenders. They took a winding route to the Grabakin family pad, via the five-star hotels and nightclubs and the shops selling luxury leather goods. Down Rue de Bellecôte, passing huge gingerbread-house chalets with snow-capped gabled roofs, until they reached a three-storeyed structure built on the side of the slope, a mile or so from the altiport.

A pair of G-Wagons were parked in the front of the property. Two guys sat in one of the vehicles; Carter caught a glimpse of them through the tinted window as they rolled past. Members of the principal's BG team. Sentry duty. Probably on eight-hour rotations. Boring as fuck. Carter had been there himself. Close protection work could be a pain in the arse. But they were doing their jobs. Reasonable to assume a certain level of proficiency.

*Going to be hard to isolate him.*

They tooled on. Swung round at the airport and cut back through the resort, mapping out the distances from Rue de Bellecôte to the nearest gondola and cable car lift stations. Quickest routes from Courchevel to the surrounding villages of Le Praz and Moriond. The police presence was discreet to the point of invisibility. Which made sense. The VIPs would have their own security details. They wouldn't rely on the local plod to come to their rescue.

At seven they returned to their lodgings in Le Plantrey. The rest of the team listened as they made their report. Then Volkova said she had heard from her source. The housemaid in Geneva.

'She says Grabakin has booked a taxi to take him to the airport tomorrow. One thirty. So he'll be in the air around two.'

'We've had an update from Six, as well,' Beach said. 'The daughter's posted again on social. Cryptic message. Says she's excited. Her hero is arriving tomorrow and she's going to crush him on the slopes.'

'Sounds like it's definitely on,' Dempsey said.

Carter nodded. 'We've done enough for today. Let's head out. Grab some food.'

'About fucking time,' said Beach. He inclined his head towards Dempsey. 'The one-man Ned Kelly fan club has been boring us senseless since you two left.'

'Pom prick.'

'Irish bastard.'

They both laughed heartily. Carter felt the tension in the room ease a little. Grim humour. The SF operator's way of coping with the stress of a high-risk job.

'Come on,' he said. 'Tonight, we're regular tourists. Tomorrow, we'll get eyes on the target.'

# Nineteen

They dined at an American-themed burger joint, had a drink at a bar on Rue de Tovets and stocked up on supplies at the local Carrefour. The town was packed. People everywhere. British and German families, Chinese tour parties, high-cheekboned women posing for selfies. Groups of rowdy young Arab guys knocking back thousand-pound bottles of champagne and leaving hundred-euro-note tips for the waitresses.

*If it's this busy on the slopes*, Carter told himself, *we'll have to tear up the plan. Back to the drawing board.*

The next morning he made the short drive into town and purchased a pair of ski passes from the ticket office at La Croisette, paid for in cash. Dempsey and Beach spent a few hours tracking Grabakin's family. The wife, the daughter and a fat kid in his early teens. They left the chalet mid-morning accompanied by two of the bodyguards and went shopping in town. The mum treated herself to some Fendi swag, then treated the kids to lunch at a high-end restaurant.

At 13.30 the soldiers returned to the chalet.

Fifteen minutes later, Carter left again with Volkova and made the short drive across town to the altiport, carrying a pair of binos in his jacket pocket. They tooled south in silence past Grabakin's huge chalet on Rue de Bellecôte. Down onto Rue de l'Altiport, then west past the approach road. Carter took the next turn off Rue de Col de la Loze, parked up in front of the Hotel Pilatus a few minutes before two o'clock.

They were facing the south-western end of a short runway that rose up steeply before sloping down again towards the far end, five hundred metres to the north-east. There was a hangar to one side of the runway with a Cessna 208 resting on the tarmac apron. Control tower, maintenance shacks and fuel dump to the north, next to a row of helipads. One of Grabakin's G-Wagons waited in the car park.

At that hour the restaurant was doing a brisk trade. People clad in ski wear and sunglasses sat around the tables. Others reclined on the deck loungers, sipping beers. Getting sloshed while they waited for the next jet to fly in. Euro dance music pumped out of a sound system. Kids messed about on their skis, chucked snowballs at grouchy parents. Afternoon sunshine blazed in the unhazed sky, reflected off the snow crust like a million scattered diamonds.

'How long until he lands?' Volkova asked.

'Flight time from Geneva is around eighteen minutes,' Carter said. 'He'll be here soon. Assuming he hasn't got cold feet.'

They lapsed into silence again. Carter dug out the binos, rested them on top of the dash. Glanced at the clock below: 1407.

'Your friend,' Volkova said. 'The Australian. The one with the bug eyes.'

'Lazarides?'

Volkova nodded. 'He doesn't trust me.'

'He's not the only one.'

Volkova glanced sharply at him but said nothing.

'Why didn't you tell us the truth?' Carter asked. 'In Minsk. You knew there was a second operation. Why didn't you say something?'

'I couldn't,' Volkova said. 'Your bosses have got me on a tight leash. They warned me not to discuss the plan with you under any circumstances. I didn't know how much you had been told. Or what was above your pay grade. When I saw your reaction, I realised they hadn't briefed you on the second job. So I panicked.'

Carter scanned the altiport. Mentally rehearsing the next few minutes. Grabakin's jet would make its approach from the north-east, touch down on the runway and park up in front of the maintenance hangar. Volkova would watch through the binos, waiting for the target to stick his head out of the aircraft. She would only have a few moments to ID him before he disappeared inside the G-Wagon and took off.

'You are angry with me?' Volkova asked.

Carter didn't reply.

'These are the rules of the game,' Volkova went on. 'In our world, everything is need-to-know. You can't blame me for not telling you everything.'

Carter grunted. 'This isn't about leaving out a few minor details. We're being kept in the fucking dark.'

'Vauxhall is worried about leaks. So am I. If it gets out that I'm helping the British, I'm dead, remember?'

Carter shook his head fiercely. 'I'm not an idiot. I've worked for them suits plenty of times in the past. I understand about need-to-know. But this is ripping the arse out of it.'

'Perhaps,' Volkova replied stiffly, 'you're worried about the wrong person.'

'How's that?'

'Those Australians. Can we trust them?'

'Totally. Them lads are solid. They've been vetted. We've got no worries on that front.'

'Are you sure? How well do you really know them? For all we know they might be phoning back to their handlers at this very moment, telling them what's happening.'

'No fucking chance. I'd bet my right bollock on it.'

'Then you're a fool, Luke. Either that, or you're not particularly attached to your manhood.'

Carter gritted his teeth. Anger pulsed in his veins, clawed at his scalp. He was tired of Volkova's mind games. 'What else are the suits keeping from us?'

Volkova sat rigid and stared dead ahead. Refused to meet his gaze.

'Tell me,' Carter insisted.

'I can't,' she replied feebly.

Something inside Carter snapped. He swung round in his seat, faced Volkova. Looked her hard in the eye.

'You've got to come clean,' he said. 'Tell us what's going on. We need to know what we're up against on this thing. Is Grabakin the only other target? Or is there another hit in the works?'

Volkova stayed quiet. She bit her lower lip, dropped her eyes to the footwell. Carter could see the struggle playing out on her face.

She looked up. Stared through the dirt-flecked windscreen at the runway.

'Yes,' she said finally.

'Yes, what?'

'There are more targets.'

Carter felt the vein on the side of his temple throbbing. 'How many?'

'Nine names in total. There's a list. Kremlin men. Spooks, mostly, but there are others on the list too. Generals, senior ministers. Key propagandists. People close to Putin. The few advisers he still trusts.'

'Jesus Christ.'

Outside the restaurant, someone popped the cork on a champagne bottle. A group of drinkers laughed. Parents shouted at their kids to behave.

*Nine names.*

*Nine kills.*

*It'll be a miracle if we make it that far without getting arrested. Or killed.*

He asked the obvious question.

'Is Six planning to kill the lot of them?'

'That would be my guess. But they haven't shared the operational details with me, you understand. I just gave them the list. That was the deal we made. The list, in exchange for a new identity in England. What they do with the names is their business.'

'Why wouldn't they tell you what they're planning?'

Steeliness crept into Volkova's voice as she replied. 'All I know is, there are a lot of factors to consider. Lots of moving parts. They're taking it one job at a time. Their words, not mine. So maybe they don't trust me either.'

Carter stared at the FSB officer. Two possibilities occurred to him. One, Volkova was telling the truth. That made a certain degree of sense. Six would want to keep their options open. See how things play out for the first hits. Some figures at Vauxhall would be wary of oversharing with a potential double agent. They were cautious by default.

The second possibility was more troubling. She might be deliberately playing Carter. Pretending to come clean with him in order to win his confidence. Gain herself a useful ally on the team. Maybe even get him to turn on the other lads.

*Right now, I don't know where I stand with her.*

'I fucking hate this spying game,' he growled. 'Nothing is ever up front. No one plays it straight. Everything has more layers than a bag of fucking onions.'

'Isn't this why you signed up for the SAS? For these jobs?'

He laughed wryly. 'I joined for straightforward soldiering, lass. Find a target, kick down a door, bang. Killing bad guys. That's my bag. Not this smoke-and-mirrors shite.'

Volkova pulled a cigarette from her packet. 'Then I have very bad news for you.'

'Aye? What's that?'

The Russian paused to light her tab. She sparked up her cheap plastic lighter, cupped a hand around the flame, took a deep hit of nicotine. Exhaled.

'You are in for a rude shock when you leave the army,' Volkova said, rolling down the window and flicking ash onto the snow. 'Life is not straightforward, Luke. It's messy, and complicated, and full of people who lie to your face. And so is my line of work.'

Carter wasn't in the mood for a lecture. He said, 'What's the end game? Why do Six want to wipe out Putin's cronies?'

'Decapitation,' Volkova said, bluntly. 'We have an opportunity to remove Putin's friends and leave him absolutely isolated. His enemies already smell blood. Once his allies are out of the way, they'll move in for the kill. Like wolves smelling blood. They'll overthrow his regime.'

'Your old man tried that already. Didn't turn out so well for him.'

'It will be different this time. You'll see. Without his friends, Putin won't have anyone to warn him. He won't see his enemies coming. They won't make the same mistake as my father.'

'And what happens if the plan works?'

'We will have a new president before the end of the year. They'll call off this senseless war.'

Carter laughed at the madness of it. 'Do you really believe that?'

'Why not?' Volkova replied earnestly. 'Not everyone in Russia is a warmonger. Many people have friends or family in Ukraine. Others are weary of the sanctions, the restrictions on our lives. We would be glad to see an end to the bloodshed.'

'But what if the new bloke is even worse than Putin? Have you considered that? What if you end up with someone who's willing to go nuclear in Ukraine? You could be paving the way for the guy who triggers World War Three, for fuck's sake.'

'That is a risk I'm prepared to take.'

'You're playing with fire,' Carter said. 'Once this shit kicks off, it'll be out of your control. Anything could happen.'

Volkova indicated the wooded slopes beyond the far side of the runway. A twin-engine turboprop aircraft broke through the cloud mist, beginning its final approach to Courchevel.

Nearby a group of drinkers peeled off from the crowd and migrated towards the snow bank overlooking the runway. Getting into position ahead of the big show. Best seats in the house.

'Get ready,' said Carter.

Volkova reached for the binos.

The engine hum grew louder.

The crowd of drinkers pointed at the aircraft, some chatting in excited voices while others held up smartphones to video its descent. The plane seemed to hang in the air for a moment before the pilot made a smooth landing on the tarmac. The aircraft swiftly dropped its speed as it glided down the runway, climbed the sharp incline and then veered off to the left before easing to a halt in front of the hangar, a hundred metres from Carter and Volkova outside the Pilatus. The propellers stopped turning; the engines were reduced to a faint mechanical thrum.

Right on cue the G-Wagon swung round from the car park and pulled up on the left side of the aircraft, following the directions from a high-vis-jacketed airport worker. The main cabin door on the aircraft sucked open. Two broad-shouldered guys shrinkwrapped in Gore-Tex jackets – Carter assumed they were bodyguards – deplaned on the left side of the aircraft. Another BG in identical clothing stepped out from the front passenger side of the G-Wagon and trotted round to the rear door before standing stiffly to attention. Ready to greet the chief.

'Eyes on,' Carter said.

Volkova focused the binos on the aircraft. As they looked on, a third figure stepped out of the cabin opening, clad in a bright-blue ski jacket, woollen hat and a pair of dark trousers. He marched towards the G-Wagon waiting a few paces away, arms swinging at his sides, his back erect. The walk of a man supremely confident of his place in the world.

The BG stationed beside the G-Wagon yanked the rear door open. The guy in the blue ski jacket dipped his head and climbed inside. The other two bodyguards joined their principal in the back of the vehicle. The wagon steered round to the access road due east of the hangar and scudded down Rue de l'Altiport.

Volkova set down the binos on the dashboard.

'Well?' asked Carter. 'Did you get a good look?'

She nodded. 'It's him.'

'Are you sure?'

'Definitely. I'd recognise that face anywhere. That's Pavel Grabakin. I'd stake my life on it.'

Carter watched the G-Wagon as it cantered past the helipad then disappeared from view past a sharp bend in the road. He cranked the engine, and felt a tingle of excitement creep down his spine.

*It's on.*

*We're in business.*

Back at the chalet they ran through the plan for the following day.

'We'll start following him,' Carter said. 'Set up an OP at the chalet and watch his routine. See what runs he likes to take, where he goes to eat. Look for weak points in his armour.'

'He'll be out early,' Volkova said. 'As soon as the lifts are open. Grabakin and his bodyguards.'

'What makes you think that?'

'Grabakin is a keen amateur skier. His father was a famous cross-country skiing champion back in Soviet days. Won gold at the Winter Olympics in St. Moritz in '48. Grabakin had ambitions to follow in his dad's footsteps before he went into the service. So he'll want to spend some time on the toughest runs before joining his family. Nice and early. Before the slopes get too crowded.'

The germ of an idea seeded in Carter's head.

He said, 'That could work in our favour. Assuming you're right.'

'I am,' Volkova insisted. 'Trust me. Skiing is Grabakin's great passion in life.'

Carter nodded. 'We'll run through the plan again tonight. Make sure everyone knows what they're doing.'

*Tomorrow, we'll begin the hunt.*

# Twenty

The next day, shortly after first light, the team left the rental property in the two Defenders. Carter and Volkova rode in the lead wagon; Beach and the Australians trailed them in the second Land Rover. They rattled through Courchevel, taking the same route to the principal's luxury pad on Rue de Bellecôte. At seven o'clock Carter pulled up outside a timber-built hair salon, two hundred metres downwind of Grabakin's chalet. He killed the motor, while the team in the second Defender carried on down Rue de Bellecôte until they disappeared from view round a sharp bend in the road. They would stop roughly the same distance beyond the chalet and pretend to fix a pair of snow chains to the wheels. Between them, they would have eyes on the chalet from both directions.

At seven thirty in the morning the area was bustling with activity. A steady flow of traffic trundled along the road: ski school minibuses bound for the slopes to begin teaching the next intake, snowploughs, laundry vans, maintenance trucks. Road clearance guys spread salt on the driveways in front of the big chalets, de-iced the front steps. Butlers oversaw deliveries of wine and food; pickups unloaded their cargoes of chopped wood for the log burners.

They waited.

Volkova left the OP to order coffees from a nearby café. She returned to the Defender with a couple of scalding hot Americanos in takeaway cups. A quarter of an hour later one of the bodyguards emerged from the front door. He descended the salt-strewn steps, started up the nearest G-Wagon, left the engine running and hurried back inside. Carter sat up.

'Target's getting ready to leave, lads,' he said into his collar mic.

'We see him, mate,' Beach replied over the line.

The soldiers were communicating over their burner devices. All five team members wore water-resistant earbuds and lapel mics clipped to their ski jackets. Carter had worried about getting a signal high up the mountains, but the reception was surprisingly clear. Better than some British towns. The local authorities had invested heavily in rebroadcasting stations, Smallwood had explained. People needed to be able to contact the emergency services from anywhere on the slopes. A matter of life and death.

Carter had changed into his skiing gear before leaving the chalet and fastened his skis to the rear-mounted rack. The team had agreed that he should shadow Grabakin down the slopes. Carter had served as Alpine Guide in Mountain Troop in 22 SAS. He'd scored top in the winter training packages. Therefore he would have the best chance of keeping up with Grabakin on the ultra-tough black runs.

Several minutes later the bodyguard stepped outside again, cradling three pairs of skis. He carried them awkwardly over to the warmed-up Defender, secured the blades vertically to the ski rack fixed to the rear bumper. Then he trudged back into the chalet again. Returned to the Defender a second time carrying a small rucksack in each hand. He stowed them in the boot and stood waiting beside the G-Wagon with his back to the road, rubbing his hands and stamping his feet in a futile effort to stay warm.

Sixty seconds later Grabakin emerged in a pair of unfastened ski boots. Three more bodyguards fell into step behind him. At which point Carter realised they had a serious problem. Because all five figures were dressed identically in dark-blue jackets, grey trousers, black boots and matching gloves. The BGs even shared similar builds to their principal and sported the same short dark haircut.

*Shit*, thought Carter.

*Once they've got their helmets and snow goggles on, we won't have any way of telling them apart.*

The bodyguards were taking their job seriously. That much was clear. They were planning to disguise the principal's identity while they were out and about in Courchevel. Deception tactics. No other reason for them to dress up in matching ski gear. He thought back to what Kendall had said to them at the briefing.

*Grabakin's bodyguards will be on high alert.*

*They'll be extra vigilant.*

The figures bundled into the G-Wagon. Two up front, two more in the back.

'Looks like you were right,' he said to Volkova. 'It's just him this morning.'

'Of course. When you're as rich and powerful as Grabakin, you don't come to Courchevel to mess around on the gentle runs. You come here to *ski*.'

The G-Wagon angled onto the road, bombed past Carter and Volkova in the Defender, then swerved round the next bend.

Carter disengaged the handbrake and said into his mic, 'They're heading north on Rue de Bellecôte. We'll take it from here, lads. Keep eyes on the family. RV back at the chalet once you're done.'

'Roger that, Geordie,' Beach's reply crackled in his ear.

Carter stalked the G-Wagon north, taking care to stay at least eight metres behind the target at all times. They got snarled in early morning traffic on Rue des Clarines, rolled past the closed shopfronts in the centre of Courchevel and steered onto Rue de la Croisette. After a few hundred metres Carter stopped outside the gondola station. Further along, Grabakin and three of his BGs jumped out of the G-Wagon. They fastened their swept-back helmets, their snow goggles pulled over the shells, collected their skis and poles. One of the Russians gave a thumbs-up to the driver. He took off again and drove round to the covered car park.

Carter said, 'Take the wheel. I'll follow them up in the gondola. Park the car and wait for me.'

A blast of cold air hit Carter as he hopped down from the Defender, stabbing at his exposed skin. He slapped on his Oakley helmet and goggles, grabbed his skis in one hand and sticks in the other and cut through the loose throng of tourists mooching about at the gondola station, maintaining a clear line of sight to the Russians up ahead.

The terminal was busy. But nowhere near as crowded as it would be later on. At eight in the morning, most people were probably still in bed, sleeping off their hangovers. This early, the slopes belonged to the enthusiasts. The hardcore skiers and snowboarders looking to beast themselves on the toughest trails.

'I've got them,' Carter said in an undertone as he stayed close to the black-helmeted Russians. 'They're taking the Verdons line. Where does that come out?'

There was a brief pause on the line while Volkova consulted the piste map.

She said, 'There's another gondola line leading up to Saulire. The Vizelle. He's either going to take that or the Saulire cable car. Or he might get off at Verdons and ski. But I doubt it. The harder runs are further up.'

Carter thought, *If it's the cable car, I'll be in that fucker with him. If he's riding the Vizelle line, I'll have to jump in the cabin immediately behind his one and catch up with him at the summit.*

*Whatever happens, I've got to stay on them.*

The Russians had already piled into the next cabin as Carter walked through the hands-free turnstile. Grabakin and two of his BGs seated themselves; the fourth guy remained standing, positioned himself to block the opening, thereby preventing anyone else from getting in. Such as a potential assassin. Carter was impressed.

*These BGs are good. They know what they're doing.*

The next gondola slowly approached the terminal. Carter hustled forward, elbowing aside a group of boorish Brits waiting to

219

board. They shouted a torrent of abuse at him as he stepped into the packed cabin a moment before the door hissed shut.

The gondola began its journey up the mountains. A German couple chatted away at Carter's side, pointing out various sights. Carter kept his eyes pinned to the Russians in the gondola ahead. A distance of perhaps twenty metres. Close enough to distinguish Grabakin's features. Through the cabin window he could see the guy staring down at his phone. The view held no interest for him. He'd probably done this route a hundred times.

The bodyguards visibly relaxed as the lift climbed towards the next station. A natural reaction. Before leaving the chalet, they would have been worried about escorting the principal through La Croisette. A crowded public space. The point of greatest exposure. Now they were in a lift by themselves, heading up to the piste. They felt safe.

At the end of the Verdons line the Russians disembarked and transferred to the Vizelle. Carter took the next available lift and sat down beside the Germans, facing the cabin several metres in front. One of the Germans, a brunette woman in her twenties, tapped Carter on the shoulder.

'Excuse me?' the woman asked him in thickly accented English. 'Is this the right line for the La Creux run, do you know?'

Carter ignored her. The woman repeated the question before she gave up and pestered someone else. Carter kept his gaze locked firmly on the Russians. He had to stay focused on the target. Couldn't afford to take his eyes off him for a moment.

*As soon as he lowers those goggles over his face, it's going to be impossible to identify him.*

They neared the holding station at La Saulire a few minutes later. The gondola ahead of Carter slowed to a crawl as it drew level with the deboarding area; the Russians stepped off, two of the BGs leading the way, Grabakin third in line, the third BG guarding the rear as they marched towards the terminal exit. Carter rushed out of the cabin as soon as the doors sucked open. He barged aside a French guy at the turnstile and emerged a dozen paces behind the Russians.

The target and his three BGs lowered their goggles against the sunlight streaming over the mountain. Carter stayed as close as possible to the Russians as they crossed a relatively flat area towards a point delineating the start of the Suisse run. One of the black routes. The highest grade of difficulty. Just as Volkova had predicted.

*When you're as rich and powerful as Grabakin, you don't come to Courchevel to mess around on the gentle runs.*

*You come here to ski.*

Carter stopped right behind the Russians, his reflective goggles concealing everything apart from his nose and mouth. He clicked his boots into his bindings and looked round while the Russians fastened their skis.

The piste was relatively quiet. Dedicated groups of skiers milled about, checking their planks or waiting for their mates to arrive. Three ruddy-faced Brits with the fattened looks of City stockbrokers passed round a hip flask and boasted about how they were going to smash their personal bests on the morning run. Giving it the usual macho bullshit. Further away, a couple of snowboarders were fre-eriding off-piste. In the distance palls of dawn mist rolled up from the distant peaks. Patches of forest clung to the lower slopes like lichen. In the valley below Carter could see the altiport two kilometres to the north-east, with Courchevel and the less glitzy resorts at Moriond and Courchevel Village further away.

The Russians went about their business in silence as they prepared to set off. Two of them carried small rucksacks. Filled, Carter supposed, with emergency medical packs, blankets, food and flasks in case they ran into trouble on the descent. He noticed something else, too. A bulge in one of the Russians' jacket pockets. The guy was packing some sort of heavy object.

Walkie-talkie, perhaps.

Or a pistol.

Impossible to tell from a distance. But a realistic possibility. The BGs could have easily smuggled a gun on their flight from Geneva. No one would have checked them for heat at the altiport.

The Russians set off.

It quickly became apparent that Grabakin and his heavies were accomplished skiers. Carter had to work hard to keep pace with them as they shredded themselves on the trail. They hit the end of the run, caught the chairlift back up to La Saulire and took another run down the same piste, pushing themselves harder this time. Massacring their legs. Whereupon they crossed over to another black trail on Mur, not far from the altiport.

At the end of the run the Russians stopped briefly at a picnic spot. Carter sat at one of the other benches, swigged black coffee from his flask while he listened to the int updates from the rest of the team. A short time later the Russians headed back up the slopes on the Aiguille de Fruit line and ripped up the Rama trail. By the time they hit the finish point at Les Creux, Carter was beginning to feel the ache in his legs. From Les Creux he followed the Russians on the chairlifts back up to La Saulire.

Then Beach came on the conference call, reporting that the second G-Wagon had slipped out of the chalet. Carrying the wife and kids, plus two bodyguards. Carter followed the Russians as they crossed back over to the Vizelle line and rode the gondola down to Verdons, before Grabakin joined his family for a bite to eat.

Carter linked up with the other team members outside an Italian restaurant. They bagged a table with a clear view towards the Grabakin clan and ordered lunch. The son stuffed his face with cream cake and apple strudel. The daughter alternated between taking selfies and picking at her salad.

In the late morning Carter tailed the family as they hit the gentle runs lower down the mountain. The blue and green trails. By eleven o'clock the pistes were jam-packed. People everywhere. Like a Tube platform at rush-hour. The starting point for the

Bellecôte route was heaving with ski instructors and students. Parents dressed unruly kids. Teenagers kicked off because they'd forgotten gloves or ski glasses. Hundreds of tiny figures bombed down the slopes. Beginners snowploughed awkwardly down on their skis; first-timers wiped out in the powder to the amusement of their fellow students.

*A lot of witnesses*, Carter thought.

*A lot of eyes on us.*

Grabakin's daughter evidently enjoyed racing against her old man. She looked reasonably confident. Whereas the son spent most of his time either fumbling with his poles or stacking it in the powder. Eventually Grabakin lost his patience and snapped at the boy for his piss poor efforts. Carter suddenly understood why the guy was so keen to get a few early morning runs in by himself.

*It's the only time the fucker can get away from his family. Get some peace and quiet.*

*If that was me, I'd be doing the same thing.*

An hour before last light the Grabakins completed their final run on the Tovets trail and caught the Grangettes line back to Verdons for hot mugs of *vin chaud* in the centre of town. After which the wife left with the daughter to hit the designer shops on Rue de l'Église while Grabakin and his son rode in one of the G-Wagons back to their chalet.

Later that evening, Carter and his team shadowed the family as they left the chalet and dined at Le Palais Alpin. Carter's mouth dropped when he flipped open the menu and laid eyes on the prices. Two thousand euros for a steak. Which was practically a steal compared to the lobster. Across the restaurant scantily clad dancers floated between the tables, carrying thousand-euro bottles of champagne with sparklers sticking out of the corks.

'Grabakin must be bloody minted to eat here every night,' Carter remarked.

'Minted?' Volkova frowned at him uncomprehendingly.

'Aye. Loaded. Rich.'

Volkova smiled, but her voice was dripping with contempt as she spoke. 'Pavel Grabakin is not rich. He is not even super-rich. He is beyond that. He has more money than you could possibly imagine. Here, I will give you an example. Do you know how many people work at their chalet?'

Carter shrugged. 'No clue.'

'Eight. Grabakin has two personal chefs, one of whom used to run the kitchen at The Savoy. He also has a butler, four housekeeping staff and an on-call masseuse. Here is something else, too.' Volkova inclined her delicate chin at Grabakin's son. 'See that watch the boy is wearing? The rose gold one with the skull on the face?'

'What about it?'

'That is a Richard Mille. Can you guess how much that watch cost?'

Carter took a wild guess. 'Twenty grand?'

Volkova chuckled and said, 'Think higher, Luke. Much higher.'

'A hundred?'

'Still higher.'

'Five hundred k?'

'Three *million*.'

'For a watch?' Carter almost spat out his beer. 'Fucking hell.'

'That is not all. Grabakin himself has a collection of many such watches. Some are worth a million dollars. Some are actually priceless.'

'How did he get that kind of wedge?'

'Sochi. The Winter Olympics. Grabakin played a key role in overseeing the various construction projects. Backhanders and sweeteners,' Volkova added, bitterly. 'All Putin's cronies had their noses in the trough. These people are destroying my country. They are the real terrorists. And the worst thing of all is, no one believes they can be stopped. Everyone who has crossed them has ended up dead. Fear is infectious. So these men feel invincible.

'You know, there was a journalist who tried to investigate the Sochi corruption,' she went on, warming to her theme. 'He did a lot of digging, at great risk to himself and his family. I know people inside the service who tried to warn him off. Don't touch it, they told him. Bad things will happen. He ignored them. Eventually he exposed the amount of money Grabakin had filched from the system.'

Volkova stared silently at her food.

'What happened?'

'He went missing.' She picked at her grilled fish. 'Of course, it does not take a genius to guess the truth. Grabakin has many people who keep their ears to the ground. They heard about the journalist, the evidence he had gathered. His plans to publish. So they got rid of him. This sort of thing happens all the time in Russia.'

She set down her knife and fork and looked at Carter.

'My father was not perfect. He had his faults. But he always put Russia first. Putin and his men, they pretend to be patriots, but they don't give a shit about Russia. They only care about taking as much from our country as possible, and screw everybody else.'

Carter tucked into his lamb chops. Beach gobbled down his food and complained about the miserable portion size. Volkova barely touched her plate. She just sat there, staring hard at the Grabakins, her jaw clenched tight with hatred.

*Is this all part of an act?* Carter wondered. *Maybe she wants us to think she loathes her own people, so we won't suspect her of working for the other side.*

Which raised another question in his mind. If Volkova *was* working for the Russians, what was her plan? Why would she be helping them to take out Putin's confidants? To lure them into a trap?

No. That didn't make sense.

Carter hadn't told the rest of the team about his earlier conversation with Volkova. The revelation about the other hits Six had planned. Partly because Carter didn't want to disrupt their focus. If the lads were distracted, there was every chance the current job might turn into a clusterfuck. But mostly because he wasn't entirely sure he could trust them.

He thought about Lazarides. The rumours about the guy blowing the whistle on his muckers. The inquiry that had resulted in the disbandment of 2 Squadron. And yet Dempsey had still enthusiastically recommended him for the team. Why?

Then there had been that business with Beach back at Hereford. His private meeting with Smallwood and Hardcastle, the CO of 22 SAS. Carter had walked in on the three of them having a private chat. Why had they called in Beach early? What had they wanted to discuss with him? What didn't they want Carter to hear?

His head started to hurt.

'Tell you what,' Beach said as he smothered cheese over a chunk of bread and crammed it into his mouth. 'I wouldn't mind a crack at one of these chalet girls myself.'

'Out of your league, mate,' Dempsey said. 'You've got to be worth a few bob before they give you a second glance.'

'You haven't seen the Karl Beach magic in action. Come back to H after the job's done and I'll show you a few tricks.'

'Yeah? What's your special move, Pom?' Lazarides grinned. 'Stick a paper bag over your face?'

Dempsey laughed. Beach gave the Aussies an evil stare and helped himself to another slab of cheese.

By nine o'clock Carter had seen enough.

They settled the bill with the AmEx card Six had issued in Carter's fake name, left a modest tip and headed outside. Nighttime in Courchevel. The air was so cold it stung Carter's throat. A fresh dusting of snow coated the ground, crunching beneath their snow-packed soles as they trekked back over to the Defender. They were grateful to get back to the warmth of the chalet – Dempsey had left the stove slumbering on a low burn before they had exited earlier that evening.

Carter gathered the team round and said, 'The original plan is a non-starter. No way we can drop the target as he gets on the gondola. Too many civilians in and around the station. People would see the shooter. Plus there's the BG team to consider. There's every chance that it might go wrong.'

'Bugging out of the town will be fucking hard as well,' Beach said. 'Traffic around that area is a nightmare at any time of the day. We'd never be able to get off the mountain before the cops boxed us in.'

Volkova looked at him sharply. 'Are you saying the mission is off?'

Carter said, 'We're not ruling anything out. Not yet. But if we're going to do this, we need to find another way of taking down the target.'

'What about dropping him at the top of the piste, as he's exiting the gondola?'

Carter shook his head. 'That's a suicide mission. At least one of the BGs is potentially carrying a piece. Could be more, for all we know. They'd drop the shooter before they could leg it.'

'There's another problem,' Lazarides put in. 'You said that Grabakin is dressing in the same kit as his bodyguards.'

'That's right. Helmets, visors, boots. Everything's identical. They're even packing the same brand of skis.'

'Then we couldn't knock him out on the pistes anyway. We've got no way of identifying the principal once he's up there.'

'We won't need to,' said Carter. 'We'll ID him earlier.'

'When?'

'The station turnstiles. You've got to show your mug to the camera so the computer can verify that it matches the photo on your ski pass. Grabakin can't slap on his goggles until after he's boarded the lift.'

'How does that help us?' asked Volkova.

'I'll be pre-positioned at the gondola terminal before the Russians roll up for their early morning runs. Once I've got eyes on the principal, I'll keep him in my sights on the way up the mountain, and when he's racing down the pistes.'

'The whole time? What if you lose him for a moment?'

'I won't. It'll be like watching someone shuffle cups around a table, and all I've got to do is follow the one with the ball underneath it. As long as I've got eyes on, I'll know which target to hit.'

'That still leaves the problem of when we can do him,' Dempsey pointed out.

Carter had been chewing over that problem since leaving the slopes. He said, carefully, 'There is one way to take him out. But it won't be easy.'

The others looked at Carter. Waited for him to go on. He took a deep breath and said, 'Here's what we're going to do . . .'

# Twenty-One

They spent the next two days running surveillance on the target. Each morning Grabakin stuck to the exact same routine. He left the chalet at the crack of dawn with three of his BGs, all clad in matching ski gear. They made the short drive north to La Croisette station, arrived just as the lifts were opening. Took the gondola up to La Saulire, followed by two sessions on the Suisse run before tackling the Mur trail. A short rest at the picnic stop ahead of a final beasting on the Rama trail. After which the Russians caught the chairlift from Les Creux to the summit and took the gondola back down to Verdons. The principal met with his family for coffee and cake at Il Refugio in the late morning. In the afternoon they hit the easier pistes above Courchevel Village.

Grabakin clearly had his preferred runs. That would have made his security detail uneasy. But perhaps Grabakin didn't care. He might have weighed the danger against getting the pleasures of a workout on the black trails and decided to take his chances. Maybe the BGs had raised the subject, but the big boss had overruled them. Which was fine by Carter.

*That's when we'll strike.*

*Two days from now.*

On the fourth day, the team carried out a dry run.

\* \* \*

Seven o'clock in the morning. An hour before the lifts opened for business. In the pale-blue light of dawn, half a mile outside Courchevel, Dempsey eased the Defender 110 to a halt on the southern edges of Lake Plan du Vah. Lazarides slid out of the front passenger seat dressed in his snow-camo jacket, trousers and mountaineering boots. He gathered his touring skis from the rack, lifted out his Osprey backpack from the boot and paced over to the lip of a trail snaking down the side of the valley between clumps of snow-dusted pine trees, carrying his skis over his shoulder. Behind him Dempsey looped round the lake and sped north, heading back in the direction of the town, tyres churning through brownish snow-slush and grit.

Lazarides laid his skis flat on the ground; the artificial skins stuck to the underside would provide him with extra grip when navigating up the slopes. He eased his toes into the binding clips fixed to the skis, lining up the inserts with the pins before locking them into place. He put on his Ray-Bans. Extended his telescopic walking poles.

Then he began his hike.

The journey to the OP took forty minutes up a punishingly steep incline. He wasn't worried about being spotted. Not at this hour. The slopes were practically deserted. If anyone did see him, they wouldn't pay him any notice. They would assume he was simply another ski tourer going for an early morning trek up the mountainside. An increasingly popular activity in places like Courchevel.

After a mile Lazarides changed direction and cut west. He crossed another track, continued climbing for two hundred metres until he reached a lightly wooded area due south of the altiport. The location the team had marked out on the satellite maps the previous night. Once he'd orientated himself Lazarides edged closer to the treeline facing the Mur piste at the point where it ran down past the altiport access road.

He walked west, parallel with the treeline, for fifty metres, cut south and turned back on himself, putting in a dogleg. A necessary precaution. If any trekkers followed his snow prints up the mountain, they'd walk right past his position, giving him plenty of advance warning. At least he wouldn't have to worry about anyone coming from the other direction. No one would be skiing towards him from the upper slopes. Not this deep in the woods.

Once he'd selected a spot with good cover and a clear view facing north towards the piste, Lazarides detached his skis, retrieved the shovel from his backpack and dug a shallow hide, working up a good sweat in spite of the cold. He dumped the cleared snow on the front of the scrape, compacted it. Took out the Magnum rangefinder, peered down the eyepiece and lined up the reticule with the Mur run to the north-west. He punched the power button, noted the reading.

A hundred metres.

Lazarides reached into the daysack again and fished out the Kestrel anemometer. He powered up the device, held it up to the sky. Pressed the capture button. At eight o'clock, according to the Kestrel, there was a one-knot breeze coming from west-north-west, 284 degrees.

Lazarides smiled to himself. He'd expected as much. At first light, as the mountains warmed up, the cold air at the top would be dragged down into the valleys. At last light, as soon as the sun dipped behind the peaks, the slopes would become very cold, and the dense air would rush down the mountain, what was known as a katabatic wind. On any mountain, dawn and dusk were the most difficult times to make a shot, in Lazarides' experience. You had to factor in windage, and other potential distortions in airflow. Eddies and turbulence and downdraughts. The way the wind hit rocks or ridgelines.

But at mid-morning the slope would be still.

Perfect shooting conditions.

Lazarides cut several branches from the surrounding pine trees with his utility knife. He unfurled his foam roll mat and spread it across the bottom of the hollow. Next he took out a Thermos flask filled with black coffee, along with a couple of high-protein snack bars and gel pouches. He set down these items next to the Kestrel. Removed the Sig Sauer Cross rifle from his backpack, unfolded the polymer stock. Rested the backpack on top of the compacted snow bank, with the barrel sitting on top and pointing at the Mur trail.

Once he'd set up his shooting platform Lazarides constructed a supporting frame from the cut branches and pulled the snow-camo netting over the top, concealing the scrape. He dropped to his belly and slipped under the net, took up a prone position with his skis and shortened poles at his side. With the net covering the top the barrel was completely hidden, so there would be no telltale reflective glare to reveal his presence.

'In position,' he said into his collar mic.

Carter's voice flared in his earbud. 'Target's just approaching La Croisette now. I'll let you know when he's headed towards your position, mate.'

'Roger that.'

Lazarides stayed utterly still.

He heard Carter relaying the Russians' movements. They were sticking to the same pattern as the previous two days. Just as they had expected. La Croisette to Vizelle, up to La Saulire, a quick run down the Suisse piste, back up to the summit. Down again on Suisse.

'Coming your way,' Carter said over the comms. 'Hitting the Mur piste in minutes five.'

Lazarides stared over the barrel at the trail. Waited. Counting down the minutes in his head. After three minutes the Russians appeared very briefly in the distance, at the point where the ground rose towards a clump of rocks. Four tiny black figures flitting in and out of sight behind patches of pine trees. Further back, fifteen or twenty metres upwind, Lazarides noted a fifth figure in lighter-coloured gear taking the same route down the slope.

Carter.

The skiers vanished again, hidden behind dead ground due east of the altiport.

Carter said, 'Approaching the bend now. Target is on the extreme left from my position. Repeat, extreme left.'

'Rog.'

The Russians popped into view again as they came round the bend immediately east of the altiport, at the point where the black run brushed its sleeve against the access road.

A hundred metres from Lazarides' OP.

Lazarides peered down the Vortex Razor scope, tracking the Russians as they careered down the valley in a rough line formation. Four figures in matching black ski helmets and visors. With Grabakin on the left of the group. The rightmost figure from Lazarides' POV.

Lazarides kept the Russians in sight as they flashed past his scrape before they carried on west down the slope towards Route Pinturleau, at the point where the Mur run merged with Cave des Creux and the easier Praméruel trail curving away gently to the south. A few moments later they were lost to sight again. Behind them, Carter parallel turned on the descent, side-sliding to an abrupt halt in a spray of snow on a flat area just up from the end of the Mur course.

'Did you have line of sight?' he asked over the comms line.

'Clear all the way,' Lazarides said. 'Can you see me from where you are, Pom?'

Carter scanned the woodland from left to right. He looked hard, searching for the slightest sign of the hollow among the mounds of snow and fallen pine needles. 'Nothing. Not so much as a fucking glimpse.'

'Let's get that test shot in before this place gets busy.'

Across the piste, Carter squirmed out of his backpack, pulled out his pair of Blackcrows skins, unclipped his boots from his bindings and brushed the snow from the underside of the planks. He affixed the artificial grips to the skis, switched his boots to walk mode and his touring bindings to climbing mode. Slid his toes back into the inserts, shouldered his rucksack and began plodding uphill. Retracing his route back up the valley.

Carter stopped again near the bend, a hundred metres north-west of Lazarides. He trekked into an area of coppiced woods on the opposite side of the run, stooped down and selected a felled log from a pile of deadwood. He traipsed back over to the piste, glanced up and down. When he was certain they were alone, he placed the log in the centre of the trail, close to the spot the Russians had passed on their descent.

'Ready when you are, mate,' Carter said as he stepped back, putting a healthy distance between himself and the makeshift target.

Lazarides folded back the mittens covering his gloved fingers, tucked the material into the wrist pouches. He lined up the sights with the log, resting his cheek against the stock. A range of a hundred metres. A straightforward shot for an elite marksman. At a longer distance he would have instructed Carter to take a wind measurement from his position to see if there were any subtle changes in the airflow between the firing point and the target. But at such short range there wouldn't be any significant variation. Nothing to materially influence the trajectory of the bullet.

He eased out a breath, relaxing his muscles.

Squeezed the trigger.

There was a light snap as the .308 Winchester round spat out of the suppressed muzzle. Minimal recoil. The bullet thumped into the timber with a sharp crack.

Carter clomped back over to the log, bent down to inspect the Australian's marksmanship.

'Direct hit. You're bang on, mate.'

'Looks like all them hours dropping roos on the farm came in handy after all.'

'Just make sure you plug the fucker when it comes to the real thing. You're only going to have the one shot.'

Lazarides laughed. 'Don't sweat it, mate. I've knocked down targets at a mile back in the day. I won't miss.'

Carter picked up the bullet-studded log, chucked it into the copse. He locked his heels back into his ski bindings, planted his poles in the snow and started down the piste again, turning south on Praméruel. At the same time he reached out to Beach on the comms and told him to RV at the drop-off point in ten minutes. Volkova and Dempsey had drawn the short straw for the day's surveillance duties: they were sitting in one of the Defenders outside Grabakin's chalet, waiting for the wife and kids to roll out of bed.

Lazarides stayed in his hollow.

Hours passed.

By late morning a steady flow of snow junkies came flashing down the piste. None of them spotted the soldier hiding in the scrape in the woods to their side. Once an hour Lazarides took measurements on the Kestrel, making a note of any slight variations in wind speed and direction. The team were confident that Grabakin would tackle the hard runs first thing in the morning, before the long queues at the gondolas. But there was always the chance that the guy might vary his routine. Maybe his wife would insist on going jewellery shopping one morning. Maybe he'd get drunk one night and sleep in.

In the afternoon a chamois ambled past the treeline, foraging for pine needles. Lazarides watched the animal out of the corner of his eye.

*I wouldn't mind bagging one of them. Stick the head up in my barn.*

*But not this time.*

*We're hunting deadlier prey.*

At last light he made one final reading on the anemometer. He collapsed the Sig Sauer Cross, gathered up the rangefinder, his empty Thermos and the protein bar wrappers, shoved everything into his rucksack, called Carter on his burner.

'That's me done, Pom. I'm heading down now. Get one of the lads to pick me up.'

'On their way, mate.'

Lazarides belly-crawled out of his hiding spot. He lengthened the ski poles, reattached his snow boots to the bindings, locking his heels securely into the clips. Pulled the mitts back over his shooting gloves, slipped his hands through the rucksack straps, inspected the hollow one last time to make sure he hadn't left anything incriminating behind. Lowered his goggles and set off down the slope, weaving between the pine trees dotting the valley until the path merged with the red run on Plan du Vah.

The sun had dipped down behind the mountains, sheathing the landscape in darkness by the time Lazarides reached the bottom of the trail. In the distance he could hear the low *crump* of snow cannons firing across the resort. Soon enough the Snowcats would be spreading out across the slopes, raking fresh snow over the tracked-out pistes.

He found Dempsey waiting for him in one of the Defenders at the edge of Route du Plan du Vah, a stone's throw from the lake. The same place he'd dropped off Lazarides ten hours earlier.

By six o'clock they were back at the chalet.

* * *

They trailed the Grabakins to dinner at Le Palais Alpin and returned to their digs at nine o'clock. In the evening they analysed local weather forecasts. A high-pressure system was coming in, the reports said. Courchevel was in for a spell of cold, dry weather for the next few days. Sunshine and clear skies. Little to no wind or cloud.

Volkova stayed in touch with the team at Ramstein, feeding back int updates. The daughter had posted again on social, Volkova said. *Staying in the Alps with a very special guest*, she'd captioned beneath a shot of her in her skiing kit, with La Saulire in the background.

*I'm going to nail him on the slopes tomorrow.*

That reassured Carter. He felt there were a lot of things that could still go wrong with the mission. Grabakin might cut short his holiday. Or he might be summoned back to the Kremlin by Putin to deal with the fallout from the Belarus shooting. But all the signs pointed to the spook staying put in Courchevel. The maid in Geneva had told Volkova that the staff weren't expecting the family to return until Tuesday afternoon. Volkova felt her contact was telling the truth. Putin would be in a rage at the death of his Defence Minister. He'd be looking for scapegoats. Who wouldn't want to spend a little longer on the slopes?

While the others went through their preparations for the next day, Carter typed out a short message to the team at Ramstein.

*We're going to execute tomorrow morning*, he wrote. *Do we have the green light? Any changes?*

He hit send.

Nine minutes later, his burner vibrated with a reply.

*No changes. Mission is go.*

*Confirm once complete.*

He stuck his phone on charge. 'It's on. We'll do him tomorrow.'

'Assuming he's gonna be doing the same runs,' Beach pointed out.

Carter said, 'Hitting the diamond pistes is the highlight of the guy's day. He's done the same thing three times in a row. You'd get short odds on him doing it a fourth time.'

'There are other black runs coming down from Saulire. Pylones, Bosses. Or he might head over to Col de la Loze.'

'He's got two days of skiing left. Sunday and Monday. Tuesday they're due to fly back to Geneva. Once this is over, who knows when he'll next get a holiday? He'll want to squeeze in a few more sessions on his favourite trails. I'm sure of it.'

Dempsey pressed his lips together. 'Let's hope you're right, Pom. Otherwise all this planning has been a waste of fucking time. There won't be time to set up another shot.'

'That ain't our only problem,' said Lazarides. He bummed one of Volkova's tabs. 'It'll be big news. Someone getting plugged on the slopes. We're gonna have a hard time getting out after it's done. For all we know they might shut down the borders.'

Volkova suppressed a laugh and said, 'For a dead Russian spy?'

'Why not?'

'Shall I give you a list of high-ranking Russians killed in Europe in the past twenty years? Because it's a very long one.'

'A killing on the French Alps will be headline news.'

'For a day or two, yes. But it'll soon be forgotten.'

'She's right, mate,' Carter offered. 'Look at that shooting in Annecy all them years ago. A week later no one was talking about it. The news cycle had moved on.'

Lazarides glared at him. 'Whose fucking side are you on, Pom?'

'I'm just saying. There's no chance they'll lock the country down. We're clear on that front.'

Volkova said, 'Just to make sure, Ruznak's people will lean on their media contacts once it's done. They'll put out the word that Grabakin was killed on Putin's orders. For getting too greedy. Stealing money from the FSB budget.'

'How does that help us?'

'People will hear that report and tune out. Grabakin will be just another Kremlin official who got too big for his boots and paid the price. That hardly qualifies as big news these days.'

'Moscow will deny it.'

'Of course. But who will believe them? That's the beauty of Russia being a rogue state. People will expect them to deny involvement. No one will give a shit what Moscow says. They'll make up their own minds.'

The team carried on with their planning late into the night. Tweaking roles, going over times and distances and RV points. They packed their bags, plotted various routes from Courchevel to Italy. Identified crossing points, toll roads. Likely choke-points.

The soldiers would regroup at Ramstein once the job was done. Six had arranged open-ended tickets for them from Turin Airport. A four-hour drive from Courchevel. They'd fly direct from Italy to Frankfurt. A Six driver would meet them airside in Germany and chauffeur them back to base.

Meanwhile Volkova would transfer to Rome and catch a connecting Aeroflot flight to Moscow. Accompanying them to Ramstein was out of the question, Volkova explained. No way she could show her face there. The place was a magnet for Russian spies. Someone was bound to identify her as soon as she got off the plane.

Carter looked at her and wondered again if she was telling the truth. Or was there another reason she didn't want to go anywhere near Ramstein? Carter wasn't sure. *Maybe Lazarides was right*, he thought. *Maybe she's afraid that one of the infiltrators in Alpha Group might crack under interrogation and blow her cover.*

*Right now, I don't know who to trust.*

The next morning, they struck.

# Twenty-Two

At five minutes to eight, on a day of searing winter sunshine, Carter and Volkova sat in the Defender outside a brasserie on Rue de la Croisette. Fifty metres away a handful of early morning skiers and park rats hung around in front of the terminal entrance, waiting for the doors to open. Carter had his rucksack at his feet, his Glock pistol tucked inside with a full clip and a nine-milli round chambered in the snout.

A mile to the south, Dempsey and Beach were camped out in the second Defender outside the target's chalet, their phones connected to the other team members across a five-way conference call.

An hour earlier, Volkova had dropped Lazarides off at the debus point near Lake Plan du Vah, at the foot of the mountain trail winding up towards the Mur run. While the Australian made his way to the scrape he'd established the previous day, Volkova and Carter had shuttled back into the centre of town and parked up close to the gondola station. Pre-positioning themselves before Grabakin and his BGs rocked up.

Now they were ready.

As soon as the G-Wagon approached the terminal, Carter would bomb out of the Defender, cross the road and get behind the Russians as they walked through the turnstiles. Once he had eyeballs on the principal, he'd follow them up the slopes. Meanwhile Volkova would steer round to the underground car park on Rue du Marquis in the neighbouring village at Moriond. She would wait there, ready to swing round and collect Carter and Dempsey from the pick-up point as soon as the job was done. Following which they would RV with Dempsey and Beach back at the chalet. Then the team would cruise out of the resort, up through Albertville towards Chamonix, before crossing down into Italy via the Mont Blanc tunnel running under the mountains. If everything went according to plan, they would be clear of the border long before the French cops could piece together what had happened.

At four minutes to eight, Dempsey reported that the G-Wagon had departed from the chalet on Rue de Bellecôte.

'Carrying six passengers, guys,' he added.

'*Six*?' Carter sat up ramrod straight. 'Who's the extra bod?'

'The daughter. Looks like she's tagging along for the day.'

'Shit.'

'Is she dressed the same as the others?' Volkova asked.

'Right down to the goggles.'

Beach's voice intruded on the chatter. 'Why the fuck is she with him?'

'She's been practising, remember? Taunting her old man on social media. She wants to test herself against him,' Carter said. 'Looks like he's taken up the challenge.'

He recalled Zarina's post the night before.

*I'm going to nail him on the slopes tomorrow.*

'What are we gonna do, Geordie?' asked Beach.

'Stick to the plan,' Carter replied. 'One more body won't make a difference. If we do our jobs properly, we'll still get it done.'

The minutes ticked by slowly. A trickle of luxury vehicles and people carriers rolled up in front of the station, disgorging skiers in groups of two or three before speeding off again. Among them Carter recognised the out-of-shape City stockbrokers he'd laid eyes on four days ago. Across the road, a couple of delivery guys loaded crates of wine into the back of a van. A pair of gendarmes patrolled the street.

'Target inbound,' said Volkova.

Carter focused his attention on his side mirror as the G-Wagon pulled up in front of the terminal. The doors flipped open; one BG dismounted from the front passenger seat, another bodyguard exited from the bench seating at the rear of the vehicle. A third guy emerged from the back seats, held the door open for Grabakin and his daughter. They detached their skis from the rack, slipped on backpacks and started towards the gondola station.

'OK,' Volkova said. 'Go.'

Carter sprang out of the Defender. He unhooked his skis and hurried in the same direction, caught up with the Russians moments before they hit the turnstiles. Two BGs walked in the vanguard, clearing a path for their principal and his daughter through the thin crowd shuffling towards the cabins. The third bodyguard moved along at their six, a couple of paces behind Grabakin. Although the Russians were wearing their helmets they had not yet put on their goggles and Carter could easily distinguish their faces. The spook and Zarina were having an animated conversation. She said something that had him bursting into laughter and throwing an arm around her shoulder.

*Daddy's girl*, thought Carter.

*Apple of his eye.*

Carter brushed past the liftie, darted towards the next cabin.

'Boarding the lift now,' he whispered into his collar mic. 'Heading up on the Verdons line.'

He dropped into a seat facing the Russians in the gondola twenty metres ahead. The first part of the job was done. All he had to do now was maintain a clear line of sight to Grabakin during the ascent, until the moment he slapped on his goggles at the top of the Suisse piste. Then it was a case of tracking that figure's movements on the slopes. Following him with laser-like focus in order to distinguish him from the rest of the group.

The door shut; the gondola began its smooth ascent towards La Saulire.

Six minutes past eight.

\* \* \*

Across the valley, Lazarides heard Carter's voice in his ear.

'Boarding the lift now. Heading up on the Verdons line.'

Lazarides had settled down into the scrape thirty minutes earlier. A light snow had fallen overnight, erasing the tracks he'd made the previous day during his walk up the mountain. The ground close to the hollow was undisturbed. No ski tracks or animal prints. No one else had stumbled upon it during the night.

Working fast but methodically, Lazarides had rolled out his foam mat, anemometer and Thermos flask. He'd taken another set of readings on the Kestrel and unpacked the Sig Sauer Cross, propping the barrel on top of his bunched-up rucksack. Took a hit of strong coffee from his Thermos, demolished a protein bar. Made sure he had a full battery and a good signal on his burner phone. Confirmed that he was in position with the other team members.

Lazarides closed his mind to the outside world. He was no longer aware of anything except his immediate environment, the rifle in his hands, the rhythm of his own breathing. The voice crackling in his ear as Carter updated him on the target's movements.

*We're going down the Suisse run now.*

*Back up to La Saulire on the chairlift.*

*We're about to hit Suisse again.*

He was happiest in this situation. The moments before you pulled the trigger. Life stripped bare of the bullshit, reduced to the ancient hunt between predator and prey. The oldest profession in the world. There was a sense of clarity in this kind of work you couldn't find anywhere on Civvy Street. Everything stopped being complicated. He felt at peace. Lying prone in his scrape, Lazarides realised how much he'd missed that feeling.

Christ, he was glad to be back in the saddle.

At nine thirty Carter came back over the line again.

'We're sweeping down to the start point for the Mur trail. Setting off in a minute. Eight hundred metres from your position.'

Lazarides had five rounds of .308 Winchester in the Sig Cross clip. But he'd only need one shot. At a range of a hundred metres, an armour-piercing round to the torso would be fatal but Lazarides had decided to go for a head shot to make doubly sure of the kill. When the bullet struck, it would turn the guy's skull inside out. There would be nothing left but bits of bone and a few scraps of brain matter.

Lazarides pulled back the mitts from his tactile shooting gloves. Index finger feathered the rifle trigger.

'I'm ready,' Lazarides said. 'Just let us know when he's about to hit that bend next to the access road.'

Carter said, 'Will do.' There was a pause, and then he added, 'Right, we're setting off now. Target on your position in minutes two.'

* * *

At the top of the Mur piste, Carter pushed off twenty-five metres behind the Russians. Throughout the morning he'd managed to keep the target in his sights. The only way to be certain they were clipping the right figure. Carter had locked eyes on Grabakin as soon as he'd slapped on his goggles, tracking him as he'd raced down the trails with his BGs and his daughter before climbing back up on the chairlift. One of the other figures had pushed Grabakin hard on the early Suisse runs. The daughter, Carter presumed. Trying to outski the old man. The three bodyguards had shown themselves to be less capable skiers and were left trailing behind the other two in a swirl of snowdrift.

Now Carter chased after the Russians as they hurtled down the trail in a rough arrowhead formation. Grabakin had the lead; a second figure, possibly Zarina, was breathing down his neck, with a third skier just behind. The other two Russians were struggling to keep up with the furious pace their boss was setting.

The Russians had the run to themselves. An hour before the late morning scramble, on a piste with the highest grade of difficulty, was the quietest place in any resort.

244

'At your position in minutes one,' Carter said.

Grabakin and the second skier had a fierce rivalry going on. They were racing along at breakneck speed, bodies tucked low, elbows at their sides. Carter's skis were chattering as he fought to stay close to them. Grabakin edged ahead, and for a moment Carter thought he might pull clear of his opponent. But as they neared the bend, the other skier started gaining on him once more, the pair of them increasing the distance between themselves and the three other figures in the group. They were only a few metres from the turn on the shoulder of Rue de l'Altiport.

'Hitting the bend now,' Carter said.

The three skiers to the rear were well adrift of Grabakin and the other figure. Carter assumed the guys at the back were the body-guards. Hence the widening gap between themselves and the big boss. Cannonballing down a steep piste could be a terrifying experience for the less experienced skier. They'd be wary of losing control and smashing into a bump, busting up a shoulder or worse. That would play on their minds, affect their speed. All their instincts would be telling them to slow down.

Carter momentarily lost sight of Grabakin as the latter carved into the turn past the thickly wooded treeline. By now the other figure had almost drawn level with the target. Carter surged past the three other Russians in the group a moment before he hit the turn. He slid round, came out at the top of the straight line running like a corridor past sprawls of pine forest.

Hidden somewhere among the trees lurked Lazarides.

Poised to pull the trigger.

Carter looked up.

Below him the two identically clothed figures were now neck and neck. Both of them schussing hard down the slope thirty metres or so from his position. Carter could no longer be sure which one was the principal.

On the comms, Lazarides was saying, 'Which one am I aiming at?'

Carter hesitated.

He had to make a split-second decision.

*Left figure?*

*Or right?*

He knew Grabakin had hit the bend on the inside. Which suggested that the figure on the right had to be the target. But Carter couldn't be wholly certain. The second figure – either Zarina, or one of the BGs – might have weaved inside Grabakin as they'd hit the straight. No way of knowing for sure.

*A coin toss.*

Lazarides came over the line again. Voice straining with urgency. 'Which fucking one, mate?'

*Make the call.*

'Right,' Carter replied. 'Target is on the right from my direction. Your left.'

A dull crack pierced the valley.

The figure on the right tumbled forward, dropped to the snow in a tangle of limbs, poles and skis. Blood spotted the fine white powder.

Carter skied on.

Someone cried in terror at his back.

Carter skidded to a halt fifty metres further down the piste. He lifted his head towards the lifeless body uphill of his position. A short way down from the victim, the other skier frantically cast aside their sticks and tore off their goggles and helmet.

'Did I get him?' Lazarides asked.

Carter didn't reply.

He looked on in horror, guts turning to ice, as Pavel Grabakin detached his skis and waded back up the trail, ploughing through ankle-deep snow and screaming dementedly. He stopped beside the dead figure. Pulled off the helmet. From his position, Carter caught sight of a wave of blonde hair, pale skin smeared with blood.

*No.*

Nearer to the bend, the three bodyguards swerved into view. They stopped in a close grouping forty metres from the teenager's corpse, shouting at one another as they hastily unclipped their boots from their skis. One of them chucked aside his gloves and pulled out a pistol from his ski jacket. Head snapping up and down the slope, scanning the treeline, looking around him for any sign of the shooter.

Zarina was definitely dead. The round would have blown a hole clean through her helmet. No way she could have survived that.

He said, thickly, 'Steve, you've hit the wrong target.'

'What?'

'I said—'

'Fuck it,' Lazarides hissed. 'Where is he? Grabakin?'

'He's taken his helmet off. Kneeling beside the victim.'

'You sure that's him?'

'Just drop the fucker.'

Carter heard the second crack. Across the piste, Grabakin spasmed violently. As if someone had applied a couple of defibrillator paddles to his spine. He collapsed beside his daughter, blood leaking out of a hole in the back of his head the size of a grapefruit.

All sense of order among the bodyguards collapsed as soon as they saw their boss go down. They were the hunted now. Not a position they would have found themselves in before, Carter supposed. The last place any good soldier wanted to be. They were paralysed with shock and confusion, and animal fear.

'Do you need help?' Carter called up.

The bodyguards stared dumbly at him. Did they understand English? Carter had no fucking idea.

He pointed with one of his sticks at the trail below.

'I'm going to send for help,' he shouted. 'Wait here, OK?'

The bodyguards didn't protest. Didn't suspect him of a thing. Why would they? He was just a regular skier enjoying an early morning session. He didn't have a gun; he couldn't have been the shooter. And maybe a tiny part of them clung to the hope that their boss and the girl might survive if a chopper could get to them in time.

The BGs swarmed round Grabakin. One of them got down on his knees, checking pointlessly for a pulse. Another tended to Zarina. The third guy, the one with the pistol, kept scanning the treeline as if he expected the sniper to reveal himself at any moment.

Carter gave his back to the dead Russians, the bodyguards and the blood-spattered snow.

'He's dead,' he said into his mic, breathing hard as he fled down the trail. 'You got him. Target down.'

'Who else did I hit?'

Carter didn't respond.

'Pom? Who the fuck did I drop with the first round?'

'The daughter,' Carter said. 'You killed the girl.'

\* \* \*

As soon as he'd clipped the principal, Lazarides sprang up from his prone position in the hollow. He had the next several minutes mapped out in his head. The result of constantly rehearsing every phase of the plan over the past twenty-four hours. Grab his kit. Clip on his skis. Follow Carter down the wooded area, join the Plan du Vah piste. Get to the finish point south of the lake. Stick their skis on the rack and bundle into the back of the waiting Defender.

RV with the rest of the gang.

Get the fuck out of Courchevel.

*We're almost home and dry.*

Then he became aware of a movement to his right. Lower down the slope.

Lazarides spun round.

And froze.

A figure stood among the pine trees. A middle-aged guy with a cyclist's physique. He was wrapped in a mountaineering jacket and

248

a pair of waterproof ski trousers; Gore-Tex-gloved hands gripped a pair of walking sticks. Locks of dark hair poked out from beneath his bright-red beanie hat.

For an instant Lazarides wondered what the fuck the guy was doing this far into the woods. Then he thought: trekker. The guy would have been following the course of the valley, climbing towards the ridgeline to the west. From there he could skirt along the top of the ridge and make his way to the summit before skiing back down. A good trail. Lazarides had spotted it himself when doing his map orientation. The route would have taken the trekker through the forest.

Right past the scrape.

The man looked nervous. Petrified. Shock and fear stamped his bony face. His wide eyes flicked between Lazarides in his camouflage gear, the scrape, the rifle in his hands.

The man said something in French.

Turned to ski back down the mountain.

Lazarides made an instant decision. He raised his rifle at the fleeing Frenchman. No need to line up the target through the scopes. Not at a distance of eight metres.

The rifle barked. A short snap, like chopping wood. There was a spray of blood mist and bone fragments as the bullet slapped into the back of the Frenchman's head. The man's arms dropped to his sides. His legs buckled; he slumped forward. What was left of his face planted in the snow.

*No choice*, Lazarides told himself.

*You had no choice.*

*The trekker had seen your face.*

*Now get fucking moving.*

He doubted the Russians would have heard the shot. Not from a suppressed rifle, and not at a range of a hundred metres. But Lazarides didn't want to put that theory to the test. He hastily folded up his rifle, stuffed it into his backpack. Fastened his clips, extended his trekking poles and skied down through the forest, leaving the slain trekker behind.

* * *

He found the Defender waiting for him at the foot of the Plan du Vah piste. Volkova sitting behind the wheel, Carter in the front passenger seat. Lazarides dumped his skis on the rear rack, vaulted into the back of the wagon. Tugged the side door shut as Volkova accelerated back up the main road towards Courchevel.

'What the fuck took you so long?' Carter demanded as the Defender lurched violently round a bend in the road.

Lazarides told him about the trekker.

'Shit.'

'I had to drop him,' Lazarides said. 'I couldn't let him get away. No fucking choice. He'd seen my face. Could have compromised the lot of us, for Chrissakes.'

'Did anyone else see you? The bodyguards?'

'I don't think so. They were too busy flapping around the target.'

They drove on. Five minutes to the chalet. Lazarides snorted and shook his head angrily.

'This was your fucking fault. You called it, Pom.'

'I didn't know. I thought – I thought we had the right target.'

'Yeah, well, you were wrong. You had one job to do and you fucked it up. We've got three dead bodies because of you.'

A sudden fury exploded inside Carter. 'Jesus, you can't blame us for the trekker. You can't pin that one on me.'

'Fuck off, Pom. If I'd dropped the target with the first shot, like we'd planned, I would have been out of there before that bloke could have got a good look at me.'

Lazarides looked out of the window, bristling with anger, his hands bunched into tight knuckles.

Carter clenched his jaw. *He's right*, Carter told himself. *I didn't perform. I should have made the right call. Should have foreseen the possibility of losing sight of the target at the bend. Should have pushed harder to keep him in view. But I didn't. I fucked up.* Now his actions had led to the death of a teenage girl and an innocent bystander.

Nausea surged up in his throat.

*Steve might have pulled the trigger.*

*But I'm the one with blood on my hands.*

* * *

They drove back to the chalet in cold silence. The town felt surreal. People were going about their normal business. News of the killings hadn't yet travelled across the resort. The gendarmes would seal off the runs. That would be their first priority. Containment. Examine the crime scene, interview the bodyguards. Try to piece together the chain of events. But it wouldn't be long before they threw up multiple checkpoints around the town. Forty minutes, Carter figured. They were looking at a triple homicide now. A much bigger deal, from a law enforcement perspective. By the early evening photographs of the victims would be circulating on the news sites. A seventeen-year-old Russian female, and a civilian hiker.

The gendarmes would concentrate their efforts on Courchevel. At least initially. Which would work to their advantage. Seventy thousand people a day took to the slopes. Seventy thousand potential suspects and eyewitnesses to process. Plus security footage and forensics. It would be a while before the gendarmes were able to widen the net.

Dempsey and Beach met the rest of the team at the chalet. Neither of them said a word about the fuck-up on the piste. There would be plenty of time for a full debrief later.

They changed out of their skiing gear, broke down their pistols into their constituent parts and secreted them in the bottom of their Alpine boots. Lazarides stashed the Sig Sauer Cross under the seat in one of the Defenders. They loaded their gear into the roof boxes and luggage compartments. Then they hit the road.

No one paid them any notice as they drove west out of the town. An hour later – at around the time the gendarmes would be sealing off Courchevel – they were passing through Albertville and headed towards Chamonix and the Mont Blanc tunnel.

By noon the team had crossed the border into Italy.

# Twenty-Three

As soon as they had cleared the tunnel on the Italian side of the border Carter fired off a message to the bods at Ramstein, on the same number he'd used to communicate with them back in Courchevel. He kept it brief. The bare bones. *We've liquidated the target. Two civilian casualties. On our way to Turin Airport now.*

Thirty seconds later, his phone hummed with an incoming call. The same number he'd just texted. Carter slid his finger across the screen, clamped the handset to his ear. Prepared to get an ear-bashing from one of the Vauxhall suits.

'Yes?'

'Luke, it's Ellen.' Kendall sounded anxious. 'Listen, there's been a change of plan. Where are you now?'

Carter said, 'We've just crossed the border. Passing through some place called Morgex. Why?'

'Don't head to the airport. I'm sending you a new address. Safehouse outside Genoa. We'll meet you there.'

Carter frowned. 'What the fuck's going on?'

'We'll explain everything later. Just get to the safehouse as soon as possible. We'll be waiting for you.'

'And Yulia?'

'Bring her with you.'

'That might be a problem.'

'Remind her of our arrangement. If she proves difficult, the deal's off the table.'

She hung up. Carter's burner trilled again with a new message detailing an address on the outskirts of Genoa. Carter copied and pasted it into his phone's built-in maps app. He reverse-pinched the screen, zoomed in on the location. A small commune nestled on the border between Piedmont and Liguria, fifteen miles north of the Genoese coastline.

'What's wrong?' Volkova asked.

Carter told her about the change of plan. The new RV point near Genoa. Lazarides made a face like someone had just told him he had English blood in his family tree.

'What do they want with us now, for fuck's sake?' he growled. 'The job's done and dusted. We're finished. Game over.'

Carter said nothing. He met Volkova's eye in the rear-view, thought back to what she'd told him at the altiport. The extra targets Six had lined up for them.

*Nine names.*

*Kremlin men. Spooks, generals, senior ministers.*

In his mind there were two possible reasons why Six had insisted on an urgent meeting. One, they were pulling the plug on the whole thing. Perhaps someone in Whitehall had panicked when they'd learned of the civilian deaths in France. They might have been concerned about the fallout.

*Or maybe that's not it,* Carter thought to himself.

*Maybe they're sending us out to kill again.*

He relayed the new orders to Dempsey and Beach in the rear wagon. The meeting with the suits. The safehouse outside Genoa. He punched the new destination into the satnav app. A three-hour drive from their present position. He took the wheel at the next rest stop, swapping places with Volkova. Followed the route south through Alessandria. Carter tried to focus on the drive, but his mind kept revisiting the Courchevel job. The dull snap of the shot. Grabakin struggling over to his daughter's limp body. His inhuman screams piercing the snow-blanketed stillness.

Carter tried to rationalise his actions.

*Take a step back.*

*Google Earth it.*

On the plus side of the ledger the team had accomplished their mission. The future director of the FSB had been eliminated. They had struck a major blow against Putin and his cronies. When you carried out an op in a civilian environment there was always a chance that something might go wrong. Carter had made a decision based on the information available at the time. He'd stepped up. Just like they taught you at Hereford. Doing something is always better than doing nothing.

But no matter how hard he tried, his thoughts always came back to the girl.

They reached Massello in late afternoon sunlight so sharp you could fell trees with it. Carter nudged the Defender along a narrow road cut into the hillside, lined with pastel-coloured apartment blocks and crumbling churches. Old men sat at tables outside cafés, playing games of dominoes. In the distance, vineyards scarred the slopes of the gently rolling hills. A mile due south of the commune they turned off the main road and headed down a gravel path, towards a stone-built villa set in a wide clearing on the valley floor and enclosed on three sides by dense forest.

A Jeep Grand Cherokee was parked in the front drive.

Carter rolled to a halt a few metres from the Jeep, switched off the engine. The lads in the second Defender pulled up to the rear in a cloud of dust and loose dirt. A moment later the front door swung back on its hinges. A suited figure wearing a Barbour jacket stepped through the opening.

Julian Heald.

'Fuck's sake. Just what we need. A debrief with this twat,' Lazarides muttered as he got out of the Defender. He joined Carter, Volkova, Dempsey and Beach at the front of the wagon. The five of them walked over to the Six officer.

'This way, chaps,' Heald said, ushering them into the hallway. 'The others are waiting inside.'

'Don't you have any other clothes, mate?' Dempsey said, nodding at the guy's quilted jacket. 'Or do you Six types get a corporate discount at Barbour nowadays?'

Heald shot him a look that could freeze the Thames. He turned on his heel, giving his back to the SASR man, and shepherded the team down the hallway into a gloomy living area.

Dust motes danced in the light bleeding through grime-spattered windows. The air carried that distinctive musty odour of somewhere that hadn't been lived in for a long time. The place looked shabby. Careworn. But it would be secure, Carter knew. Rigged up with jamming devices and frequently swept for bugs. Six had many such places around the world. Bought up on the cheap through one of the many front businesses run by Vauxhall. Probably a cleaning lady showed up once a month, kept the place tidy.

A pair of chintzy sofas occupied the centre of the room; an old bookcase sagged under the weight of dust-coated hardbacks. Vallance, Kendall and Ruznak were sitting at a long dining table facing the rear patio doors. Ruznak nervously puffed on a cigarette; Vallance and Kendall rose to greet the new arrivals. Kendall smiled nervously at Carter.

'Geordie. Good to see you again.'

Carter didn't reply. He was still busy processing Ruznak's presence in the room. He decided that Six wouldn't have invited the Ukrainian to sit in on the meeting unless the mission was still live. Therefore, they weren't going to pull the plug. Not today.

*They've invited us here for another reason.*

Vallance kept looking down at his watch, like a businessman at lunch waiting for a tardy client to arrive. 'I'm sorry for the last-minute change of plan, but we had to meet with you as soon as possible. Please sit down, guys.'

Lazarides stood his ground. 'What the fuck is going on?'

'We'll get to that in a moment. Take a seat.'

They dropped into the sofas. Vallance leaned against the edge of the table, arms folded across his chest. Heald, Kendall and Ruznak adjusted their chairs so they were facing the team. The SBU officer's cigarette smelled foul, and he watched the soldiers through a veil of smoke.

Next to the ashtray on the table Carter spied a small stack of passports, Samsung smartphones and driving licences. Five of each. And a waterproof plastic case the size of a laptop bag.

Carter wondered about that.

'I'll cut to the chase,' Vallance began bluntly. 'We've got a lead on another target, and there's only a small window of time in which to act.'

'Another job?' Dempsey repeated disbelievingly. He turned to Volkova. 'Did you know about this?'

'Yulia's not in the loop on this one,' Vallance interrupted before she could reply. 'This job is coming from another direction. All the same, we'll need her expertise. Hence why we've asked her to attend this briefing as well.'

'Fuck's sake, how many of these things are we gonna have to do?'

Vallance stared at him. 'There's no time for this discussion. You've got to leave tonight if we're to stand any chance of pulling this job off.'

Lazarides shook his head. 'That's too fast. We've only just bugged out of Courchevel. Which, as we all know, turned into a shitshow,' he added, shooting a dark look at Carter. 'We should be keeping our heads down for a few days.'

'I'm afraid that's quite impossible. The information Eduard has given us,' he paused to tip his head at Ruznak, 'is extremely time-sensitive. Emphasis on extremely. We must act at once before the opportunity slips through our fingers.'

Beach said, 'Where's Smallwood?'

Kendall said, 'On his way back to Hereford. His work is done. He's handed the operational baton to us, so to speak. We're taking the lead on this one.'

'Who's the target?' asked Dempsey.

'Not who,' Heald replied. 'But *what.*'

Carter stared inquisitively at the suits. Heald cleared his throat before he went on.

'There's a special train. Scheduled to depart from a military airbase outside Volgograd tomorrow night. Bound for a private retreat on the Black Sea coast south of Gelendzhik. Carrying a number of high-value targets. You're going to destroy it en route to its destination.'

'You want us to carry out an op in Russia?'

'Yes.'

'What about the Grabakin job? Things went south on them slopes. It's all over the news. People are going to sit up and take notice. They might start joining the dots between that job and the one we did in Minsk. We might already be compromised.'

Vallance said, 'We're not concerned about that. You shouldn't be either. Everything's been taken care of. Nothing will come out.'

'You knocked the target on the head. That's the main thing,' Heald added flippantly. 'The rest is just detail.'

Lazarides glowered at him. 'I've just killed a teenage girl and a French citizen. I wouldn't call that a fucking detail, mate.'

Vallance drew up sharply. 'How do you suppose the Russians would react if they were in the same position? Do you think they would feel an ounce of guilt about a couple of innocents caught in the crossfire?'

'That's Russia. That ain't how we work.'

'Perhaps we ought to. We're preparing to fight a war. The drumbeats are sounding, and when it kicks off we're going to have to fight dirty to win. No one will give a damn about the Geneva Conventions when the nukes start dropping. So bloody well get used to it.'

Lazarides shot to his feet. 'Fuck this for a laugh.'

'Where do you think you're going?'

'Back to Oz. I'm done. I didn't sign up for this shite.'

'You can't quit.'

'Yeah? Just watch me. See you, fellas.'

He started towards the front door. Vallance raised his voice and called out to him, 'Leave now, and tomorrow morning your face will be on the website of every major news outlet as the prime suspect in a triple shooting in the French Alps. You'll bring the SASR into disgrace. Who knows? It might even lead to the disbandment of the rest of your beloved unit.'

Lazarides stopped in the living room doorway. He looked round at Vallance, the colour draining from his face.

'You wouldn't. You wouldn't fucking dare.'

Vallance sneered, 'Then you obviously don't know what we're capable of, do you? Now for God's sake, sit down, man. We've wasted enough time already.'

Lazarides hesitated for a long beat. Vallance stared him down, daring the Australian to defy him. Lazarides sat back down, cursing under his breath.

'Let's get back to business,' Vallance said. He squinted at his watch. 'You're boarding a private jet two hours from now, departing from Genoa airport. We've got a lot of ground to cover before then.'

'Who's on this train?' asked Carter.

'High-ranking targets. Multiple. That's all you need to know.'

The spook looked meaningfully at Volkova.

Carter said, 'Any civilians on board?'

Kendall said, 'It's a private train. Armoured carriages. The only passengers are the HVTs, their bodyguards and personal advisers.'

'What about the drivers?'

'All train staff are vetted by the FSO prior to their employment. The Kremlin's Federal Security Service. We're talking about individuals whose loyalty to the Kremlin is beyond question. Everyone on that train is complicit with Putin's regime to some degree.'

'There won't be any innocents on that train,' Heald said, 'if that's what you're worried about.'

'As far as you know.'

Heald merely shrugged.

'Where are the targets going?' asked Dempsey.

Vallance said, 'They're heading for a high-level conference on the Black Sea. The details aren't relevant to your mission. All you need to know is that we have a once-in-a-lifetime opportunity to eliminate the Kremlin brains trust. But we must move quickly.'

'Why not get them at the retreat?'

Ruznak swatted away the question. 'You can't. It's a fortress. Like fucking Fort Knox times a million. Prohibited airspace. Frequency-jamming equipment. Guards everywhere. A small army. Believe me, they'd cut you down before you could get within a mile of that place.'

'Hitting them at Volgograd is equally difficult. The train really is our best bet,' said Kendall.

Volkova, who had been silent so far, sat forward and said, 'Where is this information coming from? I have heard nothing about a meeting in Gelendzhik.'

'You wouldn't. This thing is highly secretive. Even the targets' families don't know where they're going.'

'Even so, a conference this big is hard to keep secret.'

'We think,' Heald said, 'we think that Putin and his remaining confidants have deliberately kept the FSB out of the loop on this one. Seeing as your people are no longer flavour of the month in the Kremlin.'

'This is true. But then I must ask – how did you find out about it?'

'Eduard has a source. Someone close to the targets.'

'Are you sure they're sound?' Carter asked.

'As sure as we can be, dear boy,' Vallance cut in.

'I wasn't asking you. I want to hear it from him.' Carter tipped his head at the Ukrainian.

Ruznak worked his lips into a hard smile. He said, 'We've got a spy on the train. An assistant to the personal doctor to one of the targets. My people emplaced her months ago. Tomorrow, she will call in sick at the last minute.'

'There's a doctor on this thing?' Beach drew his head back in surprise. 'Who are we fucking hitting?'

'HVTs,' Vallance snapped. 'That's all you need to know.'

'I don't like it,' Carter said. 'We're basing everything on this spy telling the truth. What if the Russians have turned her? What if she's leading us into a trap, and there's no train?'

Vallance brushed lint from his trousers. 'Pattern of life, dear boy. Digital shadows. You Special Forces types understand the principle, I presume?'

Carter drew his eyebrows together, nodded slowly. He'd heard of the term from his previous jobs with Vauxhall. The first rule of going after a top-level target. You didn't look at the main target. Penetrating the inner cordon was too tricky. You had to factor in early warning systems. Tripwires. Counter-surveillance. The enemy might realise they were being watched and change or cancel their plans. Or set a trap. So you widened the lens. Focused on the outer cordon. You watched the people who watched the target: the bodyguards. They were more likely to be slack with their personal security because everything they did was geared towards protecting the principal. You could monitor credit card activity. Social media accounts. Online bookings. Anything that left a footprint. Could be something as simple as noting what the wives and girlfriends of the BG teams did when their husbands and boyfriends were out of the city. Did they meet up with secret lovers? Fly down to Milan for a shopping trip? Hit the nightclubs in Moscow? Listening in on a target's conversations was almost impossible, but a bodyguard might call his missus on an unsecured line to say he wouldn't be able to talk for the next three days because of opsec. Then you'd know the target was on the move.

Kendall said, 'We've been watching the BG teams around the HVTs. Specifically, their mobile phones. There's been a frenzy of activity over the past few days. A large-scale detachment has moved down to Volgograd. Fifty bodyguards.'

'Must be a bloody long train to carry that many bods,' Beach remarked.

Kendall nodded. 'There are twelve carriages. There's an on-board gym. Beauty spa. Medical facilities. Cinema. There's even a casino.'

'We've been following the train personnel too,' Heald said. 'Guards. Engineers. The driver. The information from the doctor's assistant holds up. There's a mass convergence centred around Volgograd station. That train is definitely leaving tomorrow night.'

Vallance pressed his hands together and said, 'Let's get on with the plan, shall we? We're on the clock.'

They crowded round the dining table. Kendall cleared away the documentation, spread out a detailed topographical map of south-west Russia, with Volgograd in the top-right corner and the Black Sea coastline on the bottom left. A vast swathe of territory. Steppe country to the north, the Caucasus Mountains to the south. A trainline coursed down from Volgograd via Krasnodar to a rural location on the Black Sea coast, twenty-five miles from the beach resort at Gelendzhik.

Ruznak stabbed a finger at Volgograd. The city once known as Stalingrad. Millions of dead. The annihilation of the Sixth Army. The graveyard of Hitler's grotesque ambitions.

'Our spy says the train is due to depart from Volgograd central station tomorrow night,' the Ukrainian said. 'There are three places where we believe you can stage an ambush. Here, here and here,' he added, indicating various points along the line.

Beach leaned in for a closer look, face scrunched in thought. He tapped on a gorge about two miles inland from the coast, at a point where the line crossed a rail bridge over a winding river. Further along, the route hit the coastline, whereupon it tracked north-west for fifteen miles towards a thinly populated belt of land.

'What's this?' Beach said.

Ruznak said, 'That's the Gorenskaya Tunnel. Three miles long. Bored into the Markotkh mountain range. Comes out over a bridge crossing a gorge. Longest tunnel on the line.'

Dempsey grinned at the British soldier. 'You thinking of blowing up the bridge, mate?'

Beach shook his head. 'Those carriages are armoured. And it's a long train. Twelve carriages. Twice as long as the bridge. Some of the occupants might escape. The tunnel would be better.'

Heald drew his brows together. 'Why the tunnel?'

'Simple physics. If you blow something up in an open area, the energy quickly dissipates. An explosion in an enclosed area causes much more damage. The energy has nowhere to go, so it's pushed back on itself. With enough charges we could take out the train and the tunnel. Two birds for the price of one.'

'I don't think that's the saying, mate,' Dempsey chipped in.

'Will any other services be running on that line?' Carter asked.

Ruznak shook his head. 'Definitely not. No other trains are allowed on the tracks while the HVTs are making their journey to Gelendzhik. Our spy is adamant on that point.'

Carter looked intently at the Ukrainian. 'Your source knows a lot for a doctor's assistant.'

'She's a spy. She's trained to keep her eyes open.'

Beach said, 'What's the train schedule?'

'It's a six-hour journey to the retreat. Line departs Volgograd at eleven o'clock tomorrow evening. It will pass through the tunnel at around four thirty in the morning. Just over two hours before first light.'

'Conditions?'

'Forecast is clear. There's no moon, so you won't be visible to anyone during the attack.'

'Should make it easier for us to sneak away, too,' Dempsey mused.

'Does it snow there?' asked Beach.

'Not that close to the coast,' said Ruznak.

'How do we get in?'

'Fishing trawler,' Vallance put in. 'Departing from Sinop, on the Turkish coast. Operated by a smuggling gang involved in the cocaine trade between Russia and the Black Sea. They'll take you right up to the peninsula, drop you off by inflatable boat.'

Carter contemplated the thought of placing his life in the hands of a bunch of criminals and grimaced.

'You've no need to worry about them betraying us,' Ruznak said. 'My people have used them before. To smuggle stuff into Russia. The other way, too.'

'Besides, we're paying them handsomely,' Heald said.

'Yeah. Because smuggling gangs are famously trustworthy.'

Vallance said, haughtily, 'It can't be helped. Overland insertion isn't possible. This is the only way in.'

'What about exfilling?'

Vallance patted the hard-shell container on the side of the table. 'Portable sonar echo-sounder. I'm sure you've used this sort of thing before. There's a navy submarine patrolling in the Mediterranean. HMS *Audacious*. Astute-class attack sub. Currently making preparations for a joint exercise with the Greeks and Turks in the Sea of Marmara. As soon as you're on the ground in Turkey *Audacious* will move up the Bosporus River into the Black Sea.'

That drew a puzzled reaction from Beach. 'But that'll cause a diplomatic shitstorm. Turkey closed the Black Sea to our warships when the war broke out. Russia's too.'

'Officially, yes. But there are breaches from both sides all the time. More than you'd imagine.'

'At any rate,' Heald said, 'you needn't concern yourself with the political side of things. People far, far above your pay grade will take care of all that.' A smug smile spread across his face.

Vallance said, 'Once you're ready to be extracted, make for the RV and activate the rescue device. It'll transmit a sonar pulse to a depth of fifty metres. Our chums on the sub will pick it up, head for the signal, send an inflatable to your location and bring you back to the sub. From there it's a straight voyage out of the Black Sea through the Dardanelles Strait and across the Med to Gibraltar.'

Heald said, 'This is an in-and-out job, guys. Should be a piece of piss.'

'Are you retraining to be a comedian?' Carter quipped. 'Because that's a good fucking joke.'

Heald suppressed a smile. 'I fail to see what the problem is. You won't be involved in any contacts with enemy forces on this mission. Good God, you won't even need to fire a gun. And there's zero chance of civilian casualties. It's outside the tourist season, so the area you're operating in will be sparsely populated.'

'This is classic SAS sabotage work,' Vallance chimed in. 'You'll be following in the footsteps of David Stirling and Paddy Mayne. Blowing up airfields and causing havoc behind enemy lines. Isn't that what you signed up for?'

'If it's so easy, do it yourselves,' Lazarides said.

Vallance looked testily at the Australian.

Beach said, 'We'll need explosives. A fucking lot of them.'

'That won't be a problem. Eduard has been liaising with his contacts in Turkey. The smugglers have friends who can supply the relevant hardware. Everything you need will be waiting for you on the boat. Bombs, weaponry and so forth.'

'When do we leave?' asked Carter.

'Straight after this meeting. There's a private jet waiting for you at Genoa airport. Direct flight to Samsun on the Turkish side of the Black Sea. Landing at midnight local time. One of our friends at the British Embassy in Ankara will meet you landside and drive you up the coast to Sinop. The trawler will be rigged and ready to go.'

'Comms?'

'You'll use smartphones while you're on the ground. Military-grade encryption. There's a rebroadcasting tower at the retreat in

Gelendzhik, so you won't have any problems with reception during the mission. We've brought new, clean passports and driving licences for each of you.'

'Yulia,' Heald said, 'will be going with you as well.'

Volkova showed no reaction. Carter said, 'Is that necessary?'

Heald chuckled. 'Are you worried about having a woman on your team?'

'Not at all. I'm worried about a civilian slowing us down if it goes noisy. We're going to be on the ground in enemy territory. We can't afford to carry any passengers.'

'Yulia's on the team, whether you like it or not. You need someone to act as a translator, and to help if things go wrong. She can get you to an FSB safehouse or help you cross overland at weak points along the border. But I doubt it'll come to that. This is going to be a breeze.'

'There's no such thing,' Lazarides said. 'If there was, cunts like you wouldn't need blokes like us. Would you?'

Heald glowered at him, lips pinched thin as piano wire.

Kendall said, 'We've prepared a target package to take with you. Mapping of the coastal area, train specifications. Arrival times at each station along the route. Information pertinent to your mission. You should study that on the flight over to Turkey.'

Vallance stood up. 'I suggest you get moving. Head straight to the airport. Your fake names are on the flight manifest. Jet's waiting for you on the pan. If everything runs smoothly, you'll be back at Ramstein forty-eight hours from now. And we'll have taught Putin a lesson he won't ever forget.'

# Twenty-Four

They took a Bombardier Challenger jet from Genoa airport and landed at Samsun airport dead on midnight. A junior Six flunky called Titus greeted them on the apron with a businesslike nod, led them wordlessly over to a waiting Caravelle. A fresh-faced embassy staffer with a jutted chin, the build of a university rowing champion and the ingrained confidence of inherited wealth. But trained well. A good boy. He said nothing as they blatted up the Turkish coast at seventy miles per hour. Didn't ask questions or try to make small talk with Carter and the others. A solid Vauxhall man in the making. He'd probably be sitting behind Vallance's desk twenty years from now, sending out future generations of Reg door-kickers to do Six's dirty work.

Two hours later they hit Sinop. Titus brought the Caravelle to a stop at the edge of the marina parking lot. The ruins of an old castle tower loomed above the wharf. Pleasure yachts, takas and fishing boats crowded the jetty; further along a handful of crewmen paced the aft deck of a berthed trawler, inspecting nets and winches.

A faint breath of salty wind murmured across the quay as the team deboarded the Caravelle; Titus pulled out a gym bag from beneath the front passenger seat and joined the others on the waterfront. A figure approached from the direction of the jetty, the glow of his cigarette cherry-bright against the oily blackness. He had the weathered look of a seaman, thought Carter. Swarthy and stubbled-faced. His face told the story of a bloke inured to the hardships of life on the waves. Dark eyes, narrow as coin slots, flicked suspiciously between Titus and his five passengers.

'Deniz?' the Six flunky asked. 'Deniz Sahin?'

'That's me.' The Turk continued to size up the team members. 'These are the guys I was told about?'

'That's right.'

'Do you have the money?'

Titus passed him the gym bag. Deniz Sahin left his cigarette hanging from the corner of his mouth as he yanked on the zip and peeked inside. Carter caught a glimpse of the contents. Thick bundles of hundred-dollar bills. Lots of them. The Turk made a brief estimation of the value and lifted his gaze to the flunky.

'Where is the rest?' he demanded in guttural English.

'Half now. The balance when the job is completed.'

'This is not what was agreed.'

'Too bad. This is the way we do business,' Titus said. 'If you have a problem, take it up with the Ukrainians.'

Sahin weighed up the situation, looking from the bag of cash to the five passengers. Making a quick calculation. A cost–benefit analysis. Refuse the terms on offer and lose the opportunity to make an easy buck carrying some extra cargo across the sea. Or bite the bullet and trust that Six would honour their side of the bargain. He zipped up the bag, slung it over his shoulder.

'My ship.' Sahin lazily wafted a hand at the trawler. Carter realised he was talking to him now. He'd concluded his transaction with Titus. 'You come aboard. We leave soon.'

'Lead the way, mate.'

Sahin flicked his cigarette into the water and set off down the jetty at a swift pace, Carter at his six, lugging the carry box containing the sonar device, the others following. Behind them, Titus drove off in the Caravelle; soon he was lost to the darkness.

A pungent odour of fish, diesel fumes and tobacco smoke hit Carter as he climbed aboard the trawler ahead of the rest of the team. Crewmen walked up and down the ship with the ease of veteran seamen, some lugging ice boxes down to the fish processing area below deck. Another guy studied a plotter in the wheelhouse. Sahin squeezed past him and hurried down the stairs to the galley kitchen and mess. A separate corridor led to the crew's bunks, captain's quarters and a cramped toilet cubicle. From somewhere below came the dull incessant thrum of the diesel engines. Turkish rap bleated out of a cheap radio.

'You stay down here until I come for you. There's coffee, tea. Food. Help yourselves. Don't come up on deck, OK?'

Carter looked round. 'Where's our kit?'

Sahin gestured towards a separate door. Carter and Beach ducked low and followed the Turk into a fish processing area, cold as a meat locker and packed with equipment for sorting and cleaning the catch prior to freezing. Sahin moved between the metal tables and fishing baskets, stepped over an unspooled hosepipe leaking water and knelt down beside one of the plastic storage boxes stacked against the bulkhead. He brushed away the top layer of ice, retrieved a rusty-looking AK-47 rifle wrapped in plastic.

The skipper set the empty crate to one side, pulled out more gear from the boxes beneath it. Laid all the hardware out on one of the benches. Carter counted a total of four AKs, all of them in equally crap condition, along with a couple of poorly maintained SR-1 Vektor pistols, with two clips of 9 x 21mm Gyurza ammo apiece. Not the best kit. Not as sophisticated as the latest NATO weaponry. But sturdy. Especially the AK-47s. The world's most reliable weapon. Almost indestructible. You could burn it, bury it, throw it into a river and it would still function. A bit of surface rust wouldn't affect its performance in a firefight.

Another crate contained a pick and a shovel, a pair of tactical flashlights; in the box below was a rucksack filled with detonator fuses, det cord, a receiver box, a radio-controlled trigger. Plus fifteen one-kilo slabs of Semtex explosive.

'You point out your destination on the map. My crew will take you close as possible,' Sahin said in mangled English. 'But we cannot land. Too dangerous, you understand? Patrols everywhere on that side of the coast. Russian navy. And shoals. Lots of shoals. You will take the tender to the shore. Then you are on your own.'

'Fine by us,' said Carter. 'How long until we get to the coast?'

'Journey across Black Sea is eighteen hours,' Sahin replied. 'Maybe longer. Depends on patrols. Usually, we have no trouble. But you never know.'

As he spoke a pair of deckhands entered the processing facility and started transferring blocks of cocaine from a rucksack to a nearby stack of ice boxes. Carter said, 'Are you sure you can get us there undetected?'

He was thinking about the dangers of making a trip across the Black Sea with a gang of Turkish crooks and a stash of Colombian marching powder. Sahin grinned slyly.

'We've been doing this for ten years. Me and my brothers. We know these waters better than anyone. If we cannot get you across, no one can.'

'I didn't know there was such a big market for coke in Russia.'

Sahin chuckled. 'You are mistaken, Englishman. Most of this product doesn't go to Russia.'

'Then where is it going?'

'The Persian Gulf. Our friends on the other side run the smuggling network to the east. The Saudi princes have a fondness for cocaine. And they're willing to pay big money for the quality stuff.' The Turk grinned again, rubbing together his thumb and forefinger. 'Good business for us.'

'Ever get the sense we're in the wrong line of work?' Beach said quietly as the skipper moved over to monitor the guys unloading the coke.

'Constantly,' Carter muttered.

Beach dropped his voice. 'You trust 'em, Geordie?'

'As far as I can spit a rock.'

'Me neither. Tell you what. Thank fuck they ain't picking us up at the other end of this job.'

'There's plenty of time for them to stitch us up before then.'

Beach pursed his lips. 'Let's hope Six is paying them a big whack to get across.'

'I don't think that matters. Even if they're getting top dollar, they might decide to double-tap us anyway. Chuck our bodies overboard and tell Six they dropped us at the RV as planned. The bods at Vauxhall would be none the wiser.'

'Would they really do that?'

'These lads are career criminals. We're five Christians on a boat full of Turks. I don't think they're going to have moral issues about knocking us off, mate.'

'You've got a dark mind, Geordie.'

Carter gave a tired laugh. 'I'm just a realist. And I know what these fuckers are capable of.'

'What are we gonna do?'

Carter sighed and said, 'There's nothing we can do. Just keep an eye on them and stay alert. You see anything suspicious, let me know.'

*   *   *

The trawler slipped its moorings shortly before three o'clock in the morning. Carter, Beach and the others heard the skipper's garbled voice over the Tannoy, bellowing orders; hands shouted at one another above deck; the engines growled as the ship pitched forward. Once they had cleared the jetty Dempsey climbed into the wheelhouse to help Sahin plot the team's drop-off point on the navigation charts. Meanwhile Carter, Lazarides and Beach descended to the hold to check over their equipment. Making sure that everything still functioned as it should. No one wanted to suffer a stoppage in the middle of an unforeseen firefight. Lazarides ran his eyes over one of the rust-coated AK-47s with a look of unmistakable contempt.

'This is bullshit.'

271

'It's a bit of rust,' Beach said. 'The guts of it are just fine. Stop moaning, for fuck's sake.'

'It's not just the guns. I'm talking about the whole package. This job doesn't feel right.'

'What's the problem? All we've got to do is get to the tunnel, bury the explosives, wait for the train, blow it up and bug out.'

'Ain't that simple. This thing is dicey as fuck. There's a lot that could go wrong.'

'Same was true for the last two ops.'

'No, mate. This is different. We're going to be on the ground in Russia. That's a whole other level of risk. Besides, what do you think will happen if we're caught? Putin will parade us in front of the cameras. We could be looking at a full-blown international crisis.'

'We're only on the ground for a few hours. And that tunnel's in the middle of nowhere. We won't come within a country mile of a Russian.'

'You're assuming the spooks are telling us the truth.'

'You don't think they are?'

'Think about it. They said they've had to move fast on this job, but they've had all the pieces in place well in advance. Briefing the navy chiefs on the pick-up point, agreeing terms with the smugglers. Getting clearance to enter the Black Sea without triggering a response from the Russians.

'They must have known about this thing weeks ago. Longer, even. They're not being straight with us. Haven't been from the get-go. So yeah, I take everything those idiots say with a pinch of salt. A fucking big one.'

'They wouldn't lie to us about the int,' Beach said with feeling. 'They've been bang on so far.'

'And if you're wrong?'

'Then we'll do what we always do. Improvise. Work round the problem. Find a solution. We've still got the edge over the Yanks when it comes to thinking for ourselves.'

Lazarides said, 'That's the problem with you Brits. Always happy to make do and mend. Don't rock the boat. But I ain't having it. After this job, it's over for me. I'm done.'

Carter said, 'What about Vallance's threat?'

'The guy's bluffing. Six throws us under the bus, it'll mean pissing all over their relationship with Canberra. You lot can't afford it. Not as if you've got loads of friends these days.'

'And if he's telling the truth?'

'I'll still quit. I've had enough of this shit.'

'You should try spending two years as an instructor teaching dems courses,' Beach said. 'You'd soon change your tune then. Me, I'm just glad to see some action at long last.'

'Be careful what you wish for, Pom. Because if this goes tits-up, we're not coming back alive.'

They passed the hours below deck, Sahin's voice intermittently blaring over the Tannoy. Those deckhands not on duty passed their time playing cards in the mess, smoking disgusting roll-ups and drinking tea from tulip-shaped glasses. Others watched shows on their phones or dossed in their bunks. Carter and Beach took it in turns to go on watch. Two guys stagged on, while the others kipped in the spare beds. That way they could always have two pairs of eyes on the crew. No one wanted to wake up to find a gun pointing at their head.

At five o'clock Sahin came down from the wheelhouse and told Carter they were four hours out from the drop-off point. He promised to bring the trawler as close as he dared to the coastline before lowering the tender. He couldn't risk hanging around the area, Sahin added. Once the tender had dropped them on the shore they were getting the hell out of there.

An hour later Carter found Volkova sitting at one of the mess tables, nursing a mug of mud-brown coffee, staring off into space. Carter recognised the look. He'd seen it on the faces of young Paras, in the moments before they deployed on their first operation. A mixture of nerves, adrenaline and restlessness.

'Can't sleep?' he said as he poured a mug and pulled up a pew next to her.

Volkova made a half-hearted attempt at a smile. 'Is it that obvious?'

'Where's Karl?' Carter asked, looking round the galley. The two Brits had another hour on stag before they handed over the watch to Lazarides and Dempsey.

'In the hold. Checking the explosives. Again. Says he needs to familiarise himself with it. But I think he doesn't trust the Russian kit.'

'Wise man.'

'Is he right? About this being an easy job?'

She looked at him hopefully. Carter said, 'A lot depends on the intelligence. If it's accurate – if that train is on time, and if it's really going through that tunnel – there shouldn't be a problem. We'll be back on the water before any nearby units can mobilise.'

'There's a lot riding on Eduard's spy.'

'Do you have any idea who's on this train?'

Volkova stared at him with widened eyes. 'I know nothing about this operation at all. That's the honest truth. I didn't even know that the train was going to be the next target. This is Ruznak's brainchild, not mine.'

Carter said, 'Whoever the targets are, they must be a big fucking deal.'

'I guess so.' Volkova fell silent for a beat as she stared at her coffee. 'Your friend Steve is right, you know.'

'He's not my mate.'

Volkova shrugged indifferently. 'Friend or not, he knows we're pushing our luck on this one. Everything is going fast. Maybe too fast,' she added softly.

Carter stared at her. 'Why did Six want you on this job?'

'What Heald said back at the briefing. You need a translator. Someone who can get you to a safehouse if you're compromised.' She saw the look on Carter's face and added, haltingly, 'What, you don't believe me?'

'I don't know.'

A tiny laugh escaped her throat. 'Do you think I really want to be here, risking my neck with you and your comrades? I could be in England right now, beginning a new life.'

'So why aren't you?'

'I can't. Six insisted I come with you on all the missions. That was part of the deal I agreed with them. They've got me over a barrel.'

Three weary crewmen trudged into the galley; two of them plonked themselves down at the next table, grousing in low voices, their clothes reeking of salt and fish guts, while the third guy fired up the gas cooker, cigarette dangling from his lips.

Volkova said, 'You know, I'm not the real problem here.'

Carter uplifted an eyebrow. 'How do you mean?'

'What happens once this is over? Has it occurred to you that your friends at Vauxhall might worry that you know too much?'

'They wouldn't bump us off, if that's what you're getting at. That's not Six's style.'

'They don't need to kill you, though. Do they? They just don't need you to come back from the mission. Maybe there's no submarine waiting for us at the end of all this. Maybe they just leave us to the wolves.'

'Even if you're right, we can't do anything about that. My brother always said worry about the things that you can control in life. Forget about the stuff you can't.'

'You have a brother?'

'Had,' Carter said.

'What happened?'

'He was killed on a job. Getting on for a year ago.'

'I'm so sorry.'

Carter nodded but made no reply.

'Were you close?'

'Yes and no. Me and Jamie were tight when we were growing up. In each other's pockets. Used to get up to all sorts of mischief together. I looked up to him, copied everything he did. He was my role model. But we drifted apart over the years.'

'Why?'

'Different outlooks, I guess. Jamie could be a hard man to get on with. He refused to play the game. Always spoke his mind, even if it meant pissing people off. That made life difficult for him in the Regiment. Difficult for those who cared about him, too.' Carter smiled sadly. 'Sometimes I think going out on an op was the way Jamie would have wanted it. Five minutes on Civvy Street and he would have been climbing the walls.'

'You're not like that? Speaking your mind?'

'Never seen the point. You can't change the system. The way I see it, life's complicated enough. Leave the political bullshit to others. I'm just happy to soldier. But that was never enough for Jamie.'

They sat in silence for what felt like a long time. The three crewmen at the other table smoked and listened to the football commentary crackling out of the radio. They stared at the foreigners with undisguised hostility.

Volkova said, 'It wasn't your fault, Luke. What happened back there on the slopes.'

'That's not how the other lads see it. Not how I see it, either.' Carter dropped his gaze to his feet.

'You made an honest mistake.' Volkova placed her hand on top of his. Her fingers were ice-cold. 'You were on the spot. You had to make a call. Could have happened to any one of us.'

'But it didn't, did it? It was me.'

Carter felt his voice cracking. The image of the teenager's lifeless body flashed before him again as he looked up at Volkova.

'Steve might have fired the bullet,' Carter added, 'but I'm responsible for that young girl's death. And I'm going to have to live with that for the rest of my life.'

# Twenty-Five

The trawler dropped anchor a mile off the coastline. The team hauled their equipment up to the deck, while a pair of crewmen lowered a Yamaha inflatable tender into the oil-black sea. A boarding ladder was dropped over the starboard side of the vessel. Sahin signalled to one of his hands. The man easily descended the wooden planks to the tender, gestured for Beach to follow him down. Beach stood up in the boat, while Lazarides and Dempsey quickly passed down the pick and shovel, the sonar box, the rucksack containing the explosives, det cord, receiver box and the two Vektor semi-automatic pistols.

On Sahin's instructions the trawler had turned off its lights to make it invisible to anyone watching from the shore. In the swamp-like dark Carter could just about discern the outline of the cliffs along the peninsula, black masses looming forbiddingly above the gloom of the sea. Once they had finished loading the kit, Lazarides, Dempsey and Volkova joined Beach in the tender. Carter was last to leave the ship. He slung his AK-47 over his shoulder, swung his leg over the side and scaled down the ladder.

Carter took his place on the gunwale next to Volkova and clasped one of the grab handles to steady himself. A stiff breeze was gusting in from the east; the boat bobbed on the surface, waves lapping gently against the sides. The Turk unhooked the ropes tethering the boat cleats to the trawler. He pulled out the choke on the outboard motor, tugged the start handle. The engine puttered into life; the tender pulled steadily away from the mothership, creamy foam trailing behind it. In less than a minute the trawler was lost to the star-pricked blackness.

The Turk worked the throttle handle, steadily increasing the boat's speed until they were planing across the water, spray dousing the six occupants. He kept one hand on the tiller, lining up the bows with the distant shore, expertly steering between the darker patches of reefs and rocks. By now Carter's natural night vision had kicked in. He could see the narrow strip of pebbled beach, grey against the black cliffs. The steeply rising headlands beyond.

Further up the coast, he spied a cluster of gleaming lights from distant villages. The nearest settlement was five miles away from their landing point. On a moonless night, with no nearby artificial light sources to illuminate the area, no one would notice the five figures disembarking from the tender.

The bluffs loomed larger as they neared the shallows. When the Turk judged they were close enough, he kill-switched the motor.

'OK, you go now,' he said.

The passengers clambered awkwardly out of the boat, splashed down into knee-deep water, started up the shingle in single file. Beach carried the rucksack; Dempsey lugged the pick and shovel. Carter gripped the box containing the sonar device. Behind them the pilot steered the motorboat round and skimmed back along the waves towards the anchored trawler.

'This way,' Carter whispered.

He led the others across the beach, towards a narrow gully cut into the bluffs. The trail zigzagged up to a wooded plateau atop the headland. From there they could move unseen towards the Goren-skaya gorge. Carter had spent the flight from Italy committing the route to the tunnel to memory, knew it as well as the back of his own hand.

They started up the trail at a deliberate pace, Dempsey as point man, Carter navigating, scanning the ground for slippery rocks or fallen debris. Anything that might result in a twisted ankle and imperil the mission. At the top of the plateau Carter paused to wait for the others to catch up and checked his illuminated watch.

Nine thirty. An hour until they reached the tunnel. Ninety minutes until the train departed Volgograd.

Seven hours until the train was due to pass through the tunnel.

They pushed inland, following a rough hiker's trail through a dense sprawl of pine trees. Volkova struggled to match the pace of the soldiers. She stumbled twice on the undergrowth, cursing in her native Russian and forcing the others to move more slowly. Carter kept a mental count of the distance they had covered, breaking it down to ten-metre increments, the way he'd learned in the Regiment. Measuring how long it took them to get from one point to the next. That would be vital when it came to bugging out, estimating their time to the RV point. Assuming everything had gone to plan.

On the far side of the plateau the ground tumbled away towards a thickly forested valley floor. Further north, barely discernible against the night sky, stood a range of low mountains criss-crossed with deep ravines. From his map studies Carter knew that the Gorenskaya Tunnel was located at the other end of that plain, a mile or so from the edge of the plateau, at the point where the bridge crossed over a narrow stream.

The team set off down the slope, Dempsey moving two metres ahead of the others, alert to potential threats. The telltale smell of woodsmoke in the air, or the distant glow of a torchlight. Anything that might disclose the presence of a lurking sentry. Ruznak had assured them that the area around the train tunnel would be unguarded, and at this time of the year they were unlikely to encounter any ramblers, but Carter wasn't taking chances. They were operating behind enemy lines now. A more perilous op than anything they had undertaken in the past. If they were compromised, best-case scenario, the Kremlin would have five high-value hostages on their hands. Worst-case, Putin would use their presence on Russian soil as a pretext to escalate the war in Ukraine. Maybe start lobbing tactical nukes at Kyiv.

Maybe further afield, too.

Not something Carter wanted to think about.

They pressed on. Carter felt the band of anxiety tightening around his chest. People assumed that SF operators were either adrenaline junkies or psychopaths, or both, and therefore immune to fear. But every guy in the Regiment felt it on an op. Impossible not to, unless you were high on something. The secret, Carter had learned, was to walk with the fear. Acknowledge it. Stare it in the face. Don't hide from it. Don't let it paralyse you. Like keeping your eyes open when freefalling out of the back of a plane. Close your eyes, give in to the fear, and you were in trouble.

That was the gift Jamie had left to him. Luke understood that now. His brother had inspired him to join the army. Shown him what it felt like to be a part of something bigger than your own life. The recruiting ads had it all wrong, in his opinion. Soldiering wasn't about seeing the world or learning new skills, although that was a part of it. In truth it was about making something of yourself. Climbing out of the gutter. In the world that Luke had grown up in, you either ended up in prison or on the dole. Or you fought back.

Luke had chosen to fight. The only way out. Victimhood wasn't an option when you were faced with a contact with the enemy. The army had saved Luke from a life of crime and poverty. He could have been sitting in a cell right now, counting down the days to his next parole hearing. Instead, he was leading the fight against the Russians. Master of his own mind and body.

They navigated around the base of a heavily wooded knoll and reached the bottom of the gorge. Carter couldn't see much of his surroundings in the darkness, but he didn't need to: he'd studied the landscape on the jet, could have found his way up to the ambush point blindfolded. On the eastern side of the ravine, midway up, the western portal of the railway tunnel emerged from the rock face. The tracks ran across a stone bridge to a broadly level area on the western escarpment, meandered around the hillside, then crossed another smaller gorge before tapering away towards the shore. From there the line ran all the way up the coast to the fortified retreat.

They began their ascent up the western scarp. The night was close to silence as dammit. Carter could hear nothing except the wind swishing through the pine trees, the faint roar of the waves, the light snap of twigs beneath their Gore-Tex boots. Carter's own breathing sounded impossibly loud in his ears.

He carried on. Focused on the next step, then the one after that. Didn't allow himself to look any further ahead than that. The first lesson they taught you in the Regiment. The soldier who thought only of the next step had the strength to walk a hundred miles. The soldier who contemplated the whole road never began his journey.

After a short climb they broke through the treeline and paused. Volkova caught her breath while Carter surveyed the area, comparing the scene in front of him with the picture in his head. They were standing on a thin strip of stony ground running parallel with the railway line curving around the side of the mountain. On the opposite side of the tracks was a sheer wall of rock capped by a lightly wooded crest.

To the east, a hundred metres away, the track spanned the bridge over the Gorenskaya gorge before it disappeared into the mouth of the tunnel. The line carried on past the team's position, through a second, much shorter tunnel, no more than twenty metres in length, then traversed another bridge over the western ravine. A river sliced through the vale to the west, emptied out into the Black Sea, a mile or so up the coast from their landing point.

'What now?' asked Volkova.

Carter couldn't make out her expression, but he detected the strain in her voice.

He said, 'We'll clear the area. Check for sentries. Steve, you take the tunnel and bridge to the west. Quade, recce the main tunnel. Soon as we've confirmed the track is safe we'll get to work.'

The four soldiers rigged up their military smartphones, jumped on the same call, plugged in their earbuds. The phones looked like standard civvy handsets but with a few special tweaks. Secure encryption, built-in GPS distress beacons and laser rangefinders, rugged waterproof housing. Ultra-long-lasting batteries allowing up to twenty-four hours of continuous talk. Each team member also carried a spare battery pack in his back pocket; if the devices started running low on juice, they would simply unclip the existing cell and slap in the new one.

Carter checked his phone. He had a good signal, even though they were in an isolated area in the hills. There was a rebro station at the country retreat, Six had explained, to give the residents frictionless comms with Moscow, eight hundred miles away. Not for the first time since they'd left Italy, Carter found himself wondering who owned the place.

*Whoever they are, they must have fucking deep pockets.*

*And a lot of clout.*

'Get moving,' he said to the Australians. 'If you see anyone coming up – guards or civilians – anyone at all – let us know.'

Dempsey set down the shovel and pick. Unslung his AK-47 and moved down along the bridge, sticking to the concrete walkway running alongside the tracks, weapon drawn, ready to put the drop on any targets. Lazarides pushed off in the opposite direction, clearing the tunnel and bridge over the ravine to the west. If any of them spotted an approaching enemy force, they would sound the alarm over the comms. At which point the team would abort the mission and bug out towards the pick-up spot on the peninsula.

Carter, Volkova and Beach settled down to wait in the dead ground close to the treeline. Carter was dog-tired. Felt the weariness deep in his bones. He'd managed a couple of hours' kip on the trawler, but now he was running on fumes. Recognised the signs. Hadn't had a hot meal since their last evening in Courchevel.

*Psuh through it.*

*A few more hours to go. Then you can rest.*

He checked the time again. Ten thirty. Exactly six hours to go. Six hours until a trainload of high-level Russian targets came rolling through the tunnel.

Thirty minutes later, he received an incoming message.

*Targets have just left Volgograd.*

At eleven thirty, Dempsey's voice came over the line. 'All clear, guys. In position at the other end of the tunnel.'

'Steve? Anything at your end?' Carter asked.

'Negative, Pom. Not a fucking peep.'

'Stay where you are, both of you. Eyes peeled. We're moving forward to emplace the charges now.'

Carter signalled to Beach. The latter removed the two high-powered tactical flashlights from inside the rucksack. Handed one to Carter, shoved the other into his rear pocket. He reslung the rucksack, stood up. 'Let's do this, Geordie.'

'What about me?' Volkova asked.

'Wait here. We'll be back as soon as we've finished mining the tracks.' Carter indicated the sonar device box. 'Don't let that case out of your sight. If anything happens to that, the sub won't have any way of locating us. Then we'll be royally fucked.'

He grabbed the pick, handed the shovel to Beach. The two Blades broke through the treeline, ventured down the bridge at a fast jog and switched on their flashlights as they reached the entrance to the Gorenskaya Tunnel. Concrete sleepers interspersed with crushed stone ballast stretched out before them, running for three miles through the mountains. According to the specs Ruznak had shared with them, the ballast ran to a depth of eighteen inches; below that was a second layer of gravel, separated from the top ballast by a trackbed mat designed to absorb vibrations.

'Come on,' Beach said.

They entered the tunnel. Like walking into an ancient cave. Beach counted his steps, paced out fifty metres. Stopped.

'This is far enough. We'll start laying the explosives here.'

'What's the plan?' Carter asked. There had been no time to consult with Beach on the amount of Semtex he'd need to bring down the tunnel, or discuss the railway mining in granular detail.

Beach said, 'We'll dig a hole every ten metres. A kilo of Semtex per hole. Make each one two feet deep. Then we're gonna need a trench running alongside the line to lay the det cord. Then we'll backfill everything. That should do the job.'

'How many holes?'

'Fifteen.'

Carter thought, *Fifteen kilos of Semtex. A hundred and fifty metres of trench.*

*A big fucking bang.*

'Isn't that overkill?'

'We've got one shot at this. Might as well go all out.'

Carter contemplated the ballast. 'That's a lot of digging.'

'Got to be that deep, mate. We don't know if anyone's going to be checking the line before that beast comes flying down.'

They got to work. Beach held the flashlight while Carter broke up the compacted rubble with the pick, taking care not to damage any of the signalling or track equipment. Carter excavated the crushed stone, heaped it to one side of the steel line. Kept digging until he hit a depth of half a metre. Beach buried one of the Semtex slabs. Then they moved on to the next hole.

It was hot work. Every scrape of the pick against the ballast echoed off the walls. Soon Carter's face was greased with sweat and dirt.

'We're going to a lot of effort,' Beach said as he planted the next block of explosive, 'to knock out a bunch of high-level spooks.'

Carter said, 'I don't think this is about the targets. Or at least, that's only part of it.'

'Then why the fuck are we here?'

'This is a show of strength. It's about reach. We're showing the Russians we can get to their people, even when they're supposedly tucked up safe on an armoured train in their own country. It's like blowing up the American President's motorcade.'

Beach stared at him. 'So we're sending a message? That's all this is?'

'It's not just that. This is going to be a personal humiliation for Putin. His cronies will start thinking if they're not safe in Russia, they're not going to be safe anywhere.'

'It'll bugger their lines, too,' Beach pointed out. He flapped a hand at the walls. 'These charges won't just take the train out. They'll bring the roof down on top of 'em.'

The digging took most of the night. Every so often they checked in with Lazarides and Dempsey. Updating them on their progress. The two Australians kept a close watch on the approaches from both sides of the line, but to Carter's relief the area remained free of enemy guards or patrols.

At three o'clock the team received another update from Six.

*Train has just left Krasnodar. Ninety minutes from your position.*

They worked faster. After they had dug out the trench running parallel with the steel line, Beach unspooled a length of det cord along the channel, linked it to the individual charges in a daisy-chain. He placed the receiver box in the hole next to the Semtex charge nearest the tunnel entrance. Took the firing device, trotted back across the bridge to the treeline while Carter watched the receiver. A total distance of around two hundred metres from box to trigger – close to the maximum possible range for the radio signal.

After two minutes the light on the housing unit flashed red.

'Is it working?' Beach asked over the comms.

'We've got a signal,' Carter replied. 'It's good to go, mate. Now let's get this thing hooked up and covered over.'

Beach scuttled back across the bridge. He connected the receiver to the charge fifty metres from the entrance, arming the device. Next Carter began the laborious work of shovelling the excavated stone back over the holes, which took a frustrating amount of time. He had to repack the gravel carefully so that the profile matched the surrounding ballast. The slightest indication that the track had been tampered with might alert a passing guard.

He was still compacting the stone on the last hole when Lazarides said, 'Torchlights approaching. Coming towards your position down the track.'

Carter stopped shovelling. 'How many?'

'I see four of 'em. Could be more. Get out of that tunnel.'

Carter grabbed the entrenching tools. Beach pocketed the hand-held firing device. They switched off their flashlights, scarpered out of the tunnel and over the bridge, dropped into the treeline beside Volkova. Lazarides and Dempsey would stay in their respective positions, hidden behind cover on the far sides of the eastern and western tunnels.

Carter stilled his breath. Voices pierced the grainy darkness. Growing steadily louder. Beams of torchlight gleamed in the mouth of the shorter western tunnel, swelled in size as they edged down the track. Dark shapes moved among them. Carter looked again, straining his eyes. The shapes resolved themselves into a pair of scruffy-looking guards packing AK-12 assault rifles and smoking cigarettes. Behind them shuffled half a dozen scrawny figures dressed in blue-and-white striped jackets, trousers and field caps. Two of them carried what looked like tree-loppers. A third man had a pair of garden shears. The other three had black bin bags and litter pickers. Another couple of guards brought up the rear of the party.

'Who the fuck are they?' Carter whispered.

'Chain gang,' Volkova said. 'Putin's special punishment for political prisoners. They get put to work as street sweepers, in the fields, on the roads. Wherever they're needed.'

'What are they doing here?'

'Keeping the track looking neat as a pin, I'd guess.'

'The whole line?' asked Beach.

'I doubt it. They'd have different teams allocated to each section of the track. Division of labour.'

Carter said, softly, 'Is this routine?'

Volkova shook her head. 'Someone must have ordered it ahead of schedule. Maybe one of the passengers doesn't like to see untrimmed hedges when they look out of the window.'

'Who the fuck is travelling on this thing?'

Volkova didn't reply.

They fell silent again as the chain gang shambled down the line. Every few paces one of the guards to the rear barked what sounded like an order at the prisoners. Pointing out overhanging branches that needed cutting, or bits of rubbish strewn across the tracksides. Carter took one look at the guards – their tattered uniforms, the slack way they carried themselves, not even bothering to scan the ground beyond the tracks – and relaxed a little. With their torches and cigarettes, they had fucked their natural night vision, and wouldn't be able to pick out the team members hiding among the trees.

The prisoners reached the eastern tunnel. One of them stopped a short way inside the opening, his eye drawn to something on the ground. In the white glow of the torchlights Carter saw the figure staring at a section of the ballast, and realised with a pang of horror that the guy was standing right over the spot where they had planted the first charge.

The one he'd been packing when Lazarides had spotted the guards.

'Shit,' Beach rasped. 'What are we gonna do?'

'Nothing,' Carter said. 'Just wait.'

He felt something heavy pressing down on his chest. Sensed the mission hanging in the balance. Ran through the next few seconds in his head. If the prisoner called the guards' attention to the charge, they would have to slip away, head straight for the coast. Dempsey would have to make his way down the gorge separately and link up with the others at the beach. They'd have to hope that sub was in position down the coast and ready to ferry the team to safety.

*As soon as those guards raise the alarm, we'll have every fucker in a twenty-mile radius hunting us down.*

The prisoner looked up. Gazed out of the tunnel.

Walked on.

More orders were barked. The rest of the group started moving on. Pushing deeper into the tunnel.

The pressure on Carter's chest lightened.

*We're clear.*

'Why didn't he dob on us?' Beach asked.

Volkova said, quietly, 'If you were living in a Russian prison, you'd understand why. These people are treated like animals by the system. Worse than animals, even. Trust me, that guy won't be shedding tears if a few Kremlin big-shots get blown to pieces.'

At four o'clock Dempsey reported that the chain gang had moved out of sight. With half an hour to go, the team moved into their designated positions. Lazarides pulled back from the smaller ravine to the west, joining Carter, Beach and Volkova at the tree-line beside the bridge. Dempsey stayed on the eastern entrance to Gorenskaya Tunnel. He'd notify the others once the train made its approach.

They were relying on Dempsey to ID the train. He would be looking carefully at the second carriage. According to the specs, that cabin had a white dome mounted on the roof, giving passengers continuous access to encrypted comms. Six had been confident that no other trains would be on the tracks at the same time, but Carter had insisted they make doubly sure the int was accurate. He didn't want any more blood on his hands. Not after the shit-show in Courchevel.

When the job was done, they would descend the gorge and link up with Dempsey on the valley floor. The whole team would then move down to the pick-up point on the peninsula, activate the pulse on the sonar device, wait for their ride to surface. The sub would take them to the navy base at Gibraltar.

Beach dipped a hand into his rucksack, took out the Vektors. He handed one of the pistols to Carter. Secondary weapons. Backup, in case they suffered a stoppage with their primary rifles. Always a possibility with a poorly maintained AK. A full eighteen-round clip pre-loaded into the receiver. Carter jammed the pistol into the waistband of his trousers. Beach pocketed the second Vektor.

Volkova said, 'Give me one of those.'

Carter said, 'No chance.'

'I can handle a gun, if that's what you're worried about.'

'It ain't that.'

'Then what is it?'

Carter didn't reply.

'You can't risk losing me,' Volkova continued. 'What if there's trouble? How am I supposed to defend myself? You're going to need my help getting out of this place.'

Lazarides laughed grimly. 'Look around you. We're in a fucking ravine. Only one way in and out. If we end up in the shit, we won't be getting out of this one alive. So you'd better pray it don't come to that.'

Ten minutes later, Dempsey broke the comms silence.

'Train's approaching, fellas.'

'Can you identify it?' said Carter.

'Wait one.'

There was a pause. Carter heard the faint clatter of a train coming down the tracks in the background. Then Dempsey said, 'Yeah, I can see the dome. This is definitely the target. In the tunnel now.'

Beach picked up a handheld trigger device, about the same dimensions as a mobile phone. Thumb over the red button, ready to depress once the train was directly over the charges. The device would send a radio signal to the receiver box; the box would send an electrical signal to the detonator, triggering the first charge. The other slabs of Semtex would explode in rapid succession, tearing through the carriages and causing the concrete tunnel walls to collapse. Burying alive anyone who managed to survive the initial blast.

*Three miles of track*, thought Carter.

The train wouldn't be moving at high speed. All that armour plating would add considerably to the overall weight, placing more stress on the engines. He estimated a top speed of around a hundred miles per hour. In an area of low mountains, on the approach to a gorge, the driver would be going carefully. He wouldn't want his passengers being thrown about on their journey. So assume a top limit of sixty or seventy miles an hour. Two or three minutes for the train to reach the other end of the tunnel.

Almost there.

A minute passed. Carter heard the distinct rumble of the train reverberating down the tunnel. Rattling towards the bridge. After another forty seconds the locomotive came surging round the bend, hood-fixed headlamps burning in the blackness, dragging the carriages along. The locomotive shuttled towards the tunnel exit. More slowly than Carter had expected. Maybe the driver was being extra cautious. At least some of the passengers were probably asleep.

*Any second now.*

Two hundred metres to the exit.

A hundred.

Fifty.

'Now,' Carter said.

Beach hit the trigger switch.

# Twenty-Six

Nothing happened.

The charge didn't explode.

The locomotive continued towards the tunnel exit.

'What are you waiting for?' Lazarides hissed urgently. 'For fuck's sake, blow it.'

'I'm trying. It's not fucking working,' Beach growled. He kept pointlessly hammering the trigger. 'Something's wrong.'

On the comms line Dempsey was demanding to know why they hadn't detonated the charges. The locomotive air-braked as it emerged from the tunnel, the screech of the wheels on steel drowning out Dempsey's voice. It came to a grinding halt on the bridge, eighty metres from the treeline. Comms dome visible on top of the carriage directly behind. Curtains drawn across the windows.

'Why the fuck has it stopped?' Beach said.

A chorus of faint cracks sounded in the distance. Coming from the east.

The far side of the tunnel.

Gunfire.

In his ear, Carter heard Dempsey scream.

'Ned? Mate?' Lazarides asked frantically.

Horror seeped into Carter's bowels, a millionth of a second before the doors on the second and third carriages flew open and a mass of soldiers poured out onto the paved area at the side of the tracks. Russian soldiers, decked out in camo-pattern uniforms, packing AK-12 rifles. Twenty per carriage. Charging straight towards the treeline.

'Fucking move!' Carter yelled.

They turned to sprint down the slope. Stopped again when Beach shouted in alarm and pointed towards a bank of torchlights swarming up from the valley floor. In among them, he heard the throated barks of attack dogs. At that instant Carter understood that the enemy had launched a blocking movement, cutting off the team's route of escape. Isolating them on the side of the ravine.

Tactically sound. Flip the situation. Turn the tables on the other side. Ambush the ambushers. What Carter would have done if he'd been in their shoes. The soldiers would have moved into position among the trees at the bottom of the gorge and waited for the signal to close the trap. A third force would have been placed on the far side of the tunnel. Hence the gunfire coming from that direction, and Dempsey's screams. Which could only mean one thing.

*The Russians knew we were coming.*

In the same microsecond he realised something else.

*We're caged in.*

They couldn't escape down through the vale. Not with the Russian attack group surging up the slope towards their position. Couldn't climb further up the escarpment either. A sheer rock face. And the soldiers deboarding from the train had cut them off from the eastern tunnel. No way out.

*Not quite.*

Carter whipped round again.

'Come on! Make for the other tunnel!' he shouted.

He took off down the treeline, Beach and Lazarides sprinting alongside him, Volkova a few paces back, carrying the sonar box by its plastic handle.

They headed away from the train, making for the shorter tunnel and bridge spanning the western ravine. Two hundred metres away. Gunshots chorused behind them, crackling in the night air, interspersed with the shouts of angry men and the baying of dogs. Rounds thumped unseen into pine-tree trunks, whipped overhead, slapped into the dirt, threw up geysers of loose soil and pine needles.

Carter vaulted over a fallen branch, glanced over his shoulder. Lazarides and Beach were hard on his heels. Volkova was further back, struggling along. Behind her the cluster of torchlights on the tracks steadily gained on them. They were maybe seventy metres away from Carter and the others. Hard to tell in the pre-dawn light, with his view partially obscured by the trees. At the same time the blocking formation pushed up the slopes, moving towards the tracks to link up with the main attack group. Closing the net.

'Keep fucking going!' Carter called out to the others as another volley of rounds zipped past them, thudded into the ground a few inches to his right. 'Hurry!'

He pushed on, running for all he was worth. As they neared the entrance to the western tunnel he broke clear of the trees and looked back again. The Russians were no more than sixty metres away now. Bullets thwacked into the ballast in two- or three-round bursts around Carter, ricocheted off the steel rails. The Russians weren't bothering to aim properly. They didn't need to. They had overwhelming superiority of numbers and firepower. Like David versus Goliath, if Goliath brought an RPG to the fight instead of a javelin. The odds were stacked massively in their favour.

'Why didn't them charges go off?' Lazarides rasped.

Carter already knew the answer. But there was no time.

He reached the tunnel entrance, heard a pained cry at his back. He looked round, saw Volkova tripping over one of the sleepers and falling to the ground six metres back. The sonar case tumbled from her grip, landed beside her on the ballast. Beach stopped to help the Russian spy to her feet. Three rounds thumped into his back. Beach jerked wildly. His legs buckled; a fourth bullet winged him on the way down, tearing out a chunk of his skull. He was dead before his body hit the dirt.

Volkova screamed for help, clutching her busted ankle.

Carter froze.

The Russians were charging down the track in a tight formation, line abreast. But their numbers worked against them, from a tactical point of view. Because the railway line was only wide enough to admit three or four guys in the front row. The rest of the soldiers had to take their places in the second or third ranks, or at the rear of the echelon. Therefore they couldn't bring the full weight of their firepower to bear on their opponents. Not until they had reached open ground.

'Leave her!' Lazarides shouted.

He'd stopped beside Carter in the black mouth of the tunnel. The Australian grabbed Carter by the arm and thundered at him to get moving again, his voice thick with anxiety.

Carter made a nanosecond decision.

*We can't abandon her. She's got the box.*

*Our only hope of getting out of here alive.*

'Cover me,' he bellowed.

He rushed out of the tunnel line before Lazarides could protest. Left the Australian at his back, shouting obscenities, hoping to fuck he would provide Carter with suppressive fire.

The horde of Russian soldiers were no more than fifty metres away now. A series of cracks exploded at Carter's six o'clock as Lazarides put down a succession of well-aimed single rounds at the Russians. Two of the figures in the front rank spasmed and fell away. Their muckers dived behind cover or went prone on the ground. Men shouted at one another in panicked voices. Amazing the effect a couple of kills could have on a large body of men. The way it sucked the confidence from others. Every soldier thought he was a hero, right up until the moment his best mate took a bullet in the face.

Lazarides kept peppering the Russians while Carter dropped down beside Volkova. He slung his rifle over his shoulder, threw an arm round the Russian, hauled her upright. Grabbed the sonar box.

Further east, a couple of the Russians were loosing off wild shots from behind cover. Muzzles lit up the semi-dark. Rounds chipped the stonework around the tunnel entrance, punched the concrete walls, zipped inches over Carter's head.

He set off through the tunnel with Volkova. Nothing he could do for Beach. He assumed Dempsey had been slotted too. No way he would have survived contact with the enemy force on the other side.

He struggled down the tunnel with Volkova, willing her to go faster. She winced with every step, hobbling along on her rag order ankle. Fifteen metres to the tunnel exit. Beyond it, Carter spied the bridge stretching over the river. So close he could almost reach out and touch it.

*Going to be fucking close.*

They hurried past Lazarides. Ten metres to the western bridge now. Lazarides was still putting down rounds on the Russians from a kneeling firing stance. Classic SF fire-and-movement tactics. Holding the enemy up for as long as possible, buying the others time to fall back. Once Carter and Volkova had pepper-potted towards the tunnel exit he dropped to a knee, set down the sonar box, deslung his rifle and opened up on the onrushing figures to the east. Pinning them down while Lazarides scuttled towards them.

The mass of Russians beyond the tunnel started to regain some of their old confidence. Figures moved forward, some singly, others in pairs, the flash of muzzles lighting up the soldiers in the attack group forty metres due east.

Carter popped off another burst, legged it towards the end of the tunnel. Behind him, Lazarides got the dreaded dead man's click as he emptied the last round from his clip. Carter stopped again, put down a two-round burst on the nearest onrushing figures, giving one of the fuckers the good news. Bullets tore into the guy's central mass. He jolted like someone had bumped him with a cattle prod and fell screaming to the tracks. His mate threw himself into cover among the trees.

More Russians flooded forward, edging past their slotted comrade. They were no more than thirty-five metres from the tunnel entrance.

Lazarides ejected his empty mag, tore out a fresh clip from his back pocket, slid it into the underside of the receiver, tugged on the charging handle. Chambering a round in the snout.

'Steve!' Carter roared. 'We have to go!'

Lazarides didn't respond. They were taking a ferocious amount of incoming now. The bulk of it unaimed fire. The Russians weren't great soldiers. Tier Two fighters at best. Drilled in the basics, and tough. But bone from the neck up. Useful as cannon fodder in Ukraine. In an equal contest, they would be no match for a couple of hardened Reg lads. But this was far from equal.

One round gouged out a chunk of the wall to Carter's right, flinging hot dust into his face.

He felt a searing pain as another round zipped past his left arm, grazing his shoulder. Any moment now they would be overrun by the enemy.

'Steve! Get moving, for fuck's sake!'

'You go,' Lazarides replied over his shoulder. 'I'll cover you.'

'But—'

'Fucking go!'

There was no time to argue. Carter snatched up the sonar box, dragged Volkova out of the tunnel. Limped over to the stone parapet at the side of the bridge. He peered down at the river below. A drop of maybe fifteen metres. They could easily break a leg on the way down, or worse. But they had no choice. The only way off the mountain.

*Either we do this, or we die.*

'Come on,' Carter said.

He helped Volkova climb atop the parapet. They stood on the capstones over the precipice.

'Hold your nose,' he said. 'Hand over your mouth. Whatever happens, don't breathe in when you hit the water. Got it?'

Volkova nodded. Carter gripped the sonar box tightly in his right hand. Pinched his nostrils with his left, sucked in a deep breath. So did Volkova. Guarding themselves against the possibility of cold water shock. The biggest hazard when plunging into icy water. The resulting jolt caused the body to gasp involuntarily. The lungs expelled air and filled with water. When that happened, you were in big fucking trouble.

He glanced once more at the tunnel at his nine o'clock. Lazarides was still brassing up the Russians, even as a savage volley of rounds spattered the ballast around him.

Carter jumped.

He hit the water with a slap, plunged beneath the surface for what seemed like half a minute but was probably no more than a few seconds while he orientated himself. Carter clawed his way through the watery darkness until he broke the surface. He normalised his breathing and looked around, orientating himself. The current was carrying him downriver at a fast speed. Volkova had splashed down to his right. She was thrashing around in the water, arms flailing, gasping for air.

Carter ferried himself towards her, one hand clutching the crushproof box.

'Keep your head tilted back,' he said. 'Arms out at your shoulders. That'll help you stay afloat.'

He kept close to Volkova as they drifted downstream like a couple of fallen logs. Carter bumped against a clump of rocks, bruising his legs. Further along they hit a small waterfall. Before they reached the edge Carter shouted at Volkova to keep her knees balled tight to her chest, so her feet wouldn't smash against unseen rocks at the bottom.

The bridge was far behind them now. The tunnel, and the trainload of Russian troops. Beach and Dempsey.

How long they rode that current Carter couldn't tell. Time became elastic. Seconds stretched into hours. All of his senses were focused on surviving the next stretch of rapids.

They plunged over the crest of a second waterfall and reached a calmer stretch of water, flanked on both banks by low hills mixed in with woodland, approximately a kilometre from the bridge. Carter decided they had made it far enough. He had no intention of following the river to its mouth. That was rule number one when escaping a hunting force. Rivers had bends in them. Which extended the distance you had to travel to reach your destination. Therefore, best avoided unless the situation demanded it. The quickest way from A to B was almost always on foot.

He grabbed Volkova by the bicep, swam at an angle towards a thicket of gnarled ash trees hugging the right bank. Carter chucked the sonar box onto dry land, caught hold of a low-hanging branch, gave Volkova a hard shove and climbed out of the water behind her. The pair of them lay choking and shivering in their drenched clothes.

Carter picked himself up. The military part of his mind told him that they had to keep moving. *Don't stop now.*

The Russians would naturally concentrate their efforts on the area around the river. Unwise to linger there. Like deciding to camp where you had fought a battle.

He helped Volkova to her feet. Volkova hissed in pain as he manhandled her towards the forest. In the map Carter carried in his head he calculated that they were about two kilometres from the shore. At that moment dozens of Russians would be streaming down the valley in search of the fugitives. Grim odds, on paper. But the Russian commander had a large area of the coastline to comb, most of it broken ground, on a moonless night. All of which would impede their efforts. There was still time to make good their escape.

*We've got a few minutes before we need to move again.*

'What the fuck happened back there?' he demanded.

Volkova needed a moment to catch her breath. 'I – I don't know.'

Something – the way she averted her gaze, the shakiness in her voice – told Carter that she was lying. He clamped his fingers around her damp, cold wrist. Pulled her towards him.

He said, 'Two of my mates are dead. Start talking.'

Volkova winced in pain, tried pulling her arm away.

'Let go of me!'

Carter ignored her pleas. 'I've just saved your fucking life. If it wasn't for me, you'd be lying on your back with a bullet in your head right now. So tell me what's going on, or I'm leaving you behind.'

Volkova read the glint of savage anger in his eyes and stopped struggling. Her head dropped in resignation.

'This was a trap,' Carter said. 'Wasn't it? You tricked us. Those detonators were shady. That's why them charges didn't go off back there.'

He was thinking about the receiver box. At first, he'd wondered if the train had some sort of on-board countermeasures. Signal-jamming equipment. Perhaps the prisoner who'd spotted the planted explosives had alerted the guards once they had moved further on. But Carter had quickly ruled it out: a signal jammer would have scrambled the mobile phone masts too. And their phones had been working just fine. He knew the trigger switch couldn't be faulty, either: Beach had tested it an hour before the attack. Which left only one other explanation.

Someone had corrupted the detonators.

*Someone wanted us to fail.*

*Lured us into a trap.*

'Not me.' Volkova said. 'I wasn't the one who betrayed you.'

She raised her eyes to Carter. Her hair was dripping wet. Strands of it clung to her dirt-smeared cheeks.

'Who?' Carter growled. 'Tell me.'

'Ruznak. He's the one behind all this.'

Carter felt something cold move through his guts. The feeling spread outward, chilled the nape of his neck, the blood in his veins. He stared at Volkova in dismay.

'Bollocks.'

'It's the truth. Eduard was the one who supplied you with the explosives,' she continued. 'He set you up. You and your friends.'

'Why?'

Carter could guess the answer, but he had to know for sure.

'He's working for the Russians. Betraying his country. Eduard organised this whole job. He supplied Six with the intelligence on the train. This was his project, remember? Not mine. He sent us here so the Russians could ambush us.'

Carter cast his mind back to the briefing in Italy.

*Eduard has a source*, they had been told.

*Someone close to the targets.*

*He's liaising with his contacts in Turkey. Everything you need will be waiting for you on the boat.*

*Bombs. Weaponry.*

It would have been relatively easy for someone in Ruznak's position to arrange for a batch of dud detonators to be delivered to the team. A simple case of making a payment to the Turks. Sahin and his mates wouldn't have given a shit about sending a few Christians to their deaths.

Carter tried to shake the dizzy feeling from his head.

'How long have you known?'

'Not long. I had my suspicions in France. But I couldn't be sure. I had nothing concrete. I needed more time to gather evidence. So I didn't say anything.'

Something didn't make sense to Carter. 'But Ruznak helped us slot two of Putin's closest allies. Why the fuck would he do that if he was working for those bastards?'

'I can only speculate. I don't know the facts.'

'But?'

'It's possible that Putin wanted Ternovsky and Grabakin out of the way. They might have been part of the plot to remove him.'

'The coup your father organised?'

Volkova nodded. Wet clothes were pasted to her eggshell-white skin.

'There were rumours that others had been involved in the plan. Powerful men, at the very heart of the Kremlin. What if the people we killed were the prime suspects? Or Putin might have sensed that they were getting too powerful in their own right.'

'Either way, they'd be a threat to his regime.'

'Yes,' Volkova sniffed. 'When I turned up at Ruznak's office with a list of names for Six, he would have shared that list with his handler in Moscow. Maybe someone put the list in front of Putin. He would have seen two of his enemies on that list and landed on a convenient way of getting rid of them without personally getting involved. He wouldn't have believed his good fortune.'

'But the Alpha Group lads. The collaborators they weeded out. Why didn't Ruznak protect them?'

'Maybe he couldn't. That's why he was fishing for information. In Belarus. When we picked you up. He was panicked about the arrests. He wanted to know if he'd been compromised.'

*The Russians were using us,* Carter realised.

*All this time, we thought we were taking the fight to them. Instead, we've been doing Putin's dirty work for him.*

'That's why Ruznak steered us onto this job? So he could get rid of us, once we'd served our purpose?'

'I think so, yes. But Putin would have wanted you taken alive. You would have made useful bargaining chips. He could broadcast your capture to the world. That would have been a great PR victory for him. A way of reasserting his strength. He could point the finger at NATO. Accuse them of escalation by carrying out an attack on Russian soil. That's all the excuse he'd need to send tanks into Poland. Or drop a nuke on Kyiv.'

'Why would Ruznak work for the Russians? What's in it for him?'

'Does it matter? People betray their countries for many reasons. Maybe they're blackmailing him. Maybe he really believes in all that pan-Slavic bullshit peddled by the Kremlin.'

'You should have told us,' Carter said. 'Or Vauxhall. Even if you couldn't prove anything, you should have tipped us off that Ruznak might be bent. Lives might have been saved.'

'I couldn't,' Volkova replied falteringly. 'They might have called the mission off. This was our chance to change everything. To bring down the regime.'

'The fuck are you talking about?'

'The target,' Volkova said. 'On the train. That wasn't a senior official, or a general. That was Vladimir Putin.'

Carter flinched his head back from the Russian. He couldn't think clearly. As if someone had scrambled all the wiring in his brain.

*High-ranking targets*, Vallance had said.

*Multiple.*

An appalling realisation stabbed him in the guts.

*Six lied to me again.*

'You can't know that,' Carter said, falteringly. 'You can't . . .'

'That train is reserved for the personal use of the President. No one else is allowed to ride on it, for security reasons. Everyone in the FSB knows this. As soon as Six told us about the target, I knew it had to be Putin himself we were going after.'

Carter tried shaking the fog from his head.

'That's why Six sanctioned the operation,' Volkova went on. 'Don't you see? They saw a once-in-a-lifetime opportunity to end the war in Ukraine and reshape the world.'

'Was he really on that train, just now? Or was that another of Ruznak's lies?'

'I doubt it. The President has many body doubles. One of them would have been on the train instead, for the sake of appearances. In case Six had a spy of their own on the staff. Putin wouldn't place himself in a situation where he might get killed.'

'Fucking hell.'

Muted voices carried on the cool night air. Men shouting at one another. Dogs barking. Coming from somewhere upriver. By now the Russians would be sweeping across the vale. Hunting their prey. Carter figured they had been out of the water for three or four minutes. Any moment now they would have to push on towards the pick-up point.

Volkova went on, 'That's it. I've told you everything I know. Believe me, or don't. I couldn't care less. Just tell me how the hell we're going to get out of here.'

Carter pointed down the coast. 'We're two klicks from the beach. There's a belt of woodland stretching from here down to the sea. We'll move through that, switch on the pulse once we hit the shore.'

'What if they find us before the sub gets here?'

'Then we'll have to go into the drink. Tread water until they can rescue us. Think you can manage that?'

He cocked his head at Volkova's injured ankle.

She smiled grimly. 'Pain I can deal with. Better than the alternative.'

'Come on, then. Let's get the fuck out of here.'

Carter stooped down to pick up the sonar box.

He heard a rustling movement to his left. Coming from the direction of the river. Carter wheeled towards the sound, bringing up his AK-47, index finger resting on the trigger. An instinctive reaction. The result of thousands of hours of work on the training ground until it became muscle memory.

A dripping wet figure stood beside the right bank.

Lazarides. Holding an AK-47 in a two-handed grip.

Black hole of the muzzle trained on Volkova.

Carter stared at him unblinking. 'Steve. What the fuck are you doing?'

'Step back, Pom.'

Volkova's eyes widened. Terror dawned on her face. Her hands came up in a pleading gesture.

'No. No, please, you—'

The rifle cracked.

Volkova fell away. She collapsed to her front on the hard ground, blood leaking out of a bullet wound in the back of her head.

'Jesus,' Carter said. 'Jesus Christ.'

'Bitch had it coming. She betrayed us.'

Carter wanted to tell him that he'd got it wrong. That he'd killed another innocent woman. But the words stuck like barbs in his throat. He couldn't get them out. They died on his lips.

'You idiot,' he barely managed.

'What's your problem? It needed doing. She tried to get us all killed.'

Carter shook his head furiously. 'The Russians. For fuck's sake, they'll have heard the—'

In that instant a volley of gunshots hailstoned through the forest. Rounds chewed up tree trunks, smacked into branches, threw up clods of hot earth and mouldy leaves. Carter heard the bee-sting of a round whiplashing inches past him, felt the warm carriage of air on his face. Lazarides swung round to meet the threat and took a three-round burst to the torso. He fell away, clawing at his bullet-stitched belly. He was still dropping as Carter spun away and darted down the hiker's trail snaking through the woods.

The Russian commander must have been close by, Carter realised. His men would have heard the gunshot, moved towards the woods. Soon the entire hunting force would be converging on Carter's position.

He still had two kilometres to go before he hit the shoreline. On foot, shivering cold and soaked through, with a group of forty-plus Russian troops on his tail. Men who were presumably warm-clothed and well fed, and therefore fresher. It wouldn't be long before they caught up with him.

He ran on as hard as possible. Every fibre of his body ached with exhaustion and hunger. He forced himself to ignore the pain. Had just one goal in his mind.

*Get to the water.*

*Don't stop for anything.*

*Pray that sub is waiting for me.*

Rounds crackled in the filmy gloom behind Carter. Men were shouting encouragement to one another. Dogs yapped and snarled. The hunters would be feeling good about themselves. One of the escapees was dead, the other was on the run. They would be confident about nailing Carter. He had the mountains on one side and the wide-open sea on the other. If the Russians were switched on, they'd send flanking forces to cover the routes east and west along the headland. No way out for him.

Carter climbed the trail towards a forested ridgeline, cleared the woods and massacred his legs on the mad sprint down the other side of the hill. He climbed the next ridgeline and stuck to the trail as it sloped towards a low headland overlooking a crescent beach. He paused to glance back in the general direction of his pursuers. Banks of white light were cutting through the gaps between the trees. Difficult to judge in the darkness, but he reckoned the Russians were no more than half a kilometre back. Not long before they reached the coastline.

Carter ran on.

He skidded down the scree, stumbled across the shingle. The black nothingness stretched out monstrously before him. Carter sank to his knees, flipped up the latches on the hardcase. Inside was a bright-yellow device shaped like an oversized torch, and a hard-wearing lanyard attached to a waterproof plastic bag.

Carter lifted the floatable sonar device out of the foam casing. He switched it on to pulse mode. The unit started beeping loudly, broadcasting a sonar signal that would be picked up by any underwater craft within a radius of five kilometres. He stuffed the device inside the waterproof pouch, clamped it shut. Looped the lanyard around his wrist so that he wouldn't get detached from the transmitter while he was treading water.

There was no time to take off anything heavy. Not with the Russians on his back. He'd have to risk it and hope the navy bods didn't leave him hanging for too long. Carter ditched his AK-47, carried the storage box with him for extra buoyancy and waded into the freezing water.

He swam out into the black void, the sonar pulse unit dangling from his wrist. He had no particular destination to aim for. He just swam deeper into the never-ending darkness.

He stopped swimming a mile or so out from the beach. His body refused to go any further. Wearily, with one last effort, Carter rolled onto his back, arms outstretched. He bobbed up and down on the foam-capped waves. Black vastness above him and below. At this distance the torchlights along the coast were as small as distant stars.

Minutes dragged by.

Still there was no sign of the sub.

After what seemed like fifteen minutes Carter started to panic. He was utterly alone, with no means of defending himself, and the very real possibility of drowning if he became too tired to tread water. Even if he managed to stay afloat, it would soon be daylight. Then he would be horribly exposed for miles along the coast. At dawn the waterways would fill up with traffic. Small fishing boats, cargo vessels, Russian patrol vessels. Any number of ships might spot him.

*They've got to pick me up before daybreak*, Carter thought.

*Otherwise I'm fucked.*

Time passed.

The loneliness was agonising. A sinister thought slowly took shape in the back of Carter's mind. One that he tried very hard to ignore. But it was there all the same, an unwelcome presence invading his headspace. Scratching at his temples.

*They're not coming.*

He wondered if the sonar device was faulty. Had Ruznak tampered with that, too? No – impossible. Vauxhall had supplied them with the unit in Genoa. The supply chain had bypassed the

Ukrainian. So perhaps it was broken. Damaged on the fall from the bridge, or the rough ride downriver. But that seemed equally improbable. The device had been stored in the protective case the whole time.

Volkova's words came back to him.

*What happens once this is over?*

*Maybe there's no submarine waiting for us at the end of all this.*

Alone, on the sea, Carter's thoughts turned to his dead brother. Perhaps Jamie had been right all along. He had never trusted Six, or the Hereford head shed. He'd tried to warn Luke. Told him that he should never believe a word that came out of their mouths, but Luke hadn't really listened. Maybe he should have done.

*Those bastards will let you down*, Jamie had told him over beers one night. *They always do, in the end. And do you know why? Because they don't give a shit about you.*

*You're expendable.*

Despair gripped Carter. Sank its teeth into his neck.

*I'm going to die here*, he realised.

*Six has left me for dead.*

*And there's fuck all I can do about it.*

Then it happened.

A black monster rose out of the water. First came the antennas and periscope. Then the fin. As tall as a block of flats, with its distinctive planes protruding from either side.

Not a monster, but a submarine.

Tension instantly drained from Carter's body. He knew then that he was saved. He laughed, absurdly, like a madman. Tiny figures emerged from a door on the side of the tower. A pair of submariners climbed into an inflatable boat and scudded along the water towards Carter. Suddenly a pair of hands was reaching down to haul Carter out of the drink. He struggled into the boat. A kind face looked down at the knackered soldier at his feet.

'Where are the others? We were told there would be five.'

Carter could barely summon the strength to shake his head. 'They didn't make it. It's just me.'

The submariner stared at him. Nodded. 'Let's get you home, lad.'

'Wait.'

Carter had one last thing to do. He slid the waterproof plastic bag from his wrist. Tossed the sonar device into the sea. The pulse would confuse the Russians. Any Russian vessels engaged in the search would zero in on that signal.

He was done. Spent. He rested his head against the gunwale as they glided back towards the sub. In the east the first pale glimmer of light was glowing behind the mountains. Dawn would soon break. A new day in Russia.

Carter looked back at the coastline. A hollow feeling spread through his stomach; he tasted something bitter in his mouth. He thought of the soldiers who had died on Russian soil. He thought of the young woman who had given her life in the forlorn hope of toppling a hated regime, and a daughter's undying love for her father. He thought of his dead brother, and the meaning of sacrifice in a world that prized self-preservation. Then he closed his eyes, the tiredness swept over Carter, like a black wave, and he felt nothing.

Absolutely nothing at all.

If you enjoyed *Traitor*,
why not join the
CHRIS RYAN READERS' CLUB?

When you sign up, you'll receive an exclusive Q & A
with Chris Ryan, plus information about upcoming
books and access to exclusive material.
To join, simply visit:
**bit.ly/ChrisRyanClub**

Keep reading for a letter from the author . . .

Hello!

Thank you for picking up TRAITOR.

Once in a while a story jumps out at you. That's definitely the case with TRAITOR.

A year ago, a group of anti-Kremlin saboteurs hit the headlines after they crossed into Russia from Ukraine and launched a series of raids across the Belgorod region. Reportedly recruited from the ranks of army defectors and emigrants living in Ukraine, their stated aim is to topple Vladimir Putin's regime. Although these groups would appear extremely unlikely to succeed, as I watched the news reports the seed of an idea quickly took shape in my head.

What if these militia forces were trained by the SAS? Or – even better – what if the Regiment found themselves in a position that meant *they* had to carry out the attacks? After all, operating behind enemy lines has been the trademark of SAS operations for decades, going back to the desert raids in the Second World War and, more recently, the attack on Pebble Island in the Falklands campaign.

The prospect of British soldiers on the ground in Russia might seem outlandish. But as we've seen in the past, wars can escalate very fast. With the conflict in Ukraine dragging on, there's always the risk that one side might miscalculate, or push the envelope too far – with potentially devastating consequences.

If you would like to hear more about my books, you can visit **bit.ly/ChrisRyanClub** where you can become part of the Chris Ryan Readers' Club. It only takes a few moments to sign up, and there are no catches or costs.

Bonnier Books UK will keep your data private and confidential, and it will never be passed on to a third party. We won't spam you with loads of emails, just get in touch now and again with news about my books, and you can unsubscribe any time you want.

And if you would like to get involved in a wider conversation about my books, please do review TRAITOR on Amazon, on GoodReads, on any other e-store, on your own blog and social media accounts, or talk about it with friends, family or reader groups! Sharing your thoughts helps other readers, and I always enjoy hearing about what people experience from my writing. You can follow me on X (Twitter) @ChrisRyanMM.

Thank you again for reading TRAITOR.

All the best,

Chris Ryan